Gordon Thomas lives with his wife in Wc
He began his career lecturing in physics at King's College, London. From
there he went to the Home Office to work mainly as a scientist but also as
an administrator. Latterly his responsibilities were in police science and
physical security. Since retiring he has become a keen writer and this is his
second novel.

To Diane

THE EMERALD OF BURGOS

I hope you
enjoy the
read !
Best wishes,

Gordon

Gordon Thomas

THE EMERALD OF BURGOS

Olympia Publishers
London

www.olympiapublishers.com
OLYMPIA PAPERBACK EDITION

A CIP catalogue record for this title is
available from the British Library.

ISBN: 978-1-84897-446-3

(Olympia Publishers is part of Ashwell Publishing Ltd)

This is a work of fiction.
Names, characters, places and incidents originate from the writer's imagination.
Any resemblance to actual persons, living or dead, is purely coincidental.

Cover picture: Diego Rodríguez de Silva y Velázquez, *Female Figure (Sibyl with Tabula Rasa)*(Detail), c. 1648. Oil on canvas, 25.5 in. x 23 in. (64.77cm x 58.42cm). Meadows Museum, SMU, Dallas. Algur H. Meadows Collection, MM.74.01. Photography by Michael Bodycomb.

First Published in 2014

Olympia Publishers
60 Cannon Street
London
EC4N 6NP

Printed in Great Britain

Acknowledgements

I thank all those who have been kind enough to help me in writing this novel. I thank those friends and family members who read the draft and told me what they thought. I am especially grateful to my son Greg and his wife Sue, to Karen Teuber, Kay Sinclair and to Loretta Proctor, each of whom read the draft for me and offered their suggestions for its improvement. I much appreciate my daughter Mel's constant encouragement.

I am supremely grateful to my lovely wife, Janet, who was first to read the draft and give me her comments. She deserves special thanks as she helped me to carry out the background research on the Spanish road to Brussels. She also patiently shared my life during writing of this book.

To Janet

PART I

CHAPTER 1

The Killing

I could see him in the twilight, swaying and staggering, as he walked drunkenly towards the house. I was ready to do it but quivering at the thought. I used all my strength to ease the granite paving stone up, on to the window sill, above the door. I steadied it with my hand and it balanced there. I could hear his uneven footsteps as he approached. I was determined if fearful: I dared not fail. While he inserted the key, I gave the stone a gentle push. It dropped straight on to him, smashing into his head with a muffled, deadly crunch. Silence.

I ran down the stairs and opened the door, fearful of what I would see. The hideous sight shocked me. His crumpled body lay there on the road. His mouth trickled blood and his broken skull gaped wide open. His eyes looked calmly ahead, as if nothing had happened. I half expected a flicker, a blink, but saw only a fixed stare. I could smell the ale and brandy on his breath and urine on his clothes. I placed my hand on his chest but could feel nothing but stillness. He was unseeing, motionless and dead. Whether or not I had meant to do it, I'd killed him. I tried hard to move him by pulling at his arms. He wouldn't budge. So I grabbed his feet and pulled with all the strength I could muster. He slid into the hall on his own blood and piddle. I sighed with relief and shut the door behind me, leaving the smashed paving slab and the trail of his redness outside.

As I washed his blood off my hands, my mind raced with the finality of what I had done. My heart beat faster and thumped in my chest. I did not panic because I knew what I had to do. I had to go and soon, if I was not to be charged with murder. I grabbed a large sackcloth bag and rushed around the house to pack my few possessions. Just two dresses, a petticoat and a pair of sandals. I took the remains of a loaf of bread, some slices of ham and a kitchen knife. I put on my coat and, with the bag over my arm, left the house, not five minutes after I had killed him.

I could not go without telling my friend Lucía what I'd done and why I was leaving our town. The door of the house where she lived, with the other orphans and stray children, was never locked so I opened it and walked in. A single candle, in its holder on the wall, flickered in the draft from the open door. I felt my way into Lucía's room, made my fumbling way to her bed and shook her.

'Who the hell is that?'

'It's me. María. Come with me. I've something to tell you,' I whispered, so as not to disturb the others.

'Can't it wait 'til the morning? I'm tired,' she yawned.

'No. It's urgent... and serious. Get out and come with me.'

Lucia, wearing her nightdress, followed me back into the hall and outside into the road. We could see each other clearly in the light of the full moon.

'What is it then? You're shaking.'

'I've killed the *hidalgo,* and I'm leaving town.'

'What? You've killed him? Never! Injured him, maybe. But from what he's done to...,' she said, shocked but attempting justification.

'Yes, he's dead.' I explained to her what I'd done and how. She already knew about what I had had to tolerate from that ogre.

'Where are you going?'

'To Madrid. I'll get a ride on a cart.'

'If you go, I go!'

'No. You can't. We'd both be in trouble.'

'Now I am in trouble. You've told me what you did and they are sure to ask me.'

'Please, Lucía, stay here. You'd be better off.'

'No. I'll pack my things now and come with you. Wait here.'

Lucía hurried back into the house. She had surprised me with the strength of her wish to come with me. I took great comfort in knowing that she was prepared – if not that well – to give up her life here and join me in a new beginning. She had always been my best friend, ever since we had escaped from the orphanage, some five years before, with my twin brother Pedro and Simón, our legless comrade. She showed her greatest value as my friend at the time of my beloved brother's disappearance. I was heartbroken and she gave me the strength to survive without him. We then shared our grief when Simón was run over, not six months later. Within a few moments, Lucia re-emerged from the house, fully dressed and wearing a short, thick jacket. She carried a small sack, full of her belongings, slung over her shoulder.

'Let's go,' I said. 'We'll find somewhere to rest by the side of the Madrid road and wait to ask someone to take us.'

We walked quickly away from her hostel, up the hill and along the north bank of the river towards the cathedral.

'Why not stay in there for the night?' I said.

'In the cathedral? We can't sleep in there, among all those tombs. Someone will see us.'

'I don't agree. Let's go in.'

My mother was a nun at this cathedral. I was named after its saint but not by my mother, whom Pedro and I never knowingly met. No one knew exactly when, but the day we were born, sometime around the year of Our Lord 1585, the nuns took us both to the convent orphanage where we lived until the day we escaped. Our father, so they said, was a priest. We could see the towering cathedral clearly by the light of the moon. We entered through the door to the north which squeaked loudly as we pushed it open.

'Someone will hear us,' whispered Lucía.

'Don't worry,' I said as we crept in.

Oil lamps, placed high on the stone columns, bathed the floor in a gentle, fragile glow. 'Let's see if there's anyone here,' I said quietly. We tiptoed carefully down the aisle, across the nave at the altar end and down the opposite aisle of this huge, echoing building.

'There's no one here,' said Lucía. 'We can sleep wherever we like.'

'Yes, but we must get up early in the morning and onto the Calle de Madrid.'

We settled down on a threadbare carpet in the Capella de la Condestable, using some pew cushions for cover and pillows.

'I still can't believe you killed him,' said Lucía. 'I wouldn't have had the courage.'

'Maybe not, Lucía. But I just could not stand to be treated that way anymore. Last night I woke up with a fright. I heard my bedroom door opening. I could see him standing there, looking at me and holding a lamp. He stood there for two threatening moments. Then he bent over. I could smell the drink on his breath. I felt his hand slide down inside the bed. I could see he was half naked and ready to do me. So I punched him in the stomach and dashed out of the room into the kitchen and grabbed a knife. He followed me shouting that he would get me.'

'You didn't try to kill him then?'

'No. When he saw the knife he held up his hands in shame and started to cry. Said it was the drink that had driven him to it. With his head down, he crept back into his room and shut the door. I swear that, if it hadn't been for the knife I held out towards him, he would have done me. That was the last straw. So I spent the day planning what to do. And I thought of that paving slab lying in the yard, round the back...'

I started to sob, more in search of sympathy than in sorrow. I could not regret what I had done.

'Now, now, don't cry, María. We'll soon be out of here and leave all this behind us.'

I didn't sleep much and neither did Lucía. My head was still spinning. If I was caught, I could be hung for this or burned at the stake. But I harboured no regrets. It was a case of me or the *hidalgo*. I could not submit to more abuse or even rape by that wretch of a man. I was certain that if he did succeed in raping me, he would kill me, and then drop me in the river. Lucía was restless, too. She fully realised that I had committed a grave act and what the consequences could be. But this wonderful friend still wanted to be with me. She supported me and gave me solace.

We heard the church bells chime out five o'clock in the morning and decided to go. First, we tucked into some of the bread and ham which I had taken from the *hidalgo*'s house and a hard-boiled egg each that Lucía had brought with her. We cupped our hands and drank our fill of cold, holy water from the enormous stone font. Then we left the way we'd come in.

Within a few minutes and in the dark of the vanished moon, we were on the uncertain road to Madrid.

CHAPTER 2

The Flight from Burgos

It felt like a typical Spanish winter morning as we walked along the side of the road, each of us carrying our possessions, mine in my bag and Lucía's in her sack. We had nothing else in the world: no money, just a few scraps of food and hardly any clothes. In vain, I longed for the lazy heat of summer but our thick coats kept us warm in the biting, early morning air and moving at a good pace helped keep the cold at bay. We were both young and healthy so could easily cope with a brisk, long walk. I did not know my birthday and Lucía didn't know hers. I was fourteen or fifteen and she was a year or two younger.

'How far will we go today?' asked Lucía.

'Depends on whether we can find someone willing to give us a free ride and how far he takes us.'

'And how many days to reach Madrid?'

'You do ask some questions, Lucía. Does it matter? We'll get there when we arrive. But as you ask, about five or six days by cart, fewer if we are lucky enough to get a carriage and a quite a lot more if we have to stop on the way.'

I wondered whether the constabulary would pursue me, and therefore Lucía, and what story we would tell anyone looking for the *hidalgo*'s killer. Each of us had to tell the same tale as the other.

'Listen, Lucía. I have thought of something. We need a story for any constable who might be looking for me. Do you agree?'

'Yes, and we should change our names. I've never liked being called Lucía and now's our chance to change.'

'That's a good idea, but maybe for later. I just wonder about telling people new names now. We can talk again about that.' I was pleased that Lucía had thought of making this change. From being what I thought was considerably dependent on me, the events of the last twelve hours or so had given her a greater sense of purpose and she had become a strong contributor to our cause. Lucía was shorter and smaller than me and I could not help feeling protective towards her, especially when she gave me that look of being lost and vulnerable. She was a pretty girl, too young to realise how beautiful she was with her lustrous, long brown hair and bright, penetrating eyes to match. She and I would have to mature quickly if we were not only to survive but to make a success of our new lives.

'You interrupted me,' I said. 'I mentioned the need for a story. We need one to tell any constable, to put him off our scent.'

'Easy,' replied Lucía. 'We are going in search of work. I can sew. We can say I am looking for a job as a dressmaker, needle working or even doing tapestry. That may even be true! We can say we are heading for Segovia.'

'Good. I could say I am a chambermaid and am looking for work in a hostelry or inn. We can say that we lived to the north of Burgos, went there to find work but couldn't get jobs so went south. The thing is to tell the same story and be sure of ourselves in telling it.'

***

The morning sun peeped through the trees and above the sprinkling of houses as we reached the countryside, clear of the town. The bright daylight lifted our spirits. We chuckled in celebration that we had not been caught so far. I suppose it must have been about 8 o'clock when we saw the first wagon rumbling towards us.

'What sort of cart do we want to travel in?' asked Lucía.

'Depends how far it's going. If a long way, something covered, to keep us from the cold. And hidden.'

There were no others walking the road at the time the next cart came creaking towards us. It stopped as it reached us.

'Whoo!' called the driver to the pair of heavy, brown horses which were panting in their harnesses. 'You're out early. Where's a couple of young girls goin' this time 'a morning? And with no chaperone?'

I spoke first and nervously. I'd never asked for this kind of favour before. 'We want a lift towards Segovia. We've no work and we're looking for jobs.'

'Can't 'elp you meself. But one of our wagons is due along in about 'alf an hour. From Burgos. 'e's on 'is way to Aranda and will stop the night somewhere on the way.'

'How will we know him?'

'Can't miss 'im. 'e's got a green painted, covered wagon, drawn by a brown horse and a black one. 'e's carrying a load of cotton so you'll 'ave a comfy ride!'

'Glad you stopped,' said Lucía, smiling gratefully.

'No trouble. I'll see 'im on the road and tell 'im to pick you up.'

With that he snapped at the reins and the cart pulled away.

'What luck!' shouted Lucía as she hugged me tightly. 'Really good.'

'Couldn't be better. But we just keep walking and staying warm.'

We were elated and still couldn't believe our good fortune. Somehow our luck and getting safely away from Burgos had taken my thoughts away from what I had done to the *hidalgo*. However, it still invaded my mind but never once took the form of contrition. We spent the half hour speculating about our wagon and driver. Would he be a spritely young man with whom we could have fun or would he be some grumpy old fellow who would hardly say a word? The half hour passed and we were still walking. We were strong and didn't tire easily but were both getting thirsty. Several wagons, carts and carriages passed us from the Burgos direction but nothing that looked like the one the wagoner had mentioned. An hour passed. We were beginning to think the cheery old fellow was fooling with us and wishing we'd stopped one of the other vehicles. And we were getting thirstier. We stopped where the road crossed a fast flowing stream and wondered whether to drink from it.

'Let me try some first,' I said. I crouched down on the grassy bank and took some water with my cupped hands. 'Here goes.' It tasted clean and fresh so we each had a good fill.

'Here he comes!' shouted an excited Lucía, as I was finally slaking my thirst.

'Wonderful!' I called out, climbing back up the bank from the river and onto the roadside. Lucía held out her hand to wave him down. The smiling young driver pulled on the horses' reins and the green, covered wagon came to a shuddering halt.

'Climb aboard. I'm running late. Carlo told me about you. He saw you by the road. Let's go,' he said in a stream of quickly uttered sentences, as he helped us up onto the bench where he was sitting and smiling. 'Bet you thought I was never coming and Carlo was teasing you!'

'Yes, we did,' said Lucía.

'At least you turned up in the end,' I added.

'Got held up by the crown constables. Put a road block on the road over the bridge and searched every cart, wagon and all. Say a man was murdered in the town last night and they're looking for a woman called María. Not one of you I don't suppose!'

'Course not,' said Lucía. 'I'm Lucía and this is my friend María. Hundreds of girls are called María but my friend wouldn't hurt a fly. Pleased to meet you!'

'My name is Pablo.'

'Pleased to meet you, too,' I said, 'and thanks for stopping for us. What more is there about this murder?' I asked, thinking that to ask him might well deflect him from being suspicious of us, rather than dropping the subject altogether.

'Nothing. Except that the woman must have been very big and strong. Apparently, she lifted up a granite paving slab and dropped it on the man's head. Smashed his skull wide open. Killed him outright. The constables want her before she gets anyone else.'

'Just doing their job, I suppose. I wouldn't want to be in her shoes,' said Lucía.

'Nor would I,' I added, resisting looking down at mine.

'So where are you two heading?'

'For Segovia, but if you're going to Aranda, that would suit us well. We can stay there and get another lift in a few days' time,' I said.

'We won't make it there tonight. We'll aim for Bahabón, stay the night there and get moving early in the morning.'

'Can we sleep on the wagon, only we've got no money for lodgings?' said Lucía.

'That's difficult,' said Pablo. 'I have to close the wagon, tie it up and seal it. That's all part of the job.'

'We'll just have to leave you there then,' I said.

'We'll see if we can sort something out when we get there. Anyway, why go to Segovia?'

We explained to Pablo that we were looking for employment, me as a chambermaid and Lucía as a needlewoman. We told him we came from north of Burgos. We said we had spent the morning, until then, walking this road. He said he did this trip two or three times a week. And so our conversation continued with this friendly individual who seemed more than pleased to have a couple of young woman to accompany him on the road.

We were surprised by the amount of traffic. Except when we pulled in for a break, nothing passed us but there was a steady rumble of wheels on the road and the rhythmic clopping of horses feet as wagons, carts and the odd, expensive looking carriage came towards us from the opposite direction. We stopped after midday and shared what was left of our food with Pablo and ate some of his. He gave us some water from a large pot which he had anchored to the inside of the wagon. After several more stops, mainly to rest and water the horses, and a final push late in the afternoon, we arrived at twilight on the outskirts of the tiny village of Bahabón.

'Got an idea,' said Pablo. 'I always stay at the inn here. The village is too small for more than one. There is a nice landlady there. We'll tell her you've got no money and ask her if you can earn your stay helping in the kitchen, doing some cleaning or something. We'll see what she says. Otherwise you'll have to stay in the stables!'

***

We approached the tiny inn. It stood no more than five *varas* from the side of the road. There was hardly enough room outside to tie up horses at the water trough, let alone space for a wagon. Pablo led us in and rang a little bell placed in the middle of the counter. A thin, middle aged, austere looking woman, in a drab, yellow dress and with a white floppy hat perched on the side of her head, appeared behind the desk and stood facing us. Her face suddenly broke into a smile.

'Hello, Pablo. How are you? Who are your friends?'

'Couple of gals I picked up on the road. Wanted a lift. This is María and this is Lucía.'

'Pleased to meet you. Do you want a room for the night?'

'That's the problem,' said Pablo. 'They've got no money. Any chores they could do to pay for your little room upstairs?'

'I'll find them something, I'm sure,' she said, cheerily. 'But if they weren't with you, I'd send them on their way,' she continued with a frown.

'We'll need some food, too,' said Pablo.

'I'll prepare something,' said the landlady. 'In the meantime, I'll show them the room.'

The landlady took a candle and escorted us up the bare, wooden stairs to the smallest double room I'd ever seen. There was a narrow bed and a tiny, old dresser. Nothing else. There was hardly enough space to move.

'I'll leave you to settle in for five minutes, then I'll find you some work,' she said, closing the door behind her.

'This will have to do,' said Lucía. 'We have to accept it. There's no choice.'

'I agree,' I said, thinking more of our safety than our comfort.

We went down the stairs and found the landlady in the kitchen. She told us she would be having a busy evening as the inn was now full and everyone there wanted to be fed. So there would be plenty of work for us. We started by preparing vegetables, sweeping out the cramped dining room and laying the tables. By the time we went up to bed, we were exhausted having washed all the dishes, put them away and made up some rooms upstairs.

'I am ready for this,' said Lucía, as she sat on the bed and started undressing.

'Not so fast,' I replied. 'We should not sleep in this room.'

'Why not?'

'I am worried about what may be happening out there,' I said, turning to face the window which overlooked the road. 'I have been thinking.

What if the first wagon driver we met, that Carlo, realised, when he got back, that one of us could be the killer of the *hidalgo*? He might have gone to the constabulary and told them. If he did, they could be on the road already, and after us.'

'But he could not have known what you did before he got back to the town.'

'True, but someone could have told him, probably the officers manning the road block.'

'What are we going to do then?'

'We are going to keep our bags packed and go down stairs when the way is clear. We'll sleep in the kitchen by the back door.'

'How will we know when to go down?'

'The sounds of conversation and laughter will have stopped and the landlady will have put out most of the lamps.'

Within an hour we were creeping down the stairs towards the kitchen. The door creaked as we opened it. An oil lamp on the wall by the oven blessed us with enough light to see our way around. We crept into the larder and took enough bread, cheese and dried fruit to sustain us for several days, dividing these items between our respective bags. We also took some little pots we could use to drink fresh water from a country stream. We then lay on the floor and, using our packed bags as pillows, fell sound asleep. At about two o'clock in the morning, we awoke to the most horrendous banging on the front door, followed by a loud utterance of the words we dreaded most: 'Open up in the name of the law!' The cue for our departure.

***

By the light of our friend the moon, we ran towards a thick wooded area about four hundred *varas* from the inn. We were soon lost within this labyrinth of trees, bushes and dead ferns.

'We'll never find our way out of here,' cried Lucía.

'That's good. They'll never find us in here then.'

We did our best to avoid the few paths which crossed the wood and decided to try to sleep in some large bushes which served the double purpose of concealing our whereabouts and providing some shelter. We were both tired having hardly slept in the cathedral. Lucía soon nodded off but my mind was immersed in working out where we should go from here, and a tentative plan of how to get there. We had to assume that our pursuers had come to the inn. It could have been the local constables who were there for some other purpose but we could ill afford to make that supposition. So we were being hunted. The two questions were: when would the constables give up? And how could we avoid them? I imagined that there were probably only two officers, three at the most, mounted on horseback, certainly armed with pistols and that they had ridden from Burgos. We had told Pablo that we were heading to Segovia via Aranda so they might assume that we would find another willing wagoner to take us. They could not possibly have the resources to search a large area, especially at night, so if they did not just give up and return to Burgos, empty handed, they would concentrate on searching for us along the road south to Aranda. So we needed to follow an off-road route to the town.

Having reached this conclusion, I too gave in to my slumbers. We were jolted awake, in the early morning light, by the sound of horses' hooves and loud voices not more than twenty *varas* from the bushes under which we were hiding.

'We'll never find them in here,' said one of the riders.

'We'll just look from the paths. We're high enough up to see a good way in to the trees,' said another. And then they vanished.

Lucía wanted to speak but I held up my finger to silence her. This could be a trap. They could be trying to draw us out into the open. So we just stayed there for about four hours but heard nothing more, other than the occasional bird song and creak from a bending tree.

'When do you think we should move on?' I said, while we were eating some of the food we had stolen from the inn.

'Soon,' she said. 'I'm cold and want to get moving.'

We tried to work out, from the position of the sun in the sky, which direction was south and made our way cautiously out of the wood into the open on the opposite side of the wood to the village of Bahabón. We soon found that the countryside nearby was criss-crossed by a network of narrow tracks and paths which were presumably used by farmers to reach their fields and barns. Using the sun's direction as our guide we followed one of the tracks and just kept walking.

'As soon as we hear anybody, we get off the path and hide,' I said.

'Fine. I still think we should use different names,' said Lucía, as we were walking along. 'What do you think?'

'Good idea. Now would be a good time. What's your new name, then?'

'I like "Susana de Rivera". How does that sound?'

'You soon came up with that one!'

'I heard of a lady with that name and I liked it. So that's my new name!'

'I like "Esmeralda Pechada de Burgos".'

'Why "Pechada"?'

'Well. It means "scrounging" and we'll be doing plenty of that in the next few weeks. And the whole name has a ring to it!'

23

'I love the "Esmeralda". Do you like emeralds? But I'm not sure of the "Burgos" bit. Doesn't that give away that we came from there?'

'Hundreds of people come from Burgos, so not necessarily. Maybe it's daring. But that's what I want. And yes, I do like emeralds. I'll have one someday!'

'That does it then,' said Lucia. 'We must start using these new names right now, so we get used to them.'

'All right, Susana. I'll never call you Lucía again. That was your past and we're in another life now!'

'And I'll never call you, María, Esmeralda!' she laughed.

'While we have been chatting we've changed direction. This road is going east surely,' said Susana. 'We need to make a turn.'

She was right but we assumed we could find a turn or bend in the path which would bring us back in the direction we wanted. The road then took a sweeping arc to the right around a large clump of trees. We followed it and suddenly found ourselves facing a group of about fifteen or so brightly coloured wagons and a number of people, men, women and children, scurrying around, talking and generally making themselves busy.

'Now what do we do?' said Susana.

'This is a gypsy encampment. Let's go in. They may be able to help us. Let's be friendly with them but not tell them we are being hunted. We can only hope they don't know! Same story as before.'

'Can't see what we can lose.'

CHAPTER 3

The Gypsies

We took a chance and, with some trepidation, walked straight into the encampment. At first nobody seemed to notice us but, when we stopped and put our bags down, an oldish man appeared from one of a dozen or so smartly painted wagons. He had black hair tied into a braid and wore a kerchief on his head, knotted at the back. His dirty, blotchy apron hung almost down to his shoes. He could easily have been a blacksmith.

'Where do you think you're going?' he asked, in a gruff voice with a heavy foreign accent.

'We are on our way to Segovia, looking for work,' I said.

'You've picked an odd way to get there. How come you're on this road?'

'We stayed at an inn in Bahabón last night and thought this would be a shortcut back to the main road to Aranda,' said Susana.

'Lies!' he shouted. 'That's impossible. To get here you would've taken about eight wrong turnings. You're heading north east now, way off the Aranda road. How about telling me the truth? Where are you from? Are you on the run? Who from?'

By the time he had uttered his last, incisive question, several more men appeared along with a wobbling, short woman who was nearly as wide as she was tall. We were stumped.

'What do we do now?' asked Susana.

'Tell him the truth.'

So, between us, we told him and his cohorts the whole sorry tale, from me killing the *hidalgo* and our escape from Burgos, to our stay at the Bahabón inn and our flight from there the night before. We also said we had changed our names to protect ourselves and were actually heading for Madrid. They all listened in rapt silence until, at the end of our story, I said, somewhat shakily and fearing the worst, 'Well, that's it.' We could never have anticipated their reaction. All of them, including the oldish man, laughed and gave us a hearty round of applause. This sudden burst of noise brought another dozen or so from their caravans and from other areas in the camp. Altogether, we were surrounded by about thirty of them.

'You have been very lucky falling into our hands,' said the oldish man, by then with a wide smile. 'We are *gitanos*, and we have our own laws and codes of conduct. Now you have told us what seems to be true, we may be able to help you. My name is Milosh. I am the gypsy leader of this camp. This is my deputy, Fonso,' he said, turning to a swarthy looking man with black hair and a curly moustache. 'And this lady is Jofranka,' he said, nodding towards the short, plump lady who wore the most colourful of dresses. 'She is our fortune-teller. You must not go before she tells you what the future holds for you,' he said solemnly.

Susana and I glanced at each other and could see the look of relief on each other's faces. This had to be the best thing that happened to us since we left Burgos. The fact that he had mentioned leaving them, after a session with Jofranka, indicated that we would not be held prisoner. That they had their own laws would mean that we would not be handed to the constabulary which worked under someone else's laws. All good.

'We are travellers and come and go on the roads around here all year long,' Milosh continued. 'Don't be afraid. We will not harm you. In fact, we will help you. We do not stand in judgment, except to say we admire you for not giving yourselves up to the constables. They do not treat us well, so we work to confound them. Aishe here will take you to a caravan where you can stay for at least a night. We can work out how we can help you reach Madrid. We have several wagons leaving in the morning, at least one of which is heading that way, if not going all the way there. Before Aishe takes you, please hand over your knife, just for your own protection. You can have it back later.'

I was shocked that he knew about the kitchen knife which I was then carrying in my bag. He could not see it. How could he know it was there? Perhaps he just guessed that we carried some form of protection, just in case we needed to defend ourselves from some vagabond wanting to take advantage of two girls. I groped around in the bag, took it out and handed it to him, without saying a word.

'Thank you, Aishe,' he said, still smiling and looking at a slim, pretty girl of about seventeen, in a long, black skirt and wearing a white bodice with a colourful, smocked front. She stepped forward and, again with a foreign accent, asked us to follow her. She took us towards the edge of the encampment, to a beautifully decorated wagon, parked under an ancient oak tree. The wagon sparkled like a gem. Its sides gleamed a freshly painted red and its wheels glowed a striking yellow. A green, almost circular canvas roof topped the delicate structure, which had a bright red door at the front. Aishe climbed some wooden steps, opened the door and showed us in.

'Here you are. Do you like it?' said Aishe, clearly proud of the pretty wagon.

The interior had been conceived in heaven. Its walls were draped in swathes of yellow and green silk. The vertical stripes made the roof look higher. Delicate, floral patterned, red and green curtains hung at the sides of the solitary window at the far end. A gilt dressing table stood under the window, which faced two beds, one against each side of the compartment. The fabric of the bed covers beautifully complemented the flower print on the curtains.

'I've never seen a room as pretty,' said a cheery Susana.

'Nor me.'

'I have to ask you a question,' said Aishe, solemnly. 'It is very personal but I have no choice but to ask you.' She hesitated and with a look of deep embarrassment said, 'Are you virgins?'

Susana paused in shock. Then, after several seconds of delay replied, 'Yes... yes. I am.'

'So am I. If only just, and despite the attempts the *hidalgo* made on my body. Why do you want to know?' I asked, feeling awkward and unsettled by the impertinence of the question.

'We have strong views about chastity. We cannot tolerate love outside of marriage. It is a crime in our society. So I am glad you are virgins because in that condition you are acceptable to us,' she replied, coolly.

'What if we weren't?' I asked.

'I would have to ask you to make a discreet departure from the encampment ... and make your own way to wherever you want to go. There is one other thing,' she said. 'I advise you to make yourselves comfortable here. Have a sleep if you wish. But please do not come out of the wagon until I knock on the door. It is already late in the day, and I will return after dark.'

Aishe left and shut the door behind her. I thought I heard a key turn in the keyhole and, sure enough, she had locked us in. Even so, we just relaxed, laid on the beds and caught up with the sleep that we had lost the night before.

***

A loud banging on the outside of the door woke us from our repose. Then the sound of the key slowly turning. In came Aishe, from the shadows, carrying a candle in a holder. 'You can come out now.'

'Good,' I said. 'We'll be two minutes!'

We used the combs on the dressing table to tidy our hair and the scent spray to freshen up. We straightened our creased dresses and put on our coats. We then descended the steps back into the main encampment. Aishe led as we followed to where other gypsies were gathered. Most were standing around a spit on which a huge animal, probably a boar, was roasting over a brightly burning fire. The delicate, smoky aroma sharpened our hunger. Nearby, two women were stirring the contents of a cauldron over another fire.

'We will be eating in about fifteen minutes,' said Aishe. 'In the meantime, I must introduce you to Ion. He'll be taking you with him tomorrow. He is going to our encampment in Buitrago. It will take him two days to get there and at night you will sleep in his wagon. The gypsy leader has decreed that he will sleep underneath it. That will not be a problem: he's done that many times before.'

I had never heard of Buitrago and had no idea whether it was on the way to Madrid or to anywhere else.

'Where is this town?' I asked.

'It's about twenty *leguas* from here, on the road to Madrid.'

'That will be perfect for us,' said Susana, smiling.

I was sure that some of the men we met when we arrived at the encampment were absent, including Fonso, probably tending to their horses and wagons for journeys they would begin in the morning. The remainder of us stood or sat on benches at long tables, talking and hungry for the meal. The two fires and several braziers, mounted some four *varas* or so from the ground, kept the night's chill at bay and gave us light. Before we ate, the gypsy leader gave a short address. He spoke in a foreign tongue but we were sure he mentioned Susana and me. It was as if we were guests of honour; but the other side of me wondered if he was warning the others about us. He sat down to a modest burst of applause which prompted four of the gypsy women to serve the spit-roasted meat accompanied by copious vegetables. The men drank ale from leather cups and the women chose from a variety of fruit juices. It was like a party in the open. Everyone was happy and the whole group laughed and joked amongst themselves.

Suddenly, and without warning, a solitary gun shot rang out and reverberated around the clearing. Terrified and shocked, we all dropped down to table level to shelter. Then another deafening shot. A voice came from the darkness.

'Stand up and put your hands above your heads,' was its shouted instruction. We all simultaneously obeyed, including the leader and all the children present. Then four armed men emerged from the darkness, each wielding a double barrelled, flintlock pistol. Their apparent leader's gun smoked from both of its barrels. The four men stood next to each other, facing us. We could see them clearly from the light of the glowing braziers and fires.

'You people have no right to be here, on this land. Get your horses. Tether them to your caravans and get out of here. In ten minutes we will kill anyone who has not gone,' their leader demanded.

'I think we will stay,' said the gypsy leader. 'If you turn around, you will see why. Drop your guns to the ground and go.'

The gypsy men who had not attended the dinner were standing a matter of ten *pies* from the intruders and aiming long barrelled muskets at their heads. There were four thumps on the ground as the interlopers dropped their weapons.

'I said go. You have five seconds to do so,' said the gypsy leader, calmly and with authority.

They turned and, with heads bowed in fear and shame, departed from the scene into the darkness beyond the encampment.

'Follow them,' instructed the gypsy leader, 'and keep your guns trained on them.'

***

The following morning, Aishe woke us early with a knock on our caravan door.

'Get out of bed and get dressed,' she said. 'Ion needs to leave within the hour. You will have some breakfast with me and my family and, of course, see the fortune-teller before you go.'

'We'll be out in ten minutes,' I called through the door.

'I'm dreading seeing the fortune-teller,' said Susana.

'I'm not,' I said. 'She can say what she likes. We can believe her or not. Our choice.'

We climbed down the steps of the wagon to be greeted by a smiling Aishe. 'Come with me.'

We followed her to a caravan she shared with her own family. It was much larger inside than the one we used. Her mother and Aishe's two brothers were already sitting at the table, drinking grape juice and eating some brown bread, tomatoes and black olives.

'Sit down and help yourselves,' said Aishe's mother. Her two young brothers said nothing but looked at us quizzically. We ate quickly and without savouring the food, realizing that we had to meet the plump soothsayer before we left.

'Not so fast,' said Aishe. 'You don't have to worry. Ion won't leave without you.'

After we finished, we said our thanks and goodbyes to Aishe's family and she escorted us to the fortune-teller's caravan. It shone in its smart, yellow livery and stood majestically on its four, large green wheels.

The brightly dressed fortune-teller sat facing us, spilling her overflowing bosom onto a table, at the centre of which was her crystal ball, mounted on a dirty wooden plinth.

'Sit down,' she said, nodding her head towards a pair of chairs which were facing the table. We sat with nervous expectation.

'Have you had your fortune told before?'

We both shook our heads.

'Which of you is the older?'

'I am,' I said.

'Then we will start with you. I will start by telling you something about your past, so you know that I am telling you the truth. Then about the future.'

She leant over, as far as her breasts would permit, and peered into the centre of the crystal ball.

'You do not know your mother... Your brother has disappeared... You were named after a cathedral,' she said, in sentences that seemed separated by an age. 'And you are one of twins. Is that all true?'

'Yes,' I said, trying to conceal my excitement, my heart beating faster in anticipation at what her forecast would be.

'Now I will predict your future...' Then another long pause. 'You will be surprised that you are able to work in your job. It is not clear in the ball why that should be, otherwise I would tell you. Maybe you won't like it much, I don't know. But you will not be ashamed of it.' Then another pause. Her eyes didn't move from the centre of the ball. 'You will be close to war. I cannot tell which war but some war, it's clear.' Yet another pause. 'Your brother will appear in your life when you least expect him.' Pause. 'You will meet the king and become his friend.' Final pause. 'And you will be unlucky in love. That is all I can see in the ball. Now you, young lady,' she said, turning her attention to Susana.

While she spoke to Susana, I dwelt on these amazing predictions. How could this woman, sitting and glaring into a crystal ball, know these things? It was strange and confusing. How could she know about my past? To her, I was a total stranger. I had not told her anything about my poor lost brother or that we did not know our mother. And I was mystified, almost frightened, by her utterances, which gave me mixed emotions. When would I find my brother and where? Would I see him in Madrid? Whatever she saw in her crystal ball, it was saying that he was still alive. That alone was a source of comfort and be wonderful, if true. Not many people in Spain enjoyed their work and perhaps I would be no different. But I detected a particular repugnance in her voice when she spoke about my future job. Could it be that hideous? And could it in some way take me to war? Spain was always at war: even I knew that. But she said I would be in contact with war. How could that be? Would this war come to Madrid or would I be going to a war elsewhere?

The most astonishing of these predictions was that I would become a friend of the king. How could a common girl, of doubtful parentage, have a close relationship with His Majesty? The answer suddenly became clear: I would make achieving that my ambition. I would make it come true! I ended up thinking that what this woman had said was nothing more than invention. The contradiction was that she had said things which were certainly factual.

'That is all I can say,' said the fortune-teller to Susana. That was enough to bring me out of my private reverie. I was not conscious of anything the woman had said to Susana but it could not all have been good because Susana burst into tears.

'Take me out of here. Now,' she pleaded. I thanked the woman, took Susana by the hand and led her down the steps outside of the wagon.

'Whatever did she say?'

'Lots of things but ended by saying there was something she couldn't tell me. That's what upset me.'

'Ignore her,' I said emphatically as Aishe walked towards us.

'Ion is ready to go now. We must collect your things from the caravan. You will have to thank the gypsy leader before you go.'

The leader smiled broadly. 'Let me give you a word of advice. Don't use this as a weapon, unless it is to save your lives. Goodbye and good luck.' He handed me back the knife, the handle towards me.

Ion smiled broadly as he helped us onto the wagon. His white teeth glowed against his mahogany skin. His black moustache curled upwards into the line of his side whiskers. We stepped into the back, under the wagon's canvas roof. A bench seat faced the two horses which nodded their heads and snapped their hooves on the ground in anticipation of the journey ahead. Pots, pans, buckets, plates, jugs, basins, chamber pots, all made of metal, formed a large pile on the floor behind where we sat. As Ion cracked the reins and the horses heaved the wagon into motion, a chorus of tinkling, clanking and banging erupted, as the metal cargo settled.

From our seat in the front of the wagon we could clearly see the way ahead. We could speak only in competition with the pounding of the horses' hooves and the grinding of the wheels on the road.

'So what exactly did the woman tell you?' I asked.

'She said I had escaped from somewhere and left many friends behind. That much is true. Then she talked about some of the things which would happen to me. She said you and I would always be friends, that I would work long hours in my job and marry sooner than I might expect. Then she said, "But there is something here I have never seen before and don't understand. It isn't that clear so I can't use it to predict your future. We'll leave it like that.'"

'Maybe it wasn't something bad, just cloudy, vague or something,' I said. 'If I were you, I would ignore what she says. I still don't understand how anyone can predict the future, just by staring into a glass ball.'

'We should never have agreed to see her. She has really upset me.'

'We had no choice. I dread to think what would have happened if we refused. We could have been thrown out of the encampment or roasted on that spit!'

***

We had been on the road for about two hours or so when Ion turned his head towards us. 'It's time we stopped and gave these old nags a break,' he said. He seemed older than us, about twenty, we guessed. He steered the wagon towards a stopping area which was partly sheltered by a jagged outcrop of crumbling slate. The wagon slowed to a welcome halt. Its cargo rearranged itself again in a cacophony of clanking metal. As Ion climbed down and helped us out of the wagon, we could feel the strength of his tall, handsome body. His long dark hair, tied at the back in a purple bow, flicked across his back when he turned. He wore a wide brimmed, leather hat and only his large earrings betrayed his gypsy origins. He offered us bread and some of the spit roast meat, now cold, from the night before. Neither of us wanted to eat what appeared to be the most unappetising of fare but we took our fill of the cold, refreshing water he offered us.

'So why go to Madrid?'

'Looking for work,' replied Susana.

'Long way to go, just for a job.'

'I know, but we are looking for adventure and work to pay for it,' I said.

'Well, you are going to the right place. Madrid is the centre of everything. All manner of things happen there, good and evil. You will have to protect yourselves. There are people there who will take advantage of you... two innocent girls. You will find life difficult, unless you already know someone there.'

Susana leapt at his last sentence, 'Know anyone who could help us?'

'Only been there once, so I don't really know. That time, I had to deliver some metal containers to an alchemist. He lived in the Calle Luna, something like that. He acted like a madman but he was harmless enough. You could call on him, if he is still there. That was two years ago.'

'How could he help us?' I asked, wanting to test Ion further.

'You never know. He might not give you a job but he might know someone who can.'

We all climbed aboard Ion's wagon and after several more stops on the way, pulled off the road on the northern edge of the Sierra de Guadarrama just before nightfall. As Aishe had anticipated, Ion, wrapped in two large brown blankets, manoeuvred himself under the wagon to sleep. He threw us a third brown blanket. 'Here, snuggle up under that.' So that is what we did. We shuffled the pots, pans and other objects in the back to find an area of the floor we could use and shared the heat of our bodies to keep us warm that night. Ion woke us the following morning early and we were on the road again shortly after daybreak. The day passed quickly and before we realised where we were, Ion pulled the wagon off the road and along a winding track to the gypsy encampment at Buitrago.

CHAPTER 4

The Surprise

Ion jumped off the wagon as soon as it came to a halt in the encampment. He left us on the cart to go to what appeared to be a makeshift office building of some kind. It was made of pine logs and smoke billowed from a tall chimney at one end of its sloping, wooden roof. Several other men, presumably also gypsies, were chatting to each other outside. Within a matter of minutes, Ion appeared again and called up to us.

'There's been a change of plan. We are going to unload our wagon and re-load with bales of cotton, which I'll be taking to Madrid. So you won't have to change wagons, as you can come along with me. If you want to, that is...'

'Excellent!' I said. I liked Ion and didn't want to get to know a new driver.

'Very good,' said Susana with genuine feeling and enthusiasm. She seemed especially fond of him. 'Could she desert me for him?' I wondered. 'Surely, not.'

'We will eat here tonight. You can sleep on the wagon again and I'll sleep in that building over there,' he said, pointing to the log cabin from which he had just emerged.

Ion smiled as he greeted us in the morning light. 'I hope you are both decent and ready to go,' he said. By then we had shared some items for breakfast, which we had put aside from dinner the night before, were sitting on the bench inside the wagon and eager to leave. Ion whipped the reins and the wagon began to move. As we passed along the winding track towards the road we spotted three, youngish horsemen, astride their mounts, who were waiting beneath a large leafless tree. As we passed by, close enough to recognise them if we saw them again, each lifted his tricorn hat, as if to wish us good day.

'Who are they?' I asked Ion.

'No idea. Never seen them before.'

So we were on the road once again. Susana and I felt quite elated as we could not be more than fifteen *leguas* from Madrid and could even reach the town late in the evening, that day, or at the latest the day after. Then our new lives would begin. With Burgos four days behind us I thought that the chance of capture was receding. It was mild for winter but we could see some dark clouds coming towards us on the horizon. After a couple of hours, Ion decided we needed a break so we pulled to the side of the road and stopped to eat a biscuit or two, washed down with some cold water.

'While I remember, you will need some money while you are in Madrid. The gypsy leader, Milosh, asked me – just before we left Aranda – to give you this.'

Ion handed each of us a small gold coin. 'It's a gold *ducat*. It will keep you in food and lodgings for about two weeks, if you're careful. He didn't want you sleeping in the streets the moment you arrived in Madrid, not if he could avoid it. And he didn't want you to have it until we'd passed Buitrago because you might start spending it!'

'You gypsies are so generous,' said Susana. 'We thought we'd be sleeping in doorways. At least until we found someone who would pay us to work.'

'We are so grateful,' I said. 'Please thank Milosh when you see him again.' We had no purses, so I put my *ducat* in my bag and Susana buried hers at the bottom of her sack.

Ion watered the horses and we were soon on the road again. We noticed that there was very little traffic, save for the odd cart and a lonely horse rider coming towards us. The dark cloud we had seen earlier was almost overhead and we could detect drops of rain falling on the road and on to the horses. The gentle drizzle intensified and, as the wind got fiercer, soon developed into a violent storm. The noise of the wind on the canvas roof of the wagon nearly deafened us.

'It's no good. We'll have to stop. The horses will stop anyway, if we don't.' With that, Ion guided the horses to a sheltered area, beneath a clump of gnarled old trees.

'Best I can do. The horses will have to stay put, but I'll jump into the wagon with you.'

We all sat on the bench, not saying much but looking out, hoping the storm would soon pass. After about half an hour, a blue patch appeared in the sky and the storm subsided.

'Let's go,' said Ion, smiling. 'I'll just wipe down the horses.' He hopped down from the wagon, dried them off with a towel, jumped back on again and cracked the reins. With the unexpected stop, the horses seemed to have renewed their energy and took to the road quickly and with determination. It was as if they wanted to make as much progress as they could before any fresh storm arrived. The short deluge had driven virtually all of the other traffic from the road. So it was a pleasant surprise to gather that there were travellers nearby as we heard the sound of galloping horses approaching in the direction from which we came. The rhythmic clopping noise became louder as the horses neared us and then stopped suddenly as they came to a halt, almost alongside.

'Stop where you are!' shouted one of the horsemen, whom we could not see from within the wagon.

'This is trouble,' said Ion. Susana and I looked at each other in frightened silence and stood to look out.

From beneath a red bandana, which covered his lower face, the lead rider shouted, 'You three. Get off the wagon!' 'Not the constabulary,' I thought. 'Not wearing bandanas. This could be much worse: highwaymen.'

Ion helped us down but said nothing. Each of the three masked men was wielding a flintlock pistol, one aiming at Ion's head. They wore tricorn hats and looked like the three men we had seen, stopped at the end of the track to the encampment in Buitrago. Susana and I were shaking in terror but did not utter a word.

'Are you all damned well dumb?' roared one of the men.

'What do you want?' asked Ion.

'Those girls!' shouted one of the others, laughing as he did so. We glanced at each other in dumbstruck horror. The fear of violent rape, being beaten and left for dead filled my mind. Susana looked scared, confused and helpless. What had I brought her into?

'Get your things from the wagon,' said the third.

We scrambled up inside the wagon to collect our bags and the few other items we had there. We climbed down again to face our gleeful captors. Susana started to cry and I tried to comfort her but failed. A pool of water formed below her as in pure fear she wet herself.

'Shut up,' said the one who had spoken first. He stared directly at Susana and then glanced at the puddle of urine.

Susana rushed up to Ion and clung to him, her arms tight around his waist. 'Don't let them take us. They'll kill us! They'll kill us!' He eased himself away slightly to avoid getting wet.

'That's the last thing we would do,' said the leader, calmly. His words gave no more than scant relief.

'What do you want with them?' asked Ion, sounding resigned and powerless.

'We are going to kidnap them. Here is a ransom note. Turn your wagon around, ride back to the Buitrago encampment and give it to the leader there. He will soon see what we want.'

'But...'

'Do what I say. Now!'

Ion walked the few paces back to the wagon. 'Don't worry girls. Everything will be fine. Just do what they say. Don't try to fight them or escape.' He climbed up, pulled the reins, to turn the cart around, and set off after we said our plaintive goodbyes and thanked him. I feared we would never see him again. Now we were totally at the mercy of these highwaymen. But if they were to rape and kill us, it wouldn't be yet, not until they failed to win a ransom. Susana, who didn't know then what the word 'rape' meant, stood and cried as she watched Ion leave us. We were scared to death, much more so now that he had gone.

'You, get up in front of that rider and you, in front of the other one,' instructed the leader. The two others helped us up so that we sat astride their horses, our backs to the kidnappers.

'Let's go,' shouted the leader, and off we set at a fast gallop along the road towards Madrid. Each of us clung on to the saddle and held our bags tight. After about half a *milla*, the horses suddenly turned off the road to the right, up a rising path and then down a steep slope towards a lake about four hundred *varas* ahead of us. As we approached the lake, we spotted a wooden hut with a wooden door. We soon realised that the hut had no windows.

'You are staying here until we are paid the ransom. Then we will release you back to your gypsy brethren,' said the leader, in a firm but not unfriendly tone. 'There is food in the hut and we will give you water. Before we lock you inside. One of us will be on guard outside. Do not... I repeat... do not... attempt to escape. If you make one attempt at getting away, we will tie you up and that will be very unpleasant for you.'

We had no choice but to comply with their wishes. I still had my knife but could see no advantage in using it, at least not at that moment. I remembered Milosh's advice not to use it unless we were in mortal danger, which we were not, at least not then. It was not long before one of them turned the key and we were locked inside. It was dark and smelt damp. But there were mats on the floor and blankets so we could keep warm and wrap ourselves in them to sleep. Once we had been imprisoned for about five minutes, our eyes became accustomed to the little light that seeped through the cracks in the timber and the gaps in the wood. We could just about see into each other's eyes. We started to assess our situation, speaking in whispers so the one of them on guard would not hear us.

'How long do you think we will have to stay here? When will the gypsies pay the ransom?' asked Susana, much calmer as she slipped on her other dress.

'They won't pay. I am certain of that.'

'How do you know?'

'The kidnappers believe we are gypsies. They spoke of "our brethren". The gypsies will soon tell them that we are not, just people they gave a lift to. I don't know what will happen to us then. But no one will be paying a ransom.'

'How can you be so sure?'

'Just think about it.'

'They gave us some money.'

'Yes, a paltry *ducat* each. The ransom will be hundreds if not a thousand *ducats*.'

I soon persuaded Susana that our best hope was clemency or to escape.

'How can we get out of here?' asked Susana.

'We could open up the side of the hut with a knife and climb through.'

'What if one of the kidnappers is out there?'

'No one will be there at night. We'll do it then.'

So we waited until nightfall to attempt to break out. First we tried forcing the lock. That was no use. But we made enough noise to prove, either that any guard out there was deaf, a sound sleeper or not there at all. We then tried pushing a wooden panel off the wall on the lake side of the hut. We banged at the panel, which was at about knee height, and shoved at it with all our might. The almost total darkness we were working in hardly helped. We pushed and heaved at it until our hands and knuckles bled. We were about to give up when we heard a squeaking sound as the wooden slat was beginning to loosen.

'Hooray,' cried Susana. 'We've done it.'

We managed to move the panel until it was loose at one end then, with both of us pushing at different points along its length, we broke it free of the hut. It fell on the soft ground outside. The sky was still cloudy and starless, so we could see hardly anything through the gap we had made.

'We can't get through there,' sighed Susana.

'I know but it should be easier now one is off to remove some more.'

I took the knife and through the opening we had made, slid it between the next panel up and the one above it. Using the knife as a lever, and taking it in turns to apply all the strength we could find, we soon stripped off the second panel. By then we were getting quite excited and felt we were on the verge of escaping. The middle panel, which we had to remove to get out, proved the most difficult to dislodge. Whatever we did to move it failed. We said that the nails securing it must have rusted solid. Then we hit on an idea: we would break it and lever off the two ends. We both held on to the panel at its centre and pulled it towards us. After several failed attempts, it broke and we both fell on to the floor of the hut, laughing as we did so. We stood and kissed each other in relieved celebration. It had taken us many hours to achieve our ends: we were free.

***

Dawn was beginning to break and the clouds had cleared. We gathered up our things and climbed out through the hole, looking around us to see whether our captors were anywhere near us. There was no sign of them.

'Which way should we go?' asked Susana, grinning all over her pretty face.

We agreed to walk along the path by the lake and away from the road, turn to the south and start walking, more or less in the direction of Madrid. Full of energy and excitement, we made good progress and within about half an hour we found ourselves approaching a large, mature farmhouse, set back about twenty *varas* from the path. The sun had risen fully by then and, despite the daylight, there were several lamps still glowing in the downstairs windows of the house.

'Shall we go and tell the farmer we've been kidnapped,' asked Susana.

'Why not and ask for something to eat and drink?'

We knocked on the door and stood waiting outside. The door opened and two men appeared, grabbed us and dragged us in, laughing. They were two of our kidnappers. The third appeared from an adjacent room. 'What a surprise. We didn't expect to see you until we came to the hut. You've save us the bother,' he guffawed.

We were devastated. We looked at each other in horror and disbelief. Susana started to quiver. I was stunned. How stupid we had been. We had not even fallen into a trap. We had created our own and stumbled into it. We had wasted all the effort it had taken us to escape from the hut and pointlessly made our hands and fingers bleed.

'You are in a mess the pair of you. You'd better come in and clean yourselves up. Your gypsy brothers will deduct some of the ransom if they think we've made your hands bleed,' the leader said, jokingly.

It was pointless to attempt to struggle or get out of the house. We could only come off worse. The two who had grabbed us at the door held our hands behind our backs and forced us into the back kitchen. It was a large room adorned with copper pots and pans that hung from hooks on the walls. A large plain table filled the central area of the room. It could easily seat eight. A fire glowed in a large open hearth and gave the room a homely touch that made us feel moderately comfortable, despite the ghastly circumstances of our renewed captivity. A large earthenware bowl stood in the centre of another smaller table. The one who had brought Susana into the kitchen released her, took a jug of water from a shelf and emptied its contents into the bowl.

'You can wash yourselves in that.'

The cool water felt good on our aching, bloodied hands. We swirled them around in the water, splashed some on our faces and dried ourselves on a towel the man gave us.

'That's better,' I said. Then, after a pause. 'What happens now?'

'We have to look after you because you're our hostages. We'll give you food and drink. But you've disobeyed us so we'll tie you up and keep you here until we hear from the gypsy leader. He has until five o'clock tomorrow evening. We've told him where he should bring the money. If he does, we will hand you back to him or whoever he sends.'

'What if he doesn't?' I asked.

'I am not going to answer that question,' said the leader. 'I believe he will pay.' We knew he wouldn't and feared the worst.

The two other men tied our arms behind our backs and led us upstairs to an oddly furnished drawing room. The windows were draped with light green curtains, tied back at the sides, and a darker green carpet completely covered the floor. Several wooden armchairs, with light green cushions, were placed at strange positions in the room. One was facing the window and another faced a side wall at which hung a portrait of a young woman. A double armchair presented itself to the door, like a four legged janitor guarding the room. Another leant against the wall, just inside the door. It was as if someone had moved the furniture to sweep the floor but had left the chairs in their new positions without returning them to where they were meant to be.

'I want each of you to sit down, in separate chairs,' said the man escorting me. We did, making sure we were facing each other.

'Now we'll tie you up,' said the other, in a calm, indifferent tone.

They left us with our hands bound and feet tied, sitting in the room. At least they hadn't gagged us so we could speak and provide each other with some degree of comfort.

'What if the gypsies don't pay?' said Susana. 'I'm really scared.' Then she started to sob.

'Assume they won't pay,' I said. 'But I don't think these men will hurt or kill us. They have nothing to gain.' I didn't say that my fear was rape and then being murdered.

We could not determine our true predicament. I was sure the gypsies would not meet the ransom demands. Why should they? We were nothing to them and our kidnappers would eventually realise that. We had, as events turned out, accurately assessed our position. The kidnappers left us locked in this bizarrely furnished room. One or two of them came in occasionally to ask us if we needed anything. They gave us food and we imagined we shared in what they had prepared as meals for themselves. They brought us water, but only water, to drink. They even asked if we needed to relieve ourselves and untied our legs and took us to a room with a chamber pot, when we did. We tried not to show embarrassment as they stood over us as we did what we had to do. They ensured we could clean ourselves afterwards from a jug of water, left by the side of the pot, and wipe ourselves with a cloth. They were, in many respects, quite kind. They obviously wanted to keep us in good condition for those whom they expected to pay the ransom.

We stayed calm and took some advantage from the situation. Although we were prisoners, we had a roof over our heads and were regularly fed and watered. We still had our *ducat* each, hidden at the bottom of our respective bags and, of course, it was intact in that we had not needed to pay for anything. We were hardened to the fact that neither of us had a mother or father who would be in anguish over our disappearance. So at least we did not have that worry but we still had serious anxieties about what our fate would be at the hands of these bandits. We struggled to work out why they had first locked us in the hut by the lake when it would have been easier to confine us in this house from the beginning. We failed to come up with an answer.

We slept surprisingly well that night, in the green room and in the chairs they had put us, with our legs and hands tied. At about five in the morning Susana woke me.

'I must do a pee,' she said. 'I'm about to burst.' With that the door opened.

'Which one of you wants the pot?' said one of the men who was, apparently, on guard outside the door.

'We both do but take her first,' I said.

It was still dark then and afterwards we each resumed our sleep. We were awoken by one of the men who unlocked the door and came in with some breakfast on a tray.

'Time for some food. Everything happens today!' he said, smiling and seemingly pleased to see us. He untied our hands and gave us some pieces of bread, some hard cheese and some grapes. He sat in one of the other chairs and attempted to start a conversation. We did not tell him that we were not gypsies but did admit that we were on our way to Madrid to find work. Nor did we tell him we were from Burgos. That would have informed him immediately that we were nothing to do with the gypsies at Buitrago and we wanted to avoid that.

At some time in the afternoon, all three of the kidnappers arrived in the green room. Without as much as uttering a word they untied our legs and led us down stairs, still with our hands tied behind our backs. The time had come. A shiny black carriage, to which two frisky black horses were tethered, awaited us outside. 'Get in,' said the leader. It was an expensive, luxury caroche of the kind owned by the very rich. Plain red velvet, buttoned into a pretty diamond pattern, covered the two pairs of facing seats and the pair of footstools. The carriage and its interior sparkled as if it had been made only the day before. It seemed as if we were to be taken to a ball, rather than to be given up for a ransom – if indeed that was to happen.

'We have no choice but to gag you,' said the leader as they tied kerchiefs around our heads. 'We can't afford to have you calling out to passers-by.' He then pulled down the blinds at the windows. The driver shouted a command to the horses, pulled at the reins and we were on our way. The carriage moved at speed along the track to the main road and we turned right towards Madrid. We were puzzled by this manoeuvre because Buitrago was to the left. We must have been driven a good hour, in the company of two galloping horses, whose riders were presumably the leader and his third accomplice, and then turned off the road to our right. The carriage came to a halt after about a further half minute. We could hear urgent talking outside and then silence.

We were there for about half an hour. The men were talking angrily to each other. Something had gone wrong. The gypsy had not arrived. Each of the men blamed the others. The leader started shouting at the other two. A gun shot rang out. We cowered on the carriage floor. Then, suddenly, the carriage moved off and headed back to the main road. We could not be sure of the direction we were travelling in but the driver was snapping the reins and the horses were working hard. We were jostled around in the carriage as the wheels hit stones and ruts in the road. We could not talk because we were still gagged. They were taking us somewhere but we had no idea where. Then I realised that there was no sound from the other two horsemen. I could hear only the carriage and its two horses, going at a steady gallop. The other two had left us in the hands of the driver. We were confused and frightened. Where were we going? What would he do to us? Would he take us somewhere and shoot us? We were in a state of total uncertainty and terror. The carriage rocked from side to side as it sped along the road. Which road? To where? We had no idea. It was getting dark. Would he drive us through the night? No. The driver stopped the carriage off the road and opened the door. He took off our gags and blindfolds.

'We are stopping here for the night. Then we set off again in the morning.'

'Where are you taking us?' I asked.

'You'll see soon enough. Come out and stretch your legs and make yourselves comfortable,' he said, while untying us. 'Then get back in.' He locked us in for the night. He must have slept up front or under the carriage. Fear, uncertainty and the total lack of information about our fate, denied anything but the shallowest of sleep.

At day break, the driver checked that we were all right and started off on the road again. He did not tarry. Wherever we were going, we were going to be there as quickly as our sole kidnapper could drive the horses. We were bound and gagged so could not speak to each other. Where was this journey to end? The carriage stopped several times by the side of the road and the man brought us food and drink.

'Where are we going?' asked Susana.

'I told you. You'll soon see,' he said replacing the gags and blindfolds. Our minds were in a state of fear and turmoil.

We moved off again. Within half an hour or so, we could hear more traffic, as if we were approaching a more populated area. Then we could hear the noises associated with a town. People shouting, horses and carts, vendors selling their wares at street corners. We could not know whether we were merely passing through or whether we were to stop here. Suddenly, after about twenty minutes, the driver stopped the carriage. We heard him climb down and approach us. He unlocked the door, climbed in and shut the door behind him. He untied us and took off our blindfolds and gags.

'Pick up your things and get out.'

We both thanked him and climbed out of the carriage. He climbed back into the driver's seat and drove off, leaving us standing in the middle of a large square surrounded by tall, handsome buildings. What an incredible relief. We hugged each other and cried tears of pure joy.

'What luck!' said Susana, smiling for the first time in days.

'Amazing,' I replied. 'I just can't believe it! Back there I expected the worse!'

'Me, too!'

We gazed around the *plaza*. It must have been midday or later. There were people everywhere, going about their daily business. Three priests walked quickly across the square, talking urgently to each other. A group of beggars held out their bowls to them. Two men, one at each end, struggled with a heavy ladder.

I approached a lady carrying a basket. 'Excuse me,' I said. 'Can you tell us where we are?'

'Certainly, you are in the Plaza Mayor, in Madrid.'

CHAPTER 5

Beginnings in Madrid

We still could not believe we were just where we wanted to be.

'Are you sure?' asked Susana.

'Course I'm sure,' said the woman. 'I ought to know. I live here. Just around that corner over there.' The woman, neatly dressed in a distinctive, orange coloured, long-sleeved jacket, over a heavy brown skirt and wearing a grey wimple, pointed to a narrow street that entered the Plaza between two tall buildings. 'How come you don't even know what town you're in?'

'We have been given a lift in a carriage. We come from near Burgos. It's a long story,' I replied, feeling uncomfortable at her questioning.

'You can tell me more over a drink,' said the woman. 'I'm on my way home and you can come with me if you want. Don't leave your bags on the cobbles. Pick them up and bring them.'

The woman led the way, across the Plaza towards a road she called the Calle Nueva. She had a friendly face and seemed kind and helpful. Susana winked at me as we walked behind her. 'Seems all right doesn't she?'

'We can leave her place any time we want,' I said, still feeling awkward and uncomfortable but grateful for her offer.

'Come on you two. Keep up.'

The woman pushed open her front door which was set back from the façade of the building, directly behind one of a series of arches. A bell rang as the door opened into a ham shop. By the light from two oil lamps at the back of the shop we could see dozens of joints of ham suspended by hooks from the ceiling. We were intoxicated by the soft, sweet smell of the cured meat. A short, plump man in a straw hat, almost completely enveloped by a large white pinafore, stood behind a wooden counter at the back, sharpening a butcher's knife on a stone.

'This is my husband, Juan Ramírez. My name is Josefina Muñoz de Ramírez. What are you called?'

We gave them our new names and said we were pleased to meet them.

'We live over the shop. Come upstairs and I'll make a drink. Follow me.'

The woman showed us into a small, dark kitchen. A wood fire burned gently in a grate at the far side of the room. Apart from a small dirty window, facing the street below, the fire provided the only light in the room. A small table and four chairs were set against the inner wall.

'Sit down and put your bags on the floor,' said the woman, as she filled a kettle from a jug of water. 'I'm going to warm up some chocolate. Would you like some? You can drink it on its own or with some water. Have some water to wash it down.'

She carefully placed a dish of chocolate over the fire. It soon melted and she poured a cup for each of us, including herself. The chocolate gave off a bitter, sweet, nutty smell.

'This tastes good,' said Susana. 'I've never had this before.'

'I mix it with sugar to make it taste better,' said the woman. 'Now. Tell me your story. I've been itching to know.'

Although it was unlikely that we would be arrested in Madrid, we needed to be careful about what we told her and not be overcome by our excitement at landing in this town. We did not want to tell her about the death of the *hidalgo*. Susana had taken the hint I had given in saying we were from near Burgos, so she knew what not to say. I started by relating that we had tried to find work to the north of Burgos, where we had come from, but had failed; that we had tried Burgos itself but to no avail; that we then decided to come to Madrid. With Susana, chiming in, I told her about the lift Pablo had given us to Bahabón and that we had got lost walking from there to Aranda; that we had stumbled across the gypsy encampment; that a gypsy called Ion had taken us to Buitrago where we were kidnapped and so on, until we were tipped out of the luxury carriage in the Plaza Mayor.

'My God, what a story! Incredible! So the kidnappers could not have been paid. Obviously not!'

'No,' said Susana. 'Why should they pay when we are not gypsies?'

'Of course! They shouldn't! You are lucky that you came to no harm... and that you ended up where you wanted to be. Very lucky. So the kidnappers weren't as bad as you thought they might be. Quite kind, in fact. So they never hurt you or anything? What are you going to do now?'

'Find lodgings and then find work.'

'I will ask my husband if you can stay here for a few days. We will find you some good lodgings. If you are not careful you can stay in terrible places in Madrid. You can work for us, doing some deliveries, if my husband agrees.'

'You are so kind,' said Susana. 'We were lucky we asked you where we were!'

'We could have asked one of those priests. They wouldn't have helped us like you have,' I said, by then feeling more confident about the señora who seemed to be genuine in wanting to help us.

Señor Ramírez was less certain about us staying at their house and unsure about our working for them.

'But we've never seen them before. What if they're a couple of thieves on the make,' he said, as if we weren't there in the kitchen with them. 'They could steal all our valuables, clear off and we'd never see them again.' His voice was shaking and uneven, as if he was afraid of us.

'I don't want to be where I'm not trusted.'

'Nor do I,' said Susana.

'Thank you for the chocolate. We'll be on our way,' I said, leaning over towards the floor to pick up my bag.

'See what you've done, Juan. You've put them off staying here.'

'All right then, they can stay. You'll have to hide your jewellery and lock the doors at night.'

'We can do jobs for you to earn our keep,' said Susana.

'They could deliver hams to your customers,' said the woman. 'You need someone now that Teresa has gone to work at the theatre. I'm not doing it all myself. Not with everything else I have to do.'

The bossy Señora Ramírez won this little argument and the couple agreed that we could stay with them, if only for a few days, and that she would help us find somewhere more permanent to live. Once again, fortune had shone upon us. A chance meeting in the Plaza Mayor blossomed into our stay at the house above the ham shop. We had offered to work for the couple and work we did. We discovered that the girl called Teresa had worked for them for several months. She had tired of carrying hams to all manner of places in Madrid and eventually found herself a job selling food and drink in the Príncipe, one of the theatres in the town. Apparently, she had stormed out of the shop complaining about the sheer amount of work she had to do for the ham seller. After a few days we could see why. It seemed that we walked every street in this town, delivering to his customers. One thing became clear. These were the best quality Serrano hams and only the well-off could afford them. This meant we had to go to the houses of the Inquisitor General, the Archbishop of Toledo, the Duke of Lerma and a number of other important officials, as well as the homes of rich *hidalgos*, and *caballeros* in the town.

We both travelled the streets together, taking it in turns to carry the heaviest of hams, or even suspending them from the middle of a pole the ham seller insisted we use to prevent us dropping them on the 'filthy streets of our town'. We must have looked a strange couple, especially when we turned the pole around in the street so the other one could take over the lead. Many of our fellow pedestrians laughed out loud at us as we swivelled around and made them clear a space for us to make this awkward manoeuvre. We delivered sometimes twenty hams in a day to houses at every point of the compass. But what an opportunity it gave us to explore the sights, sounds and smells of our chosen town and, of course, to get to know its people. Its enormous size frightened us. Burgos seemed like a village in comparison. You could walk from one side of Burgos to the other in a matter of a half an hour. Not so in Madrid which seemed to go on forever. We never stopped telling each other how well off we were here. We glowed with happiness.

***

After we had been staying with the ham seller and his wife for about a week, he asked us to deliver two of his exquisite products to a house at the eastern corner of the Calle de la Luna and the Calle de la Madalena. The Calle de la Luna snaked down in a south easterly direction, off the Calle de los Convalecientes de San Bernardo, which was on the main thoroughfare out of the town to the north. I had a strange feeling about this task. I don't really know why. It seemed just like any other delivery the señor asked us to do, but I felt something odd would happen at this house. Something we didn't expect. The señor gave us the hams and off we cheerfully went with these huge objects, each shrouded in a white net, dangling on the pole, with one of us holding it at each end. People in the town were scurrying to work as we left the Calle Nueva on our way there. The sun shone brightly for a winter morning and we glanced at many smiling faces lit up by its orangey, golden rays.

'Where you off to now?' asked a beaming flower seller who always spoke when we passed her little stall on the corner of the Calle Nueva and the rambling Puerta de Guadalajara.

'Up to de la Luna,' said Susana, returning the smile. 'A house on the east corner with the Calle de la Madalena.'

'Don't know that one or who lives there,' she said.

'It's the house of Señor Benito Ortiz de Navarette,' I said.

'Never heard of him,' she called after us.

We crossed the busy Puerta de Guadalajara, across the Plazuela de los Herradores, where the stall holders were setting up their usual Tuesday morning market, and up the Calle de los Ángeles. Our noses were deluged by the smell of the human excrement which had been tipped, the night before, from the houses onto the street.

'This stink is making me feel sick,' said Susana, before coughing loudly.

'Put a handkerchief over your nose.'

'I would if I had one.'

'For God's sake keep your end of the pole well clear of this shit. Señor Ortiz de Navarette won't sign for the hams if they're covered in it.'

We decided not to go up the Calle de los Convalecientes de San Bernardo because that would mean coming back on ourselves to reach the junction of de la Luna and the Calle de la Madalena. The streets were likely to be busy with all kinds of early morning traffic, which might jostle and bruise our valuable hams. So we took a short cut, up the narrow, almost deserted Calle de los Tudescos instead. We soon wished we hadn't. A group of scruffy beggars, who emerged from an alleyway, followed us. One of them tried to snatch one of the hams, which swung away from him as he tried to grab it. Then it came back and hit him in the face. He fell to the ground swearing as we started to run up the road away from them. The beggars gave chase. One of these hams would have fed all five of them for three days, if not more. We held the pole high and ran as fast as we could, holding the hams to steady them. At the top of the street we turned to the left on to the Calle de la Luna. The street was thronging with people, some on horseback, gingerly picking a way down the road, through the crowds of people on foot, who were dashing to and fro and talking quickly to each other as they went. I looked round to see where the beggars were. To our great relief, they had stopped at the end of the street. We had shaken them off. We caught our breath and walked the rest of the way to the house.

***

The majestic three-storey property proudly overlooked the street. Its two bay windows, each of which was low enough to allow passers-by to see inside, flanked an imposing, heavy-looking front door. We paused to peer through the window we passed but could see no one there. We were about to pull on the bell cord when the door burst open and a tall, thin, grey bearded man ran out of the street coughing with all his might. He was followed by a cloud of grey, black smoke.

'Run down the street,' he shouted and spluttered at the same time. 'There's been an explosion in there!'

Surprised, and mildly amused, we followed him for about twenty *varas* and looked around. The black grey cloud had ascended skywards and was dispersing as it went.

'We should be all right now,' he said, after he had coughed one final time and was then at the panting stage. 'I was just conducting an experiment and it all went wrong. I am Señor Benito Ortiz de Navarette, the alchemist of la Luna'.

I looked at Susana and she looked at me. We just about avoided laughing out loud. Then everything fell into place. This was the alchemist whom Ion had mentioned while we were on the way to Buitrago. I knew there was something about this delivery. Señor Ramírez' mention of the Calle de la Luna had made me feel uneasy but I had completely failed to connect the name of the street to what Ion had said while we were on the road. So much had happened to us since then that my mind refused to make the association. Now all became clear.

'I love the look of those hams,' he said. 'I can always rely on Señor Ramírez to save the best for me. Do you have time for a drink and a snack before you go back?'

'I think so,' I said. 'Our next delivery is at midday so we have time to spare.'

'Yes, I'm thirsty,' said Susana.

The alchemist showed us into his magnificent house. As we stepped into the hall we were greeted by the acrid smell of some kind of acid or alkali. It stung our noses and we each stopped spontaneously by the door. He could see we were uncomfortable.

'Let me open a few windows. Wait here, please.' He returned a few minutes later and by then the bitter smell had all but vanished. He couldn't resist showing us into the two front drawing rooms. The most extravagantly furnished rooms I had ever seen startled my vision. The floors shone with their polished glass finish and some expensive looking, Turkish mats decorated the tiling. Armchairs, scattered with red silk cushions, rested in front of an open hearth. Portraits and various landscapes hung from the luxuriously papered walls. He then took us through to the kitchen and sat us down at the table.

'So where do you carry out your experiments?' I asked.

'I'll show you in a minute. Would you like some fruit juice first and a biscuit?'

'Yes, please,' said Susana, reminding us of her thirst.

'Now come through to my laboratory.' He opened the door to a room which was about as large as the three substantial rooms we had already seen put together. We could detect the residue of the sharp smell which confronted us when we entered the house, but it was only a trace and by then quite tolerable. Shelves around the walls bore the weight of hundreds of bottles, of different shapes and sizes, filled with crystals, powders and liquids, each a different shade or colour from the other. Greens, blues, yellows, orange, purple, whites, greys and black. Each bottle was labelled with the name of its contents. Some names were etched in the glass; others written in manuscript on paper or parchment. Oil of vitriol, brimstone, calomel, aqua fortis, arsenic glass, lunar caustic. Some of the bottles were coloured. Others were shaped like giant teardrops and filled with coloured liquids.

Three well worn, wooden benches filled half the floor space. The alchemist had regimented his huge range of apparatus upon them. Dishes, retorts, evaporators, measuring vessels, tripods, crucibles, pestles and mortars, flasks, oil burners, empty bottles, tongs, spoons and stirrers stood in organised groups.

'What made all that smoke?' asked Susana.

'I was trying to make copper from blue copperas but something went wrong. I shall have to check my notes to work out what caused the explosion. I'm lucky it didn't blow the windows out!'

'Can I ask you a question?' I asked him. 'Did a gypsy bring you some pans some time ago? Maybe two or three years?'

'Yes,' said the alchemist. 'He was a jolly, young fellow with a moustache that joined up with his side-whiskers.'

'That's him,' said Susana, laughing.

'How do you know that?'

We explained to the alchemist how we had met Ion who had told us that the alchemist might be able to help us find work in Madrid. The alchemist was as surprised as we were that we had met him by chance through a delivery of ham.

'I may just be able to help you,' he said, smiling excitedly. 'I am looking for an assistant who would help me in the laboratory. But I couldn't take you both. And I could not give you lodgings. I will pay well. Three *reales* a week.'

'Can we think about that and let you know? That doesn't seem much to me. And which of us would you want?' I said, sounding ungrateful.

'You have a think and come back at 9 o'clock on Saturday morning and we can decide. If you don't come, I'll take it that neither of you want the job,' he said, his face having suddenly lost its glow.

With that, the alchemist politely showed us out and we walked back to the ham shop to make our next delivery. We didn't take the shortcut in case we saw the beggars again but talked to each other, the whole way.

'What did you make of that?' asked Susana.

'I'm not quite sure. I liked him and could work for him but we don't have anywhere else to live. Other than with the Ramírezes.'

'She said she'd help us find somewhere but she's done nothing so far.'

'That's because she's afraid we'll leave them and she'll have to deliver the hams on her own.'

'Which of us would work for the alchemist?' said Susana, with a note of uncertainty in her voice.

'I'm not sure, Susana, but if we're interested we should allow him to choose. It would be wrong of us to say only one of us is available. Or that he must have you.'

'But if he chose you, I could be left with no job. I might as well go back to Burgos if that happens,' she said, her eyes looking towards the floor.

'But if he chose me, we would find you a different job. And me one if he chose you. Don't forget what the gypsy told you. We would be friends for ever. We won't be if you go back to Burgos.'

'That's true,' Susana said, becoming more cheerful but still a little downhearted.

'It's simple, really. We have to decide whether one of us should work for the alchemist. If yes, we both go to see him and let him chose. I think we should do that. That's because the Ramírezes are only giving us food and lodgings. No money. That three *reales* a week would at least give us something to spend. I'll tell you what we should do. Go to see him on Saturday. He'll decide which of us he wants. We then try to persuade him to let us both stay in his house. That way we have somewhere to live and some money. We won't say anything to the Ramírezes until one of us gets the job. They may let the other one carry on working for them. I still think Señora Ramírez won't want to do the deliveries on her own.'

'You are clever, Esmeralda. I agree with everything you've said. We'll see the alchemist on Saturday, 9 o'clock.'

Saturday soon came around and we left the Ramírez household on the pretext that we were going to explore more of the town. As he opened the heavy front door, the alchemist welcomed us like lost children, which I suppose we were in a way.

'I'm so pleased you came back. So, so pleased,' he grinned, his moustache sweeping upwards as if it was just as pleased as him.

'Now which one of you would like to be my assistant?'

'We thought you should choose,' I said.

'What are your names?'

'I'm Esmeralda Pechada de Burgos.'

'I'm Susana de Riviera.'

'How old are you?'

'I am fourteen or fifteen, maybe sixteen. We are orphans, you see, and don't know when we were born exactly.'

'I am thirteen or fourteen.'

'I think I would prefer to take you, Esmeralda. You are just that bit older and you will be stronger. Do you mind, Susana?' he said, being as sensitive as he could about her feelings.

'Well, I am disappointed but I do have a job working for Señor Ramírez.'

'Can I ask you a question, Señor Ortiz de Navarette?' I asked.

'Of course.'

'Susana and I were wondering if you could think again about us staying here. You have a lovely large house. We would have your smallest room and be no trouble at all. In fact, we could help you with the cleaning, the cooking and other jobs you might want us to do. We would not expect to charge you and we'd be more than happy to accept the three *reales* a week for everything you asked us to do. We are utterly trustworthy, as Señor and Señora Ramírez will tell you.'

'I'm still not very willing. I have a housekeeper to do the cleaning and she comes twice a week. But if you can cook, make the beds and run errands for me that would be most useful. Let's agree to have you here for a month. We can think again then. You start here on Monday, Esmeralda, and both of you can move in then.'

Susana dashed up to the alchemist and hugged him. I thought she was going to kiss him, she was so pleased. I was, too, but less open about showing it.

On the way back to the Calle Nueva, we decided to tell the Ramírezes exactly what the alchemist had agreed. Señor Ramírez was furious. 'What the hell have you two been up to? I send you to one of my customers and the next thing is you are asking him for a job? I knew we couldn't trust these two, Josefina. We should throw them both out now. Go and pack your bags.'

Señora Ramírez defended us like a fairy godmother. She was just as angry but with her husband, not us, 'Just you stay put, girls. No, Juan. You are wrong. We said we'd help them find somewhere to stay. We've done nothing to find them lodgings or paid work. We've selfishly made the most of their willingness to do deliveries. So they've found something themselves. Well done you two! As far as I'm concerned, and if Señor Ramírez agrees, you, Susana, can continue working for us. How much should we pay her, Juan?'

'Maybe you're right, Josefina,' he said softly, immediately acquiescing to his wife. 'We'll pay Susana three *reales* a week, the same as Esmeralda will get. She can help you with the deliveries. Do you agree?'

Susana was overwhelmed. She rushed up to Señor Ramírez as if to kiss him, too. She placed her arms round his waist and hugged him. 'I love you, señor. You are so kind.' Then she did the same to the señora, squeezing her so hard her eyes almost popped out.

'Thank you, both of you. You are wonderful,' I said and truly meant it.

'Everybody's happy then,' said the señora. 'We will celebrate tonight. I'll cook my speciality pork dish and we'll all have a little drop of wine.' Once again the overbearing Señora Ramírez had won the battle with her plump, little husband. We were mere onlookers.

True to her word, the señora concocted a spectacular meal for the four of us. She cooked a pork casserole for several hours over the fire in the kitchen. She boiled up some artichokes, carrots and beans and served the dinner on the little table in the kitchen. We all managed to sit around it, even though we were breathing down each other's necks. Señor Ramírez opened a bottle of the finest rioja.

'Let's drink to you girls,' said the señor.

Neither Susana nor I had tasted wine before. We didn't like it much so we switched back to water. Señora Ramírez drank the rioja with fervour, to the extent that she instructed the defenceless Señor Ramírez to open another bottle. As he pulled the cork, he looked at me, smiled broadly and winked.

'I think ...we should ...go to bed ...now,' said Señora Ramirez, speaking awkwardly and slurring her words. By then we had been sitting in their drawing room for at least an hour and the Ramírezes had told us about their life before the ham shop: that they had met in Toledo; that they had married young; that he was her second choice; that because a doctor had found something wrong with Señor Ramírez, they had not had children; that they owned the ham shop and the rooms above it. We exchanged our 'good nights' went to bed.

About a half hour afterwards, when Susana and I were almost asleep, we were disturbed by some strange, groaning noises coming from the direction of the Ramírezes' bedroom. By then, they trusted us and none of the rooms was locked at night.

'Whatever is that?' asked Susana.

'I'm not sure,' I said.

'Let's go and see,' said Susana.

We crept out of our room onto the landing. The Ramírezes' bedroom door was partly open and two oil lamps flickered inside. The shrieks and groans sounded as if they emanated from Señora Ramírez. We approached the bedroom door and peeped in. Señora Ramírez was stark naked and sitting astride her husband's unclothed body. She was riding him like a horse, her little white bottom pounding up and down to the rhythm of her squeaks and squeals. Her tiny breasts, the size of chickens' eggs, were moving in time with her bottom. She pulsated like some grotesque machine. Señor Ramírez' hands were supporting her unsubstantial buttocks, so helping her frantic pulsations. He kept her pulled towards him to stop her sliding off his plump round tummy and himself from falling out of her. We froze in shock at this incredible sight. Susana grabbed my hand, as if to seek protection.

'Come, you bastard! Come! Finish fucking me!' Señora Ramírez yelled, with total inhibition, oblivious to our presence as her guests.

I gently pulled Susana away and we tiptoed back into our bedroom. 'What did she mean by "come"?' asked Susana. 'They aren't going anywhere are they?'

'Remind me later. I'll explain it to you.'

CHAPTER 6

The Alchemist

I rang the alchemist's doorbell early on the Monday morning. The excitement and anticipation of starting in my new job completely possessed me.

'I'm ready to begin, Señor Ortiz de Navarette. What d'you want me to do first?' I asked, standing outside, holding my bag. The knife was still inside it, as was the gold *ducat*. We still hadn't spent any money in Madrid.

'First, I'll show you to your rooms,' said the alchemist, leading the way to the attic. 'I've decided to let you have a room each. There is no extra charge. You will be helping me because, without you, the rooms would stay unused. They haven't been lived in for years. Here, this one would be yours and that would be Susana's.'

My heart sank. The shock at what I saw and smelt stunned me into silence. My room was strewn with empty boxes, old news sheets, a roll of threadbare carpet, odd pieces of broken furniture and clothes, too worn and too dirty to wear. A musty, damp odour wafted out of it. Susana's room was worse. The stench of it hit my nose. It reeked as if someone had left rotten food in there. The room was piled so high with rubbish I couldn't possibly see the cause of the smell. I wondered then whether we should have asked to see the rooms first before agreeing to stay. We didn't so we had to accept what the alchemist provided.

'Is there a bed in here?' I dared to ask.

'As a matter of fact there is. Over against the far wall, under all that junk. You can see why I wanted someone strong to work here. Your first job is to sort out the bedrooms and make them habitable. When you can get to the window, open it and let some air in and the smell out. I will help you, of course,' he said with a slightly worrying smile.

We laboured all day to make the rooms decent. I lost count of my overloaded journeys down the stairs. The more things we moved, the more dust we made, until the whole house swam in a choking grey suspension. It was as if a nearby volcano had erupted and blown its debris inside. The alchemist set a bonfire in the back garden. It burned so hot he risked setting himself on fire. His clothes smelt scorched by the clamouring flames. Acrid smoke mingled with the fog indoors.

This working collaboration provided an opportunity I had to take. To discover more about this man. To begin with, I felt nervous talking to this stranger, who seemed very clever, but I soon found the courage to ask him about himself.

'So, what made you become an alchemist?'

'Well, when my father died he left me a small fortune. He owned a shipping company in Cádiz. And worked the trade routes to the West Indies. His luck held out well and, although he lost a few ships to the Dutch, he still had fourteen square riggers in his fleet when he sold the company to a sugar importer in Seville. Must have been twenty years ago. My mother died of the plague and my only brother was killed in the battle of Lepanto. So when my father passed away, I was the sole beneficiary of his will.'

'Your brother? Killed at Lepanto? I've heard of that.'

'Yes. An Ottoman arrow straight through his heart. Thirty years ago and I still miss him,' he said.

'So how is it you became an alchemist?'

'Be patient young lady. I am getting to that. I was a teacher in Álcala de Henares. I lectured in mathematics and science at the University. I decided that, with the money my father left me, nearly 100,000 *ducats*, I could afford to resign my job as a teacher and become an alchemist. I'm interested in the stars so at night I watch the skies in the observatory I've had built at the bottom of my garden. I am therefore an astronomer as well! I'll teach you and Susana about the stars.'

'We'd love that. Thank you! That will be so exciting. I love to hear about new things. Tell me, are you married?'

'No. I am wedded to my studies. They give me great satisfaction. But I have a lady friend who sees me about once a week. Usually, I go to her house but sometimes she comes to mine. She lives in the Calle del Postigo de San Martín so only a few hundred *varas* from here. You will meet her. She is Angélica de la Torre. She is a lovely lady and I'm certain you will like her.'

As we were removing all the rubbish from the rooms, washing the paintwork, brushing the floors and reinstating the beds and wardrobes, we talked about Susana and me. I told him as much as I thought I should but, of course, did not mention my killing of the *hidalgo*. By the time we finished our day's work, both bedrooms could be slept in. Neither would impress a queen but they would be sufficient to meet the needs of two poor girls from the country. Each bedroom looked over the alchemist's beautiful garden towards his little observatory and beyond, to the north of the town. Each would benefit from the rising sun in the morning so we would, as the alchemist put it, have no excuse to oversleep.

With the job done, I went to meet Susana, only because I felt unhappy about her coming all the way from the Plaza Mayor alone. Susana couldn't wait to see what the alchemist and I had done in our new home and explore our freshly prepared quarters.

'This is far better that our tiny room at the Ramírezes,' she said, 'and look at that lovely view. I shall miss sharing a bed with you, Esmeralda but I'm sure we'll both manage.'

**

It wasn't long before we each settled into our daily routine. We would both have breakfast with the alchemist and Susana would go alone to the Ramírezes to work for them and leave me with him. With my three *reales* a week, we bought things for ourselves and got things done. Sometimes we bought food and prepared it together in the kitchen. Occasionally, we prepared dinner for ourselves and the alchemist who loved to join us as our 'guest' for a meal. We bought some new dresses, new shoes, stockings, new bags and some orange blossom scent. We took our dirty clothes to the laundry in the Calle de Flor Alta and took our worn-out shoes to the menders in the Calle Nueva, a few doors away from the Ramírezes' shop.

I worried about Susana arriving safely at the ham seller's. At that time of the morning, all kinds of beggars, thieves and vagabonds roamed our streets and any one of them would regard a pretty little fourteen year old as a tasty victim. So, for her own protection, I gave Susana my knife which she kept in a bag she carried to and from the Plaza Mayor.

I would spend the day working with the alchemist doing all manner of work, including assisting him in his laboratory. Apart from the days when his cleaning lady appeared and rushed round the house with her brush and her duster, I spent most of the time alone with this interesting character. I soon felt I could trust him and we became a good working partnership. Unlike the *hidalgo*, he never once made an attempt to abuse or molest me. Quite the opposite, he treated me – and Susana for that matter – with constant respect. He didn't stop teaching as he regarded me to be his more than willing student, which indeed I was. In days when he did not feel like working, he might spend some time showing me how to read and write and to do simple arithmetic. I had hardly accomplished any of these skills at the convent and, at fifteen or so years of age, I was more willing to learn. And, of course he showed me the rudiments of working in his laboratory, what chemicals were dangerous, what not to touch, what not to mix with what, how to clean the glass vessels without damaging them, how to measure out volumes of liquids and how to weigh out quantities of materials. I thoroughly enjoyed working with my new master.

***

Susana and I spent some time speculating about Señor Ortiz de Navarette's lady friend, Angélica de la Torre, guessing what she looked like, what she wore, what size she was, how pretty she might be and even about what they did together. Then one bright spring day, after we had been staying with him for about three months, Susana and I, who were both alone in the house, heard a loud ringing on the door bell below. I dashed downstairs and opened the front door only to be confronted by a comfortably large but well formed lady wearing a full, salmon pink dress, which reached down to her feet, and a wide brimmed, bright red hat. She was carrying an attaché case.

'Hello. I have come to see Señor Ortiz de Navarette. You must be one of his lodgers,' she said trying to smile, as if she was expecting the señor himself to answer the door and not some poor girl.

'Is he expecting you?' I asked.

'Yes. As far as I know. Mind you, I may be a little early.'

Then she turned around in the direction of a plaintive voice from no more than twenty *varas* up the road. 'Angélica. Angélica, it's me, Benito.' The alchemist had returned from the shops and was waving frantically. 'I'm sorry I'm late.'

'No matter. Anyway, I may be early. It's good to see you,' she said, planting a wet kiss on each of his skinny, bearded cheeks.

'Have a seat in one of the drawing rooms. There's a fire in the one on the left. I'll get you a drink. Esmeralda, come with me. Now.' His instruction sounded urgent and pained. I followed his hasty steps into the kitchen.

'Esmeralda, I have made a mistake. I wasn't expecting Angélica today. I thought she was coming tomorrow. I beg a favour. I need some private time with her so I don't want you and Susana in the house for a few hours. There's a new play at the Príncipe theatre. It starts in an hour or so. Here is some money. Take Susana and go to see it.' He gave me a handful of coins which I later counted to be five *reales* and a few *maravedís*.

Susana and I walked to the theatre which is in the Calle del Príncipe, just off the Calle de San Geronimo. It wasn't at all what we expected. It was situated in an open courtyard between two large houses, the backs of which faced each other. The stage was a raised platform at one end and the rest the main auditorium. The women were separated from the men and had to sit in the *cazuela* which was a gallery built into the house on the right as you faced the stage. We paid our *real* each and entered about half an hour before the start of the performance. As we did, and accompanied by the stench of stale urine, we were deafened by the outrageous noise of the audience. Most of the women in the *cazuela* were standing and shouting obscene abuse to men. As their retort, the men threw banana skins, apple peel, bits of stale bread and screwed up balls of paper at the women, who simply picked up the rubbish and lobbed it back at the men. A piece of melon hit Susana on the head. Like a true pikeman, she picked it up and threw it back in the direction from which it came.

'I didn't expect this,' said Susana, half enjoying the debacle. 'I thought theatres were places where nice people went for entertainment.'

'Not in this bloody town,' said a woman next to us. 'This is mild. Some tart is sure to get her tits out before long.' Within moments of this prediction, a woman along from us, in a white floppy hat and greyish dress, dropped the dress from off her shoulders and wobbled her massive bosoms in the direction of the men. Another woman, just along from the first exhibitionist, did likewise, exposing the top half of her moving, somewhat smaller body. The men cheered with rowdy enthusiasm. 'Told you,' said the prophetess, laughing all across her face.

Within moments of this display of female flesh, a drum banged out from the direction of the stage and a man appeared from behind the curtain. He wore blue tights, a green buttoned up jacket and a fancy hat with a long feather sticking out of it. 'Order! Order! Unless you lot behave yourselves, I'll call in the constables. They'll soon shut you up.'

Gradually, the crowd calmed down and the play began. It was called The Imperial Otón but, apart from realising that it was about a king of Bohemia, we simply could not follow the plot. The audience booed and whistled as each actor nervously appeared on the stage and vanished as the mob shouted them off. The cast failed to perform the play and even an order restoring interval failed to quell the fearless disruptors from wrecking the second act. Disappointed with the afternoon's entertainment but educated by the behaviour of a Madrid afternoon audience, we left the theatre and made our way back to the alchemist's house.

'Not sure I want to see another play,' said Susana.

'Nor me. I can't get over those women showing off their breasts. That wouldn't happen in Burgos.'

'Or many other towns. I wonder if Angélica will have gone by the time we get back?'

We were away from the house for the prescribed two hours but she was still there, sitting on one of the armchairs in the left hand drawing room. Something, however, differed dramatically. She no longer wore the striking salmon coloured dress but had changed into a short black frock which exposed a considerable depth of her cleavage. Her legs were graced with red stockings which reached to the centre of her thick, white thighs, which generously displayed themselves from the inelegant position she had adopted on the armchair. We did not dwell on this change of apparel but merely offered our greetings to the couple as we passed the room on our way up to the attic.

'You can tell me later what you thought of the play,' said the alchemist, looking discomfited by our returning before the señora had left.

*****

'I don't get it,' said Susana, as we flopped onto the bed in her room. 'Why did the señora change her dress?' At that moment, I confirmed to myself that poor Susana knew nothing about lovemaking. I suspected as much when she reacted with such astonishment to the Ramírezes' session that we witnessed through their bedroom door. I had never discussed my own incomplete knowledge of such delicate matters with anyone before, except my brother Pedro. I therefore felt a degree of reluctance to touch on such details with my friend, Susana. I thought though that she'd probably prefer to learn from me than from someone she didn't trust so much. I also felt she'd be protected by knowing enough about the subject to realise when she might be the subject of a proposition or worse. So I steeled myself to tell her some of the relevant facts. That moment, in her room, seemed as good a time as any.

'Susana, my dear friend, I feel have to ask you a sensitive question.'

'Go ahead, Esmeralda.'

'I don't want to offend you at all. You understand?'

'Please, Esmeralda, I'm sure I won't be offended as long as it isn't something sad. I don't want to cry!'

'All right then. Do you know how babies are made?'

'Yes, a bit about it. The mother makes a wish and months later a baby comes out of her bottom. One of the nuns at the orphanage told me. That's all I know.'

'No, Susana, that's not right. I'll tell you some of the facts.' Susana's face was a picture as I told her what happened between a man and a woman. I explained the preliminaries, the movements and what happened at the finish. She seemed shocked and disappointed. Nor did she feel I was telling her the truth. She thought I was joking or making it up.

'I don't believe you! Where does the man put his cock? Where does it go?'

I thought for a moment and realised that it would not be out of place to demonstrate to her where the man entered the woman's body, even if I could show her little more.

'As we are friends, I'll show you,' I lay back on the bed and lifted my dress up to my breasts. Then I eased myself open so she could see inside.

'See this. The man's cock goes in this hole. Not the little one you pee out of but the one below. It opens up, wide enough to take it. He moves in and out and eventually he comes. Some white juice shoots out the end into the woman and if they're lucky – or unlucky if they don't want one – it goes to make the baby.'

'I get it,' said Susana. 'That explains why Señora Ramírez shouted at her husband to "come." Do you remember, I asked you where they were going? Silly me! The only thing is that I don't think I could do that.'

'Why not?'

'I've only got a pee hole, no other hole like yours.'

'Yes, you have. I'll show you. Lift up your dress.' As I dropped mine down, she lifted hers to expose her prettiness which was just beginning to show signs of hair. 'If I open you up, as I did with myself, I can move my finger around you and you can feel where it is. Just now, it is on your pee hole. Can you feel that?'

'Yes. It is nice to have someone touching it. I feel all prickly!'

'Now I'll go lower and put my little finger on your lower hole. Can you feel that? It's just inside.'

'Yes, it feels nice. I want you to push it in further.'

'No. I mustn't do that. You must stay tight and that way you will still be a virgin. I am because it is only the tip of my finger that has gone into mine.'

'Thank you, Esmeralda. I am so grateful. I would never have known these things.'

'There's a lot more and I'll tell you about that later.' I made mental note to tell her about the monthly bleed before she had one herself and thought there was something badly wrong, as I did when I had my first one.

**

We each enjoyed our new lives in Madrid. We explored this wondrous town at every opportunity. We would go on long walks, laughing and joking to each other as we saw a funny sight, like a cat jumping on a man's shoulder, or a woman chasing some chickens through the market in the Plazuela de Selenque, and we gazed in awe at the spectacular buildings or the views from the north over the town. We loved to wander up to the palace and giggle at the stern-faced guards to try and make them laugh. One day, the king smiled at us as he climbed into his ornate carriage. Our waiting in hope, near the palace entrance, had paid its dividends. Susana reminded me of what the gypsy fortune-teller had said about my becoming friends with him. That still puzzled me, but I was still determined to make it happen, one way or another.

***

One day, as summer was approaching, the alchemist shouted up the stairs. 'Esmeralda, come down straightway!' I dashed down, jumping them three at a time. There was a man standing at the front door carrying a paper. A horrible thought crossed my mind: not a constable from Burgos who had come to arrest me. This fear died as another was born.

'Susana has been arrested. She's supposed to have stabbed a man while she was walking down the Calle de los Ángeles.'

'I don't believe that! It cannot be true!'

'It is true, Esmeralda. I'm sorry to say. It is true. This prison warder says so.'

'Poor Susana. Where is she now?'

'She's in the town prison,' said the warder, without any sign of compassion. 'She gave this house as her address. She's been charged with attempted murder. You can pity her as much as you like but the man she stabbed is in the General Hospital fighting for his life.'

'I've got to see her,' I said. 'Can I see her now?'

'No. Visiting is at five o'clock this afternoon. You won't be let in before then.'

I felt sick and guilty for bringing her here and getting her into this mess. I tried to remain calm because this would help me to help her. I could see that the man's story could be true. If so, she must have used the knife I gave her. But surely she wouldn't have used it without being provoked. The man must have attacked her first. Or so I convinced myself.

'Are there any witnesses?' asked the alchemist.

'Yes, some street vendors and four beggars. They all say she tried to rob one of the beggars. He's the one she stabbed.'

'I can't believe that. She's got a job at the ham shop in the Calle Nueva. She doesn't need to rob a beggar.'

'Say what you like, young lady. I'm just telling you what she's been charged with,' he said coldly, as if he was talking about a lost pigeon, not my beloved friend.

I walked to the town prison and waited outside the main gate for visiting time. A crowd of about fifty had arrived there before me. A small group of women were all crying, as if they had been told that a loved one had died there. Some street sellers were offering refreshments to the throng. A man in a tall hat was using the prison wall as a urinal. The whole Plazuela de Ville, to which the prison faced, smelt like a sewer. I could not bring myself to watch others eat in this vile place. Let alone do so myself.

Eventually, the gates opened and we were herded into the prison yard. It was strewn unevenly with human waste, clearly the main source of the stench in the Plazuela. Poor Susana, left confined in a place like this.

A completely bald, stocky warder, with a bunch of keys the size of a bouquet of flowers, escorted me to Susana's cell. I could hear her crying as we approached. Her arms were tied to metal rings in the walls. She stood on tip-toe to take her weight.

'Esmeralda, look what they've done to me. It was self defence and now I'm accused of murder,' she said, her eyes streaming and her voice shaking. 'What can you do to get me out of this shit hole?'

I tried to console her. I asked her to tell me exactly what had happened. I told her to start from the beginning and tell me every detail. That would serve two purposes: to settle her down and to give me any facts that I could follow up.

'You know I left a little later than usual this morning, so I thought to save time I would take the short cut, down the Calle de la Luna into the Calle de los Tudescos where the beggars chased us before. I looked down the road and could see other people going to work so I thought I was safe going that way. I went down the Calle and from there into the Calle de los Ángeles. I kept my eyes open for anyone suspicious and kept the knife near the top of the stuff in my bag, just in case.

'When I reached the point where the passage straight through to the Plazuela de Santa Catalina joins the Calle de los Ángeles, I felt someone behind, making a tug at my hair. I turned around quickly and it was one of the beggars who attacked us before. He wanted my money and said he'd kill me if I didn't give it to him. I put my hand into the bag and pulled out the knife. I saw the flash of a knife blade in his hand but I was too quick for him. I stabbed him once in the stomach and he dropped to the ground. Another beggar came and took the knife from his hand and another grabbed me around the waist.

'"Hold her while I get a constable," said a third.

'I tried to struggle free but two street vendors helped the beggar to hold me as the other beggar went for the constables. There was a lady carrying a baby who saw the whole thing. She looked frightened and disappeared back up the street. I am sure I recognised her as a lady who lived in the Plazuela de San Domingo. Señora Ramírez and I delivered two hams to her, only a few days ago.' Susana began to stutter and sob again.

'Two constables ran down the street towards us blowing their whistles. One took my knife and the other tied me up. Then one of their carts came. They bundled me into the back and took me to the judicial office in the Puerta de Guadalajara. I was terrified and screamed all the way. When I calmed down, they made me sign a statement of some kind, shoved me back in their cart and brought me here. What can I do, Esmeralda? Help me,' she pleaded with her brown eyes and still sobbing. 'Honestly, I was just defending myself.'

'We'll soon have you out of here,' I said, not really believing what I was saying. 'I'll see if I can find the lady who bought the hams.' The jailer appeared at the cell window to say my time was up. I hugged and kissed Susana, who was frightened and distraught, told her I'd visit her the day after and left. On my way back to our lodgings, I plotted how we could rescue her from this hell in prison. I had to find the lady with the baby. We could only hope that she would be courageous enough to help. I would ask Señora Ramírez to tell me where she lived.

CHAPTER 7

The Explosion

The alchemist greeted me as I walked through the front door. I cried immediately and fell into his arms.

'Esmeralda. I am sorry.' He hugged me and eventually I stopped the tears.

'I'm sorry, too, Señor Ortiz de Navarette. I was all right until I saw your friendly face.'

'I understand, Esmeralda. Don't worry. Best to let it out. How was she? How is she coping?'

'In an awful state. She wouldn't stop crying. They'd tied her up so her arms were above her head. Her bare feet could hardly touch the ground. She told me the whole story. She stabbed a beggar in self-defence. He threatened to kill her if she didn't hand over her bag.'

'Where did she get the knife from, my kitchen?'

'No. I was worried about her being attacked on the way to work. So I lent her the one I brought from Burgos. I feel so guilty. Terrible.' I started sobbing again.

'If you hadn't given it to her, she could be dead by now. So don't be like that... it's not necessary.'

'You are kind, Señor Ortiz de Navarette. I think I'm better already.'

I told the alchemist the whole story, just as Susana had related it.

'Two things occur to me. First, you must track down the lady with the baby. Early tomorrow morning, go to Señora Ramírez. Tell her that Susana has been wrongly imprisoned. Ask her... No... beg her to keep the job for Susana until she is free. Volunteer to work for them at the weekends when you are not working for me. That is sure to help. Ask her to go with you to the Plazuela de San Domingo to speak to the witness with the baby. She will have to go to the judicial office in the Guadalajara to give a statement. Second, I will pay for a lawyer to defend Susana at her trial. We will find the best lawyer in town.'

'Trial?'

'Yes. She will have to be tried for attempted murder. The authorities have no choice.'

'But she is only thirteen or fourteen.'

'If she had been ten she may have just been reprimanded. But she is old enough to know the difference between right and wrong so will be tried before a judge.'

I broke down again. I had never felt so bad. It was all my fault. The alchemist put his arm around my shoulder to comfort me again. He helped me settle. I could see that there was nothing to be gained in feeling sorry for myself when it was poor Susana who was in trouble.

'Thank you, señor. You are so good. Spending your own money on a lawyer. That's just wonderful.'

'Don't worry. I can afford it.'

The wait for Susana's trial was the worst three months of my life. It seemed endless. Poor Susana almost gave up hope. She stopped eating. She stopped drinking. She almost stopped breathing. She suffered all the cruelties of hell: the constant stench of human excrement; the shouting; the sound of beatings and the screaming of the other accused. I did all I possibly could to comfort her. I went to see her every day. I kissed her, as a true friend would. I told her I loved her. I said everything would be the same when she got out. I did my best to share her misery and pain. I explained to her that Señora Ramírez was keeping her job and that I was helping with Susana's work. I said we had found the lady with the baby who would act as our main witness and that we had engaged the best defence lawyer in Madrid.

After about a month in prison she could begin to see that there might be an end to her suffering and she became more positive. From becoming so thin and emaciated that you could see her bones though her skin, she began to gain some weight. She even raised a smile when I went to see her. She began to eat and drink regularly. What a relief.

***

Life had to go on and, especially while awaiting the trial, Señor Ortiz de Navarette gave me plenty to do and explained his work to me. He said that the main goal of alchemists was to change ordinary metals into gold, a process they called 'chrysopoeia' a word I struggled to remember. He told me several times that he had long given up the quest to make gold from any other substance. He had proved to himself that that was impossible by doing the exact opposite. He had tried every method known to him to convert gold into another compound. He had used the most powerful acids, the strongest alkalis and still he could not convert even the smallest measurable amount to another substance, let alone a metal. He was a man of great care and paid every attention to the smallest detail. So after every attempt to convert any of his gold, he weighed it. Not the smallest amount detectable on his most sensitive balance was missing.

He did however have other ideas for making metals. Metals of a kind that had never been seen before. About two weeks before the trial, Señor

Ortiz de Navarette received a large heavy box which was delivered to his house by postal cart. He explained that this was a new type of ore which he had imported from Brazil. It bore the name manganesum crystallite. The alchemist believed that this ore contained a metal. He didn't know what the metal was but he knew a method of 'reducing' the ore, as he called it, to this new metal.

He wasted no time and the following day we set about making this intriguing element. He was so excited he could hardly sit down. He even refused to stop working to have lunch. He wrote a list of chemicals for me to weigh out and, as I did so, he constructed his apparatus. It was, for an experiment that had not apparently been performed before, amazingly simple. It comprised a large metal bucket, filled to the top with sand. He hollowed out a large hole in the top of the sand and placed within a large earthenware crucible.

'Have you weighed out those chemicals yet?'

'Yes, señor. They are in these pots. What do I do now?'

'Give them to me. I need to mix them together. Now grind up the manganesum crystallite in a pestle and mortar.'

Within minutes of me smashing the ore into a powder, he had placed one of the mixtures in the crucible and was carefully pouring the other down a narrow tube of paper he had made and holding it over the end to prevent the mixture from spilling on the floor. He pushed the tube into the centre of the mixture in the crucible.

'Next, I light the top of this paper fuse,' he said. 'I'm not sure exactly what will happen then so I want you to go outside the laboratory and close the door behind you. Once I've lit the fuse, I'll go to the back of the room to watch what happens.'

I stood outside and waited on the stairs and listened. I heard a steady, gentle fizzing noise as the fuse burnt down into the mixture in the crucible. Then there was the loudest bang I had ever heard. It almost burst my ears. The force of the explosion hit the door of the laboratory like an escaping bull. It smashed it clean off its hinges and blew it across the hall. A fraction of a second later, I heard the sound of bottles of chemicals bursting. The blast threw me to the bottom of the stairs where I curled up in a heap, absolutely petrified, if not unconscious. After about a minute, I opened my eyes and saw a cloud of black smoke drifting from the laboratory.

I dashed in and faced a scene of devastation. Broken glass covered the floor. The walls had turned black and grey. Half of the ceiling had fallen on the benches and floor, exposing the joists of the room above. The window panes had shattered and the curtains flapped carelessly in the breeze. Fumes rose from the acid which had spilled onto the floor and was etching its way into the wood. The pear shaped bottles had simply gone. At first I couldn't see the alchemist but then I heard him call me.

'Over here, Esmeralda. Help me,' he pleaded, almost silently. The blast had thrown him to the end of the centre bench where he had landed in a dishevelled heap on the floor, his left leg twisted round beneath him. He looked at me with his blackened and blood bespattered face. 'I have broken my leg. Look at my chest. I think something has stuck in me.'

I carefully unbuttoned his shirt and could feel a shard of glass embedded in him, just below his shoulder. 'Stay there, señor, I will fetch a doctor.'

'Go to see Angélica de la Torre. Tell her what has happened,' he whispered and then passed out.

As I opened the front door, I was confronted by about ten people, men, woman and one skinny child, who all looked at me anxiously.

'What's happened in there? What has exploded?' asked a tall man I recognised as living in a house a few doors up the road. I told him I desperately needed a doctor to see the alchemist.

'I am a doctor,' he said. I was so relieved to hear him say so.

'Come in. He is in the laboratory, over there on the floor.'

The doctor knelt down by the alchemist. 'Benito, it's me, Alvaro, from up the road. Can you hear me?' The alchemist did not respond.

'He's breathing but he's in a bad way. His leg is broken and I've just eased this piece of glass from his chest. He is bleeding quite badly. We must get him to the hospital. There is a man who lives on the other side of the road who has a horse and cart. Ask one of the people outside to get him.'

I dashed out and did what the doctor had told me. Within moments a cart drew up outside. Three of the neighbours and the doctor carried out the alchemist, still unconscious, and gently placed him on the back of the wagon. The doctor and the driver went with him to the hospital. I decided that, as my boss had instructed, I should go straightaway to see Angélica de la Torre. I soon found her house in the Calle del Postigo de San Martín and knocked on her frog shaped door knocker. I waited several minutes and knocked again. Just as I did so, the señora appeared and ushered out an embarrassed male visitor.

'Oh. Hello. You are the girl who works for the alchemist, aren't you?'

'Yes. Something dreadful has happened.'

'Come in and tell me,' she said, sounding unconcerned.

I followed her into her house. I remember being impressed by the quality of furnishings when we first entered the alchemist's house but the señora's displayed an altogether higher degree of opulence. She took me along the hall, the walls of which were decorated by gold framed pictures of nymphs in various erotic poses. A huge mirror hung over a mahogany side table. A gold gilt and white staircase, carpeted in white, rose to the floor above.

'Come into this drawing room and sit in the armchair over there,' she said pointing to a pink leather sofa which matched three others, arranged in an arc to face the fireplace. A wood fire burned with a soft, welcoming flicker in a large stone hearth. I glanced nervously around the room to see a large cupboard adorned with beautiful china plates, a further series of painted erotica on the walls, a cabinet filled with crystal glasses and bottles of drink, and a shelf of large, leather bound books.

'What happened then?' she said, tucking a leg under her thigh as she sat in an armchair next to mine.

I told her what had happened, from the delivery of the new ore to the explosion in the laboratory and the carrying of her friend the alchemist to the hospital.

'Hmm. Very interesting,' she said, as if to calculate in her mind what the effect of this could be on her. She seemed hardly interested at all in the poor alchemist and the fact that he was near to an early grave. She betrayed the total absence of feeling.

'Let me pick you up on one point you made in your account,' she said. 'I have no particular relationship with your employer, the esteemed Señor Benito Ortiz de Navarette. You may be surprised to learn this, but I am a prostitute and the señor is merely one of my many gentleman clients. You saw my most recent one leave the house as you were entering.'

I was shocked into silence. I just could not reply. I had seen the street prostitutes showing their wares in the town and I imagined, quite wrongly it seemed, that they were all the same, sorry looking individuals, desperate to work for a few miserable *maravedís*. This one was living a life of luxury and hearing that a loyal, regular customer was being beckoned by death himself, hardly meant a thing to her.

She helped me recover from my astonishment, even showing some emotion at my plight. 'What are you going to do? You can hardly go back and live in Señor Ortiz de Navarette's house. It could collapse around you for one thing and you could die of acid fumes.'

'Thank you for your concern, señora, but I must go back. There are things that have to be done. I must sort out the laboratory. I don't know what to do about the windows. The curtains are flapping outside and the weather can come straight in.'

'I have an idea. I have a man who does jobs around the house. His name is Jesús. I'll get him to sort out your laboratory. He can put something over the windows and do enough to make it safe.'

'You are so kind,' I said. 'It will be good to have a man in to see what needs to be done. He'll need to put the door back on its hinges.'

'An easy job for him. I suppose you will not be able to work for the Señor Ortiz de Navarette while he is in hospital.'

'I hadn't really thought of that.'

She walked in silence towards the window and paused to look out. Then, after a minute or so, she turned towards me smiled and said, 'I have another idea, too. I have been thinking about engaging an assistant to help me. You could do that job for a month or so until he gets better. I haven't had an assistant before so we would be helping each other. I would see how it worked for me and you would have a temporary job, at least until the alchemist was well again.'

'What would I be doing exactly and what would you pay me?' I didn't hesitate to ask.

'Basically, you would help prepare my room for clients and prepare me. It would not be difficult work. I would buy you some new clothes so you looked nice for my clients and I'd pay you, say, five *reales* a week?'

'You wouldn't expect me to....'

'Goodness no. That would be my job. You would answer the door and escort them in, that sort of thing. You would have no contact with them in that way.'

Rightly or wrongly, I warmed to the idea. I felt sure the alchemist would be happy about my working for Señora Angélica de la Torre. I would still live at his house so would be able to watch over it for him. 'When would you like me to start, señora?'

'Let's say next Monday. I will sort out some clothes for you. I can see what size you are. If you arrive after breakfast, I can show you what to do before the first client is due, at ten. Monday is never a very busy day. It's too near the weekend.'

Having agreed the terms with my new employer, I was bubbling with excitement and could not wait to go to the prison to see Susana and tell her this incredible story. She had reached the stage of her confinement at which she had become more accepting of the miserable situation she found herself in. She even became optimistic about her release, especially as the lady with the baby, who had witnessed her encounter with the beggar, had signed an excellent and convincing statement. The jailers had not been tying her against the wall since she convinced them she would do nobody any harm nor hurt herself. 'How many days to the trial, Esmeralda?' she said after our usual exchange of kisses.

'Not long now. Fifteen. I hope you are not worrying. The lawyer thinks you will be acquitted.'

'Yes. He came to see me yesterday to tell me what was going on. He seems a nice man. And he's tall and handsome. He said he'd come later to tell me what to say and how to get the sympathy of the judge.'

I then told her about the extraordinary events in the laboratory that day, that the alchemist had been badly injured and about my meeting with Señora Angélica de la Torre. I was not surprised when Susana told me that she had learnt quite a bit about prostitutes while in prison. Half the women in there worked the streets or the brothels in the infamous Calle de Arganzuela. In fact, she had become good friends with some of them. They had taken pity on her, especially as she was so young and innocent.

'I'm amazed that she offered you a job. And at such good money. I hope she chooses some clothes you like! When do you start?'

'Monday. I'm dying to see exactly what she wants me to do!'

***

I knocked on the frog shaped doorknocker not too early in the morning. The señora opened the door immediately, as if she had been looking for me and, for some reason, did not want me to be seen waiting outside.

'Welcome to your new job,' she said, smiling with her mouth and eyes. 'First, I want to show you to my bedroom and you can change into your new clothes.' We climbed her ornate stairs and entered her opulent bedroom. It was furnished completely in white, as if she wanted to be reminded of her long, lost virginity. Even the dressing table, the bed frame, the mirror surround and the chairs were white, as was the bed linen.

'Here is the dress I bought you and here are some stockings. Try them on!' The dress was pure white and the stockings pink, similar to the ones we saw her wearing at the alchemist's when Susana and I returned from the theatre.

I lifted my dress over my head and dropped it on the floor by the bed, then slipped into the new dress. It fitted beautifully. I sat on her dressing table stool to put on the stockings. I looked at myself in her mirror.

'The dress is very short,' I said, feeling a little embarrassed at complaining. 'If I bend over I will show everything to your clients.'

'I'm sure you will be fine. If you are worried you can wear some pantaloons under it.'

'I'll try it as it is for now.'

'Now come into my boudoir and I'll show you what I want you to do for me in there.'

She opened the door to a fairly large room with a canopied double bed at the centre, its headboard almost touching the wall. It was draped in the finest mauve coloured silk. 'I call this the play room. I get up to all sorts of mischief in here.'

She placed a bowl of water close to one side of the bed. She then removed her dress and stood naked on the carpet, facing me. She possessed the most imposingly voluptuous figure. Her breasts were well-shapen and hung gracefully to the sides of her chest. She had rouged her nipples which stood proud of the surrounding, tender flesh. Her hips were wide and graced with a light brushing of hair which pointed down where her legs met. 'I hope you won't be embarrassed or shy about what I want you to do,' she said sitting on the side of the bed next to the water. My heart fluttered as I wondered what she expected of me. I could not imagine.

'After each customer has finished what he comes to do with me, I want you to wash his fluid out of my body with this douche. You will need to fill it with warm water and squeeze it inside me. I will sit astride the bowl as you do it. Let's have a practice run.' So this was it. At first, I felt a certain revulsion at touching the woman's body in such an intimate place.

She filled the douche and opened her legs. Her whole area there smelled like a special blend of exotic perfumes, orange blossom, myrrh, rosewood, oil of cedar, lavender and frankincense... I could feel my heart beating and my hands shaking slightly as I pushed the end of the douche inside her. It was as much as I could do to hold it steady. 'Further up,' she said. I did as instructed and squeezed it until a gush of water came from her. 'Lovely. That was nearly perfect. You'll get even gentler with practice. And you'll be less nervous! Now take that mauve towel, dry me and talc me from that pot on the shelf beneath the table. Then refresh the perfume around the hair with a small dab from the jar.'

I had never been as close to another woman's secret garden before, except Susana's. But Susana's buds had yet to flower. I had just touched the glowing sex of a mature woman and, to my astonishment, found it quite exhilarating.

'You'll be fine,' she said, giving me a good feeling of confidence which added to the sense of intimacy. 'You'll have to show my guest into the boudoir and I'll ring this bell when it's time for you to enter. You'll escort him out and I'll await your attentions here. He will pay me, of course,' as if there could be any doubt.

'I know it sounds a little odd, but I'm going to let you go now, back to the alchemist's house. I've arranged for my man Jesús to be there, waiting outside for you. You can show him in and he can help clear the place up. Tell him I'll pay. You can start work proper tomorrow. Now off you go!'

I still couldn't believe I had accepted this strange job. But the señora seemed likeable and, considering her sophisticated life style, she possessed an aura of charming innocence. After all, she delivered a much needed service and, as far as I could determine, took great care to perform it well; and to take care of her delectable body. While walking back to the alchemist's I reached the view that I should be immensely grateful to her for offering me the work. She had honoured me with the responsibility of preparing her and I would do my utmost to serve her well. But I wasn't sure how I would react to spending so much time in such intimate contact with a mature woman.

As I turned the corner into the Calle de la Luna, I could see Jesús leaning against the wall of the house, next to the alchemist's front door.

CHAPTER 8

Susana's Trial

The señora selected her clients with the skill of jeweller selecting gems. Or were her clients so shrewd in choosing her? What a charming assortment of men. Several were doctors, one of whom we already knew, there were lawyers, many were civil servants, some of whom worked at the palace, one was the captain of a ship which sailed on the trade route to the East, others were of the minor nobility, *hidalgos* and *caballeros*, two were extremely rich *titulos* in land, some were owners of their own businesses, a flour miller, a brewer, a gunsmith, a property agent, several were senior members of the priesthood and another was, of course, an alchemist. They treated the señora with the utmost courtesy and respect. I would show one into the boudoir and close the door behind him. As I shut it, I could hear her greet him with a, 'come over and give me a kiss', a 'lovely to see you once again', a 'you are looking as handsome as ever' or 'it's so good to set eyes on you'.

Sometimes the señora rang the bell after just a few minutes, fifteen or so minutes or, if they were having an exceptionally pleasurable time, after nearly an hour, depending on whether he would have to make way for her next customer. As I stood by the door and he stepped towards me, he almost always smiled and sometimes even blushed. He often still had his purse in his hand and would proffer me a modest tip, maybe a two *maravedí* or even a four. I'd be happy and so would he. Then I would escort him to the door and show him out with a smiling 'goodbye, señor. I hope we see you again soon', always the same farewell. He would acknowledge me with a nod of the head, then don his hat, if he wore one. Only rarely would he utter a word.

As I did what I had to do to her perfumed body, she would always comment. 'He came so quickly, I could hardly draw breath' or 'I wish more were like him. He knew how to pleasure a woman' or 'God he stank. About time he had a wash' or 'he kept talking all the way through' or 'I wriggled and squeezed him, moved with his rhythm and I still couldn't make him come' or, sometimes combined with the previous one, 'then I thought he'd never stop'.

Although I doubted, before starting, whether I could enjoy being the señora's assistant, I thrived on the job. I much preferred it to working for the alchemist whom I seriously liked and to whom I would be eternally grateful, especially for teaching me to read and write. I hoped somehow I could continue working for the señora after the alchemist had recovered. I pondered hard on how I might achieve that. Then, a few days before Susana's trial, the señora said something which seriously shocked me. So much so I could not reply because words would not come out of my mouth. 'Esmeralda, you have the right personality for this work and a good body. All my clients like you. You really should become a whore. You'd make a fortune. I have.'

***

Everyone wanted Susana to present herself well. Her fellow lady prisoners had made a collection and one of their visitors had bought her a new cotton dress, a print of blue flowers on white. She was proud of it and glowed while wearing it. She sat with a jailer below the stand, waiting patiently to be called.

Justice had not only to be done but be seen to be done. So the court was open to anybody who wanted to attend. As I walked to the prison, I noticed a complete absence of beggars on the streets. Usually, they congregated on the steps of the churches, at the entrances to the market places or on busy street corners. Each had left their begging bowl in its usual place so that it continued to expect the odd piece of change to be dropped in by a generous passerby. It was as if the beggars had become invisible but were, at the same time, still begging. I could see and hear why these mendicants were absent, as soon as I entered the forbidding, panelled door to courtroom. It seemed that the whole community of beggars in Madrid had given up their pitches for a day to witness the trial. After all, one of their brethren had been stabbed by the accused and justice, to them, meant that she should be jailed, flogged or even executed. They argued, joked, laughed, coughed and shouted at each other. They played cards. They ate their breakfast. They swigged from jugs of beer. They spat on the floor.

This untidy rabble had recruited other street workers to join them: pickpockets, vagabonds, tricksters, street women and vendors. Their friends magnified the level of hubbub created solely by the beggars. The usual audience of women, knitting, crocheting, passing food to and fro and randomly chatting, contributed to the general clamour.

I sat in the area reserved for friends or relatives of the accused. While entering, Señor and Señora Ramírez greeted me heartily. I felt good to be reunited with them. Clearly fond of Susana, they said how concerned they were about what might happen to her that day. I could offer little reassurance. The court room was packed so the latecomers were forced to stand or sit in uncomfortable and awkward proximity to some stranger.

'Si...lence in court!' a blue uniformed usher cried. As if to give the last vestiges of noise time to die away, the judge, a skeletal figure in a black gown, eased himself, at a measured pace, into the room, climbed the six steps to his throne on high, stood before it and bowed. He leant over so low that his large white wig almost fell from his head. He urgently grabbed it and pushed it back, to the accompaniment of a cloud of talc, which settled on his shoulders like so much dandruff, and of the laughter of the more daring in the crowd. He cast a deprecating eye at the gigglers, then sat firmly against the chair's high back, upholstered in red leather with a carved crown at its head.

'Br...ing in the accused,' bellowed the usher.

With her head bowed and serious-faced, but looking pretty in her new dress, Susana entered, sat in the dock and looked up, like a shy faun, towards the judge.

'Are you Susana de Rivera?' he asked, in a friendly, sympathetic tone.

'I am,' said Susana.

'You are accused of attempted murder. Do you know what that means?'

'I do, your Lordship.'

'How do you plead?'

'Not guilty, your Lordship,' she replied, calmly and politely, just as she had been taught by her lawyer. Her words provoked loud booing and hissing from the vagrants and their entourage.

'Silence!' shouted the judge. 'Any more of that and you'll be removed from this court.'

'Who is prosecuting this case?' asked the judge.

'I am your Lordship,' said a meek, baldheaded lawyer, who jumped to his feet as the judge spoke.

'What is your case?' asked his Lordship. The prosecutor, in a diminutive voice, explained what he understood to have happened. He gave the date and time. He named the victim: Gonzalo González. In his support, he called two beggars who, like other witnesses, had been confined to a room outside to await their moment of glory. The first beggar took the stand and swore to tell nothing but the truth.

'Tell me, in your own words what happened,' said the prosecutor.

'Me an' me mates were walking down the Calle de los Ángeles, mindin' our own business, when this girl appeared from nowhere, stabbed poor old Gonzalo in the stummick an' tried to grab the money bag tied to his waist. We grabbed 'er, took 'er knife, still bleedin' with Gonzalo's blood, and 'eld 'er ta the law came and took 'er away.'

'Can you see the said girl in this court?' said the prosecutor.

'Yes. That's 'er over there,' he said pointing an accusing finger at Susana who visibly cringed.

'Who is defending the accused?' asked the judge.

'I am, your Lordship,' replied the lawyer whom the alchemist had engaged. His name was Estaban Ganado. My heart fluttered at the sight of this handsome specimen of manhood. Then I realised that I had seen him many times before. He lived not far up the Calle de la Luna from the alchemist and often visited Señora Angelica de la Torre. He performed rather well, or so she said.

'Do you have any questions you would wish to address to the first witness?'

'No, your Lordship. Not at this stage.'

'Then call your next witness, prosecutor.'

The second beggar took the stand and swore the oath.

'Tell me in your own words what you saw,' said the prosecutor.

'Me an' me mates were walking down the Calle de los Ángeles, mindin'our own business, when this girl appeared from nowhere, stabbed poor old Gonzalo in the stummick an' tried to grab the money bag tied to his waist. We grabbed 'er, took 'er knife, still bleedin' with Gonzalo's blood, and 'eld 'er to the law came and took 'er away.'

'Can you see the said girl in this court?' said the prosecutor.

'Yes, that's 'er over there,' he said, pointing an accusing finger at Susana who, looking at him, seemed more relaxed to be in the line of his finger than that of the first.

'Do you have any questions of these witnesses,' asked the judge, addressing Susana's lawyer.

'All I can say, your Lordship is to point out the identical words that these two have used. They have put their heads together to concoct their story which is a falsehood and I shall show that from what my client and my independent witness will say to this court.'

'Before we question the accused, I would like to ask the prosecutor if he wishes us to hear the evidence of any other witnesses.'

'Yes, indeed, your Lordship. Two street vendors witnessed this appalling crime and I wish to call them to address you.'

The first of the street vendors swore the oath and gave his account. The second gave his story which was put in different words but consistent with that of the first.

'Do you have any questions of this witness,' the judge asked Susana's lawyer.

'Yes, your Lordship. I have a question.' Then turning to the second vendor, 'Did you see the accused stab the beggar?'

'No, señor. I saw no stabbing. I only helped one of the previous witnesses, the second one, in fact, to hold the girl while another went to fetch the constables.'

'How many constables arrived at the scene?'

'Two, señor.'

'I now wish to call the accused to the stand,' said Susana's lawyer. She swore the oath and gave her account of events. It matched exactly what she had told me when I first saw her in the prison but, of course, it differed markedly from what the beggars had said. She admitted to stabbing the beggar but pleaded that she did so in self-defence.

'Where did you get your knife?' asked her lawyer.

'My friend Esmeralda gave it to me?'

'Why was that?'

'So I could defend myself, if I had to, going to work. It's a long way from where we live. All the way to the Calle Nueva.'

'I now wish to call my independent witness, my Lordship.'

'Call Señora Clara de Herrera to the stand, usher,' said the judge.

Our witness swore the oath and gave her story. Her voice shook with nerves as she did so. When she said she saw the beggar's knife their colleagues in the audience erupted. 'No. No. He didn't 'ave a knife. Only the girl 'ad a knife. She stabbed Gonzalo with it.'

'Silence! I've already warned you once. I'll clear you and your friends from the court if you say just one more word,' said the judge.

'How many knives did you see?' asked Susana's lawyer.

'Two,' said Señora de Herrera. 'The beggar who threatened Susana had one and so did Susana.'

The judge asked the prosecutor if he had any questions.

'Indeed I do, your Lordship. How can you be so sure that there were two knives? You could have seen the same one twice.'

'I saw them with my own eyes, señor,' she said, her voice shaking even more uncertainly than before, as if she didn't quite believe what she herself was saying. 'When I realised the beggar had one, too, I ran back up the road with my baby. I was scared we might be attacked. Me or my little one.'

By then, it was nearly midday and the judge decided he would adjourn for lunch. Before he did so, he spoke to the court.

'I will deliver my verdict when we reconvene but I have grave misgivings about this case. Gonzalo González is still suffering from a stomach wound that Señora Susana de Rivera admits to causing. She claims she acted in self-defence and has a witness to support that. That witness is Señora Clara de Herrera. I am unsure about what this witness saw. While I am sure she is being honest in her testimony, I do have doubts about whether she saw Señor González with a knife. There is no other evidence to support that, other than what Señora Rivera says in her defence. My doubts are increased because Señora de Herrera admits to being frightened and running off with her baby. I may, therefore have to give a verdict of guilty.'

There was a roar of approval from the beggars and their friends. Susana burst into tears.

'Silence!' said the judge, once more. The motley group of beggars ceased their premature celebration, fearing ejection from the court. So silence was restored. Then to everybody's surprise an old lady who was sitting in the back row of the court stood up and spoke hesitantly.

'Excuse me your Lordship. May I say something?'

'Is it relevant to this case?' asked the judge.

'Yes, your Lordship. I saw everything that happened from the balcony of my house in the Calle de los Ángeles. I would like to tell you what I saw.'

'Does anyone have a good reason not to hear from the lady who is standing?' asked the judge. No one said a word. 'Then we will delay lunch and listen to this lady. Señora, please take your place on the witness stand.'

The lady slowly made her way to the front of the court, passing the beggars and their compatriots who hissed at her, believing that she would say nothing to help their case against Susana. She serenely ignored them. She climbed up the one step to the box, clambered in and looked around the court. She wore grey hair, tied neatly in a bun and had a round, motherly face. She smiled broadly and looked up at the judge.

'When should I start, your Lordship, your Honour?'

'What is your name?'

'I am Constanza Pérez.'

'You need to swear the oath to tell the truth and then you can begin.' She did so and, without faltering, started. 'Well, it's like this, your Honour, my Lordship. I live in one of the terrace houses on the east side of the Calle de los Ángeles. I was hanging out some washing on my balcony when I saw this pretty girl coming down the road from the direction of the Calle de los Tudescos. She was walking towards a group of three beggars who were standing by the side of the road. They are often in that spot and can be a nuisance the way they treat us passers-by.

'As the girl came near them, one of them walked behind her and grabbed at her hair. He was carrying a shiny knife and threatened her with it. He said something like, "Give me your money or I'll kill you." I heard him. The next thing was the girl took a knife from her bag and stabbed him. Another of the beggars took the knife away from the stabbed beggar and hid it inside his jacket. Another one grabbed the girl and held her. She struggled and two street vendors, the two who were in the stand just now, helped him to hold her while another came to the aid of the beggar the girl stabbed. Someone went for a doctor. Two constables later turned up and took the girl away.'

'Can you see the girl you saw that day in this court?'

'Yes, my Lordship, your Honour. She is the girl in the dock over there.'

'Thank you, señora. Do you have any questions of this witness?' the judge asked the prosecutor.

'Yes, your Lordship. How can you be so sure that the beggar, you say threatened the girl, had a knife?'

'It was a shiny knife, señor, and as he turned it to point it at the girl, it shone in the sun. It nearly dazzled me blind, it did. No. He was carrying that knife all right.'

I looked at Susana and she looked at me. 'God bless this stranger,' her eyes seemed to be saying.

'I think we can safely adjourn now,' said the judge, 'that is if nobody else wishes to take the stand.'

After lunch, the judge appeared and climbed the stairs into his seat on high. He shuffled some papers in front of him, coughed twice and began, looking around the court as, in a formal tone, he spoke. 'I have reached a verdict in this case. Before I give it, I must give you a brief summary. I have not been impressed with the accounts given by the principal witnesses of the prosecution. These two men clearly colluded to ensure that the untruths they told were consistent. The two street vendors, on the other hand were helpful. But they were unable to corroborate what the beggars had said. The beggars were the only witnesses who claimed the attack by Señora de Rivera was unprovoked. Nor were they independent because they are friends of the victim.

'Señora Clara de Herrera sounded unsure about whether a beggar threatened Señora de Rivera. It wasn't what she said but the unconvincing way in which she said it. It wasn't until Constanza Pérez offered, from the gallery, to tell her version of events, that we were able confidently to confirm that the beggar who was attacked possessed a knife. The two main witnesses for the prosecution failed, despite their efforts, to conceal this fact.

'I believe that the attack on Señor Gonzalo González was provoked. Señora Susana de Rivera acted in self-defence. She is therefore not guilty of attempted murder. She is free to leave this court.'

I looked across at Susana who burst into tears as soon as she heard the verdict. My tears came out in sympathy. We were both overjoyed. Her smiling, friendly jailer allowed both of us back to her prison cell where we picked up her few belongings and put them into a bag he gave us. The other women prisoners came in to wish Susana good luck. Some of them were in tears. They hugged her and kissed her. One gave her a *real*. Another gave her a hat which she had knitted from wool she had pulled from the prison blankets. They all wished her happiness in the world outside. Susana thanked them for their support and for the blue patterned dress they had given her and promised to visit them. I doubted whether she would but said nothing.

We still had a home at the alchemist's house and walked back there in the weak, autumn sunshine. During my visits to the prison, I had regularly kept Susana up-to-date with events in the 'outside world'. She knew that, true to her word, Señora Angélica de la Torre had paid her handyman to put wooden slats over the broken windows in the back of the house and to clean up the laboratory, so the house was habitable. I had visited the alchemist several times in the General Hospital and had told him about the Señora de la Torre's generosity, not only in tidying up his house but also in giving me a job while he was still in hospital. He said he was pleased that I was being looked after.

Susana could not stop talking while we walked from the town prison back to the alchemist's. She told me about the people she had met in the prison. She had spent many hours talking to the women inmates, most of whom were much older than her. In effect, they had carried on from where I had left off in giving her lessons in reproductive biology. She told me that she had had two bleeds while she was in prison and had been prepared for the first by a street woman who had been convicted of robbing her clients.

'You'd never believe she'd rob anybody,' said Susana. 'She's just such a nice lady. I learnt so much from her. I had this bad tummy ache one morning and she asked me if I had started my bleeds yet. I had no idea what she meant but she explained it to me, just like you would, Esmeralda. And do you know what? That's what it turned out to be! She even lent me some of her bits of cloth to soak it up.'

I felt guilty that I hadn't taught her myself but I would have done so, if she hadn't been sent to prison. I couldn't see anything to be gained in admitting to that, so I just listened. She said she had learnt more about reading and writing and that the women had told her about their various trades. A murderess showed her how to crochet; a forger how to make gloves out of waxed paper; a baker, who had assaulted a constable, showed her how to make bread, buns and cakes in the prison kitchen; a teacher, who had tried to kill her husband, stimulated her interest in history, current affairs and geography and taught her the basics of arithmetic and numbers.

'Several of the women told me how to make a good living,' she said. 'Become a whore. You can make a fortune. The men pay you anything from half a *real* upwards, depending on what they want. You can earn in a morning what we earn in a week.'

'You know I am working for one? Señora de la Torre. She has made it into a profession. She's made a fortune, enough to buy that beautiful house in the Calle del Postigo de San Martín and to fill it with luxury furniture. She loves her work. You can tell that from the way she treats her customers and the way they treat her. She said that I could do well in the profession. She told me that the worst thing to do was to work on the streets. She had known several women who were killed doing just that. In one case, the man did what he wanted, took out a knife and killed her there and then. It saved him less than a *real*, the price of her sad life. Another had been shot by an angry wife who had caught her husband doing her in a shop doorway. The señora told me that the best way to start was to work in one of the town *mancebías*. She knows several of the women who run the ones in the Calle de Arganzuela. She even said she would recommend me to one or two of them. Isn't it a coincidence that we are thinking the same way?'

'Would she recommend me? Do you think? If we wanted to do it?'

'I don't see why not.'

***

I showed Susana the mess the explosion had made in the laboratory. 'My God. It's a wonder the poor man wasn't killed. When will he come home?'

'I don't know. He is much better now. Let's visit him tomorrow in hospital. You'll be going to the ham seller, I suppose and I'll be assisting the señora.'

'We'll go tomorrow.'

By the time we had eaten, sorted out Susana's things and chatted even more it was time to go to bed. Poor Susana. She said she didn't want to sleep on her own on her first night back so she cuddled up with me in my bed. We shared the heat of each other's bodies until sunrise.

***

Susana carried on where she left off before she went to prison. The Rodríguezes were delighted that she returned to work for them and literally welcomed her with open arms. Señora Rodríguez was especially pleased because Susana's return meant that she did not have to distribute the Serrano hams alone or with her husband in tow. The señora was never really happy sharing the task with her husband, protesting that she saw enough of him anyway without plodding the streets at his pathetic pace. We never again saw the knife with which Susana stabbed the beggar. Presumably, it was kept by the court. Who knows? We still felt it dangerous for Susana to walk to the Calle Nueva alone so we thought of an altogether less offensive weapon: a small bag of hard boiled chickens' eggs.

We visited the alchemist several times. The explosion had seriously injured him and he almost died in his hospital bed. The burns alone almost killed him and he had broken his left leg in several places. He made slow but sure progress and, when Susana first visited, he erupted in joy at seeing her. Susana told him all about the trial and how lucky she had been that the lady with the balcony had come forward to give her evidence.

'You deserved that, Susana. From the moment Esmeralda came to see me, I thought you were innocent.'

Although he seemed chirpy and cheerful, he told us about a bad shock he had had the day before our visit, which was the day of the trial.

'They brought a man in and put him in the bed next to me. He screamed out in pain from his stomach. They gave him something for the pain and he eventually calmed down. I asked him what was wrong and he said he had been stabbed in the stomach about three months ago. He said he was taken to hospital and made a good recovery but, the day before he was due to give evidence in court against his attacker, he became doubled up in pain. It got worse and worse until he passed out. A friend of his brought him round with some brandy and took him to hospital that day.'

'What was the shock then?' I asked.

'About an hour after he told me all this, I heard a horrible croaking noise coming from him and called a nurse. The nurse came and almost immediately he died in her arms.'

'Who was he?' asked Susana, by then in a raging panic.

'They said his name was Gonzalo González.'

'I killed him! I killed him!' cried out Susana. Her eyes rolled up in their sockets and she collapsed on the floor in a faint.

'I should never have told her,' said the alchemist, flushing with regret. 'Get a nurse, Esmeralda.' The nurse brought some salts and placed them under Susana's nose. When she came round she didn't know where she was. Then she looked at the alchemist. Her eyes lit up in fright.

'I'm scared! They will retry me,' she said, with tears streaking down her face.

'No they won't, Susana,' I said. 'You did it in self-defence. That was the judgement. You didn't kill the man. He must have got something else wrong with him. That was nothing to do with you.'

Eventually the alchemist and I consoled her and she stopped crying.

'If you want to be sure, go to Susana's lawyer. He lives five doors from me up the street. He will tell you that everything is fine, now that the judge has made his decision.'

So we took the alchemist's advice and, on our way home, knocked on the lawyer's door.

'Come in,' said the handsome man. 'I think I recognise each of you,' he said.

Susana immediately hugged him and thanked him for all his efforts the day before. 'I am so grateful. I cannot tell you.' Then she began to weep again.

'This is a time for celebration, not for sadness,' said the lawyer, showing us into his study. 'Why are you sad?'

'You tell him, Esmeralda,' so I did, repeating to him exactly what the alchemist had told us about Gonzalo González' death.

'Um,' muttered the lawer, as if deep in thought. He stepped up to a tall bookcase, removed a volume from a shelf and flicked through it until he came to the pages he wanted. 'According to our law, you cannot be tried twice for the same offence. This means that, once you are acquitted, as you have been, you cannot be tried for it again, whatever new evidence appears or is discovered. Technically, you could be charged with a new charge of murder...'

'Oh no!' cried out Susana, in tears again.

'Don't worry. Just let me finish. I can be confident that they won't do that. There are two reasons. Firstly, it was proved beyond reasonable doubt that you acted in self-defence. Even if you had killed him the fact that you had defended yourself again his threat to kill you, while he was holding a knife, would not change. Self-defence is total mitigation. Secondly, after this much time, no doctor worthy of his profession could say beyond reasonable doubt that his death was due to your actions. It could be completely independent of what you did. This means that you have nothing to worry about. When the judge said you were free he meant it.'

'I'm so, so happy,' said Susana, smiling from ear to ear and hugging the lawyer again.

'What a relief,' I said. 'Such a relief.'

***

I told the alchemist that Señora Angélica de la Torre was happy for me to continue working for her after his discharge from hospital. His gratitude showed clearly on his face.

'My dear Esmeralda, I will have nothing for you for weeks, maybe even months. It will take an age to replace my chemicals, the apparatus and repair the damage to the benches. I am seriously thinking of giving up alchemy. My carelessness has caused too many accidents. I may just publish a few papers on my recent work and restart my astronomy. There would still be a job for you but it would mean working at night.'

This gave me the escape I was hoping for. 'Señor Ortiz de Navarette, I would love to carry on working for you. But I would hardly see Susana if I worked nights. How would you feel if I continued with Señora de la Torre?'

'No problem, Esmeralda. Carry on with her. You and Susana can continue staying at my house, if you like. You are looking after it while I'm in here.'

So we agreed and we would stay there rent-free.

CHAPTER 9

Time for a Change

A few weeks later, while we were sitting on her bed chatting, Susana again raised the subject. 'Esmeralda, this work for the Ramírezes is boring and I'm fed up with it already. I'm fed up with plodding the streets dropping off the hams. I love the customers but I know them all now and there is nothing new in it. And the money is poor. So why don't we become whores? Think of the money we'd make!'

'I'm quite enjoying my job but my pay isn't good either. The señora clearly enjoys her job. She smiles every time one of her clients goes in and again when he comes out. So it can't be bad. She likes it but would we? We couldn't expect to start at the level she's working at. We wouldn't be serving the gentry of Madrid. We'd have to do what the ordinary men of the town wanted, whatever that might be. I dread to think! They'd want to shove themselves in every hole in our bodies! And we'd have to perform God knows how many times a day and halfway through the night. How long would we be able to stand it? We'd go to bed as sore as galley slaves, every single night,' I said, with an air of knowing seriousness, but not really knowing at all. I wanted Susana to realise that this would not be easy work; that we'd have to do things for clients that we may not want to do and suffer any painful consequences.

'You are trying to put me off, Esmeralda. I thought you sounded quite keen when we talked about it before. I'm disappointed.'

'No, but we need to be sure of ourselves before we decide. That's all I want. If we go ahead and can't bear it, we might find it hard to get a normal job. Not everyone will take on a woman knowing she's been a *puta.*'

'How would they know?'

'They'd find out from gossip. Someone would know and be certain to tell. Once a *puta*, always a *puta*, even if you're not one anymore. It's a bit like being a killer. Once you've killed you are a killer, even if you only killed once. But a *puta* isn't a killer, of course, but could be I suppose. That's the truth of it.'

'I agree with all you've said but I still want to be one. We are both young and would soon get used to it. Whatever the men wanted us to do. I just don't want them to hurt me. But there must be limits to what the men can do? The woman-in-charge would surely set some rules?'

'I don't know. But you are right about us being young. We should be able to adapt. And there are plenty of women doing this, not all out of desperation.'

Susana convinced me, and we convinced each other that, from what we knew about the work of a *puta*, we would like to enter this dubious profession. We would go ahead and find jobs. There were certain things the men might want that we decided we would avoid doing, if we possibly could.

'Why don't we ask Angélica de la Torre if she could introduce us to one of the madams at a house of pleasure in the Arganzuela? You suggested that before.'

The following day I asked the señora just that.

'But I would lose you, Esmeralda. What would I do?'

'Do you really need an assistant, señora? My main job, apart from bringing the clients up to you and taking them down afterwards is to clean you up and to add a dash of perfume to your lady hair. Maybe you could take that on yourself or find another girl to do it for you? I hope you don't think I'm being rude.'

She sat back on her bed and thought for a few moments, looking towards the ceiling. 'You are right, I mustn't be selfish. I must not hold you back in your career. I remember saying that you could make a fortune doing this and I should encourage you. Not stand in the way. I will recommend you to a couple of the madams in the Arganzuela. My only problem, Esmeralda, is that, despite all the hours we have spent chatting to each other, between customers, I hardly know anything about you. The next time we have a break between clients you must tell me your story.'

Within an hour or so, the señora was sitting in one of her gilt framed armchairs and, in deep concentration, listening to me. I told her I was rejected by my mother who was a nun and how I arrived with my twin brother at an orphanage in Burgos. 'It was fine while we were little babies and they treated us well. Even when we were little children. But when we were able to work, things changed. They exploited us in every way they could. They made us do the work while the nuns spent all day praying and sitting in their cells reading the bible. They told us that God meant them to pray and us to work. They said we were sent by God to work for them. They sent us into the fields at the back of the orphanage and we worked. They said they were praying for us as we laboured. Sometimes we were out in the fields all day, with hardly a break. The nuns in charge of us would bring out some food, usually oat cakes or bread and water.

'This was our life. It was as if we had been sentenced to hard labour in a prison. They gave us specific titles and tasks. They made me a hoer. There were three hoers and we hoed in a line together, cutting out the weeds, as the weeders came behind us to pick them up and put them into baskets. By the end of the day my hands bled from the sores the handle made on my soft skin. I'd have to put them in cold water to ease the pain. The nuns just ignored my cries. "God is punishing you today. What bad thing did you do yesterday?"

'The older, stronger children were given more skilful tasks. One of them was the ploughman. Another was the tiller. They could both ride horses. At harvest time we changed jobs. I became a picker. My friend Susana became a loader. I would put the vegetables in a box and she would load them onto the back of a cart. One of the older children then drove the cart back to the nuns who would sort through what we'd harvested. They would send the best to the vegetable market and keep the worst to feed their orphans.

'There were four of us who were friends: my twin brother, Pedro, our legless friend Simón and Susana who shared a bed with me in the dormitory. Simón was born with no legs. That is why his mother dumped him in a bag on the steps of the orphanage. But he developed the strongest arms you'd ever seen. He could walk on his hands if he wanted to. He would swing his body in front of him, land his bottom on the ground, swing his arms ahead of him, pick up his bottom and swing it in front of him again. It was as if he was walking with three legs. He always wore a pair of pantaloons with a small pillow sewn into the crotch for his bottom to land on. He became so good at moving himself around like that, he could go nearly as fast as we could run. He laughed and made a joke of his disabilities, saying that he was the only one of us who was normal. "What do you want those ugly legs for anyway?"

'Susana's mother died in childbirth and her father, a boy of fifteen, couldn't cope with her so left her with the nuns. He felt so guilty about leaving his little baby and so sad about his lovely wife that he jumped off the bridge into the river and drowned himself. Or so we were told by the nuns. Susana never accepted that story and to this day believes they lied to her about him. Susana is a few years younger than me and we became best friends while working in the fields at the back of the orphanage.

'The four of us, my brother Pedro, Simón, Susana and I, decided, after years of being abused by the nuns, to escape and live on the streets. It didn't take long for us to work out a plan. The nuns locked us all in the main part of the orphanage at night. It was surrounded by a twelve *pie* wall so we stole some sheets from the bedding store and tied them together to make a rope. We stole food from the kitchen and packed some bags with clothes. It was in the spring so we had a summer outside to look forward to. We got out of bed and dressed when the clock on the cathedral tower struck two in the morning. We all gathered in the back kitchen where there was an outside door. There was just enough light to see what we were doing. Pedro was first over the wall, then Susana, then Simón who hauled himself up the rope by his hands and I followed close behind him. We were free!

'That morning we worked our way to the edge of the town and found a derelict barn where we decided to live. Believe it or not, we were so happy there. We could do what we liked when we liked. We lived well, partly by stealing vegetables from the fields and cooking them over a fire. "Getting our own back on the nuns," my brother used to say with his twisted sense of justice. We went to the markets and robbed the stalls. We'd distract the stallholder and Simón would sneak around the back and grab a handful of fruit or a few buns. Then we would creep away before the stall holder suspected anything. Most times they didn't even realise they'd been robbed so we'd fleece them again when we were hungry enough. It was in one of these sorties to the markets that Simón was killed. He was stealing a loaf of bread from a baker's wagon when the baker saw him. The baker chased Simón across the market square into the road outside. Simón didn't see a horse and cart coming around a corner and was crushed to death under the wheel of the cart. It was horrible. The worse thing I have seen in my entire life.' I became overcome at recalling this terrible event and the señora comforted me.

'Now, now, Esmeralda. Please don't cry. I should never have asked you to tell me all this.'

'Don't worry, señora,' I sniffed, wiping my tears away as I did so. 'There is not much more to tell. Shall I continue?'

'Please do, Esmeralda. Just take a minute to settle yourself.'

'Not long before Simón died, Pedro went out to meet some beggars who had a pitch near the cathedral. They knew he was one of our little gang and they had told him the day before that they had a job for him. Anyway, that's what he told us the night before he went. To make a long story short, we never saw Pedro again. We looked everywhere. We even broke into the convent one night to see if he'd gone back there or had been taken back by the nuns. We've never seen him since,' I said, again mopping tears away.

I told her about some of the jobs we had done and that I worked for an *hidalgo* for a time. I did not tell her I killed him or that we had changed our names to avoid being arrested. I described our perilous trip to Madrid and how we were kidnapped and held to ransom and how the Ramírezes were so kind in giving us food and lodgings.

'Well, that is my story, señora, and that of Susana I suppose. I thought I would give you these details because you can see from what I've said that neither Susana nor I know our ages. We don't know when we were born.

I think the nun gave birth to me around 1585 and Susana was born a year or two later.'

'So you are about sixteen and Susana about fifteen, maybe. You cannot work the brothels if you are under fifteen and Susana looks that old. It's the law. Luckily they don't need proof. Another thing. They cannot employ virgins. So I have to ask you, Esmeralda...'

'Yes, we both are.'

'That's a nuisance. But there is an advantage. I'll tell you what it is but I first want to check your virginity. I promise it won't hurt. Come up to the boudoir.' I followed her up the sumptuous stairs, onto the landing and into the room of boundless pleasure.

'Lie down on the bed, lift up your skirts and open your legs.'

I did as she told me, if a little nervously and wondering how gentle she would be. She cast her eye at my parts and paused for a moment and then spoke. 'My God, Esmeralda, those are the most beautiful labia I have ever seen.' She touched me with her warm fingers. 'They are so large and pliable. They alone will make you a fortune. The men will never tire of gazing at them. Beautiful.'

I smiled, grateful for her reaction. Although I had seen Susana's, I hadn't realised that my lips were quite so different from other women's. A warm sense of pride enveloped me. The señora then examined me. 'Yes, Esmeralda, you are certainly a virgin,' she said excitedly and smiling her broad smile. 'Are you sure Susana is a virgin, too?'

'Yes. At least before she went into prison.'

'How do you know?'

'I did to her exactly what you've just done to me. I was showing her where it was.'

'Then I have a plan for making you, Susana and me a nice little pile. There is a very rich marquis who lives in this town who just loves virgin flesh. He could be your first man. Let me tell you, he is very gentle. If you agree, I will tell him I have found two pretty girls for him.'

'I must tell Susana first.'

'Of course.'

Susana reacted with surprising enthusiasm. 'We've got to lose it sometime. We might as well be paid to. Yes, I'm for it. Tell the señora... tomorrow!' So that's what I did and she spoke to the marquis.

'It's a good deal, Esmeralda. You and Susana will get two *ducats* each and I will get four. I will give you one of mine apiece so you'll get three each. See how generous I am!'

'Goodness, señora! That's as much as I earn in six weeks.'

'Yes, for half an hour's work! And with any luck a lot less.'

'You are so kind... dividing your share.'

'Don't worry. The least I can do,' she said, smiling widely with her whole face.

***

The marquis proved to be a clever man. He laid down four conditions. The older of us, namely me, would be first. There would be an interval of four days before he indulged himself in the other. Both sessions would take place in the señora's boudoir. The señora explained that he wanted to ensure that I had prepared Susana for her deflowering by telling her how easy the whole experience would be for her and he did not want us, for reasons of his own anonymity, to know where he lived. A gap of four days would simply add to the intensity of his anticipation and pleasure.

I was terrified that day when I knocked on the señora's frog shaped door knocker. I didn't know what to expect. I had only seen one erect penis before, the *hidalgo*'s, the night before I killed him. I wondered how big others would be and whether they would hurt me. The thought of pain filled me with an agonising fear. 'Come in, Esmeralda. You look pale. There is nothing to be afraid of. Honestly,' she said. She could read my mind. Then, as she took me by the hand, 'Come with me into the drawing room. I'm sure he will be here soon. He wants to see you in the boudoir. He asked that he goes in first and you follow, after no more than a minute. You will be fine.'

Just a little later, we heard the door knocker. I quivered. The señora answered and ushered her visitor upstairs. I heard them both talking as I sat waiting anxiously below. She then appeared in the drawing room again. 'Come on up,' she said with her beaming smile.

She opened the door and ushered me in. The marquis was sitting in an armchair opposite the door, looking very relaxed and confident. He beckoned me in with, 'It's Esmeralda, isn't it?'

'Yes, señor,' I replied. 'I'm charmed to meet you.' I didn't feel charmed at all.

'Likewise,' said the marquis as he stood up, came towards me and softly shook my hand. He broke into a smile as he did so and that made me feel more relaxed but still tense and fearful. 'We are going to make love. It is your first time,' he said, 'and I want you to enjoy it. That is my challenge. To give you pleasure and at the same time to have my share, too. I first want you to take off your dress, lie on the bed and open your legs, just a little. You can keep your stockings on if you wish.' I did as he asked, still feeling nervous and frightened. I forced a smile.

'Now I am going to take my clothes off,' which he did with the total absence of inhibition. I looked straight at the object which was going to penetrate me. Although it had yet to prepare itself, presumably with his help, it was tiny. My fear of pain evaporated like a rain drop on a hot roof. 'No wonder,' I thought, 'he specialises in virgins. One as thin as that would hardly touch the señora's.' I had to look away from it, to stifle a chuckle, so peered upwards to his blue eyes.

'You are strikingly beautiful,' he said, by then sitting on the bed and stimulating himself, as I looked on. Even when as ready as he could be, it was remarkably thin and not that long either. 'I'm now going to try to enter you,' he said. I was beginning to feel quite excited, relieved and much less tense, now I'd seen the size of his diminutive monster. I opened my legs a little more and felt him insert the first half a *pulgada*. He then paused.

'How is that, Esmeralda?' he grinned.

'Fine,' I said, hardly feeling a thing. Maybe a slight twinge but nothing much.

'A little more?'

'Go on,' I said and meant him to take up my invitation. In a few further, hesitant steps the short length of him was right inside me. I had hardly noticed pain and, to my surprise, felt quite a bit of pleasure. 'Susanna will like this,' I thought, no longer a virgin.

'Why are you laughing?' he said, as he climbed off, expended and breathing heavily.

'Just with pleasure, My Lord,' I replied, thinking of my three *ducats*.

***

'You were right, Esmeralda. Dead right! I did enjoy it. It was a little painful when he started but something kind of snapped in me and from then on I liked it,' said a happy Susana, as she came to the front door.

I felt concerned before she went to the señora's because she looked anxious and vulnerable; but then I just glowed with relief. That meant we could take the next step together.

***

Not many days later, we visited the house of pleasure the señora had recommended. It was at the north end of the Calle de Arganzuela, just down on the right from the Calle de Toledo. We arrived at about 9 o'clock in the morning, following the advice of Señora Angélica de la Torre. She said that, if we arrived later, we would be subjected to heavy banter from the men queuing outside which we would probably find embarrassing, especially as we were not yet working there.

The madam greeted us. 'I've been expecting you two. From my friend Señora de la Torre aren't you? She used to work here. Come into my office.'

She was a plump, friendly, older lady, probably around fifty and shuffled along rather than walked. She had tied her greying hair into a bun and wore a long red dress which exposed a huge area of her cleavage. Under a window, which overlooked the rear garden, stood a small single bed. She had arranged two chairs for us in front of her desk, behind which she squeezed her well rounded form.

'Take a seat. My name is Isabel Jiménez. And yours?'

We introduced ourselves.

'I believe you are looking for work?'

We nodded in anticipation.

'Well, you've come to the right place. I have just two vacancies at the moment and we'll see if you meet what I want. First how old are you?'

We told her that we didn't know accurately and that I was about sixteen and Susana about fifteen.

'That's not a problem. Just about legal. Are you virgins?'

We told her we weren't.

'When did you lose your virginity?'

We told her that, as well.

'Who to?'

We explained that it was to a marquis that Señora de la Torre had found for us.

'Hm,' she breathed. 'His cock is so small, it hardly counts. But if you're sure, that will be fine. The señora has told me all about the two of you. You have lived a pair of interesting lives, so far. Starting off in Burgos and all that. And you, Susana, getting off for attempted murder. Well done!

'Just a few other things. You will be inspected by a doctor twice a month. To make sure you haven't picked up something nasty. I'll show you how to make a pessary which will stop you becoming pregnant, and we now need to work out my cut. I only charge my girls for the room they use for business. That's five *reales* a week each, if they live out. If they live in, nine a week. Staying in means buying your own food and cooking it here. I'm giving you the bedroom sharing rate of seven. It's all that's free for now. If another room comes up you can have it. But I've got separate rooms for each of you to work in!

'Now for our prices. You charge our fixed rates, half a *real* for a fuck with your clothes on, laying down or standing up. A *real* with you naked. Half a *real* to bring him off by hand. A *real* and a half by mouth. Anything else and you settle the price before.

'I have some strict rules, too. I won't have you working for anyone else. Not at any time. Don't make arrangements to see clients away from here. That's to protect you as well as me. Break either of these and you're out. You can talk with the other girls and argue with them as much as you like but I won't tolerate fighting. You must treat each other with respect, especially in front of the clients. On no account must you be rude to the clients. If one of them tries to hurt you, you can defend yourself and shout for help. Do not use knives or other weapons here. If I want any girls to work away from here at a special event, I will have the final say on who the girls should be. That's about all.

'Oh, just one other thing, I need to inspect you to make sure you are all right to start. Who wants to be first?'

I said I would be.

'Right, lay down over there,' she said, pointing to the bed, and pull your dress up...'

I did as she instructed.

'I think you'll both fit in well here, if what Señora de la Torre tells me is true.' she said. 'I've got a lot of belief in her.' As she spoke she was opening me and craning her neck to have a look around. My body tensed as she gently inserted her index finger. Once she had taken it out, she looked at it intently and sniffed.

'You'll do nicely. Now you, señorita.'

Susana passed the test, too.

'When can you start then?'

'Can we see the room we will be sleeping in?' I asked, not wanting to be caught having to sort out the mess the alchemist's rooms were in. The madam showed us upstairs, along a landing to the end, opened a door and pointed inside.

'Treat it as your home,' she said. There were two single beds, quite close together, a wardrobe, a dressing table with a stool and two small armchairs, one at each side of a small fireplace.

'I think I like it,' said Susana, looking at me.

'Good thing we are friends. It's a bit small,' I said.

'It's all I've got, señorita. Afraid it's take it or leave it.'

'Can we see you downstairs?' I asked, wanting to talk in private with Susana.

'Suppose so,' said Señora Jiménez.

'What do you really think, Susana? It's small but maybe all right?'

'I think we could cope, especially if we take it in turns at the dressing table. I think we should take it. Sounds like she'll have another room soon enough.'

So we agreed with Señora Jiménez that we would work in her establishment and have the room. We told her we would inform our current employers that we were taking the jobs with her and agreed to start on the following Monday.

Predictably, Señora Ramírez barked in disgust when Susana told them but Señor Ramírez was far more sympathetic, even congratulating her. When Susana told me, we remembered the little wink he gave us, the night he got his wife drunk before their noisy love session. 'What do you know about it, Josefina? Susana will earn much more there, far more than I'll ever afford to pay her.' At first, Señora Ramírez's reaction upset Susana but she soon recovered. It delighted Señora de la Torre that we'd taken the jobs and she kissed me in her excitement. 'I do hope you like it there. I really do.'

***

We decided, for mutual support, that we would arrive at the brothel at the same time, 9 o'clock on the Monday morning.

'You're far too early for business,' said Señora Jiménez, 'but come in, put your things in your room and we can introduce you to some of the others.'

She knocked on the door of the room next to ours. A tall, well dressed woman answered the door.

'Beatrix, have you got a minute? Here are the new girls I told you about. I want to introduce you to them.'

The girl asked the three of us into her tidy little room and said her name was Beatrix de Mendoza. She was about eighteen. She had the most striking red hair, tied at the top of her head so that it hung loosely over her shoulders. Both Susana and I instantly liked the girl's friendly attitude and saw her as a potential ally. The madam left us to talk to Beatrix and asked her to introduce us to some of the others, before 11 o'clock.

'Why 11 o'clock?' I asked, after the madam had disappeared downstairs.

'That's when the men start appearing in earnest. We might get the odd one or two before, but not many.'

'Got any tips?' asked Susana.

'I think you should tell me about yourselves first. It's not often we get two starting at the same time.'

We told her why we were in Madrid, avoiding mentioning my killing of the *hidalgo* and changing our names. We did tell her about Susana's trial and about the jobs we'd already had in Madrid.

'I suppose I should tell you a bit about myself before telling you about working here. I am an orphan. My poor mother was Italian. She died when I was three. I was pawned here by an uncle who looked after me until I was sixteen. The madam gave him twenty *ducats* for me and he can claim me back at any time for fifteen. He won't though, I guarantee. This means I only get half of what I earn and Madam Isabel gets the rest.'

'Do you like it here?' asked Susana.

'It's all right. But you need to keep your nose clean. Any trouble and you're out. The madam will tell the other houses in the Arganzuela and you'll have a job finding anything as good anywhere else. You'd probably have to move to another town, Guadalajara or Toledo or somewhere. The old gal is pretty fair though and she won't chuck you out without a good reason.'

'What did you do before coming here?' asked Susana.

'My uncle was a property agent. I worked in his office, mainly sorting papers and fixing meetings. Then with the property slump, his company folded up. He owed money to some speculators so he pawned me to work here. He owed a hundred times what he got for me. I hate him for what he did to me.'

'I'm sorry to hear your story,' I said, then, changing the subject. 'As Susana said, got any good tips?'

'Quite a few,' said Beatrix. 'First, make sure you keep yourselves clean. Wash yourselves every day, at least once and make sure you are clean down there,' she said pointing to below my waist. 'Make sure the clients are clean, too. Don't be afraid to have a good look at them before they touch you. Some of them have some real filth underneath their foreskins. Check them out. Offer to wash it, if you don't want it inside you.'

'Did Isabel tell you about the Mule?'

'The Mule?' asked Susana, her eyes wide open as if fearing copulation with an animal of some sort.

'Yes, we've got a woman here who will do anything. If one of the men asks you to do something you don't want to do, ask María Nuñez. She'll do it. She'll do anything. Some things you'd never imagine. She'll fix her price. Just leave it to her!'

'What sort of things will she do that we won't?' asked Susana.

'You'll find out soon enough.'

'Anything else?' I asked.

'Do your best to get on with the other girls. They will help you if you get into trouble. Come and I'll introduce you.'

Elvira rented the room opposite ours. She looked quite a lot older than Beatrix, probably around forty, if not older. As we entered her room she glared at us like a fox cornered in an ally. I felt an involuntary shudder as her eyes drilled into mine. For some, as yet unknown reason, she saw us as a threat. 'Did I ask you in?' she said, making us feel uncomfortable and awkward.

'These are the new girls,' said Beatrix, raising her voice to reveal an unexpected fearlessness. 'I only wanted you to say hello to them, Elvira. There's no need to be so nasty.'

'Hello,' she said. 'I'm busy now. I'll see you later.' She then eased her room door closed.

'I'm sorry about that,' said Beatrix. 'She's not good with new girls, but her customers love her. She'll soon warm to you both. Just one more introduction. Melchora Cabello. She's right down the end.'

As we approached her door, we could hear someone singing inside.

'That's her,' said Beatrix. 'She used to be an actress and singer but had a serious attack of stage fright so came to work here.'

Beatrix knocked softly on her door and let herself in. Melchora continued her singing. She stood before a music stand and seemed, to my untrained eye, to be following the words and the music from a manuscript. Beatrix lifted her index finger to her lip. Melchora, instantly stopped singing and turned towards us. Her face beamed as she set eyes on Beatrix who soon explained our presence.

'I shouldn't be here really. I'm a singer actress at the Príncipe. I shall be going back there soon. Welcome to the whore house! I hope you like the work. You may or you may not. I hate it but it pays my bills.'

'You'll like it,' said Beatrix. 'You will be working in a community. We all help each other. Let's take you down to Madam Isabel. She will want to show you where you will be working.'

Madam Isabel first showed us my room which was not far from the front door. I expected a cold, stark dungeon of a room but this was the exact opposite. The pretty little room purred with a warm glow. A dark red cover draped the single bed which stood on a red carpet, against the wall opposite the door. A small chair stood in the corner by the door and a coat hanger was hooked over a nail on the wall. There were red drapes to the small window. A silver mirror hung from the far end of the room and several erotic drawings, all in dark red frames, were dotted around the walls. One showed a man on top of a woman and in union with her; in another a man was licking a woman's genitals as she pleasured him with her mouth; another showed a woman on her knees with a man penetrating her from behind; in a fourth the woman's back was to the wall and the man was standing but obviously inside her. The artist had used the same couple in all the sketches.

'I like your drawings, Madam Isabel...' I wasn't so sure.

'Just call me Isabel.'

'... but I don't understand why they are here.'

'Very simple,' said Isabel. 'Many of our customers are from abroad. From Greece, Italy, Flanders or the Spanish Netherlands. They don't speak the language and the pictures are to show them what you can do. Once your client is in here, and you have shut the door behind you, you'll have to find out what he wants... Do you like the room?'

'It's lovely and nicer than I expected.'

'My aim is to make you and your clients feel relaxed and comfortable. I'll show you Susana's room now.'

Susana's was equally welcoming but furnished in a soft green. A similar set of drawings, but in dark green frames, decorated the walls and, as in mine, the window overlooked the back garden. Susana smiled as soon as she entered and glanced around it.

'Well, have you any questions, you two?'

'When do we start?' asked Susana.

'As soon as someone comes through the front door,' said Isabel.

CHAPTER 10

Working Girls

Madam Isabel decided, once again, that I should take the lead. So I entertained my first customer before Susana. Maybe, because I was the elder, Madam Isabel believed I would help Susana by describing the experience to her before she dealt with hers. To me, that didn't seem unreasonable.

As I sat on the bed in my work room, waiting for that encounter and turning over in my mind, with quite a degree of dread, how the first one would treat me, I heard the madam welcoming a client at the front door.

'Come in Father, come in,' I heard her say. Not a priest, surely. I could not believe my ears.

'Good to see you again, Father,' she said. So I had heard correctly. I couldn't work out whether a priest would be a good customer or bad. I only hoped he would be good and not hurt me. At least he'd been here before and none of the girls we had met warned us about him. The madam knocked at my door.

'Come in,' I said, in a puzzled, slightly raised voice.

'I'd like to introduce you to Father Sebastian Gutierro. He is your first customer,' said the madam, with a smile.

The priest stood in his long black cassock with a black biretta, a size too small for him, atop his large head. He was a youngish man of about twenty five to thirty. 'Good morning, my dear. You are a pretty girl,' he said still wearing a friendly smile. Madam Isabel left the room, shutting the door as she did so.

At first I was stuck for words. The last person I expected was a priest. The thought of my supposed father flashed across my mind. I thought I'd better smile, too. 'Welcome to my little room,' was all I could say at first. Then, 'Sit down if you wish.'

'I'd rather start straight away, if that's all right with you. I have a number of calls to make this morning, so I need to leave in about twenty minutes, if not before. Would you mind lifting your dress over your head and putting it on the chair. Now lie in the centre of the bed with your head on the pillow and you legs open.' I did exactly as he had asked and while I did so he took off his biretta and placed it gently on the floor. He undid the buttons down the centre of his cassock and slipped it off, over his broad shoulders. He took a rosary from a large side pocket and held it in his right hand. And there it was: his member needed no stimulation but stood at the ready, as if in contemplation. Without saying a word he climbed onto the bed, made the sign of the cross above me, and gently eased himself inside me, while I held myself open for him. He still held the rosary and as he took his weight with his left arm eased the rosary beads through the fingers on his right hand, reciting the rosary prayer, 'In the name of the Father, and of the Son, and of the Holy Spirit. I believe in God the Father Almighty, Creator of Heaven and earth... And in Jesus Christ, His only Son, our Lord, Who was conceived by the Holy Ghost, born of the Virgin Mary, suffered under Pontius Pilate, was crucified, died and was buried; He descended into hell.' He yelled out at the word 'Hell' and continued: 'On the third day He arose again from the dead; He ascended into Heaven, and sitteth at the right hand of God, the Father Almighty.' As he performed this holy recitation he slid himself slowly in and out of me.

While I was laying there and going through this ritual, something came suddenly into my mind. What, I wondered, would Pedro think of my doing this work. Would he be ashamed and disgusted? Would he reject and disown me? I doubted that. I was still his twin sister and he would surely admire me for finding a well-paid job with the other girls at number seven and not working alone on the streets. He would probably feel the same about Susana. I longed to meet him again to hug him and tell him my story.

'Amen! Amen!' he called out when, after no more than two minutes, he came in a bursting shudder. 'Thank you. Thank you.' Then, after a pause in which he slid off the bed, 'Is that for the usual one *real*?'

'Yes Father. Thank you.' He took a small purse from his cassock pocket as he was dressing himself, took out two coins and put them on the pillow as I lay, still naked, on the bed.

'Thank you. You never know, I may see you again. Goodbye and God bless you.' He then opened the door, went out and closed the door behind him. I didn't know what to feel or think. Not only had he been here before, he'd clearly been a client. But why did he play the ritual with the rosary? Was that for his benefit or mine? And was it a coincidence that he was my first customer or was that planned?

I concluded, probably rightly, that his seeing me was a coincidence. It might have been that Madam Isabel was expecting him and she had selected me for him. I had no intention of asking. The rosary was to benefit each of us. It was mainly for him, almost to forgive himself in advance for breaking his vow of chastity, probably for as many times that he could not remember. For me, it was an attempt to make me feel the presence of God during the act. At least that was my conclusion. My emotions were mixed. I felt relief that my first client had been well satisfied and that I had not suffered into the bargain. I felt that I had performed nothing more than a service. Although I had dutifully smiled at him while he was having me, there was not a hint of emotion or feeling towards him, other than a sense of contempt for his breaking of his vows. How many priests were there who behaved like this? He couldn't be the only one. Far from it.

The whole experience with the priest was not physically unpleasant. But I took little delectation from it. He had not satisfied me and had probably ignored that aspect of our encounter. However, I could see how, with a little more practice, I could find the whole thing quite enjoyable. But until then...

The door burst open and Susana stood at the threshold, as I noticed he'd left a two *maravedí* tip. 'A priest, who would have thought?' she said in utter astonishment. 'Wonder what mine will be!'

The answer to that question soon became clear: hers was an undertaker's assistant. 'He said his name was Salvador de Cantos. He couldn't stop talking. It may not have been his first time but he was a bit clumsy and he came in about ten seconds. He was more nervous than me. And he had this odd smell.'

'Embalming fluid, I expect.'

'Don't say that. Esmeralda!'

'Well it could have been!' I said, laughing. 'What do you think of the work?'

'I quite liked what he did and I felt in charge. He almost forgot to pay. I should have charged him a *real* but I let him off a couple of *maravedís*, only because he was so quick and he was very nice.'

'You're not meant to let them off paying the lot. He's got away with it. He'll ask for you the next time!'

'Well, I told him to ask for me, if he wanted to,' said Susana.

So we had each survived our first customer. There were only a few more for us that day. Susana had one and I had two, one against the wall and another on the bed. The first was an Italian and the second a hat maker in his siesta. Again, I felt little or no emotion. Nor did I feel abused. It was that I had something to offer and customers were prepared to pay for it. I felt no guilt either. I had done no wrong, as far as I was concerned. Quite the opposite, this was a reasonable way for a girl to earn a living. I was already beginning to feel committed to my new profession. I was going to enjoy it and, as Angélica de la Torre had said, I would make by fortune from it. I vowed to myself to keep a record of the number of customers I would have: day 1: three.

With the exception of Elvira, who remained distinctly cool towards us, the other girls were all curious about how we had managed and felt about our first day. That night, after the madam had taken in our last customer, we chatted as we helped each other to cook a meal in the madam's kitchen.

'Always take the payment in advance, not after the job. Learn from our experience,' said Beatrix. 'You'd be surprised how many try to leave without paying and once they run for the door, there's not much you can do. I was cheated a couple of times, in the early days. Not any more.'

'How many customers have you all had today?' asked Susana.

'Sorry. I don't answer questions like that,' replied Elvira.

'I've had twelve,' said Beatrix. 'That's a normal load for the day. Pretty active lot they were, too! Well, most of them.'

'How is it I've only had two?' asked Susana.

'I've had eight. You girls are new and Isabel is breaking you in gently,' said Melchora.

'What I don't understand is to what extent we can like the customers?' I asked.

'That's a difficult one. We are not here to fall in love with them or to have a relationship with them outside. Isabel will have told you that. She will dismiss you if you have a paid customer, other than here. But there is nothing wrong with liking the customers. If you get on well with them they will come back and ask for you again. It's a bit like a rider going to his favourite blacksmith. It's no different. The blacksmith knows the horse and is careful with it in the hope that the customer will go to him again. And if they like it a bit rough and you are rough then they may ask for you again.'

'I like the gentle ones best,' said Melchora. 'There is one who likes me to sing to him before we start. He always asks for me.'

'Honestly, Melchora, you are fooling yourself that you are a singer when you're a whore, the same as the rest of us,' said Elvira.

'No need to be unkind. She's just saying what she does to gain favour from her clients. If you could sing you'd do the same,' said Beatrix, over the sound of Melchora's whimpering.

'Well damn the lot of you,' said Elvira, her voice shaking with anger. She turned her back and stormed out of the kitchen.

'Why does she always get on her high horse?' asked Melchora, recovering herself. 'There is always something we're doing she doesn't like.'

'I suppose you can't please everybody,' I said, trying to regain calm.

'Why does she think she is so special?' asked Susana, missing my hint to change the subject.

'Well, um,' said Melchora, giving herself a moment to think. 'Elvira is a kind of specialist and if a customer wants what Elvira has on offer he has to ask.'

'So what does she do?' asked Susana.

'She specialises in subjecting men to pain and humiliation,' said Beatrix. 'Some of them want that. Don't ask me why. Her room is in the basement, down the back stairs. It is like a dungeon. She can tie them to the wall, the bed or even to the floor. She has canes and whips, chains, shackles and ropes. Madam Isabel had to put a thicker door in because the yelling from Elvira's customers was annoying the other customers... and us. You could hear her whipping and beating them.'

'Maybe she is taking revenge on the men who come to her for something some man did to her. She could have been abused or raped as a child,' I said.

'She's never said so,' said Melchora. 'She is the odd one out. She prefers to go out at night and leave us here. God knows what she does.'

'She stops and chats to the street girls and hawkers. I've seen her,' said Beatrix. 'She's going to land herself in trouble soon. Just you wait and see.'

'Where is María?' I asked.

'She doesn't stay here. She lives in a rented apartment in the Calle de San Pedro, not far from here. She has done well here and can afford to pay a high rent. It is a small apartment but it's nicely furnished. I stayed the night there once,' said Melchora.

After our meal of stewed beef, beans and artichokes, we all went to our rooms.

'They don't like Elvira. Do they?' said Susana.

'And I'm not sure what María does to make her so well off.'

'Isabel said we'd find out soon enough. I'm tired. It's bedtime.'

***

That was the end of our first day working at number seven, Calle de Arganzuela. We still had a lot to learn, about the clients, the others working there and how to make the most of the work without punishing ourselves or getting into trouble. As Melchora had said, Isabel was breaking us in gently. I dealt with four customers the following day, five the day after and by the end of the week, my total had risen to twenty seven and Susana's to twenty three. We worked Saturday afternoon and almost to midnight but had all day Sunday off. I had earnt three *ducats*, exactly plus a dozen or so *maravedís* in tips and Susana, two *ducats* and seven *reales*. So, even after paying Madam Isabel her seven *reales*, we had each made a handsome profit. We needed to work out what to do with our money so we asked Beatrix. 'Bank it. You must set up an account. There is a bank in the Calle de Tenerías on the corner of San Pedro, where María lives. The name of the street reminded me of my brother again.

That week, I sent only one customer to María. I didn't like him from the moment I saw him. He was an untidy individual with a black and grey beard, sharp features and penetrating eyes. He said he worked as a stonemason and had a job at the new cathedral being built in the Calle de Toledo. He had a strange request, or it seemed strange to me. He came in and asked me if I had a chamber pot in the room. I said I did and he nodded with approval.

'Do you need to use it?' I asked. 'I can look the other way if you do.'

'No. Not now. But I'll need it later.'

'What would you like then?' I reeled of the usual list of possibilities and the prices.

'None of them.' Then he told me in detail.

'Sorry, señor, but I won't do that but we have a girl who will,' I said. I opened the door and took him quickly along to María who smiled and took him in.

'I'll leave you then?' I said, not quite knowing how she would react as she stood and listened to his bizarre request.

'That's fine. Only too willing to oblige, señor. Whatever you want.'

Needless to say, over the following weeks, I sent many more to María. I hated the thought of being constrained in any way which would give the man physical control over me. One night, about 8 o'clock and just before we were about to finish work, Madam Isabel brought me a tall, young handsome man of about twenty five. He was dressed in leather pantaloons and a sparkling clean white shirt and had his hair tied in a braid. 'Come in,' I said as Isabel brought him to my door. Unusually, he was carrying a large, canvas bag.

'Been shopping?' I asked, smiling at him.

'No. I've brought some rope. I need to tie you to the bed, if you'd like to take your dress off.'

'Not me, señor, but we have a girl who will oblige. Come with me.'

In another case, Isabel showed in an excessively plump man wearing a battered top hat. His paunch was so large he couldn't possibly see his penis, not without the aid of a mirror. I had two immediate thoughts. First, if he lies on top of me, I'll never breathe again. Second, how can he possible get himself in with that enormous paunch in the way? All was soon revealed. Tucked into the belt of his trousers lurked an iron chopper with a wide wooden handle. I was horrified.

'What do you think you are going to do with that?' I said ready to scream and thinking he was going to butcher me.

'No need to worry, señorita.' He then explained his request.

'Not with me, señor, but one of my colleagues will be pleased to do that.'

María, it seemed could and would do anything. Susana thought the same. We agreed that our María was a godsend. She deserved ever *maravedí* she got.

This was not to say that I would refuse to use the acceptable tools of the trade. Madam Isabel was well acquainted with a wood turner who lived in the Calle de la Ruda, off the Calle Toledo, not far from number seven. To her exact specification, the wood turner made a range of '*consoladores*', as Isabel called them. No one knew whether she had invented these pleasuring objects, whether she had picked up the idea from someone else or whether they had indeed, as she claimed, been used by the Romans and the ancient Greeks. The wood turner created these penis shaped objects from mahogany or oak. He had made them in a range of lengths and widths and polished them until they glistened.

***

I was armed with a range of these instruments, when Isabel sent me to the strangest assignment I could contemplate. 'Whatever you do, only use the larger ones!' she said, making a joke of it. She sent me to an extravagant house in the Calle de San Nicolás, not far from the palace. Carrying a small bag of these various implements, I knocked on the door and waited a few moments. To my complete astonishment the marquis who had, admittedly for a good price, taken my virginity, opened it.

'I know you, don't I?' he said with a cheeky grin.

'You should do! You deflowered me about four months ago!'

'And your friend ...about four days later?'

'That's right,' I replied, still in shock but managing a smile.

'Come in and let me explain. First, have you brought the tools?'

'Yes.'

'You may be a little surprised to hear this but today you will be working with my wife. She will tell you what she wants you to do. Here are three *reales* for looking after her. I don't want to inhibit either you or her, so I am going out to meet some friends in a tavern. I'll put my coat on and go right away.'

So I was to serve a woman. That would be a change I may not want. I couldn't see a way of escape, if I wanted one. I could hardly refuse to go back on a mission the madam had asked me specifically to undertake. As the marquis disappeared through the front door, the marchioness appeared from a drawing room. She looked beautiful in a pretty floral dressing gown, which hung precariously from her soft white shoulders. Her blonde hair was tied into a knot on the top of her head and she had decorated her fine features with a dash of rouge which accentuated her high cheekbones.

'You are Esmeralda, Filipe tells me. I don't want to waste time, yours or mine, so let's go straight up to my bedroom and we can start to play. Goodness, you are a pretty girl. I'm sure we will have fun,' she said, in obvious contemplation of the events which were about to commence.

'Yes, but I think I am due a word of explanation. My job is to pleasure men. Am I expected now to make love to you, a woman?'

'You could say that, but explain I will. My honourable husband, the marquis, has been blessed with one of the tiniest members in the Empire. It is so small, he'd have trouble taking the virginity from a mouse. Of course, he makes love to me regularly but only to his own satisfaction. You have brought a range of toys with which I think you can satisfy me. So, the sooner we start the better! Follow me,' she said, excitedly.

She dashed out of the room and had reached the top of her stairs by the time I had only just entered the hall. 'Come on,' she said. 'You're not shy are you?'

I thought for a moment before answering her question. I wasn't shy, just in mild shock from learning about this peculiar assignment. I had never before felt inclined to lovemaking with a woman and I didn't then, although I believed there were women who did. However, whatever the lady wanted she could have it from me. I had nothing to lose and, for certain, she could not make me pregnant. I decided that I should do her with alacrity. This could be a new and profitable line of business.

'No señora, I'm not the least bit shy. I just wanted to give you a head start!'

As I entered and peered around the door, the marchioness lay sprawled across her bed stark naked and, in due deference to her modesty, with her legs crossed. She had thrown her nightgown to the floor.

'Put your bag of toys by the pillow and take off your clothes. We should be naked together! Then lay down here, beside me,' she said, giving me precise instructions.

I did exactly as asked. As I moved my naked body alongside hers I could smell the aroma of the exotic perfume which enveloped her. It was the fragrance of orange blossom and cedar wood. By good fortune, I too had perfumed my body that day, exactly where Angélica de la Torre used to treat hers. The lady's skin was silken and, apart from the blush on her face, almost totally white. It was as if she had deliberately avoided exposure to the sun, even for a moment.

'Now I want you to kiss me, on the lips. Make your tongue penetrate.'

I felt no compunction to do what she wanted but, against my nature, did so. She reciprocated and our tongues mutually explored our respective mouths. Her breath tasted and smelt of honey and her mouth was wet inside. I had never kissed a man in as intimate a way as this but, here I was, kissing a woman.

'Now I want you to fondle my breasts and I will do the same to yours.' Again, totally against my natural instincts, I did so, touching her firmness and gently moulding her nipples in my fingers. I could feel by the movements of her body, which she silently brought closer to mine, that she thrived on this form of stimulation. I began to feel a compulsive force within me which wanted me to submit to her and take maximum enjoyment from her body.

'Now touch me there,' she said, pointing, 'but be gentle.' By then she was wet with her own juices and as she, without as much as a gentle request, touched me in mine, I could feel my own wetness beginning to form. She knew how and where to touch me, how to make me squirm with pleasure, how to give me the nicest feelings. This woman knew the way around her own exquisite body and how to give herself such pleasure, so without a doubt, would know the exact points on my body she would have to touch to pleasure me. She was in every way totally unlike any other customer I had served. I could not believe any man would go to such extremes to please me. Indeed, in their case, the role was reversed: my function was to give them pleasure; not one customer, at least until then, had seen my pleasure as part of the equation. This was a completely different kind of assignment. The marchioness, bless her lovely soul, was clearly and unashamedly pleasuring me at the same time I was pleasuring her.

'Now we go head to tail and you taste mine as I taste yours,' she instructed. 'You lay on the bed and I will go down on you.' Accompanied by the sounds of the groaning bedsprings we manoeuvred ourselves around so that I lay with my legs apart with my head resting on her fluffy pillow. She shuffled herself into position with her mouth over my charms as I began to explore hers. Then, quite to my surprise, she shouted out. For a moment I thought she had seen someone watching us but no. 'My God. I have never seen lips like those before. They are wonderful. I could eat you all day long. Where did they come from?' I felt embarrassed somewhat by her question. What did it mean? How could I know where they came from or even that they were at all unusual. Señora Angélica de la Torre had, of course, admired them before.

'They just developed like that, when I was becoming a woman.'

'They are the most beautiful things I have ever seen on a woman's body.'

Hers, too, made a delightful picture. They were still glistening with the warm juices I had made by fondling her. I touched her with my tongue and felt I should offer a compliment in return. 'Yours is a pretty thing too, and it tastes of musk and rose petals.'

'Thank you, Esmeralda. You are so nice. Take your tongue to my little button, under that hood-shaped piece. Flick it rapidly on that.'

As I did so my nose touched the surrounding area, sure enough, she had perfumed herself there too! On about the twentieth of my tongue flicks she began to purr, just like a cat drinking a dish of cream.

'Oh! Oh! I enjoyed that so much. Let me do the same to you. Put your hands underneath your bottom and lift yourself up a bit so I can reach you with my tongue.'

I felt the same kind of pleasure as she did so didn't want her to stop. It was as much as I could do not to shout out in ecstasy. I barely controlled a yell but could not prevent a shudder as she skilfully brought me to a mighty climax. Eventually she paused and said, 'The tools. We've forgotten to use them. Start from the smallest and work up.'

Within a few moments I was pleasuring her with the smallest *consolador*. 'Are you happy with me looking down on you like this?' I said from the advantage point of my head on her pillow and hers still down between my legs.

'Of course! You can see where to put it from up there. That's no good. Try the next one up.' So I inserted a larger one. As I moved it gently in and out it made a squelching, sucking sound as her juices swished around inside her. The smell intoxicated me.

'That's better. Faster! In and out.'

I did as instructed, wondering what she'd ask me to do next.

'Better. But still not as good as it should be. Get the biggest one.'

'Do you realise how big it is?' I asked her.

'Show me!'

'Here it is!'

'My God! What a monster. I'm sure you'll get it in, Esmeralda. Give me the one you've just used. I'll try it on you.' As if I had any choice in the matter. I gradually and gently pushed the monster into her. I didn't want to hurt her or make her bleed. I had never seen a cucumber as wide as this and some marrows weren't that much larger.

'Fantastic, Esmeralda. Just what I wanted. By the blood of Christ, that's tight! Oh! I'm coming again.' With that she let out a strange, stifled yelp, almost as if someone had accidentally trodden on her toe and hurt her. 'Move it in and out, but slowly and gently.'

Once again, I did as I was told and at the same time could feel her pleasuring me with the smaller one. What a pleasure to give pleasure and accept pleasure in return for pleasure. The more pleasure I give the more I must take. Where does this pleasure end? And I am being paid for this!

'Thank you, Esmeralda. Thank you. I think I have had enough. I am exhausted. I do not want to pass out. Yet I can feel, from the lightness in my head, that I am heading that way. But that would be bad for both of us.' I slid the monster out of her, a far easier operation than its insertion. She wriggled off me and eased her feet to the floor. 'Esmeralda, you were magnificent. We'll just have to do that again. Maybe next week!'

'That would be excellent, señora,' I said, not knowing whether I meant it or not. We got dressed and she showed me downstairs towards the kitchen.

'Would you like a drink or even something to eat before you go?'

'Señora, you are too kind. But no thank you. I ought to be getting back to the Arganzuela.'

'That will be fine then,' she said, as if to consent to my release from her house. 'That will be fine. Follow me.' She led me down the hall towards the door but, before opening it, planted a soft kiss on my lips. 'Goodbye, Esmeralda,' she said and I went, carrying the bag of tools with me and with the three *reales*, the marquis had given me, buried in my purse. As I began to walk back down the Calle de San Nicolás, towards the Calle del Humilladero, I didn't know what to feel. I certainly couldn't say what I thought because I had no clear idea. My mind jumped from recalling this complex of experiences, and wondering whether I should have enjoyed them so much, to seizing itself with guilt at finding such pleasure in another woman. Then as I opened some distance between me and the marchioness's house, I began to feel better. I should not scourge myself after satisfactorily performing a duty, for which the marquis rewarded me so well; and if a craftswoman is not permitted to enjoy her work then there is something wrong in the world. At least that was my immediate conclusion.

***

'What sort of day have you had?' I asked Susana, as I put my bag on my bed.

'You'd never believe. Without you here, I've had to work twice as hard. In the time you've been gone, I've had six men. I can't even remember them all. One was black, from the Maghreb. He had a cock and a half.'

'What did you do with the half he had to spare?'

'Don't be silly! You know what I mean! Another one was big and fat. A brewer, or so he said. He couldn't get it up.'

'Brewer's droop,' I said. Susana chuckled.

'Then there was this old man from north of the town. I'm sure I'd seen him in the Calle de la Luna. He was well over fifty. Said he'd been a *tercio* and had fought the French at Arras. Said he was a widower and had two daughters. One had married a corn merchant. The couple moved to Burgos about five years ago.'

'Did you tell him we're from there?'

'No. I kept away from that. Anyway, he said he didn't want to make love but only wanted to sit with me and chat. "Are you sure?" I said. "Certain," he said. "How long have I got?" I told him he could have half an hour and he just talked away and paid me before he went. Easiest half hour I've ever had.'

'What did he say?'

'He talked about his wife, who died of a mystery illness. But mostly about his mother who used to beat him and his father. I didn't know what to say, so I just sat on the bed and listened.'

'You did right. What about the others?'

'They just wanted to do it and went. I can hardly remember them. What about you? Did you have to perform with those *consoladores*?'

'You'll never believe this, Susana. I had to make love to a woman, the marchioness.' At first Susana didn't know whom I was talking about but I soon reminded her of her acquaintance with the lady's husband. I described the encounter with the marchioness in all its intimate detail. Susana reaction was interesting but it did not altogether surprise me.

'I couldn't have done it. I'd have had to go. No. I couldn't touch a woman like that. It's unnatural. It would have made me sick. I'd have been sick on her bed! How could you have done it, Esmeralda?'

'Well, to start with, I was inside the señora's house before the marquis told me what was in store. Then no sooner had he told me I would have to work on his wife, he shoved three *reales* in my hand and cleared off, leaving me with his already excited woman.'

'So you didn't have a choice then?'

'I suppose I could have said no and left, but I didn't and stayed. I hate to confess this, Susan, but I actually enjoyed it... once I had... well, kind of accepted what I had to do. I'll tell you something. That woman had washed herself so thoroughly. She was spotless, even around her bum. Totally clean. And perfumed. She'd dabbed herself with a fragrance of orange blossom and cedar wood and I could smell something sweet in it, like bougainvillea. There aren't many men who come here smelling of roses. It's mainly piss and beer. And if you looked at their bums, they'd be spotted with shit.'

'I see what you mean,' said Susana, 'but you still didn't have to go that far did you? You didn't have to. It's disgusting!'

I could have become angry with Susana but I couldn't bring that on myself. Although I had to admit to doing something with the woman that was out of the ordinary, that made no difference to the fact that I enjoyed it, at least up to a point, part of which was due to the obvious pleasure the woman took from me.

'No, Susana, you are right. Of course you are right. I didn't have to do it, but I was doing something I had been handsomely paid for and I wanted to do my best.'

'I think I get that.' she said, albeit with reluctance. I wasn't enjoying Susana's interrogation so I decided to drop the subject at that point. 'Are we going out tonight?' I asked.

CHAPTER 11

The Party

Much had changed in our lives since, a little over a year before, I had killed the *hidalgo* and we had fled from Burgos, fearing for my life, if not for Susana's as well. I had had four different jobs and Susana two. We had worked hard. In our four months or so at the house of pleasure in the Arganzuela, Susana had made love to 710 men and I had dealt with 853. Numerous of our customers had become 'regulars' and we appreciated return business from several points of view. First, it meant that the men were satisfied with our work. Second, having had the same customer a few times, we could predict relatively easily how he might behave the third and fourth time, and so on. We even knew some of them by their first names and they called us by ours.

Madrid is a small town and, maybe it is no surprise that we knew some of our clients from our previous work or lives in the town. Doctor Alvaro de Peralta, who came to the aid of the alchemist after the explosion that almost killed him, turned out to be one of our strangest clients. He always asked for Susana. Perhaps not surprisingly for a doctor, he always gave her the most intimate of examinations before anything would happen, even to the extent of putting his nose right down to her charms, but then he would masturbate himself over her breasts, pay, bid Susana farewell and go.

The lawyer who defended Susana, Estaban Ganado, always asked for me. At first I was astonished that this wealthy lawyer, one of Angélica de la Torre's customers, came to number seven, which was a lesser establishment than the señora's palatial mansion. I declined to ask him why he did so. I imagined that he just needed a change. I did ask him why he didn't go to Susana and he replied that he would never use the services of one of his clients. To do so would be in breach of his professional standards. What his professional standards had to do with often visiting a whore house, number seven or the señora, was one of those puzzles better left unsolved. To our overwhelming surprise, we discovered that Señor Ramírez indulged himself quite regularly at our brothel. He never asked for anyone in particular and Susana was quite shocked when the madam knocked on her door with him at her side, smiling and willing for business. Susana did not know what to say at first but soon saw the funny side of having her previous employer stretched between her legs and pumping at her with all his might.

We were surprised by the number who willingly paid who didn't want any more than to talk. Not just our more senior clients who might have difficulty in making themselves ready for business with us but quite young men who seemed to need advice rather than comfort. We took them seriously and spoke to them about whatever they wanted. Their topic for discussion often, if only eventually, clarified itself to be about a woman or women and who better to talk to than another woman. They often discussed their own wives: how to satisfy them, how to make lovemaking more enjoyable for the two of them and how to avoid pregnancy. Some had never seen their wives bodies in anything like the detail we were willing to display so some of our clients just wanted a 'closer look' than they had ever had before.

My encounter with the marchioness led to other business with the women of Madrid. I visited the marchioness several more times over those months and she must have spoken about me to several of her rich lady friends. So, at these ladies' request, Madam Isabel sent me along to their houses and I set to work with them. As usual, I took my array of *consoladores* and pleasured them, much in the same way as I had delighted the marchioness. Some, but not all of them, reciprocated the pleasure on me. Susana still found this difficult, if not revolting, but I had to admit to enjoying it as an aspect of my job. I did it to the best of my ability and these lovely ladies paid me well into the bargain.

While we were far from wealthy, we had by then accumulated a useful amount of money. We bought some nice clothes, shoes and some perfumes and still had about 40 *ducats* each at the bank. This seemed a fortune, about three times what a farm labourer could earn in a year and we had little idea of what to do with it.

'We should buy our own house,' said Susana. 'Eighty *ducats* is a lot of money and with a mortgage we could afford something modest, maybe not far from here.'

'I'm afraid we won't get far on eighty *ducats*, not in this town. Maybe, in Burgos or Guadalajara but not here. And I'd be amazed if a money broker would lend to two young whores. We'll just have to be patient and keep saving. I agree, though. Buying our own place is a very worthwhile ambition.' So we left it at that.

***

Isabel Jiménez excelled in her skills as a business woman. She knew so many people in the town whom she could rely on to give her girls work. Not that she would openly ask those she knew to visit us here at the Arganzuela. She cultivated her friends and contacts so that they knew that our services were always available. For example, she kept closely in touch with the local crown constabulary. Their job, of course, was to protect us citizens from all manner of ills which could befall an innocent person in this town. So having a regular but infrequent and discreet visit by a parish constable or sergeant could give us a degree of protection which we might not otherwise be afforded. Similarly, she mixed with the priesthood and regularly visited the convents and monasteries near the Arganzuela and in other parts of the town. Hence the occasional visit by a priest. My first customer, rosary beads and all, turned out to be a regular, if infrequent, customer.

We found out eventually that Madam Isabel made frequent visits to the *Tercio* barracks near the palace, not far from the marchioness's house in the Calle de San Nicolás. Needless to say, soldiers returning from the battlefields of Europe were among our most prized customers. They were always young and virile, mostly unmarried and usually desperate for physical love. They also had plenty of money which they had earned or gained from objects they had plundered, or of course from both, and were usually generous with it.

One morning, after Susana and I had been working for Madam Isabel for about six months, she asked all of us girls to gather in her office.

'I have had a slightly unusual request from one of the colonels at the barracks just off San Nicolás. A hundred and twenty of his *tercios* have just returned from fighting in Flanders and he wants to celebrate their successes by holding a party at the barracks.'

'Don't tell us, we are all invited,' said Elvira. 'We go along and they treat us like ladies and escort us back after a pleasant evening's singing and dancing.'

'No need for the sarcasm, Elvira, but apart from some pleasuring duties you would be expected to perform for our heroes, I imagine you will be dancing and singing if you feel like it.'

'Tell us more,' said Beatrix.

'The colonel has given me a programme for an evening with the soldiers. It will take place in two days' time, on Friday night and begin at nine o'clock. There will be a sumptuous meal with beer and the best wine in town. You will each have a place at the table. There will be a small orchestra playing. After the meal the soldiers will mix with you and you will do your best to pleasure them. You will not be expected to do all one hundred and twenty. A couple of other houses of pleasure in this street have also been approached. The colonel wants twelve girls in all. He will arrange for each girl to be escorted home.'

'Is he expecting us to do ten men apiece?' asked Beatrix.

'I asked him about the amount of contact. Many of the men are married and will only want to watch what happens. Others are of a God fearing nature and won't want anything to do with the... shall we say... after meal activities. And others will be too drunk to do much anyway! So I'd be surprised if you had to do more than half a dozen apiece, maybe even fewer. And you will be paid a *ducat* and five *reales* each.'

'Fantastic!' said Maria. 'It'll be good to do military service. Good money, too!'

'I agree,' I said. 'When will we be paid?'

'The morning after. Say, about ten o'clock.'

'Sounds good to me,' said Susana.

'Count me out,' said Elvira. 'I'm not interested in fucking a cart load of soldiers. I've got better things to do on a Friday night.' With that she walked out of the meeting and closed the door behind her.

'You can't please everyone,' said Isabel, smiling as if relieved at Elvira's departure.

So on Friday evening, five of us spent an hour or so preparing ourselves for our 'military encounter'. I put on a new dress and petticoat, which I had just purchased, and Susana did likewise. We liberally sprinkled ourselves with the best perfume we could afford and off we walked up towards the barracks. We arrived close to nine o'clock and were greeted at the door by the colonel himself.

'Good evening ladies. I believe you are our guests from the Arganzuela?'

'Yes,' said Melchora. 'We are from number seven.'

'Good. There are some girls from number five and they are already here. I am honoured to meet you. Do come in.'

We were surprised that the dinner had been constructed to be such a formal affair. Each of us sat among a group of soldiers, all dressed smartly but not in anything resembling military attire. The dining room had been arranged with a top table, at which sat the senior military figures and two priests, and three other tables at right angles to the top table. These tables filled about two thirds of the dining hall. About a third of the room had been left unoccupied but a range of musical instruments had been placed on seats in that part of the hall and a harp was standing like a forsaken bride-to-be, between the chairs. Once we were all assembled, one of the priests said grace and sat. The colonel shouted 'Ready' and a parade of waitresses arrived carrying bowls of soup and plates of bread which they distributed amongst us. Wine waiters appeared from the sides of the hall, which were draped in heavy damask curtains, and filled the glasses on the tables. 'Red for you, sir, or white?'

Once the wine and the soup course had been served, conversations began. The *tercio* sitting to my right was a handsome but nervous man of about twenty. He wasn't going to start so I did. 'How did you cope with Flanders? It must have been horrendous.'

'It wasn't too bad, actually. We were defending Brussels against the French. They had no chance against us and the cavalry and eventually retreated. Saw a lot of deaths though. Mostly French but hundreds of our lads were killed. I suppose I was one of the lucky ones.'

'What role did you play?'

'I was one of the pikemen. I never thought I would kill men but I did. I can't feel guilty either. It was them or us. We beat the bastards, well and truly. What are you doing here?'

'I'm one of the ladies of pleasure, brought in to entertain you,' I said, thinking that I wouldn't mind serving this one. He seemed normal and he looked clean and healthy. I could do far worse.

'My name is Antonio de Salazar,' he said. 'Maybe we'll get to know each other later.'

'Yes, I'd like that. My name is Esmeralda. And what about you?' I said, looking at the older *tercio* across the table from me.

'Yes, I served in Flanders, too. My name is Juan Gallegos. I served as part of the hospital corps so saw some bad sights I can tell you. I hope you won't ask me too much about them... I'd rather forget and enjoy myself. I could fancy you, young lady, given half a chance.'

'Let's see how things develop, after dinner. But, yes, why not,' I said, not quite taking to this one, mainly because of his missing teeth and rank smelling breath. Still, I'd had worse at the Arganzuela.

'And you?' I said, smiling at the *tercio* to my left.

'My name's Lucio. I'm a musketeer. I liked the action in Flanders but I'm hoping it's better here!'

It looked as if we might have some say about whom we would be serving, if I had interpreted events correctly. I looked round to see if I could locate Susana. Oh no. She had already had enough to drink and was babbling freely to all of the soldiers around her. So much for the formality. The other girls, too, had taken the trouble to speak to their neighbouring soldiers and seemed to be enjoying the flattering company.

Right at the end of this hearty meal the little orchestra started to play some soft, slow dance music. This signalled our guests to invite us women to the dance floor. 'Fancy a dance?' asked the young *tercio*, Antonio.

'Be delighted,' I smiled. We moved to the dance floor at the same time as about another dozen or so couples. Looking back at the tables, there were still quite a number of women sitting, chatting with the men so, somehow or another, the crafty colonel had invited many more of us women than Madam Isabel had suspected. In fact, I recognised several as street *putas* who worked the area near the Plaza Mayor that spilled out onto the Puerta de Guadalajara. One, a plump, well-endowed girl of about thirty had already pulled the top of her dress from her shoulders to allow the men near her a view of her glorious breasts. I think her name was Anna. Another, who frequented the area around the Calle de la Luna, had wrapped her arms around one of the youngest soldiers there – he couldn't have been more than fourteen – and was kissing him with the passion of Venus.

Antonio pulled me close to him and we began a slow dance. I put my arms around his neck and gently kissed his cheek. Then I placed my hand on his face and rubbed his smooth, shaven skin. He put a hand on my forehead and touched my eyebrows. Then, smiling lustfully, he pushed his fingers through my hair. I could feel something further down becoming firm as he then placed both of his hands on my bottom. For several minutes we continued rocking each other to the music. He returned my kisses and then took his right hand from my waist and softly touched my breast. I cast a secret eye around me and saw others in a similar, pedestrian embrace, most fondling and kissing each other. It was good to feel the pleasure of this man's gentle touch and to see others of us working girls having similar fun. Poor Elvira. She didn't know what she was missing, or maybe she did!

'It's no good, Esmeralda, I shall have to do something about this,' he whispered, unhitching my hand from his shoulder and placing it down the front of his breeches. I can't say he shocked me because he didn't. 'Let's go to the back of the hall.'

I looked over his shoulder in the direction he was peering and was surprised to see that the three parallel tables had been removed and replaced by a scattered array of beds of various sizes. By then, several couples were indulging themselves on them, one couple in particular were writhing completely naked and all but falling to the floor. And there, with his bottom waving in the air, a handsome young soldier was having his way with a smiling Susana, whose dress was so far up her front, it looked like a thick scarf, keeping her neck warm. A girl from number five was laughing, naked and astride a bearded *tercio* who lifted her up and down on his erect flesh. By the time Antonio and I found a bed for ourselves, only three or four remained, albeit temporarily, unoccupied.

'I'll kneel and take you from behind,' said Antonio, urgently. So I climbed on the bed and pulled up my dress, presented my bottom to him and let him start. 'That's lovely,' he said as his tummy gently knocked rhythmically at my rear and his chest brushed my back. 'Lovely.' He controlled himself well and maintained a steady pace, like a runner going around a track.

'Can I join in?' I heard a familiar voice ask Antonio. It was the older *tercio*, Juan, who sat opposite us at dinner.

'What do you think?' said Antonio, still taking his pleasure.

'Can't do much from here,' I laughed.

'You can take me in your mouth?' said Juan.

'Go and get some wine,' I instructed. Within moments he appeared again carrying a glass brimming with a rich-looking red.

'Swish your cock around in that. Yes, and under there,' I said, looking up at him. He did precisely as instructed. 'Now get it up and I'll take you.' Within a few moments he had placed himself in my mouth and I could taste the fruitiness of the remaining wine. Glancing around, I could see that the dance floor had been all but abandoned for the random array of beds which were all by then occupied and heaving with all kinds of carnal activity. A sixth sense told me that the old *tercio* was about to finish so I whipped him out of my mouth and aimed him over my shoulder to the still pumping Antonio. The shock of the old *tercio* spurting over his back must have triggered Antonio, unless it happened as a total coincidence, and he came as well, snorting, 'That was great, Esmeralda, but why get that God damned idiot to shoot all over me?'

'I'm so sorry, Antonio,' I said, when I wasn't sorry at all. I didn't want it all over me, on my face or in my hair. 'I meant to aim him at the floor. Let me get a towel and dry you off!'

'I should think so,' said Antonio, now laughing and giggling with the old *tercio* who could see the funny side of this extraordinary incident.

'Less of the idiot, *hombre*. It wasn't me who tried to drown you!'

'I'm sorry, *amigo*. It was just my reaction to yours landing on my back.'

'Off you get. My turn now.' Such were the impatient words of Lucio, the musketeer sitting on the other side of me at dinner. 'Is that all right, Esmeralda,' he said, standing naked from the waist down and already firm.

'I have to get a towel first, to clean up Antonio.'

'Don't worry about that,' said Antonio as he slid off the bed.

'You can have another go later,' I offered Antonio in consolation as Juan went to gawp at the cavorting on a nearby love nest.

'Not in there!' I said to Lucio, as I took him from half way up my rectum, wiped it in the bed sheet and put it where it was designed to go. 'If you want that kind of action you'd better try someone else.'

'I'm really sorry, Esmeralda. That was purely an accident. My mistake!' As if it was.

I knelt with my elbows on the bed and glanced around me. Just about all the girls were being penetrated and only a few seemed to regard it as work. The rest of us were bantering happily with our suitors and enjoying being appreciated. Queues were beginning to form by some of the beds – there were three of the lads by mine – as most of these wanton but disciplined soldiers were prepared to wait their turn. But some weren't so willing to wait. A minor skirmish broke out near an adjacent bed when each of two men thought they were next in line. They were naked and too vulnerable to fight but a sergeant intervened and decided for them.

This orgy of rampant activity continued for about an hour and, by then, I had had seven or eight. The air by then was permeated by the smell of sweat, perfume and fresh semen. As invited, Antonio returned for a second round after, by various means, I had brought off several others. It pleased me that no one else had attempted entry in my rear. Then the action froze as a bugle sounded. Intercourse stopped in mid-stroke. One of the colonel's assistants instructed that the men should, 'Give the girls a break for twenty minutes. They might want to use the chamber pots or have a drink. You can leave your clothes where they are, if you want to, girls.'

Many of the girls, naked from the waist down, drifted towards the table where fresh cups were brimming with wine or warm beer. Others, including Susana, her dress still decorating her neck, dashed to the other end of the room. There they each relieved themselves in a chamber pot, picked up from a neat pile of these useful but bland looking receptacles which had been assembled on the floor. The sound of so many of the girls, standing or sitting, and simultaneously gushing into these pots, was like a mountain waterfall in spring. The sight of them, mainly nude or wearing only a blouse or camisole, was akin to a scene of frolicking nymphs in an erotic Greek play.

'Well, what d'you make of this?' a stark naked Melchora asked me as she held a cup of frothing beer.

'To tell you the truth, I haven't had such fun since we started at number seven. These men are so polite, so grateful and as gentle as any man could be. One tried to take me up the rear but that may have been an accident. And I've washed several in wine before taking them, one way or another.'

'I'm having a good time, too, Esmeralda. It's so good to be appreciated. They are all such fun and most want to be slow and gentle. I haven't had a hard fuck once! Hearing all that pee splashing has made me want to go,' and she sped off towards the chamber pots.

'Hello, Maria. Are you enjoying yourself?'

'Yes, and I can't believe how normal they are. I haven't had any requests to do anything nasty. So yes, definitely!'

'And you Beatrix?'

'Yes, I'm enjoying it and can't believe we get a whole *ducat* and more for our efforts. They are an energetic lot and I enjoy a vigorous romp. I haven't laughed so much in ages. Now I need a pee, too.'

The bugle sounded again and we, as it were, took to our beds. I went back to the one I had occupied before – we all did, I think. My dress was still there – I stood naked apart from my sandals – and Antonio was standing there behind his already erect penis which was leading a queue of three.

'One more time, Esmeralda?'

'Why not try another?'

'I have tried a couple of the others but I like you the best!'

'All right then,' I giggled.

'Do you want to lie on your back this time?' What a relief to have a more relaxed position. Antonio climbed aboard and with great care found his way in. I still could not believe how gentle this band of men was, certainly with me and by all accounts with the others, too. He wanted a quicker session this time which suited me because of the building queue.

'Finish as quickly as you like,' I said grinning into his face. 'There are a few more watching and waiting. Is it more enjoyable with an audience?'

'They can always go somewhere else,' he stuttered, just as he let himself go, probably by accident. Every bed betrayed a scene of continuous but changing action, which I could see, even from the prone position I occupied. I could only just keep tally of the number of soldiers I'd hosted – thirteen by then – and after a time the bugle sounded again.

'In ten minutes we have something special for you, so finish what you are doing and gather on the dance floor. You can go back for more later.'

The flunkies who were helping out at this extraordinary event had mounted a bed on a wooden plinth so that anything that happened on it could be seen by anyone standing nearby. 'Let's begin,' said the voice again. At that moment, the plump woman, whose name I think was Anna, climbed onto the bed. She was completely naked and as she turned one way the fat on her frame seemed to want to go the other. She bowed to the gathered and expectant crowd and stood swaying her body in the centre of the white mattress. Then, through the door at the end of the hall, appeared two men, each holding the reins of a donkey. My heart beat hard against my rib cage. Whatever obscenity would unfold before us now? I felt afraid, afraid for my colleagues, especially Susana, and for myself.

The men took the donkey up to the bed. Anna, if that was her name, knelt and offered her naked, massive rear end towards the ceiling. One of the men stroked the innocent donkey's dappled penis and quickly brought it to firmness. Then they covered Anna with the donkey, one of them placing its firmness right inside her. With the men holding the donkey in position, it copulated with her, just as if she was a female donkey. I could not believe that I was witnessing this scene of horror and depravity. Some of the men cheered. Others gasped in amazement at what was happening before them. One heaved and in seconds spewed on the floor. Others drifted away and turned their backs on this ghastly spectacle. Apart from some of what seemed to be Anna's acquaintances, all the women, including us girls from number seven, retreated to the drinks table at the far end of the room.

'God, that was revolting,' said Susana.

'What a shock. Disgusting. And the woman seemed to enjoy it,' said Melchora, with a frightened, serious look in her eye.

'Not even I would have done that,' said Maria. 'I couldn't do it. Anything with a man but I couldn't do that, not for any money.'

'I suppose there might be an amount that I would do it for,' said Susana, 'but no one would pay me, say, a hundred *ducats*.'

'Someone will always do some disgusting thing for money. Yes, I suppose there is always an amount that some people would find acceptable. But let's not lose sight of the idea of human dignity and honour. I wouldn't do that for any money. I simply wouldn't do it,' I said.

'No, nor would I,' said Susana, quietly and slightly rueful at what she had previously admitted.

'I knew a woman once who would let her dog lick her vagina. She loved it and so, she said, did the dog,' said Beatrix. 'She would perfume herself and lay back and enjoy the attention of her sweet little pet. I can't see much wrong with that.'

'Nor can I,' said Susana, 'but being done by a donkey is different again.'

'That woman you knew needed a man. She should never have taken to a dog. I suppose the point is the dog never penetrated her, did it, Beatrix?' I asked.

'That's where it all became unclear and I didn't dare ask her that question,' said Beatrix, laughing. We all chuckled and that made us all feel more relaxed, even willing to indulge some of our new found clients again. Antonio came over to see me.

'Can I have a private word, Esmeralda?'

'Certainly.' We moved away from my colleagues and sat on the bed where we had pleasured each other. I was still naked and he wore only a shirt. I picked up my dress and held it over me in a pointless gesture of modesty.

'Tell me the truth, Esmeralda, I am not looking for a future wife or anyone to love. I am a soldier and could be killed tomorrow. But I have enjoyed your company, not just making love to you, but your personality and especially your vivacity and zest for life. I want to meet up with you, occasionally, maybe in a tavern for a drink or something like that. What do you think?'

'I would love that, Antonio. Where do you live?'

'I live here, in the barracks. I won't be here long because, as the colonel says, we will be going back to Flanders in not many months' time. But I'm free until then and would love to meet you, maybe a few times before I go. We could walk the Tela, down by the river, or go to the theatre. Something like that.'

'How can I contact you at the barracks?'

'Just call in and ask for me at the gate. Someone will fetch me or bring you in.'

'What if I call in on Monday night? The madam generally lets some of us off on Mondays because business is never that good then.'

'Won't you need a chaperone?'

'That's something us working girls don't need!'

'I'll see you on Monday, then. I think I'll retire to my bed. Thank you again for making love to me.'

By then, and after the huge misjudgement of the display with the donkey, many of the soldiers had drifted off but most of the girls were still there and available on the beds, or anywhere else for that matter. Susana came over to the bed on which she had left her dress and Beatrix and Melchora found their beds, too. Most of the men had had their fill of lovemaking but some of the very young were keen to indulge once or twice more before the end of the party. The young soldier who had earlier made love to Susana came up to me as I sat on the side of the bed, still completely naked. He was naked, too.

'Your friend tells me you are called Esmeralda. Please could I make love to you Esmeralda? I'd really like to, if you are still available.'

Although I was beginning to feel as if I had had enough, I decided I should agree to having him. 'Of course you can, young man,' I said, smiling and looking him in the eye. He could hardly be more than fourteen years old and still had a boyish look about him. 'How should we do it?'

'We both lie down on the bed and we kiss each other and see what happens. Does that sound alright to you?'

'It sounds good to me,' I said easing myself onto the bed. He followed me and we started to kiss and pet each other. His breath smelt a little of wine but I enjoyed the touch of the young soft skin of his fingers.

'How is it that your hands are so soft,' I asked.

'I am a company drummer, so I do not fight. I don't really do anything which could roughen my hands.' It wasn't long before he was ready to make love to me. 'How should I do it, Esmeralda? Do you want me on top or would you like to lie on your side?' This young drummer possessed the manners of a gentleman. Surely, he would go far with a personality like his.

'I really don't mind,' I said, 'maybe on my side. That way you can easily touch my breasts if you want to.' So that is what we agreed. As he enjoyed me – and I enjoyed him – I looked at the other beds. Far from all were in use but our girls were serving until the end, and clearly still relishing this unusual experience. The drummer boy had made love several times before but still had sufficient energy to keep going. I was beginning to feel tired and felt so relaxed with him gently thrusting at me. I closed my eyes and was beginning to fall asleep. As I began to enter a state of dreaming I heard a shout.

'Get him off me! Get him out!'

I looked around at the other beds. Melchora shouted out again. 'I am not here to be treated like this! Get him off me.'

'I'll have to help her,' I whispered to the drummer. 'I'll be back soon.' He withdrew and I dashed over to Melchora. Lucio, the musketeer who claimed that sodomising me was an accident was buggering her. Two of the colonel's assistants arrived at Melchora's bed before me and were pulling him off her.

'God! That was horrible,' said Melchora. 'He said he just wanted normal intercourse but then he shoved it in my ass! It was like a rolling pin. I've had it there before but not without some warning. Brutal man!' She started to cry and I comforted her. Poor Melchora. Of all of us girls from number seven, Melchora was the one who enjoyed the job least. So she would be the one who would complain if an encounter with a customer didn't work out the way she expected. Lucio said nothing and drifted over to another, possibly more willing partner on another bed. I went back to the drummer who just lay on the bed, watching the incident. We continued as we had left off. He didn't last much longer and finished in a shuddering spasm.

'Thank you, Esmeralda. That was lovely. I so enjoyed you.'

We both climbed off the bed and I made my way over to Melchora and sat on the bed with her. On my way, I glanced around. No one wanted to make more love, dance or drink. We were all finished and tired. The few men left – there couldn't have been more than a dozen – were lying next to their mostly naked bed partners and chatting and enjoying a joke with them. All of the women from number five, and the lady with the donkey, who I think was called Anna, had gone. A few street girls were still milling around, and apart from them, only us five from number seven were dotted around the beds. Susana lay naked against her latest partner, a soldier whom I had satisfied earlier. He lay on his side with his eyes closed.

Melchora and I rounded up Susana, Beatrix and Maria and we decided to go. By then it must have been well after midnight and we strolled back towards the Arganzuela, chatting and laughing among ourselves. We all felt safe walking back to number seven so didn't take up the colonel's offer of an escort. Melchora had all but forgotten the shock penetration from behind. We left Maria at her house in the Calle de San Pedro and eventually arrived back at number seven still giggling and joking.

CHAPTER 12

Three Murders

As we rounded the corner from the Calle de Toledo to the Arganzuela, we saw three armed constables standing at the door of number seven. What a shock. I wondered what to do, whether to simply walk past them into number seven or ask them why they were there. Curiosity won the battle in my head.

'What's the matter?' I asked the largest, most senior looking of the three.

'There have been three murders. Each a client of this place.' My thoughts became chaos. Our clients murdered? Impossible. But that's what he said. Three of them. Who could do such a thing? Could it be just a coincidence that they all used number seven? Hundreds of men came to us. My mind jumped back to my killing of the *hidalgo*, which suddenly became real again. I wondered how these murders had happened, remembering the grinding sound of the paving slab as I slid it over the window sill.

'How can that be anything to do with the women who work here?' asked Beatrix. I was stunned into silence as she stood with her hands on her hips and her feet planted firmly on the ground as she let fly. 'We are decent and hard working. It's nothing to do with us!'

'Do you work here?' asked one of the other constables, placing his musket over his shoulder.

'Yes we all do. And we live here. But can't you tell us more? Who were the men who were murdered?' I asked. I couldn't resist.

'We are not at liberty to tell you that. All we can say is that there are three men who are no longer alive and that all three visited this place. Frequently. We have reason to believe there is a connection between their deaths and the fact that they were customers here,' said the third constable, a thin-looking man with a narrow face masked by a huge growth of beard.

'Where is Señora Isabel Jiménez? She's the madam here,' said Melchora, looking grey, shocked and sounding as if she was asking for the whereabouts of her own mother.

'She is at the judicial office in the Puerta de Guadalajara, being interviewed under oath. If she's not arrested and charged she'll be back before dawn.'

'She couldn't have done it. Why murder your own customers?' said Susana. 'Can we go in? Otherwise we'll have to sleep outside for the night.'

The three constables walked a few steps away from us and spoke to each other in whispers. Then the senior-looking one came back to us and announced his decision.

'Yes, you can go in. One at a time... and one of us will escort you. We will want to see something you can identify as yours, in your room, before we leave you there.'

'What nonsense,' I thought but decided that it was better to say nothing. The second constable instructed me to go in with him and I led the way. I half expected him to touch me in some way so I kept well ahead of him.

'That's my room, there,' I said, pointing to the door.

'Tell me something you can show me in there,' said the constable.

'My green dress is on the bed,' I replied. I opened the door with my key. 'There it is,' I said.

'Fine,' he said and left.

Within a few minutes we were all indoors and sitting in the kitchen, wondering what had happened and where all this would lead.

'I just can't believe this,' said Melchora. 'I'm frightened. What if they shut us down?'

'We'd all be out of work,' said Susana, looking distinctly pale. 'Didn't you have a go at them, Beatrix?'

'I'm trying to work out what's going on,' I said. 'They said there is a definite connection between the deaths and this place. I wonder how they know that. Maybe the murderer has left a note by the bodies explaining the connection. Who would want to kill men who came here and not to one of the other *mancebías* in the street? Maybe they frequented some of the others, too. No, I just don't understand it.'

'I wonder if Elvira is here?' asked Beatrix. 'She might have a clearer idea of what is happening.'

'She's probably in bed... Asleep. I don't think we should wake her. She wouldn't thank us for that. She'd tell us to sod off!' Susana said.

'True,' I said. 'One consolation is that the constabulary don't suspect us. Otherwise, they'd have arrested us.'

Our bodies had worked hard at the party in the barracks and tiredness reigned. So we adjourned to our rooms. As soon as we reached ours, Susana showed her feelings.

'I'm sorry, Esmeralda, but this is all too much to bear. I'm frightened for both of us and our future. What will we do if number seven is forced to close? What if Madam Isabel is arrested?'

'Let's not worry ourselves sick before we need to. Tomorrow may just reveal what has happened. The best result will be if the constabulary arrest someone we don't know and charge him. The one thing I am certain of is that Madam Isabel is not a murderess.'

We each drifted into the land of sleepy images from the waking land of fresh nightmares. I woke from a dream and, still partly in the world of sleep, wondered if I had dreamt of what we had heard from the constables when we returned from the party. Then, as I was laying there its hideous reality hit me. I wondered how the day would unfold, whether Madam Isabel had returned, whether this nightmare would fall apart to reveal some kind of error or misunderstanding. But no, it didn't. I shuddered in response to a hard banging on our bedroom door. Susana's head shot up from her pillow.

'It's me. Isabel. Get out and come down. I've something to tell you.' She quickly transmitted the message through the other bedroom doors and within a few minutes we had returned to the kitchen to see her standing cross-armed against the stove waiting for us all to gather. Elvira came in looking shocked and shaken.

'I have bad news,' said Isabel. 'Those of you who went to the party at the barracks will know that three of our clients have been murdered. Are you aware of this dreadful news, Elvira?'

'No. I had no idea. It's awful. A tragedy. Who are they?'

'I'll get to that in a moment. Last night, around midnight, I was taken to the judicial office to be told about it and interviewed. They brought me back at four o'clock this morning. All three victims had had their throats cut. All three were married. A note had been left next to each body which read, "In the name of the Father, and of the Son, and of the Holy Spirit, this is the true price of what you did at number seven. God rest your soul." This is what the constables told me. I was horrified.'

'We're finished now, Isabel. Who will come here now, if the price is that he will be punished by death? We are out of work, girls,' said Beatrix.

'Not so fast,' said Isabel. 'I left the constabulary with a list of all our regular customers and they will bring them in for interview. They think it's someone who is a customer here. Or someone who has been spying on our customers. They think it could be a mad priest, carrying out some twisted form of summary justice.'

'My first customer was a priest,' I reminded Isabel.

'I know, dear. I remember. I know him well. I doubt that it was him.'

'Tell us, please, Isabel. Who are the three murdered men? You must tell us.'

'Doctor Alvaro de Peralta, a lawyer called Estaban Ganado and an undertaker's assistant, Salvador de Cantos.'

'My God! Not my lawyer! The poor man who defended me!' said Susana who then collapsed on the floor in a flood of tears. Then she shrieked again, 'And Salvador, a regular of mine! Oh no!'

As I bent over and knelt by her side to comfort her, I could feel tears coming to my eyes. 'Yes, the lawyer. It's just evil. How could anyone kill that lovely man? He was so gentle and considerate,' I said, sobbing out loud.

'Well, whoever it was cut their throats with a knife as sharp as a razor.'

Madam Isabel was far from being right. Over the following days, business at number seven decreased, markedly but in a way this played to our advantage. During that time, each of us girls in turn was interviewed at the judicial office. I think Beatrix went first, then Melchora, Maria, me, Susana and finally Elvira. The interviewers were firm, penetrating but fair and polite. They asked us where we were on the night of the Thursday before the party, which they believed was the night the murders took place. They asked whether we knew anyone who could verify our whereabouts for the time between about mid-afternoon and two o'clock the following morning. They asked us which clients we had pleasured that night and any we knew of who had not been at number seven. I felt as if the judiciary suspected me of committing at least one of the murders and probably suspected some of the other girls of being my accomplices. It was all very frightening but, even knowing we were all *putas*, they treated us well. Then several more days passed and no arrests were made.

Because business was lower, Madam Isabel gave us some time off and during an evening's break, I went to visit Antonio at the barracks. He knew about the murders and that there appeared to be a connection with number seven. He didn't know what it was but realised that we were all suspects. One of the guards went to tell him that I had arrived and he came to greet me.

'Esmeralda, what a lovely surprise. I really didn't think you'd come here!'

'Why not? A handsome man like you! How could I resist?'

'Let's go for a drink. There is a tavern in the Calle de San Juan. Come on let's go.'

So we walked arm-in-arm to the inn. I had never been inside one of these drinking houses before, so the novelty excited me and made me smile. But I wondered if any of the drinking customers would recognise me as one of the whores from the Arganzuela. I asked Antonio and he simply said, whether anyone recognised me or not, if they were rude or unkind they would have him to deal with. So with little hesitation, we walked in, Antonio leading the way. Apart from two women serving jugs of beer, there were no other females there.

'I'm the only woman, Antonio. I feel uncomfortable. What should we do?'

'Just brazen it out. There is no reason to feel awkward. You are with me!'

The place smelt as if the floors had been washed with beer and rinsed with urine. The stench hit my nose as I walked in but somehow, within a few minutes, my nostrils became used to it. Men stood or sat in little groups and argued, pointing their fingers at each other between liberally swigging from their jugs. Antonio escorted me to a table in an alcove where we could chat, away from the general din.

'What's the latest news on the three murders?'

'It's been bad in the Arganzuela. Everyone knows that there is a connection between the murders and number seven, so no one can walk by without stopping and looking in. It's all everybody wants to talk about. It's no surprise: business has been affected badly. It dropped away quite a bit as soon as word got around. It's strange what influences people. The ones who are still loyal have an odd sort of fascination for the place... and us workers. I'm sure some think one of us did it. And want to claim ... suspecting it's one of us... that they've made love to a murderess.'

'Surely not. Can you tell me about the link between the killings and number seven?'

'I don't see why I shouldn't. The murderer left a note by the side of each of the bodies which read something like, "God the father, God the son and God the Holy Ghost. This is the price of going to number seven. May your soul rest in peace." Something like that. Our *burdel* is known as number seven, Calle de Arganzuela, even though the houses are not actually numbered. Some clever constable made the connection and sure enough, each of the victims was one of our regular customers.'

'Well, I don't believe it could have been one of you. You've got too much to lose. You'd hardly kill off your customers. Only if you were insane.'

'You're right. I cannot think of any reason for any of us killing a customer. It has to be someone else, maybe connected with number seven, but not working there. Anyway, let's change the subject. When do you think you will be going back to Flanders?'

'I'm not really sure. The colonel certainly wants us back there, sooner rather than later. We'll be leaving in a few months I imagine.'

'Will you go back by sea?'

'No. Definitely not. But part of the way, yes. We'll probably go overland to Cartagena, from there by ship to Genoa and then we'll be marching past the Alps, across our territories to the north and up to the Spanish Netherlands. Probably via the Duchy of Luxembourg.'

'Good God. What a route. It will take an age to get back there. Why did you come back here in the first place?'

'Your question is easy to answer. We had to escort a number of senior officers from Flanders to Madrid. Two field marshals, three sergeant major captains and a judge advocate auditor. They had to report to the king. They also had to make some arrangements for financing the army. They didn't have enough to pay us so we had to collect our pay when we returned here! It will take about three months to get back, from the time we leave Madrid to our arrival at Brussels. They say we will be joining an army under the command of an Italian general. General Ambrosio Spínola.'

'Why not go back by sea.'

'Too dangerous. The Dutch navy would blow us out of the water. If they didn't, the English would! So that's why we use the road from Genoa to Flanders.'

'Sounds sensible, at least to me.'

We stayed and chatted in the tavern for about an hour. I wasn't used to drinking wine or beer and after a glass of each my head began to spin. I felt I'd need Antonio's help to get me on my feet. I told him that I felt a bit queasy and he suggested we go back to the barracks. I thought this would be a good idea and decided that if he wanted to make love to me there in his room I would oblige. He helped me to my feet and, with his arm around me, we made our way, if clumsily, to the door.

'Is she pissed?' said one of the barmen.

'No,' replied Antonio, 'Just a bit unsteady. She's not used to drinking and I shouldn't have given her so much.'

'Now you can take her home and fuck her,' I heard another barman say, under his breath. Antonio didn't comment.

It wasn't long before we were sitting in Antonio's room in the barracks. A prison cell would have been more comfortable. I could feel and hear the straw stuffing of the mattress as I sat on his bed. A small wardrobe rested itself against the wall, a wooden chair stood in a corner and a tiny chest of drawers sat at right angles to the wardrobe. The room had been cleaned, probably by Antonio, but cried out for a fresh wash of whitening.

'I've been thinking while we've been chatting to each other. I've got an idea. But I'm not going to tell you about it because you'll walk out!'

I could imagine that he wanted to make love but didn't quite know how to tell me. He had guessed how I might react. He wanted me to make an offer to him. Men!

'Unless you tell me now what it is, I'll go. You've got until the count of five,' I said, laughing. 'One, two...'

He paused teasingly and then spoke. 'You said that the level of business had dropped at number seven. I've thought of a new job for you, and maybe for Susana and one or two of your colleagues.'

'Go on,' I said, puzzled and not sure where this could be going.

'Well...' he hesitated, seeming to doubt whether he wanted to tell me. 'When we are in the battlefield or on our way to fight, there are women who come with us. We call them the followers. Some call them our battlefield wives. They are the women who are paid to look after our, shall we say, manly needs and I don't mean food or drink. They make love to us and we pay them.'

'My God! I couldn't do that, Antonio. Maybe I could. I don't know,' I said, my mind in a state of turmoil. The very idea shocked me. I didn't know what to think.

'Esmeralda, you were one of the most popular of the ladies at the party the other night. You were wonderful to us men. You were friendly and accommodating. Not only that, you enjoyed our company and laughed with us. It was so funny, even to me, when you shot off the old *tercio* down my back. No one else would have dared do that! We loved you and you were the talk of the barracks the morning after. You are a very attractive young woman: your lovely long, black hair and perfect long legs, right up to your slim bottom. You'd make a fortune as a follower. I guarantee.'

His talk of a fortune made me feel more positive about this idea and somehow took away the initial fear of what would be a totally new experience. I had to tease him and test him with some other questions.

'You do flatter me! But I know nothing about fighting. And I don't want to be killed on the battlefield. I enjoy my home comforts too much to take up a life of travelling. It's not something that interests me... where do the women live... as "battlefield wives" as you put it?'

'In houses we rent or commandeer. On the way there they travel by wagon. No one expects them to march. But you could lead the parade, Esmeralda. We'd all follow you.'

'Straight to my bed, I'm sure!' I laughed.

'No I was only joking. You'd be comfortable on the journey. Well fed and well looked after.'

'I couldn't go alone. I'd have to take Susana with me. We are such good friends and I feel responsible for her. I need to protect her. It was my idea that we came to Madrid and I wouldn't want to leave her here.'

'Susana would come with you. There is no job at present but the army is always discreetly looking for women to come with us. I can ask one of the colonel's assistants if you like.'

'Let me think about it first and try the idea on Susana. Then I'll let you know,' I said, and meant it.

We chatted a little longer while sitting on Antonio's bed. He didn't ask me to make love to him and I can't say that that bothered me. In a way it made me feel that he respected me. He could easily have asked me and I would have found it difficult to refuse. But he seemed not to want to take advantage of my presence there and my vulnerability. After about half an hour he asked if he could escort me back to the Arganzuela and I accepted. As he left me outside of number seven, he planted a firm kiss on my lips.

'When shall we meet again?' he asked. 'Maybe in a few days' time?'

'Good idea. I'll let you know then what Susana thinks about becoming a follower!'

As I stepped inside number seven, Susana greeted me. 'You'll never believe this Esmeralda. Do you remember that priest, your first customer here? Well he's been arrested for committing the murders.'

'I can't believe it. Yes, Father Sebastian Gutierro. How could I forget him? What with his rosary beads, but I thought he was a really nice man. He wouldn't kill a fly.'

'I don't know about that but it's true that he's been arrested. He's in the town prison. Waiting for trial.'

I became enshrouded in fog of shock. Had I completely misjudged this man whom I thought was sincere in blessing me after he had been my first customer at number seven? I could not believe that I had been penetrated by a killer. Surely, I hadn't. The court would probably acquit him and the true murderer would be brought to justice.

'What do you and the other girls think, Susana?'

'We are all stunned by the news and no one can believe it. He has made love to all of us at some time and seems a nice man. Alright, his vows of chastity meant little but that is true of so many of the priests in our town. Oh... Elvira thinks he's evil and is sure he is the killer. She is the odd one out and doesn't want to talk a lot about it.'

That night, before we settled down to sleep, I told Susana about the idea of becoming women who followed the soldiers and stayed with them in the battleground.

'No. I want to stay in Madrid. We are earning good money here and business is sure to pick up, now the priest has been arrested.'

'I'm not so sure, Susana. Number seven has a death cloud hanging over it. Business may well improve but I'd be surprised if it picks up to what it was before the killings.'

'Let's talk about it in the morning. We are great friends. I love you like a sister. I don't want you to leave me here on my own while you go off to Flanders without me.' She started to sob, partly, I thought, because of the shock arrest of the priest, but mainly no doubt because of what I had just said about serving the Spanish army. I put my arm around her shoulder to comfort her and we settled down to sleep. We resumed the discussion in the morning.

'I woke up in the night thinking of what you said about following the army and serving their needs, Esmeralda. I thought of the gypsy saying I would be lucky in love. You remember, the fortune-teller?'

'Of course I remember.'

'She said I would marry sooner than I might expect and that there was something she couldn't tell me. You told me not to worry.'

'I did,' I said softly.

'Well. I thought, if things turn bad here and the brothel has to stop because we don't have enough customers to keep going, it may just be a good idea to follow the army.'

'All right. But what's that got to do with what the gypsy told you?'

'Simple. We would meet a lot of soldiers, mostly while we were making love to them. So I could find a husband maybe. That is the thought that came into my head.'

'So you are happier about the idea this morning than before we went to bed?'

'I think so, Esmeralda. Even so, we need to know more about the job, how we would be paid, how much and what we would do with the money while we were in Flanders. We need to know much more.'

'I am so pleased you are seeing it differently today. I will find out more from Antonio.'

***

The news sheets proclaimed Father Gutierro's trial as 'The Trial of the Century' which was hardly a serious claim because it took place in 1601 so the century had hardly begun. Even so, none of us would forget these spectacular proceedings, if only because the church put forward such a strong defence of their brother. The trial took place at the court in which Susana had been tried, almost exactly a year before, and a month after the murders. To our astonishment, the same skeletal presiding judge had been appointed. His sympathetic approach to Susana's case made me think that the priest would be acquitted. We had to wait and see.

Madam Isabel instructed us girls not to attend the public galleries to watch the trial. It was bad enough that three of our customers had been murdered. She didn't want to give anyone the opportunity to accuse us of using the trial as a venue for advertising our services, simply by our presence there. Needless to say, it would be a different matter if any one of us was summoned to give evidence, as indeed some of us were.

I will never forget my dread, that mild autumn morning, at receiving the summons from the court to appear as a witness for the prosecution. I feared the worse. I could anticipate that the prosecutor would ask me about every move and every touch the priest made on my body. How would I cope with questioning about such intimate detail? The day I took to the witness stand, the court thronged with all manner of people from our town. It reverberated with the cackling of the mob in the public gallery and reeked with their assorted aromas, from the perfumed, bewigged and extravagantly dressed ladies of the court to the foul smelling beggars whose clothes were stained with cheap beer and other unmentionable fluids.

'Do you recognise the accused, Father Sebastian Gutierro, standing in the dock?' said the prosecutor, his head thrown back and thumbs placed arrogantly under the lapels of his gown.

'Yes. I do,' I said, my head bowed low.

'Speak up young lady!' he said.

'Yes. I do,' I said, more loudly but still with trepidation. I could sense myself shaking.

'Are you a prostitute who works in the brothel known as number seven, Calle de Arganzuela?'

'I am, sir,' I said, as shamelessly as I could.

'Have you ever, shall I say, conducted business with the accused?'

'Yes. I have, sir,'

'How many times?'

'Once, sir.'

'Are you sure?'

I paused to think. 'Yes, I'm certain, sir.'

'Tell me what happened.'

'I can't do that,' I said. 'What happens between a lady of pleasure and her client is private and cannot be told, either here in court or anywhere else for that matter. You wouldn't expect me to describe the details of any business I had conducted with you would you, sir?'

A shocked gasp filled the court. The public gallery erupted. Those who supported my stance cheered and laughed. There were boos from the disappointed who expected a salacious account of what I had done with the priest.

'Silence in court,' bellowed an usher who was immediately obeyed.

'I know this is difficult,' said the skinny judge, in an intimate and quiet way, as if he was speaking only to me and the prosecutor. 'But the court needs to know about your meeting with the accused. We will need to know whether the accused penetrated you and if anything notable happened which you think the court should know. I am not going to permit the prosecution to ask you anything else at this moment. So you may resume questioning along the lines I have indicated, prosecutor.'

'I, of course, demur to that, your Lordship. Well, did the accused penetrate you?'

'Yes, he did,' I said, with confidence and fully accepting the judge's proposals for questioning me.

'And did anything unusual or of special note occur at the time?'

'Yes, while doing so, he fed his rosary beads through his fingers and recited the rosary prayer.'

Again the court erupted with laughter and feverish exchanges in the public gallery. The usher regained silence.

'I find it difficult to imagine how he did that while penetrating you at the same time,' said the prosecutor.

'Then you will continue to find that difficult,' said the judge, again respecting my modesty. 'The court has heard sufficient from this young lady. Thank you, señorita. You may step down now.'

I felt a great sense of relief that this session was over. I thought, too, that I had conducted myself competently and that I had done well to win my battle with the prosecutor. I couldn't wait to get back to number seven to tell Susana and the other girls, who had of course been banned from attending the trial, what had happened there. I anticipated that Susana would certainly be called because both the doctor and the undertaker's assistant were solely clients of Susana. The defence council were sure to want Susana to testify, if only to attempt to discredit the victims for visiting our *burdel*. The girls laughed out loud as I told them how I had reacted to the prosecutor's initial questioning.

'How did you get away with it?' asked Beatrix.

'The judge came down on my side and said he didn't want the detail of what happened between me and the priest! It was quite funny, really. I told them that as he did me, he was reciting the rosary prayer and working the beads through his fingers, which is true. It amazed the court but the judge stopped the questioning right there and sent me home!'

Sure enough, they called Susana, too. It upset her terribly. For some reason which none of us could divine, the judge wanted much more detail about what she did with the victims, naturally before they were victims. She had to recount how the doctor masturbated over her and how the undertaker came back many times to ask for Susana and how she would not charge him the full amount because she liked him so much. The doctor's wife yelled out and fainted as Susana testified. She was distraught at what her husband had done to Susana who cried several times in the witness box. The judge at least allowed her to pause to regain her composure. She broke down again as she related the story to us when she got back. We all felt sorry for her, except Elvira, who, not unexpectedly, showed not a *maravedi*'s worth of sympathy. Susana soon settled herself again and became her normal self. Elvira also testified and none of us was surprised when she returned and went straight to her room, pointedly refusing to say a word about what had happened to her.

The court found the priest guilty and sentenced him to death by burning at the stake. None of us, except Elvira, who refused to express an opinion, could believe the verdict. But, talking over what had happened, none of us could find a reason why he should have been acquitted. He just seemed a decent man to the rest of us, someone quite incapable of killing a soul. Just how wrong could we all have been?

***

The day after we learned of the verdict on Father Gutierro, I went to the barracks to see Antonio. One of the guards summoned him to meet me at the gate and he took me to his room.

'What a lovely surprise, Esmeralda. You haven't been here for ages! I thought you had deserted me in favour of one of my colleagues,' he chuckled.

'I suppose I should have,' I joked. 'Most of them are better looking than you!'

'You've got a cheek!'

After our initial chaffing, we settled on his bed. I told him about the verdict on the priest and the sentence for his execution.

'That is the only just punishment. When will the sentence be carried out?'

'In a month's time. None of us can believe he killed those three men. Just can't believe it,' I said, excluding Elvira's view from our collective opinion.

'Well, the court has found him guilty and, in my opinion, that is all there is to it. Can we change the subject? Have you thought any more about becoming a follower of the army? Did you ask Susana if she would come with you?'

'Yes, I spoke to her. At first, she became frightened that I would leave her alone in Madrid and go with the army. I reassured her and, once she had slept on it, she became more interested. Like me, she thinks it's a good idea, especially if business at number seven doesn't pick up to what it was before the murders. In fact, she came up with some good questions which I promised to pass on to you.'

'Go on. What were they?'

'She asked how we would be paid, how much we would be paid per client and what we would do with the money in Flanders.'

'Smart questions. You will find the rates are the same as you are paid here. You will be paid per customer. The men pay you direct. You have to be careful because some will leave you a promissory note and not many are honoured. Only take cash unless you are really sure. Then there is a bounty. For every day you spend with the army, from the moment you leave Madrid to when you arrive back you will be paid three *reales*.'

'I like that idea and so will Susana! What will we do with the money, while we're in Flanders?'

'Easy. You bank it with the paymaster. You will each have a bank book recording the amount in your account. The money goes around in circles. The paymaster uses it to pay the men and they pay it to you for services you provide them!'

'So, no one gains anything then!' I teased. 'Except the soldiers by our pleasuring them!'

'No, no, no! The amount in your bank account goes up every time you pay money in. That's the important number. What the paymaster does with the money is up to him!'

'I was only playing with you! I'll let Susana know what you are saying. The more you tell me the better I like the idea. It will be an adventure!'

'The last thing I want is to push you into making a decision you may later regret. But if you want me to go ahead and ask the colonel's assistant to take you with us, the sooner he knows the better. So what I think you should do, Esmeralda, is to go back to Susana and work out what you want to do. I think you should come with us but I think you already know that. In my opinion, what the future level of business might be at number seven shouldn't be part of your thinking. You need to decide whether to come on this adventure as you put it, or stay here. Simple as that.'

'You're right, Antonio. I'll go back and discuss it again with Susana.' So that is what I did but not before asking Antonio if he would like to make love to me. He agreed and we spent some time entwined with each other on his creaking, uncomfortable bed. What bliss.

Susana and I spent some time discussing Antonio's proposal. We concluded that we would, if they accepted us, follow the army to Flanders. Having mentioned our plans to Beatrix, she said she wanted to come, too. At first, we were none too sure. Beatrix was older than us and we didn't want to be led by her. She could also be sharp and temperamental, often when you least expected it. However, we liked her and could see advantage in the three of us going, rather than just Susana and me. This would make our adventure even more exciting and we would put this proposal to Antonio. After all, Antonio had talked about two or more women being recruited. We thought it only fair to tell Madam Isabel about our plans. Her reaction did not surprise us. While she regretted that we could be leaving her, she half welcomed a fall in the number of us working at number seven because, after the murders, she too anticipated that business would not pick up to what it was before. We thought she stretched her generosity to it limits in saying that we could continue working at number seven until the moment we would be leaving for Flanders. We would be forever grateful to this generous and understanding lady.

After we had told Madam Isabel of our thoughts, all three of us, Susana, Beatrix and I, went to see Antonio about our decision. He was surprised that Beatrix wanted to come as well. Antonio had anticipated our interest and had already spoken to the colonel's assistant about our almost certain interest in joining the woman followers. According to Antonio, the assistant shook Antonio's hand with joy and relief. Try as he did, although he had recruited a number of women to go with them, most were inexperienced and he had simply not been able to find as many girls as he had wanted for the job.

'I'll ask him to come to see you,' said Antonio. We waited in the mess room for a few minutes for him to arrive.

The assistant was a large young man with a red, friendly face. 'Am I pleased to see you girls,' he said, making a statement rather than asking a question. 'You've got me off the hook. I've scoured the whole town looking for women to come to Flanders with us. Then Antonio comes up with two to start with and now three! Can't believe my luck.'

'Do you want to interview us or anything?' asked Beatrix. I wished that she hadn't, fearing that 'anything' might mean gratuitously trying us out in a bed. But he made no such request.

'Not necessary. You've all three got a job with us. Congratulations and thank you for your interest.'

He placed some papers on a table and asked us to write our names on it and our dates of birth.

'Sorry,' said Susana. 'I don't know mine and nor does Esmeralda.'

'We won't make that a problem,' he said. 'Just give me a year.'

'1584,' I said.

'1585,' said Susana, both of us erring on the side of being legally able to offer the men our services.

***

Having received agreement from the colonel's assistant that we would be going, and as we were making detailed preparations for our sojourn to Flanders, something entirely unexpected happened. It was the day before the authorities were due to execute Father Gutierro. Susana and I were talking to each other, probably anticipating our perilous journey with the army or guessing what the level of work with the soldiers might be or how we might be organised to serve them, when Elvira appeared. She frightened us with the severity of her mood and glared at us as if she was possessed by demons.

'That bastard, cock wielding priest. He dies tomorrow, consumed by the flames of hell. Serves him right. How dare he prey on us women? His fate is the fate of the damned. I could not have killed to destroy an individual worse than him. Killing three was the price and he carries my guilt.'

'Your guilt? What are you guilty of?' said Susana, responding to this barely intelligible rant.

'I'll tell you something that I've told no other and you must tell no one what I tell you. I killed those three men. Your customers. I killed them with a knife. Cut their throats. They are my victims. Not his. But he will die for it. Tomorrow!'

'Do you know what you're saying, Elvira?' I said.

'Of course I do and I'm proud of what I did. God will judge that bastard, perverted priest, just as I have judged him.'

Susana looked at me in horror and I looked at her, equally stunned by what Elvira had said in her frenzied, insane confession.

'Well, it will be all over tomorrow!' I said, feigning careless laughter. 'Will you go to see justice done?'

'I'm thinking about it,' said Elvira, as if she had said nothing strange about the deaths.

'Well, we are going out for a walk. Care to come with us?' I said.

'Rather not,' she replied.

'Let's go then,' I said to Susana.

As soon as we were outside we hurriedly discussed what we should do about what Elvira had said.

'We go straight to the judicial office and tell them what she told us. We cannot allow them to execute the priest. Not now. Not until they have arrested Elvira and tested the truth of what she told us of it. Let's go,' I said.

We turned right at the top of the street on to the Calle Toledo and walked quickly up to the Guadalajara. A constable sat at the desk inside the door of the judicial office.

'What do you two want?'

'We've come to ask you to delay an execution. The execution of Father Gutierro,' I said.

The constable just laughed. 'What is he a friend of yours or something?'

'No,' said Susana. 'We've just heard someone else confess to the murders and we think you should investigate.'

'Don't be so damned daft. The sentence of the court must be carried out. The Father will die tomorrow. Go away.'

'No. We're going nowhere until you let us speak to someone senior,' I said.

'Blast you. What have I got to do to get rid of you?'

'Take us in and either listen to what we've got to say or sit us in front of a senior officer and we'll tell him,' I said. 'If not you could be responsible for a miscarriage. A serious miscarriage of justice. Father Gutierro's execution must be delayed.'

We were so relieved that after this awkward and argumentative exchange, he let us in. We sat opposite him and a sergeant and told them both exactly what Elvira had said. The sergeant reacted with astonishment.

'My God. Are you two sure of what you are saying? You're not telling me this just because you like the priest and want to get him off. If so you yourselves would be perverting the course of justice and that is a very serious offence. You could be sent to prison for it.'

Susana made her mark on the discussion. 'I guarantee that we're telling you the truth. Just what Elvira said. We were as shocked as you are now. We do like the priest but that has nothing to do with this.'

'Hmm,' muttered the sergeant. 'We are going to have to look into this. I don't think we've got a choice. We will have to take a statement from each of you before we can do anything. Can you write?'

'I can,' I said.

'I can't, at least not very well,' said Susana.

'All right, you write down what you told me,' he said, looking in my direction. 'And you young lady, tell the constable what you said and he'll write it down for you.'

It didn't take long for us to produce the two documents and to sign them.

'Thank you, señoras. Those will be fine. Now constable, go to the charge room and ask a colleague to go with you and to number seven and bring Senora Elvira Delgado in for questioning.'

'What do we do now?' asked Susana.

'If I were you, I'd find a different way back to number seven and take your time getting there. You won't want to be there when Señora Delgado is told she will have to come here to be questioned. The constables will have to tell her that you have given us sworn statements. About her confessions. All hell will rise up.'

'And what about the priest?' I said.

'I will have to go to the judges' parlour to ask them to put a stay on the execution. Obviously, I'll show them your statements and the rest will be up to them.'

The sergeant must have kept to his word. The following day the town news sheets were full of the story. 'Judges give convicted priest a stay of execution', 'Prostitute arrested for triple murder; priest's execution stayed'. We were not mentioned by name but Elvira's appeared all over the news sheets as well as the fact that she worked at a brothel known as 'number seven, the Calle de Arganzuela'. By the time we arrived back at number seven, Elvira had gone.

'Guess what?' said an excited Melchora. 'Elvira's been arrested.'

'We know,' said Susana.

'How can you know? You've only just come in.' The other girls appeared and were giving us puzzled looks. We had no choice but to tell them what Elvira had told us and, indeed, relate to them the rest of the story. They were astounded and divided on whether Susana and I should have reported to the authorities what Elvira had said.

'Why did you have to do that?' said Melchora.

'We just couldn't let the priest burn to death after she had confessed to the killings,' I said.

'Why not,' said Maria. 'The court had found him guilty and it's right that he should be punished.'

'Not for something he didn't do,' said Susana.

'Just wait a minute,' said Beatrix, leaping to our defence. 'All the girls have done is to tell the constabulary what Elvira told them. It's up to them to decide whether the court's decision still holds. The priest is still in prison and won't be released until someone else is found guilty. That could take an age. We'll just have to wait to see what happens.'

Madam Isabel then appeared, looking worried.

'Well done, you two. You did exactly the right thing. Maybe you should have told me first because this could well affect the future of number seven but I'd have agreed that you should repeat to the constabulary what Elvira told you.'

'I'm sorry, Isabel. You are right. We should have come to you first. We have no excuse.'

'Don't worry. I'd have probably done the same.'

***

The following day, two constables and the competent sergeant we had spoken to at the judicial office visited number seven with the sole aim of searching the room in the basement where Elvira worked and her bedroom. They discovered two bloodstained dresses, a knife and a note beginning with the rosary prayer that its author probably intended to leave beside the body of the next victim. This evidence, our statements, the evidence Susana and I and others gave in court and the impassioned confession which Elvira all but shouted to the court, served to convict her of the triple murder. Despite the efforts of the council for the defence, Elvira could not convincingly explain why she committed these awful crimes. She spoke about the vengeance of God, about the evil of men, about just punishment and retribution. She delivered to the court little more than an extended version of the incoherent rant she gave Susana and me before she was arrested. So neither the judge nor the council for the prosecution could work out why she had committed the murders and falsely blamed Father Gutierro for them. We of course had our own views: she harboured an insane jealousy of our working relations with the three victims. Her insanity led her to kill them. This was stimulated in part by the obvious consequence that they would never see us again. As for attempting to incriminate the priest, and successfully testifying against him, she saw him as a deserving person to implicate. The fact that he, a man of the cloth, saw no guilt in using number seven served in her mind as something to be severely punished. Indeed, she almost succeeded in achieving his execution. The day she was sentenced to death by burning at the stake, Father Gutiero was freed. Needless to say, his family and all of us at number seven were delighted.

Sadly, the three murders and Elvira's conviction for them led Madam Isabel to close number seven. The level of business collapsed to a mere trickle. Melchora found a job with a theatre company and Maria was offered a job with number five. Thankfully, these events had less of an effect on Susana, Beatrix and me. We were about to embark on a new adventure.

PART II

CHAPTER 13

The Start of a Journey

All three of us, Susana, Beatrix and I, were surprised by the suddenness of it all. Madam Isabel had let us stay at number seven long after she had closed it for business. Right until the spring. Then three letters arrived telling each of us that we were departing for Barcelona in two days' time. That we would travel from there by ship to Savona and then by road to Flanders.

'Doesn't leave much time for packing,' said Beatrix.

'Doesn't leave much time for anything,' said Susana.

'We'll go to the bank and tell them to keep our accounts open and to expect payments into them from abroad,' I said. 'Isabel won't want us leaving anything here so we'll put the things we don't take into the storage house off the Calle de Toledo.'

'Won't be much,' said Beatrix. 'Mainly clothes and odd items for cooking.'

'Same for me,' said Susana.

'Another thing. We must write our wills and get them witnessed,' I said.

'Wills?' asked Beatrix.

'Yes,' I replied.

'Who gave you that idea?' said Susana.

'Madam Isabel. She told me to make out a will before I went. Then if anything happened to me, my wishes could be dealt with.'

Susana became fretful. 'I am feeling very unhappy now. You are reminding me about that horrible gypsy woman.'

'I'm not sure about your gypsy, Susana, but I agree with Esmeralda. We should write our wills. And get them witnessed.'

'Yes,' I said. 'I've got an idea. If one of us dies, the other two will have what she leaves... divided equally between them?'

'Good point,' said Beatrix. 'We are the only people we are close to and we'll be even closer, working and being together on the way to Flanders.'

'I suppose I agree,' said Susana.

'Can you tell us what the gypsy told you?' asked Beatrix.

'I already know,' I said, in a voice which sympathised with Susana. I wasn't sure if she wanted to tell Beatrix what the gypsy had told her or not told her. So to give her some time to decide what to say, I told Beatrix what the gypsy said about my future. 'Let me tell you what she said about me. She said I would not be sure about whether I would like my work. And I was far from sure! I'm not sure now a lot of the time. Having to put up with what some of those brutes want to do to me.

'She said I would find my brother. He disappeared just after we all escaped from the orphanage. We looked everywhere but couldn't find him. It broke my heart to lose him. I still cry when I think of him. I could cry now.'

'Don't get upset,' said Susana, putting an arm around my shoulder.

'But I wouldn't know where I should look. He won't be in Burgos if he's still alive. We searched that place high and low.'

'But the gypsy must have thought he was alive,' said Beatrix, smiling with her eyes.

'Sometimes that thought keeps me going,' I said. 'Then she said I would get to know the king. I ask you? A whore like me? Knowing the King of Spain? So I made that my ambition! And who knows...? Then she said I would be involved in war. And here we are, about to head for Flanders! Finally, as if to want to finish me off, she told me I would be unlucky in love! But I haven't dwelt too much on that...'

'It wasn't all bad then,' said Beatrix. 'Could have been worse.'

Then Susana spoke. 'It was worse for me. I wish I hadn't ever seen or had to listen to that horrible woman. She told me that Esmeralda and I would always be friends. I could cope with that. No trouble. Then she told me there was something in the crystal ball she couldn't tell me about. She said it in an odd tone, as if it scared her. Esmeralda and I have argued about what she saw. But I try not to think about it and get on with my simple life. All this talk about making wills brings it all back.'

Poor Susana then flooded with a torrent of tears.

'I'm sorry,' said Beatrix. 'I now feel bad that I asked about the woman. I should never have mentioned her.'

'Don't worry,' said Susana, sniffing and wiping her eyes with the bottom of her dress. 'Please don't. You weren't to know what she said.'

So the following day, the three of us walked to the bank, told the accountant that we would be receiving money from abroad, and persuaded him to witness three wills. We then returned to number seven, packed our bags and took what little we had left to the store house in the Calle de Toledo. We were ready as ever we would be to go to Flanders.

***

Poor Madam Isabel cried into her handkerchief as she said goodbye to the three of us. Her quiet sobbing prompted us also to shed a tear or two as we thanked her for giving us work, taking care of us and letting us stay at number seven until this moment, our time of departure. We turned to wave to her and walked up to the barracks near the Calle de San Nicolás. Our feelings were mixed.

'What are we letting ourselves in for?' asked Beatrix, firmly directing her question at me, as if I possessed some knowledge that I had not yet shared.

'I cannot know more than you or Susana,' I said. 'I know Antonio told me first about this need for women to serve the troops and what he told me I've passed on to you, word for word.'

'But you are the wisest of the three of us,' said Susana. 'We expect you to know more about what is lying in wait for us.'

'Flattered though I am, I just don't know, Susana.'

With that we arrived at the gates to the barracks, to be confronted by the seething activity you might expect when a hundred and twenty soldiers, their equipment, wagons and horses were organising themselves to leave for Flanders. Antonio spotted us as we looked quizzically through the bars of the heavy gates.

'There you are! Right on time! Good to see you. I've been looking out for you three.'

With the total absence of formality, a guard took a key from inside his waistcoat pocket and let us in.

'We'll be leaving soon so would you load your bags onto that wagon over there,' he said, pointing to a cart that looked so battered and worn that it would hardly reach the end of the street, let alone survive a journey to Barcelona.

'You're not expecting us to travel in that are you?' I asked.

'That's the plan,' said Antonio sheepishly.

'No. You can take our luggage in that but not us,' I said. 'Show us some respect and take us in something half decent.'

'It's all we've got,' said an Antonio, shrugging his shoulders and lifting his open palms in to the air. 'There's nothing else available.'

'I'm not travelling in that heap. Not me,' said Beatrix, suddenly raising her voice.

'Nor me,' said Susana.

'Then you can forget the whole idea,' I said. 'Let's go back to number seven, girls.'

'I'm not sure what to say,' said a wide eyed Antonio, bowing his head. Then, with a desperate air of resignation, 'I thought this was all going too well.'

We were each unsure of our ground but, even so, made a move to pick up our bags and look towards the gates. Then the colonel's assistant, the one whom we spoke to two or three weeks before about working for the army, appeared and spoke.

'What's going on here?' he said. 'Sudden change of tune? Don't you want to go?'

'We are still prepared to go but not to travel in that open wagon. It's a wreck. And apart from that, we don't want to be on view to all and sundry as camp followers, obviously earning a living as whores to you lot,' I said.

'I agree,' said Beatrix. 'There are limits, you know.'

'Get the carriage from the stables,' said the colonel's assistant, directing his instruction to Antonio. 'I'll probably be shot for this but at least it'll keep them happy.'

We stood and waited for about five or ten minutes. Antonio then emerged from around a corner, riding one of a pair of chestnut mares, tethered to a beautiful, black, two-door carriage.

'That's more like it,' said Susana. 'I could enjoy riding in that!'

'Beautiful!' said Beatrix, smiling.

'That's it,' I said. 'Now we are happy!'

Next we could hear the clatter of horses' hooves as dozens of stable lads brought the soldiers' mounts into the parade ground in front of the gates. Horses' heads were flicking from side to side, anticipating a lusty gallop ahead.

Then an important looking soldier walked over to speak to us. He was the only one wearing an elaborate, lace fringed, white collar that all but reached his shoulders. 'My name is Lieutenant Jorge Castillo. I am in charge of the troupe going to Flanders. I want to tell you girls what is going to happen. You may already know that we are going to Barcelona to go by galley to Savona. From there we go by road to Flanders. It is a very gruelling journey but we will do our best to make you comfortable.

'We will ride as quickly as we reasonably can. We will be changing horses every five or six *leguas*. Those pulling your carriage will be changed just as frequently. Your driver will be Leo here.' He gestured towards a scruffy looking, unshaven old soldier in a beaten, tricorn with his breeches tied below his knees with pieces of string.

'I hope I don't have to have him on top of me,' I thought. 'Not the most pleasant experience.'

'I'm charmed to meet you, Leo,' I said, putting on a slightly superior tone which I hoped he would find off-putting, if not offensive. Susana and Beatrix detected the nuance.

'I am equally charmed to meet you,' said Beatrix.

'I too,' chimed Susana.

The lieutenant continued. 'We will provide you with everything you will need on the journey. I can't promise you the best food but we are taking a small team of army chefs and they will prepare us some good, if simple meals. We will also be using local taverns on route. They have been told in advance of our needs and will be expecting us. Do you have any questions?'

'What if we want to stop for a pee?' asked Susana, staring the lieutenant straight in the eye. He frowned and looked towards me. I raised my eye-brows and shrugged.

'Easy,' said Leo. 'If it's urgent, just call out and I'll pull over. Somewhere you can do it without being seen. Try and hang on until we are due to stop, though.'

'What happens when we get to Barcelona?' asked Beatrix. 'Do we stay there or get straight on the ship?'

'That depends,' said the lieutenant. 'We will be taking the regular galleys that sail between Barcelona and Genoa. If the fleet is already in Barcelona, we get straight on board. If they're a day or two late, we'll have to wait there. We'll put you up in local inns, in that case.'

'When do we start performing our duties?' I asked.

'Hm...,' muttered the lieutenant. 'That depends.'

'On what?' Beatrix said.

'On where we stop for the night and what facilities we have available when we get there. Why do you ask?'

'It's obvious, isn't it?' I said. 'We need some notice to prepare ourselves. We are not instantly available.'

'I see,' said the lieutenant. 'I hadn't fully appreciated that. I personally will make sure you get at least twelve hours notice. At least on the journey to Barcelona. My role changes when we are on the ship but resumes when we get to Savona.'

'One more question,' said Beatrix. 'I thought we were going by road to Cartagena and from there to Genoa. Has there been a change of plan?'

'Not quite but something like that. For tactical and financial reasons we are going to Savona and overland from there. It will all become clearer when you are on the road from there to Flanders. We save a small fortune by disembarking at Savona rather than Genoa so that's why we are going there.' He failed to mention Cartagena or explain his 'tactical' thinking so, having interrogated him quite intensely, we relented and saved any further questioning until later.

'Well, señoritas, would you please come this way and step into your carriage. We are all but ready to depart.'

By then, Leo had climbed onto the driving seat and a hundred and twenty or so soldiers had mounted their horses which were champing to go and swirling around in circles on the parade ground, as if preparing for a race.

***

We each in turn lifted our skirts to step into the carriage. It rocked gently towards us and then away as we entered. Beatrix first, followed by Susana and me at the rear. We cast our eyes around its sumptuous interior as we took our seats, which were made from red stained leather, cut and sewn with incredible precision from narrow strips. The side walls and doors were lined in a rich, red damask which may have been a tone or two darker that the leather of the seating.

'Bet you've never travelled in anything like as smart as this,' said Beatrix, still looking at the elegant interior.

'You may be surprised,' I said, recalling the frightening journey Susana and I had made from Buitrago to Madrid.

'Tell me more!' said Beatrix.

'Definitely. Later,' I said. 'We need to settle ourselves for this journey now. Maybe, once we are well on the way.'

Susana and I sat facing the team of two horses and Leo, while Beatrix faced Susana. By the time we had climbed aboard and had taken our places, we could see through the windows that the company had started to move. The lieutenant, riding a black, bright-eyed mare, led the parade. A smiling young soldier, bearing the company's colours on a flag pole, followed. We moved at an excruciatingly slow pace: the horses were merely walking. But about half an hour after we had left the barracks, at the point where we reached the Puerta de Alcalá, on the road to Guadalajara, we heard the lieutenant shout an instruction. While we could not decipher its meaning, its effect was immediate: the horses broke into a fast trot. Leo responded by cracking his whip over our pair which also began to move fast enough to keep up with the others.

'About time we speeded up,' said Susana. 'We'd take a month to get to Barcelona at that rate.' She had to raise her voice a little, over the sound of the horses' hooves and the carriage and wagon wheels riding the firm ground. But we could still hold a conversation, despite the noise from outside, which we decided to reduce anyway by sliding up the windows.

'This is quite comfortable, don't you agree?' asked Beatrix.

'Not bad at all,' said Susana. 'As long as the road stays like this and the carriage doesn't have to go much faster. Otherwise, we'll be thrown all over the place.'

'I'm wondering how long we'll take to get to Barcelona,' I said.

'I'll guess five days,' said Beatrix.

'No idea,' said Susana. 'Not even sure where it is.'

'Well it must be on the coast for a start,' said Beatrix. 'Not many ships will pick you up from somewhere on dry land!' We all chuckled but Susana seemed none the wiser.

After about two hours fairly hard riding, our military procession came to a halt. 'Get out and stretch your legs, girls,' Leo shouted, still from up on the carriage driving seat. 'We've just reached Guadalajara.'

You would think that some of these men had rarely seen a woman. As we stepped out of the carriage we felt a hundred and more pairs of eyes staring at us, as many of the army riders, especially the younger ones, turned their horses to snatch a better view.

'Good God!' said Beatrix. 'Look at this lot staring. I have a feeling we could be working hard tonight!'

'Are there any other women in this convoy?' asked Susana.

'I haven't seen any,' said Beatrix. 'What about you, Esmeralda?'

'No, I haven't seen any either.'

'Then we will be working hard tonight!' said Susana.

'Not necessarily,' I said. 'Most of these boys will be so tired by the time we reach wherever we are going to stay, they won't be able to raise a flag, let alone get ready to do us!'

'I'm not so sure,' said Susana.

'We'll have to wait and see,' said Beatrix.

'We can always say no,' said Susana.

'Don't forget what the lieutenant told us,' I said. 'We'd get twelve hours notice. And it's past midday now!'

'Yes, I'd forgotten!' said Susana, looking relieved. Three *reales* a day seemed good compensation for travelling across our country in a luxury carriage and not having to do much.

We stepped out of the carriage and, just as they would have treated senior officers or members of the nobility, a red faced sergeant escorted the three of us towards a roadside inn, set not more than four *varas* from the edge of the road.

'Sit in here girls, while I get you something to eat and drink,' said the sergeant, ushering us towards a private room at the back of the inn.

'Where are the soldiers taking their refreshment?' asked Beatrix.

'Don't worry about them,' said the sergeant. 'There are three inns here so the soldiers don't all have to use this one. We always stop here on the road to Barcelona. We change horses, have our refreshment and take off again. All within half an hour. Not bad, eh? My job is to look after you girls when we stop and make sure you are comfortable before we restart our journey.'

'I didn't expect that,' I said. 'I thought we'd have to fend for ourselves. What's your name?'

'I am Sergeant Luis de Alvarado of the 7th Company of the Madrid *Tercios*. Do you want some juice or something to eat?'

'What I want most of all is a pee,' said Susana, predictably.

'If you go through that door at the back you will be outside and you can relieve yourself there, if you wish.'

Susana rushed towards the door, quickly followed by Beatrix. The sergeant passed me a plate and invited me to help myself to some pie, pickled walnuts, some bread, cheese and fresh grapes. He put a cup of water in my hand.

'There you are, love. Get some of that inside you.'

I wondered whether to use this opportunity to ask the sergeant about what would be happening to us, on this journey and further along, on the road to Flanders itself. 'Tell me Luis, is it alright to call you by your first name? Where will we be stopping tonight? Not sleeping in the open, I hope?'

'You are all welcomed to call me Luis, señorita. I'd be pleased with that. We are heading for a little town called Alhama de Aragón. We sent an advance party four days ago to reserve places in a number of inns there. We are only a small company so everyone will sleep in a bed tonight!'

That was good news. None of us would want to sleep in the carriage, comfortable though it was. 'How long will we take to get to Barcelona,' I asked.

'We have to be there in three days. Otherwise we will miss the galleys.'

'The galleys? How many of them?'

'Usually three,' he said, holding up three fingers of his right hand, as if I might be deaf. 'Two will take the troops – and you girls – and another will be heavily armed and be our pilot. The Mediterranean waters from Barcelona to Genoa are thick with pirates. But we know how to deal with them.' He smiled, knowingly.

'We are going to have to travel quickly to be there in three days aren't we?'

'Yes, but with enough changes of horses we'll do it. I don't know where we'll be stopping tomorrow night but it will have to be further on than Zaragoza.'

I thought of asking him about when we would start serving the troops but decided that I shouldn't. I didn't want to embarrass him, for one thing. The girls reappeared during my conversation with the sergeant. Once we had taken sufficient of the food and had enjoyed the fresh, cool water, we thanked him and returned to our carriage.

'That was good!' said Susana. 'Free food and a nice place to stop for a while.'

'I can't believe the *tercios* are so well organised,' said Beatrix.

'I couldn't either, but they clearly are. The sergeant told me we must reach Barcelona in three days or we'll miss the galleys. We'll be staying tonight in a place called Alhama de something... I forget exactly what he said.'

'Sleeping in beds?' asked Susana.

'Yes, for certain. At least, that's what he told me. In a tavern they've reserved in advance.'

***

We maintained a good pace until nightfall and, having made three more stops, either to rest or change the horses, arrived in the sleepy town of Alhama de Aragón. True to what Sergeant de Alvarado had told us, the landladies of four inns were standing guard of their respective establishments, with arms open to welcome us. It was as if they had been waiting there all day and, for all we knew, they had been. There seemed something strange about this town and none of the three of us could work out what is could be. The air seemed warmer and more humid than it should have been. We thought we could see, from the light of oil lamps, vapour clouds enveloping the roof tops. We just thought it odd.

Sergeant de Alvarado showed us to our rooms in the inn. What luxury to have a room each! We quickly explored our own rooms then sped to look at those of the others. All were small but provided sufficient comfort, most importantly a double bed in which we could each spread out.

Just after I had returned to my room, having explored Susana's, there was a knock on my room door. I opened it to be confronted by the lieutenant.

'I want to ask you a question, Esmeralda. Would you three be available to consort with my men tonight?'

'What do you mean by "consort"?'

'Well... to be available to serve them... to make love to them?'

'Hell, Lieutenant! There are over a hundred of them! Are you expecting us to do all of them before we go to sleep? It's late enough as it is. Anyway, you said you'd give us twelve hours notice!'

'I apologise, Esmeralda. I know...I know. But you know what they are like. A soldier is a soldier!'

'Please stay here while I speak to my colleagues.'

I spoke to Susana first and suggested we meet with Beatrix in her room. I explained to them what the lieutenant had asked.

'No. that wasn't the deal,' said Beatrix. 'We need reasonable notice and I for one don't feel like it tonight. We've been sitting all day and my bum is sore through being jolted on the road here!'

'Mine too,' said Susana whom I felt was simply following Beatrix.

'I'll tell him,' I said.

'I'm not sure I can accept that,' said the lieutenant. 'You have been engaged by the army to service the troops. What am I supposed do?'

'That's not my problem,' I replied. 'You should have had the courage to tell them about our deal... rather than pandering to them and coming to us to find a way out of it. Good night, lieutenant.'

He grimaced and turned quickly around so I found myself facing his back. I closed my bedroom door and chuckled to myself. At least we had won our first argument with the lieutenant, if that could be construed as a victory. At what price, I wondered.

Each of the three of us was tired and slept well in our comfortable beds. I woke well before dawn to a sharp knocking on my door.

'Who's that?' I shouted, fearing to open up.

'It's me,' said Sergeant Luis de Alvarado. 'The lieutenant wants us all to assemble outside the inn in fifteen minutes.'

'What's the time?' I asked, rubbing the sleep from my eyes.

'Six, by the church bells!'

'I'll get the others.'

Despite this sudden and unheralded call to a meeting, the three of us managed to dress and get outside within the allotted time. We were not the first, nor the last, to arrive. It was still quite dark but there was just about enough light to see human shapes and almost enough to identify them. The lieutenant stood on a wooden box to address us all.

'We had a hard day yesterday, men. You did well to get us here in good time. I've got you up early for a special reason. Many of you know that there is a lake here, fed by hot springs. It is wonderful to bathe and swim in. I want to give you all, including our lady companions, the opportunity to use the waters before we leave. I want you to reassemble here in an hour, after your dip and after your breakfast. I forbid you to touch any of the ladies who decide to join you in the water. I will ask them to make themselves available to serve you later. Now dismiss.'

Almost to a man, the soldiers made their way to the huge lake which was the source of the vapour we saw the day before, as we arrived there. 'What do you think?' asked Beatrix, directing her question to me.

'We join them. We strip naked as the men are sure to do and we dive in. Let's forget our modesty. It's almost dark so they won't be able to see us that well. They'll see a lot more when we start to work for them!'

'Yes, but they'll be getting a free look now. No one's mentioned paying us,' said Susana.

'Don't be mean, Susana. We're being paid three *reales* a day for being here. And we haven't yet shown a nipple for it,' said Beatrix.

'You're right. We'll get good credit for playing along. In fact we shouldn't try to cover ourselves up at all,' I said.

'I agree with you,' said Beatrix.

'All right. I agree as well,' said Susana. 'I think I can see. It'll do us no harm.'

So the three of us made our way up to the lake but stayed behind a group of the men. As soon as we reached the lake we removed our clothes. 'God, its cold,' said Beatrix, shivering in her nakedness.

'It ain't in there, love,' laughed one of the soldiers.

So we ran down the bank together and dived in. I felt the gentle heat on my skin. It caressed me like a hot towel and was lovely. It touched every surface of my body and felt even better as I completely immersed myself in the lake.

'This is so good,' said Beatrix, lifting her upper half from the water. 'I could stay in here all day. It's like a hot bath. It's a pity we have to get out so soon!'

'It is a hot bath,' I said.

'It is good,' said Susana. 'I'm glad we did it!'

By then it was getting lighter and we could sense many of the men turning towards us for a curious look. But none came close so no one touched us. One shouted out, 'Come on show us your breasts. Give them a wobble!'

'Shall we?' said Susana, in a smiling voice and getting into the spirit of things.

'Yes,' said Beatrix and I, in unison. So the three of us put our arms around each others' shoulders and gave the men the swinging breast display they wanted, even though only one had plucked up the courage to ask. A hundred and twenty soldiers responded to our smiling naughtiness by letting out an almighty cheer which echoed around the lake.

'Thank you girls,' said the lieutenant. 'Well done! You've made some friends for life! Right! Off to breakfast now!'

Along with the soldiers, we climbed out of the water, only to realise that we were soaked from head to toe and had nothing with which to dry ourselves.

'Now what do we do?' asked Susana. 'Wipe ourselves with our clothes?'

'Definitely not! We bundle them up so they don't rub against us and get wet. We then walk with our heads held high, back to the inn and go up to our bedrooms. We towel ourselves dry when we get there and then go down for breakfast.'

'That's brave,' said Susana.

'And brazen,' said Beatrix. 'But what fun. We'll do it. I'll even go first!'

So, we followed Beatrix back to our rooms. The men delighted in our little parade, especially as it was getting lighter by the minute. Instead of cheering, they applauded us, all the way to the inn front door.

'Now we cover up,' I said. 'We don't want to embarrass the landlady, even though she'll have seen it all before.' So we each covered our front, leaving our rear exposed, and walked in and up the stairs.

***

We travelled even faster that day than we did the day before. The sky was dark to begin with and the lieutenant didn't want to ride the horses in rain. So he pushed the men and horses to the limit, so as to make as much progress as we could while the weather held out. By the time we arrived at our first stop, where we refreshed ourselves and changed mounts, the poor animals were perspiring so much it ran down their legs and were panting to retrieve every breath of air. They, if not we, were exhausted. Leo hurtled the carriage along its path, as if his life depended on keeping up with the riders, irrespective of how much we were thrown around inside.

'I'm sorry,' said Susana as she was tossed across the carriage into Beatrix's lap, when Leo negotiated a tight corner.

'Don't worry, love. No damage done!' he shouted. It was just as well. We were depending on this comfortable but fragile vehicle to transport us to Barcelona.

We thumped and pounded the roads and, after changing horses five times during the day, including making a stop in the city of Zaragoza, arrived at about six o'clock in the evening in the historic town of Fraga, in Aragon, apparently not far from Huesca and the French border. Once again, Sergeant Luis de Alvarado, who was proving himself to be a kind and sympathetic man, escorted us to separate rooms in an inn near the centre of the town.

'Just make yourselves comfortable girls. I'd have a rest if I were you. You've had a rough journey today and it sounds to me if you could be in for a busy night.'

We didn't need reminding that, at our first stop in the morning, Lieutenant Castillo had asked us to be available for service that evening. None of us knew quite what to expect. There were only three of us and over one hundred and twenty men. Surely, they wouldn't expect us to work with up to forty each, between then and whenever we would retire for the night.

'Well, how do we think this is going to work out?' asked Beatrix.

'I don't know,' said Susana. 'If we fuck with all this lot, we won't be able to sit down tomorrow!'

'We're not going to,' I said. 'I'll go to see the lieutenant and set down some rules. What if I say we'll do two an hour each from seven o'clock until midnight? That'll be ten apiece. Thirty in all and we'll say we'll have another thirty tomorrow.'

'You'll never get away with that,' said Beatrix. 'He'll want one done every quarter of an hour!'

'And we haven't got a clock between us,' said Susana.

'I'll see what I can get out of him. Agreed?' They each nodded and I went.

***

I couldn't have expected a worse reaction. The lieutenant fought hard. Perhaps I shouldn't have felt so confident after my success of the day before.

'You women were more than pleased to accept the three *reales* a day to come with the army. Now you are dictating your terms. It's not good enough. Would you rather return to Madrid? I can arrange for that easily enough.'

'You tell me what you think is reasonable, then. Do you accept that we can't do the whole company between now and midnight. With forty apiece, we'll hardly be able to stand up tomorrow. Let alone cope with a ride as rough as today.'

He looked away from me. His eyes glanced at the ceiling. Then at the door, his escape route possibly?

'Esmeralda... um... well... I hoped you would come up with something... something I could take back to the men.'

I'd cornered him. 'Right, lieutenant. This is what we'll do, if you agree. We will start work in half an hour. We need a little time to prepare. We will work from seven until midnight. There will be a break of five minutes between customers. Just to clean ourselves up and prepare for the next one. We'll do as many as we can. You and Sergeant Luis can start organising a queue, starting with your youngest men and saving the oldest until last. They won't all want to have us tonight. Maybe a third will. We'll see. Cash payments before anyone can start. Understood?'

'Esmeralda, I think you have solved a problem. I have no intention of second guessing or negotiating with you. I've said enough. We'll fit in with what you propose. I'll go now and organise my men. We'll send some up from seven. I'll tell the men to stay a respectable distance from your doors. You won't want them hanging around listening! In the meantime, go and take some refreshment.'

By midnight we were completely exhausted. We convened in Beatrix's room to share experiences. 'I counted fifteen,' said Susana. 'And I'm really sore. They all want to fuck. No hand work or oral. I just want to sleep now. Have you any cream I could use?'

'I did about the same. Two wanted oral and one a hand job while he looked down at me below. He couldn't see much anyway, by the light from a candle on the dressing table. One thing. They didn't smell too bad. They'd had a bath this morning,' Beatrix laughed.

'Sounds like I had the most: twenty one. Most were over and done within a minute or two. Oh, and another just wanted to fondle my breasts. He said he'd been thinking about doing that since he saw us naked in the lake.'

'Did yours all pay?' asked Susana, looking at me.

'Yes. I made them pay before they did anything. What about yours?'

'All but one. I hadn't the heart to say no. Said he'd lost his money playing cards last night but would pay me when we reached Barcelona.'

'He probably won't,' said Beatrix.

'I'm not that bothered. I made fourteen *reales*. A good night's work, as far as I'm concerned.'

***

We slept well, having travelled hard all day and assiduously satisfied our customers at night. The lieutenant thanked me at breakfast for helping him out that evening and asked me to pass on his appreciation to Susana and Beatrix. Another busy day was ahead of us. The soldiers were already mounted as we stepped outside the inn. Their mounts were flicking their heads expectantly, anticipating a punishing run. We climbed into the carriage at about eight o'clock and set off, once more, at a frightening pace.

As night began to close in we could sense, by the clamouring noise and the pungent, dungy smell that we were nearing a very large town. Many more wagons and horses were travelling the road than we had seen on our journey before, except as were leaving Madrid. We were approaching a great city. We had reached Barcelona.

CHAPTER 14

Of the Sea and Ships

'My God!' she said. 'It's so big. I've never seen anything like it. Its size is frightening. It scrapes the sky! I'm scared! Will it hurt me?' She began to sob and was soon brimming over with tears.

'Don't cry,' said Beatrix, putting an arm around Susana's quivering shoulder. 'It is not some kind of monster or a giant. It cannot hurt you. It can't even try. It's a ship! You must've seen pictures of them.'

'No. Never. But I have heard of ships. My little friend, a boy in the orphanage, had a toy boat. He'd hide it from the nuns. But I didn't expect anything as big as this. I'm terrified,' she said, cowering into Beatrix's breast.

'Don't worry, Susana,' I said. 'We will be travelling in one of those to Savona. There is nothing to worry about. You will love being on it. You will even sleep on it. And we'll both be with you. So don't cry.' I didn't tell her that she would be spending half her time serving our customers on the ship. Somehow, it didn't seem right to mention it.

I did agree with Susana though about the overpowering size of the ship. It seemed to have a strength in its own shape and form that should be possessed only by something living. Its sails seemed to be attached to straight, strong arms and its hull was like a huge body, lying in the water and moving and creaking with the swell of the sea. I could understand, with not much imagination, how some who saw it for the first time could be shocked and frightened by it, especially someone who had never seen anything bigger than a cathedral, large though it would be, firmly attached to the ground.

The following morning, having spent the night in a scruffy inn not far from the quay, we packed our bags and made our way back to the moorings. The sergeant was right. There were three of these behemoths tied to their moorings, ready for us to clamber aboard. We stood in amazement and watched the seething activity needed to prepare the ship for its voyage to Savona. Men were climbing high above the decks, securing the sails to the yardarms. To us, looking from a distance, they looked like ants working on an elevated nest. A badly crippled porter laughed as he limped towards the ship carrying six live chickens by their legs, three in each hand.

'These could be on the plate in front of you tonight, loves! They're fresh and ready for the table!'

We chuckled as a woman heaved against two goats which pulled against her and did not want to go aboard.

'Why is she taking those goats on the galley?' asked Beatrix.

'They use them for their milk,' said Susana, without a moment's hesitation.

'Well, I didn't know that,' said Beatrix, as surprised as I was that Susana knew.

We looked on in sympathy as three men struggled to lift some heavy barrels from a horse drawn cart onto the quayside. They heaved and shoved at them as they rolled these heavy objects up the gangplank. We shrieked out as one lost his grip and a barrel starting coming back down the slope. Then we sighed as they regained control over the wayward drum.

'What do you think is in those barrels?' asked Susana.

'Who knows?' said Beatrix. 'Could be beer. Could be wine. Could be brandy. But it's probably water.'

'More likely water,' I said.

'Why water?' asked Susana. 'There's plenty in the sea.'

'Yes, but there's salt in that. And you'd die if you drank it!' said Beatrix.

Porters and teamsters brought all manner of things to the ships. Baskets, parcels, bags, barrels full of food. And objects the ship would be taking to Genoa or Savona for sale or export. Wood, grapes, olive oil, wool, cotton, clothes and pottery.

We stopped at the quayside to watch this important and organised activity. Then a bugle sounded in a street near the ship. We looked around. And there they were: our soldiers. They marched in line and in formation to the sound of a single side drum, played by a one-eyed drummer. Susana spotted a tall pikeman, somewhere near the back.

'See him,' she yelled. 'He's the one who lost his money the night before. He still hasn't paid me, the lanky shite.'

'Don't worry,' I said. 'I'll get it out of him. Or he'll wonder what hit him.'

Our lieutenant, sitting astride a frisky white stallion, led this motley parade. Two paces behind him was the young flag bearer we had seen many times before. He smiled cheekily as he saw us grinning at him.

'Do you know something?' I said, looking in turn at Susana and Beatrix, and then nodding towards the youthful flag bearer. 'He had me while we were staying that night in Fraga. He was a virgin. Or so he said. He wanted to have a look before I let him in. So I showed him. He was up and ready in seconds and that's as long as he lasted!'

'Why didn't you tell us before?' asked Beatrix.

I couldn't think of a convincing answer so just said, 'I forgot! It was over so quickly.'

'I've got a confession to make,' said Beatrix. 'Last night I served the lieutenant.'

'You're joking,' said Susana.

'No, I'm not. He surprised me. For a man who seems so unsure of himself when he speaks, he was very confident in bed. Quite experienced I would say. A good, boisterous lover and I quite enjoyed him. So thank you, Esmeralda, for agreeing the same sort of arrangement last night as we had the night before! And he left me a four *maravedí* tip!'

The lieutenant dismounted right next to us as we stood at the quayside. He came over to us and spoke.

'Good morning ladies. I hope we've all had a pleasant night,' he said making a clear if tangential reference to his experience with Beatrix. 'I have to tell you about your journey to Savona. You will each be travelling on a different galleon and be serving the crew and soldiers on your ship.'

'No, we won't,' I said. 'We three travel together. We work as a team and we stay as a team. And we perform better as a team. We all stay on the same galleon and serve whoever wants business on that ship and that ship alone.'

'You've put me in a very difficult position. I have a hundred and twenty men to keep happy and you only want to work for a third of them.'

'Not the case. How often do we call into port?'

'We stop every night.'

'Simple. Whoever wants our services will have to come aboard our ship. You'll have to organise that. If not we keep our legs together until we get to Savona.'

'In which case you will lose your daily allowance.'

'We don't care,' said Beatrix, glaring at him with her eyes afire. 'We three work together and that's the end of it.'

'You lot will end up back in Madrid, if you're not careful. The carriage and wagon drivers will be leaving by midday. Any more of this awkwardness and you'll be going back with them.'

'Just listen to me, lieutenant,' I dared to say. 'We've each got something that just about every single one of your men wants. You make a move to send us back and you could have a hundred and twenty mutineers. You'll be left with nobody.'

'I wish you'd all stop arguing,' said Susana. 'I'm frightened of being on one of these big things and I need my friends with me.' She started to cry.

The lieutenant came across to comfort her. 'Don't worry, my love. I'll sort something out. Just be patient and you'll soon see.'

'Thank you, lieutenant,' said Beatrix, sarcastically. 'I hope you can.'

'Let me start by taking you to one of the galleons.' He led the way to the gangplank of the centre ship in the row. If anything, it was a quite a bit larger than the other two.

'I'm even more scared of this bigger one,' said Susana, breaking into tears again.

'Please, Susana, the lieutenant is doing his best for us. We must go along with what he is saying. We'll all be together and that's what we wanted most.' Susana let out one more sob and smiled back at me.

Standing at the top of the gangplank was a handsome young man with a hair braid, partly covered by a flat-topped, brimmed hat.

'This is Captain Domingo de San Martín. This is his ship.'

'I'm delighted to meet you, ladies. Welcome aboard *El Crisantemo*. We will do our utmost to make your journey as comfortable as we can. This is a new ship, made here in Barcelona and I'm sure you will enjoy your time on board.' He looked sideways at the lieutenant while concluding his welcome, as if to acknowledge that we had certain duties to perform.

'Captain San Martín is fully in charge of this ship. Although I am still responsible for the actions of my soldiers, he reports to his bosses on what happens to his vessel.'

'Ladies, I want to ask you a serious question. Could you make your services available to my crew? We'd be so grateful to each of you if you did.'

'I'd be grateful if you would give us time to discuss your request, señor captain. We can let you know by...'

'Say two o'clock this afternoon,' interjected Beatrix, looking a bit sharply at me.

'That will be fine,' said the captain. 'Let me show you to your quarters.' He had surprised us with the use of the word 'quarters' but we went along with him, leaving the lieutenant, standing at the head of the gangplank.

'Well, here we are,' said the captain, showing us three beds, less than few *pies* apart, in a cabin in the stern.

'I'm sorry, Captain San Martín. This will not be sufficient either for me or the others,' I said, in my most diplomatic voice.

'Definitely not,' said Beatrix.

'Why not?' exclaimed the captain.

'Well. It's like this. You are fully aware of the nature of the duties you are expecting us girls to perform. We only ever conduct them in private.

We cannot possibly share a cabin, like this. We need separate rooms to do our work. To do otherwise would be an invitation either to an orgy or to embarrassment for any customer, working with us in the presence of another. For example, you wouldn't want anyone watching you, would you?'

'I understand,' said Captain San Martín. 'I will find you separate cabins, even if that means upsetting a few of my men. They may also want to be your customers so, hopefully, they will be willing to accept a change in accommodation, even if it means sharing with the troops.'

Within the space of thirty minutes, the captain returned and escorted us to three individual cabins in the forecastle, above the crew's deck. Small though they were, they were each equipped with a single bed, secured firmly to the floor, a small chest of drawers and, most luxurious of all, a small wardrobe, each of which was incorporated into the sides of the cabin. Mine was an especially odd shape as it was situated right in front of the prow. The others were on each side of mine and were equally well appointed.

Within moments of Captain San Martín leaving us in our respective cabins, we were rushing into each other's to see what he had allocated to us.

'You've got a mirror!' said Beatrix to Susana. 'You lucky thing! I haven't!'

'Yours must be right in the middle,' said Beatrix to me. 'Judging by the way those beams fan out each side.'

'The good thing is we've got what we wanted. Now we can work with our men to our hearts content without another one looking at us!' I said.

'Well done, Esmeralda,' said Beatrix. 'You are our chief negotiator. You are the leader of us three and that is so obvious.'

'I'm only too pleased to help,' I said, breaking into a grin, relieved that Beatrix accepted my leadership and seemed to have no ambitions to take my place.

***

It wasn't long before we had left our cabins to explore the ship. By then a number of *tercios* had arrived on board. Eventually, we found out that there were seventy on our ship and twenty five, or so, on each of the other two which were mainly cargo vessels, taking cotton to Genoa for their famous lace makers and brandy to Savona. Apparently, the Savonese preferred the Spanish varieties to their local brands. We found our way on to the deck, into the fresh breeze which caressed us and this beautiful ship which responded by swaying gently on its moorings. We admired from this considerable height the great city of Barcelona and wandered around, taking care not to trip over the ropes and bulwarks. We were surprised by the number of cannons facing outward and ready. We felt sure that these aggressive looking, black guns could defend us against any ship that wanted to cause us trouble.

'Didn't expect you to be on our ship!' said Antonio de Salazar, who was on deck with some of his colleagues and whom we last saw in Fraga. 'I thought they were putting one of you on each of the three! Pity the poor men on the other two, if they want a woman.'

'Not so quick,' said Beatrix. 'The lieutenant is sorting all that out. He relented when we told him we wanted to be together. Admittedly, we've left him with a problem. Interesting to see how he deals with it!'

'Come and look at our quarters,' said Antonio. 'Come to see what we've got.'

'I'm not sure about seeing that,' said Susana.

'You know what I mean!'

So Antonio and a couple of his friends took us down some steep stairs, walked us through the main deck, also lined with cannons, even larger than the ones above, and down yet more steep steps to the crew's quarters. It was packed with bunks, hammocks, suspended between the uprights, and the narrowest beds I had ever seen.

'I see what they mean when they say, "I could sleep on a plank",' said Beatrix, chuckling at her own wit.

'If there is anything like a strong wind out there, you have to join your arms together underneath, if you want to stay on,' said Antonio.

After teasing us about how sick we would be if the sea was rough, and about having to work our bodies during the day as well as at night, we left them and returned to our cabins to unpack.

***

The youthful Captain San Martín was delighted when I told him that I had spoken to Susana and Beatrix and that we were more than willing to serve him and his crew. He was less pleased when I said that we would have to give priority to our soldiers, but that seemed only reasonable when we were there to work with our men and not his. And, of course, I explained our terms.

'Not bad,' he said. 'About the same as the *puterías* in Barcelona. Is there anyone with you at the moment?'

'I'm sure I know where this is going,' I thought. 'No,' I said. 'There was no one there when I left to see you.'

'What if I came a long now and you served me?'

'But you are busy aren't you, preparing this ship to leave?'

'I can spare the time and I'm not the only one working on board!'

'All right,' I said. 'Let's go to our cabins. I'm sure one of us will oblige.' I could quite enjoy this handsome specimen myself but thought I would offer him to the other two first.

'The captain's come to see us!' I shouted, knocking on both Susana's and Beatrix's doors. 'He's looking for love!'

'Not so loud,' he said. 'I don't want them all to know I'm here!'

Both girls appeared from Beatrix's room. 'What can we do for you, captain?' asked Beatrix, smiling and feeling she knew perfectly well.

'Well...um...'

'He'd like to make love to one of us, one of you two, I think.'

'Me?' said Susana, hopefully.

'Agreed,' said a generous Beatrix. 'Maybe, me next time!'

The captain and Susana disappeared into her cabin. Beatrix and I adjourned to her cabin and sat on her bed. Hers was on the other side of mine, so we couldn't hear any of the goings on in Susana's, even if we wanted to.

'I wonder if the soldiers realise we are available for work,' said Beatrix.

'Hard to know for sure', I said. 'Mind you, we've served them well since we left Madrid and maybe they've had their fill by now. Some of the older ones, at least!'

'Maybe when the ship is out of the port they will be more interested. When there's nothing to look at other than the sea!' she laughed.

'We'll just have to wait. I'm willing to get on my back at any time. It would be good to have a nice, clean youngster. I could fancy doing that young flag bearer again. At least he won't be a virgin, next time around!'

'Changing the subject, I'm wondering how everything will work out when we join up with the rest of the troops going to Flanders. The soldiers we've been serving up to now will be joining a much bigger group. Numbered in thousands, so one of the customers told me.'

'Didn't you say some general was going to be leading an army or something. First time you mentioned all of this to us. Someone with a name to do with honey?'

'Ambrosio. Ambrosio Spínola. He's the general. He'll be leading the troops up this... Spanish Road... I think they call it. How many camp followers do you think they'll need to service say two thousand men? Any ideas?'

'Let's work it out, Esmeralda. I'm quite good at arithmetic. Say each man needs a woman once every four days. This means there should be five hundred services a day. We never did more than about fifteen, twenty at the outside. So that means five hundred divided by say twenty. That gives twenty five women. They'd all be working flat out so I imagine there would be quite a lot more, say about fifty.'

'I've no idea what sort of figures the army would use but my betting is that you aren't far out, Beatrix. Basically, you are saying that they'll need twenty times as many as the three of us who are serving a hundred and twenty men.'

'I suppose I am. Where will they get that number from? Italy?'

'Probably. I don't see many coming from Spain.'

With that we heard Susana's door close and her bidding her farewells to the captain. Within moments she was also sitting on Beatrix's bed, telling us what happened between her and Captain Domingo de San Martín.

'It was incredible. It was the first time anything like it has happened to me. Before we did anything, Captain Martín placed a tiny, paper package, not much bigger than his thumb, on my chest of drawers. It was screwed up at the top which was tied with a piece of fine ribbon. He undid the ribbon and opened it carefully. Inside was some fine, light brown powder. He asked me to sniff it up my nose. At first, I refused but then he said it would make our experience more intense and pleasurable. I asked him if he would take some but he said he had brought it for me. And that if I didn't want to try it he wouldn't be offended.'

'What did you do then?' said Beatrix, raising her eyebrows in puzzlement.

'I sniffed it up. Other than making my nostrils tingle, it had no effect. Not then, anyway. He undressed and so did I. We were then completely naked. He asked me to lie on the bed with my legs over the end so that he could kneel on the floor and put his head between my legs. He then started to kiss. At first, I didn't feel anything different from how it usually feels when a man does that. And he just carried on.

'Then I don't know what happened to me, but I think whatever it was in the powder started to have an effect. Suddenly, I had this sensation of really needing a man. I became overcome by a mad passion. A real need. I just had to have him, right there and then. Not just have him but to make him do me really, really hard. I began to itch like hell. It was as if I had something tickling me deep inside. I told him to put himself in me, quickly or I would pass out.'

'So then what did he do?' I asked. I had heard of these potions but decided not to mention that then.

'He had been concentrating so much on kissing me, that he was only partly ready. But between us we soon sorted that out. I slid back up the bed and, within a matter of seconds, he was doing me really hard. God, it was wonderful. I'd never felt like it before. Most of the men I've done up to now were only interested in satisfying themselves. But he made sure I got as much pleasure as he could give me. If it was the powder, it worked like magic.

'I don't know how long he carried on. I was in an odd state of mind and completely lost track of time.'

'Couldn't have been very long,' said Beatrix, dismissively. 'We were only chatting here for about ten minutes, if that.'

'Anyway,' continued Susana. 'It came to a really strange ending. I seemed as if I was going to explode and had the biggest shivering sensation I've ever had, much more intense than anything I've felt before. I've not had many anyway. I let out a shriek.'

'We didn't hear anything,' said Beatrix.

'Just as I cried out, he whipped himself out of me and took a little phial from his pocket, took the cork out of the end and placed it right by my *vava*. I felt myself release some liquid, quite a lot and I had no control over it coming out of me. He collected it in the bottle and put it on the chest of drawers. Then he finished off. "That was a delight, Susana. I think you enjoyed it, too!" he said, smiling with creased up eyes. I felt exhausted but good. Really good.

'He had his back towards me while getting dressed and while he did so said how we would like the voyage to Savona. He then picked up the phial, left a silver *real* on the chest of drawers and left, without as much as saying another word.'

'What an experience. I've had a number of nice climaxes, some of which I've brought on myself,' laughed Beatrix. 'But I don't think I've had anything as intense as that. I definitely haven't had anyone bottling up my come!'

'I can still feel that powder making me itch. I could still do with something inside me.'

'I'll give you one of my *consoladores* to play with!' I said. 'That'll keep you going. At least until we get a customer or two coming along!'

'Any idea what that powder could have been?'

'I think I may know,' I said. I didn't want to appear boastful so I mentioned the context in which I had learnt about such things. 'I remember when the alchemist showed me around his laboratory. He told me about this brownish powder called Spanish Fly. He only had a small bottle of it. It was made of crushed up beetles, I'm pretty sure.'

'Do you mean to say I've sniffed up something as horrible as that? I'd never have done it if I'd have known!' she said, screwing up her whole face so her eyes almost closed.

'That's why he didn't tell you!' said Beatrix.

'That mad alchemist told me to ask Angélica de la Castillo, his *puta* and girlfriend, if she used the stuff! Needless to say, I didn't have the nerve! I think he was joking anyway!'

'An alchemist? How did you know an alchemist?'

'I'll tell you another time!'

***

By the time we had finished chatting about Susana's encounter with Captain Domingo de San Martín, the galleon had slowly, almost imperceptibly, left the quayside at Barcelona. It was almost as if this colossus had waited for the captain to have his fill of Susana before it decided to leave the city at its stern. Our soldiers soon tired of looking over the gang rail at where the ship was going and what it was leaving behind. They began to trickle towards our quarters where a small queue formed to partake of our delights. None, however, offered us an experience anything like the one Captain Domingo de San Martín gave Susana. We worked hard during that first day at sea and well into the night, so much that we all three felt well deserving of a good night's sleep when we disembarked near a waterside inn in the tiny port of Agde, on the French coast.

Before going back on board to bed we chanced upon Lieutenant Jorge Castillo, who invited the three of us to have a drink in the *tasca* there.

'I'm interested to know how you managed to deal with the consequences of your kind decision to let Susana, Beatrix and me stay together on *El Crisantemo*,' I dared to say.

'That was not as difficult as I first imagined it would be,' said the lieutenant. 'I discovered that two other working girls from Madrid were staying on the quayside in Barcelona. Like you, they'd decided to join the army on its way to Flanders. They, however, were making their own way to Genoa to join the troops. They went without any certainty of employment but, from what they'd heard from others, settled on chancing their fortune.'

'Do we know these girls?' asked Susana.

'Quite possibly,' said the lieutenant.

With that, two women appeared from outside and wandered into the drinking area. One was a plump, quite tall, well-rounded girl whom I felt sure I recognised. The other was shorter and much thinner. Seeing the two together, made me realise who they were. They peered around the room and each smiled as they recognised the lieutenant. They then came over towards our little group.

'Let me introduce you to Ana and Marina,' said the lieutenant. 'I hope I remember your names! This is Esmeralda Pechada de Burgos, Susana de Rivera and Beatrix de Mendoza.'

We each shook hands with the new arrivals.

'And this is Ana Blas and Marina de la Cueva.'

Susana winced, coughed and screwed up her face. Beatrix moved her head to look the other way and then contained herself and turned back. Each of the three of us recognised them. Ana Blas was the street *puta* who worked in Madrid in the Plaza Mayor. We well remembered feeling a sense of disgust when she allowed her body to be penetrated by a donkey. Marina used to work the Calle de la Luna. She provoked little but a sense of questionable neutrality and a degree of trepidation only because she had associated herself with the shameless Ana Blas. I could recall her enthusiastically riding a young *tercio* at the party but we couldn't condemn her for doing what she was asked to do and for which she was well rewarded.

'What are you doing here?' asked Susana, not directing her question at either in particular.

'We could ask the same of you,' said Ana Blas, bluntly and staring vacantly at the ceiling. She betrayed no intention of giving a meaningful reply.

'Well, aren't you going to tell us?' asked Beatrix.

'What's it got to do with you?' said Marina de la Cueva.

'I don't know why you are being so secretive,' I said. 'I can't imagine you've come here to see the scenery. You've come for the same reason as us. To be camp followers. Are you saying you're not?'

'I'm not telling,' said Ana Blas.

'Nor am I,' said Marina.

The lieutenant listened silently to these abrupt exchanges, with his mouth open and his eyebrows furrowed. Then he spoke. 'Well, girls. You are all from the same town. You all work in the same profession. And you are fighting each other. I don't understand.'

'I'm sure we'll get on better as we work more closely together,' said Beatrix, nodding her head gently. 'We'll have to.'

'No we won't. I'll see to that,' snapped Ana Blas.

'Let's go,' said Marina de la Cueva.

The two of them turned away from us and the lieutenant and quickly made for the door.

'What was that about?' asked the lieutenant, his eyes wide open.

'It's hard to tell. They were both street workers in Madrid. They don't like *putas* like us who work in the brothels. Life is too easy for us. Having a bed to work on. In the warm. When they mainly work at night.

And do it in the street, up against a wall or tree or in a doorway. They envy us and envy causes tension,' I said.

'Hm... I'm just concerned about relationships. If you don't get on with them, they won't be too willing to help you out,' said the lieutenant.

'Don't worry,' said Susana. 'They'll help if it means money for them.'

'Anyway, how do you know them?' asked Beatrix who was as puzzled as I was.

'One of my men was talking to them in a quayside tavern in Barcelona and I just joined in the discussion. It soon became clear what they did for a living. They said they were making their way to Genoa to join the camp followers there. I said I was looking for a couple of girls to serve on my other two ships. And they accepted the work.'

'They should be grateful to us then, not angry,' said Susana.

I feared that our unpleasant exchange with these women might signal problems with them in the future and we wouldn't want that. The journey to Flanders would be difficult enough without having to fight them.

***

As we anticipated, we were compelled to work harder on board the ship than during our journey overland to Barcelona. The men took the opportunity of a sea voyage to relax and, rather than riding their striving horses, took to riding us instead. We worked our youthful bodies from early morning until late at night. We enjoyed having the same man again and once again. As we discovered at number seven, what would happen on these repeated encounters was predictable, or usually so, from the previous one, maybe with slight variation.

We spent the next night in Marseille. Some were not keen to disembark there because we were not then enjoying the best of relations with the French and didn't want trouble. While we stood on deck waving to the motley throng who had gathered on the quayside to wave us off, we could not help noticing that our ship was leaving the port much later than the others which we could see some half a *legua* or so ahead. Mother Nature kindly provided a strong tail wind that day, so we made good headway. The ship rocked noticeably in the wind but that did not agitate us. If anything, the crests and falls gave us a nice rhythm to work with in satisfying our customers who enjoyed the added, regular motion.

Working below deck ensured we had little idea of where the galleon was heading or, indeed, how far it had distanced itself from land. We laboured away in our quiet cabins in the forecastle, peacefully oblivious to the world outside. After we had been laughing and drinking in the aft galley with about a dozen or so soldiers and crew while enjoying some fresh olives, some cheese and some French bread for lunch, we returned giggling and joking to our cabins without giving a moments thought to our location on the Mediterranean sea.

'I wonder who we'll be working with this afternoon,' said Beatrix. 'Those cups of beer Antonio gave me are making me feel quite sleepy. I'd like a slow mover who can rock me off to sleep and wake me up before he goes.'

'He could always leave you, dead to the world and the cash on the chest of drawers,' said Susana.

'Better that than sneak out without paying,' I added.

We each kissed each other gently as we passed a short queue of three jolly, expectant soldiers chatting noisily while they were waiting for us to serve them.

'Here they are!' said the one at the back.

'About time!' said the one at the front grinning with the thought of his pleasure to come.

We each went into our respective cabins, accompanied by one of them. I selected the soldier at the front, a very young harquebusier whom I had seen several times before who blurted out his name as Felipe Sanz. Susana opened her door to a large musketeer called Carlos, whom she greeted like a lost friend, and Beatrix grabbed the hand of a timid but eager looking older man who said his name was Cristóbal Gutiérrez and a member of the galleon's crew.

My encounter with Felipe was progressing in the manner of routine business when he and I suddenly heard loud banging on Beatrix's cabin door. He paused for a moment and looked at me straight. 'What in hell's name is that?' he said. It sounded as though some madmen were smashing the door down with hammers or hatchets. Then we heard gunshots coming from up on deck.

He then uttered that dreaded word: 'Pirates!' He gently but quickly withdrew and put his pantaloons on. 'I'm going. Now!'

'I'm coming too,' I said, speedily doing up a few buttons on my dress. 'Sounds like Beatrix's cabin's being raided!'

We dashed out of mine and into Beatrix's. Our mouths dropped as we cast our eyes on the hideous scene which confronted us. Beatrix's shy customer lay on the floor, naked and dead in a pool of blood, a long handled dagger embedded in the back of his neck. His erection was still intact. Beatrix in her nakedness, with blood splashed over her face and breasts, was pitifully flailing her arms, attempting to fight off two black men who by then were also stripped naked and fighting between themselves for the prize of doing her. Felipe Sanz grabbed one of the men by the throat and smashed him hard against the wall, shouting, 'Help, Carlos! Help!'

In a trice, Carlos, having stopped his enjoying of Susana, appeared at the broken doorway, followed by Susana whose face contorted at the sight before her.

'Get him off me!' yelled Felipe while struggling with the man against the wall and being punched on the back by the man's companion. An almighty blast assaulted our ears. We could suddenly smell burnt gunpowder. Carlos's flintlock pistol, smoked from its single barrel, which he had discharged into the face of the second attacker. Blood poured from the side of the man's head as he collapsed to the floor. Beatrix let out a tortured scream and rushed into my arms, which I clenched tightly around her shaking, incarnadine form. Susana cried out as she rushed her arms around me and Beatrix who passed out and slid to the floor.

By then, the man against the wall had pulled the knife from the neck of Beatrix's dead customer and held it at the neck of Felipe. As Carlos hit the man in the face with the barrel of his pistol, Felipe wrestled the knife out of the man's hand and pushed it into the side of his throat. Blood gushed from the wound onto the floor and Beatrix's bed as this man collapsed in a shuddering heap. More soldiers appeared carrying guns and daggers.

'Bit late now lads,' said Felipe. 'We've done with these two. They're dead.'

'Come up on deck. There's one hell of a fight going on up there,' said one of the new arrivals. 'We've been attacked by pirates!' As if we didn't know. We three girls were too frightened by what was going on in Beatrix's cabin to notice much of what was in the background on deck but we could still hear the shouting and gun fighting above. The men left us, so Susana and I wrapped Beatrix in a towel and eased her into my cabin. I locked us in and we began to clean her up. The feel of the cold water on her face brought her round. She coughed, spluttered, and then cried uncontrollably.

'That was hideous,' she said, still shaking with fear. Then she started sobbing.

'I'm scared too,' said Susana, looking at the floor. 'How is this going to end? They could come down and kill us.'

'Let's just concentrate on getting Beatrix back to normal. Clean that blood from between her poor breasts.'

'We need more water. I'll get some from my cabin.'

'Not now. We'll manage with what we've got here.'

We were little short of terrified by the surprising happenings in Beatrix's cabin and the sound of the gun fighting, which continued above us on deck. We were numbed by fear and helplessness and cuddled up to each other silently on my bed. We gazed at each other and shook at the explosions which rocked us. Then after about ten minutes or so, which our fright had extended to hours, the frequency of the discharges decreased and then stopped. Silence. Nothing. Not a sound.

Who had prevailed? The soldiers and crew or the pirates? We could not know. We sat motionless on the bed fearing to make the slightest sound. Then after a few moments we heard a shout outside our cabins.

'It's over. We've won!' But who had won? 'The crew and us *tercios*. We've beaten them! You can come out now!'

We covered Beatrix's modesty and hesitantly emerged. This could not be some trick because the pirates did not speak Spanish. Our cautiousness could only have been due to our residual sense of fear which we could not dismiss in an instant. So we went out on to the deck area outside. A familiar face. And a familiar voice. It was Antonio de Salazar.

Susana rushed up and hugged his strong torso then cried on his shoulder. 'You've saved us! We are alive!'

'Not just me, Susana,' he said. 'Our men and the crew were heroes! You must come up on deck and see the pirates. We've tied them all up! Must be twenty of them. The rest are dead!'

We three, still anxious and shocked, followed Antonio into the fresh, windy air above. A sense of renewed security came over us as we saw the pirates, tied up and sitting, blindfolded and gagged, on the deck. Their defeat showed on what we could see of their faces. Their heads hung low, bowed in shame.

'What are you going to do with them?' I said to Antonio. 'You can't leave them here.'

'We'll have to wait and see. It depends on what Captain San Martín wants to do with them.'

It soon became clear. Captain Domingo San Martín appeared, wielding a wide curved cutlass. He stood in front of a group of his crewmen, facing the pirates. His men were holding flintlock pistols. 'What sort of barbaric spectacle are we about to witness?' I asked myself. The crew then tore the blindfolds from the pirates' faces, untied their legs and made them stand. They forced them at gunpoint onto their own galleon, which they'd tied alongside ours, retied their legs and made them sit on the deck. A dozen or so of Captain Martín's men climbed aboard the pirate ship and set the sails and rudder before climbing back onto *El Crisantemo*. They untied the ropes by which the pirates had tied their vessel to ours. Their ship drifted off silently away from us. It looked so peaceful and a gradually decreasing threat, the further away it drifted. Then, at about three hundred *varas* from us, a series of massive explosions rang out from it. Beatrix cowered at the sight as Susana and I hugged each other in horror. The pirate ship burst into flames which were so high they seemed to singe the sky. I felt a deadening disgust as I witnessed the spectre of their burning ship break up and slide beneath the waves. What a hideous, agonising death. This cruel, heartless captain, who had pleasured Susana with such alacrity, had without mercy, executed them.

***

We had to recover quickly. We had work to do. The captain sent some of his crew to clean up and freshen Beatrix's cabin. It must have taken them an hour to remove the blood and other excretions which had leaked from the dead pirates. Some of the crew unceremoniously threw their corpses overboard. Fortunately, we did not see that.

The effect of their battle with and bloody victory over the pirates surprised us girls. To all but a man, they had to have us. And have us...and have us! So we celebrated with them!

A day later all three of our galleons docked in Savona. Our frightening voyage was over.

CHAPTER 15

A shock in Turin

After the hideous experience with the pirates, we were greatly relieved to arrive safely in Savona. As we disembarked from *El Crisantemo*, a smiling Captain Domingo de San Martín stood on Savonese land, at the bottom of the gangplank, holding an umbrella and waiting to bid us farewell. The three of us didn't stop as we ran past him and shouted a peremptory, 'Goodbye'. The heavy rain almost drowned us as we ran, giggling stupidly, to a tavern overlooking the harbour where the three of us, and about twenty of our men, were to stay the night before starting on the next stage of our journey.

The lieutenant must have learnt his lesson. He had ensured that three nice rooms were awaiting us, albeit for a damp arrival, on the first floor of the pretty, white-fronted tavern.

'I'm soaked to the skin, right through my coat and it feels as if my skirt is sodden too. My feet are sloshing in my shoes! I'm going to dry myself off before I do anything else,' said Susana, unlocking the door to her room.

'Let's all do that,' said Beatrix. Her voice still trembled after the shocking encounter with the pirates. I couldn't stop thinking of that ghastly scene: the timid man's body, lying on the floor, his blood spattered on her face and breasts. The effect on Beatrix, who must have been terrified when they broke through her door, had to be much more severe than it was on me. She succeeded in losing her feelings in her work, immediately after the attack but, in the few days since, she had seemed vacant and generally far from her usual cheerful and sparkling self. I could see that I would have to help her to overcome this setback, as would Susana. Within ten minutes we had dried ourselves, dressed in dry clothes and were in Susana's room chatting.

'How busy do you think we'll be tonight?' said Susana.

'I don't care,' said Beatrix. 'Anything to get my mind off those pirates.'

'You'll soon be over that, Beatrix, but we both understand. And we love you. It was bad for all three of us. But much, much worse for you. You'll be better in a few days,' I said.

'I agree,' said Susana. She got off the bed, walked over to Beatrix and planted a kiss on each of Beatrix's cheeks.

'I'm so glad I've got you two,' said Beatrix. 'I'd be broken without you, but I'm feeling a bit better already, especially as we are talking so openly about the attack and how it affected us.' Tears began to trickle down her face. Susana gently wiped them away with the edge of a sheet and Beatrix then settled.

So we moved on to another subject. 'I suppose our journey really begins tomorrow,' said Susana.

'I'm not sure what you mean,' I said.

'Well, we've raced across land to Barcelona and come to Savona by sea. Won't we be following walking soldiers from now on? We'll be walking too, won't we?' said Susana.

'No we won't,' I said. 'The soldiers will be on foot but we'll be in wagons or carriages when we go with them to Flanders.'

'How busy will we be?' said Beatrix.

'I can't imagine that there will be much need for us while they are actually on the march. I suppose that's obvious! But who knows about when they stop. It's at night we'll be in demand. Before they go to sleep,' I said.

'You must be right,' Beatrix said.

We all cowered slightly at the sudden banging on the door, still anxious after the banging on Beatrix's door only two days before. Susana slowly opened it, her eyes wide open.

'Hello!' said Antonio de Salazar. 'A number of the lads are drinking at the bar and we wanted to know if you'd like to join us. Maybe have something to eat as well.'

'Good idea. I'd like something to drink before we start our evening's work. I don't like working on a full stomach but a little food would be nice,' said Beatrix. At least she didn't seem sorry for herself.

'Let's go then,' said Susana.

The men in the packed bar applauded and cheered as we three walked in. We smiled and waved back as we struggled through, with Antonio leading the way. We felt more like royalty than busy, young *putas*. The men showed amazing respect towards us: none of them moved a hand to touch us as we moved across the floor. We assumed that physical contact with them would come later.

Two plump barmaids, talking and laughing with the men as they did so, sloshed beer from large jugs into earthenware cups. Wasted beer flowed from the flat surface onto the floor. The bitter, oaty smell tickled my nostrils as we reached the bar.

'So what do you want to drink?' asked Antonio. 'Have what you like!'

'Just a cup of grape juice for me,' said Susana. 'Anything stronger and I'll fall flat on my face!'

'I'll have a small cup of beer,' said Beatrix. 'It'll make me relax. Like it did yesterday. And I'll be ready for work later.'

'I think I'll try some beer, too,' I said.

We pushed our way to a small table at the back of the tavern and chatted with Antonio, Felipe Sanz and Carlos Pinero de Albuquerque, all three, in their own way, heroes of that day before. They probably knew as much as anyone about what would happen on the march to Flanders so we couldn't wait to ask them.

'We'll be doing the walking, girls, and you'll be in the wagons. Of that I am sure!' said Felipe.

'What about carriages? We were in a carriage going to Barcelona. You know that. You should have seen your face when Esmeralda refused to let us go by wagon!' said Susana.

'You were lucky,' said Antonio. 'If the colonel's assistant hadn't stuck his nose in, you would have been going by wagon or not at all!'

'We'd have stayed in Madrid,' said Beatrix. 'Anyway, the wagon would never have got there at the speed we went. You'd have all been waiting there at least a fortnight until we turned up!'

'I don't see why we can't go by carriage' said Susana, quite sternly.

'I'll tell you,' I said. 'The army won't supply carriages for all... How many *putas*, did we say, Beatrix, about fifty? And there's no reason why they should treat us differently from the others. Right? Anyway, we travelled by wagon from Burgos to Aranda. And from the gypsy camp to Buitrago. So we know what it's like to go in one. Not bad as long as it's not too fast!'

'I can tell you something,' said Carlos. 'The lieutenant told me, on board the ship, that I'll be your wagon driver. I'll be taking you to Flanders. Hasn't he told you?'

'No. Not a word about it. We are so pleased!' I said, sure that I could speak for the three of us. Susana and Beatrix smiled in agreement.

'You are a strong man,' said Beatrix, casting an eye over the young man's heavy frame. He wore his hair long and loose, a well worn tunic and a leather wide-brimmed hat. He couldn't be more than three or four years older than me.

'Good to have a handsome, brave man looking after us,' said Susana.

'What else can we tell you?' said Carlos. 'Not much, I think.'

'You can tell us how much work we'll be expected to do?' said Susana.

'What do you mean? Are you afraid of how much you might have to do? You were serving me well enough when the pirates broke Beatrix's door!'

'Thank you, Carlos. And you paid me! But I want to know whether I'll be expected to work twice a day or twenty times a day or even more!'

'How would we know?' said Antonio. 'The answer to that depends on how many other *putas* there are on the road. If you are the only three...you're finished!' and he laughed loudly.

'Not funny,' said Beatrix. 'And unrealistic. None of them has got a clue.'

'I understand that,' I said. 'How would they know? As long as they get enough! That's all they want to know! I'm more interested in the food and water. How often will we get food and where will the water come from? There could be thousands of us altogether. How will the little towns on the way be able to feed us all?'

'You are with the army now. And we know how to organise supplies. You'll soon see. We order the food and drink in advance. And it's ready for us when we get there.'

'And the lodgings?' asked Beatrix.

'And the lodgings,' said Carlos.

'Sounds too good to be true,' replied Beatrix

***

We didn't know how they knew which rooms were ours but, when we returned from the bar, there was a group of about a dozen men waiting by the doors.

'You could be in for a hard time tonight,' said one of them, laughing as he did so.

'Where do you get your energy from? We did all of you lot last night,' said Susana, chuckling back at him.

***

We made an early start the following morning. Lieutenant Jorge Castillo sought us out at breakfast and told us about travelling in the wagon. He looked down at the floor as he did so, as if he was expecting an argument. When Beatrix said that that would be fine, he looked at her wide-eyed with surprise. All three of us laughed. Then he laughed too.

'You knew all along,' he said, smiling as he did so.

Once again, but now on foot, the lieutenant led the company, followed by the young flag bearer. Susana looked at him and smiled before glancing at me, still smiling.

'I know,' I said. 'A virgin then but not now!' The three of us chuckled.

Carlos's wagon and pair followed our *tercios*. Behind us, a smaller wagon contained Ana Blas and Marina de la Cueva. 'What a relief that we don't have to share with those two,' said Beatrix.

'Don't speak too soon,' I replied. 'This is the closest to them we've been so far!'

***

We crawled along the road. The horses walked so slowly they looked bored, as if they were about to fall asleep. In some ways the pace benefitted us. The three of us sat on a bench behind Carlos, in the same way Susana and I travelled behind Ion on the road to Buitrago. This ensured that, from a slight elevation, we had a good view of the passing scenery. The green of the grass on the plain between Savona and the foothills of the mountains glowed with a brightness I had not seen in Spain. We covered little more than five *leguas* in that first day and arrived at twilight in the town of Millesimo, where we all stayed the night. By then our company had grown to about one-hundred-and-forty because a number of newly recruited soldiers had joined us at Savona.

Once again, Sergeant Luis de Alvarado arrived at our feet to take us to our rooms in a tavern in the town square. Five such inns overlooked the large open area and we and our *tercios* would be occupying them but for no more than one night. You could feel the tension in the air as the sergeant also had to escort Ana Blas and Marina de la Cueva and brought them in alongside us. We hardly looked at them, let alone exchanged pleasantries. By then our soldiers understood well our need to have separate rooms, if we were to work for them that night, and we were given the choice of five rooms on the first floor.

'Well, which room would you like, Esmeralda?' asked the sergeant.

'I'll have that one, nearest the stairs please.'

'Tell me. Why are you giving her the first choice?' said Ana, staring intently at the sergeant and then transferring her glare to me.

'No special reason. Someone has to have the first choice. Thought it might as well be her.'

'I'm having the first choice and I'm having the room nearest the stairs. The one she wants,' said Ana, nodding her large head in my direction but looking the sergeant in the eye at the same time.

'Let her have it,' I said, having more to think about than arguing with these two. 'And she can have second choice, don't you think girls.' I looked towards Susana and Beatrix while putting an open hand out towards Marina.

'I'm happy with that,' said Susana.

'Me, too,' said Beatrix.

'Good we've beaten them,' said Marina.

'You haven't,' said the sergeant. 'I gave these three the first choice and I told you why. You'll get the first one another time. You are working for us; not us for you.' The sergeant looked Ana straight in the eye and spoke in an unconcerned monotone. They had to accept his decision and bowed their heads towards the floor.

We selected our rooms and went into Beatrix's.

'God, that was nasty,' said Susana.

'We don't want too much of that nonsense,' said Beatrix. 'I could get really angry with those two.'

'I agree,' I said, 'but I don't see how we can avoid it. Let's do our best to be friendly towards them and see how they react.'

***

Having to walk all day seemed to affect the soldiers' need for our services, exciting and varied though they were. Only a trickle of men found their way to our area of the first floor of the tavern. We shared them with Ana and Marina. The men themselves decided whom they wanted by standing outside of the relevant door. The sergeant must have given some indication of who of us was where. We later discovered that he had pinned up a notice, in the form of a little map, by the bar. We admired him for treating all five of us girls the same. The fact that the other two had been difficult about the choice of rooms hadn't influenced him at all.

The soldiers struggled hard for the next four days. Having enjoyed the relatively easy walk on the coastal plain from Savona, they were faced with the walking in the foothills of the Apennines. They were compensated by having more frequent stops but the lieutenant made them pay heavily by insisting on covering at least five *leguas* a day and pushing them to seven if he felt he could. Several times we felt anxious as we saw soldiers, weakened by the hard walking, stop by the roadside to rest their weary legs. The last overnight stop before Turin was the town of Moncalieri which is less than two *leguas* from the centre of the city itself.

The army had again excelled itself in making arrangements for us all to stay. For that night, and to the delight of us three girls, we and all the men slept in the magnificent, fortified old castle that presided over the town. Its sprawling construction reminded me of the Alcazar palace in Madrid, itself a military fort. While extended only decades before, the castle had a mature and weathered look which gave it a comforting grandeur. His usual polite self, Sergeant Luis de Alvarado showed us to our rooms on the fourth floor of a tower.

'I thought I'd show you to your rooms first. I didn't want a display like the other night, especially in the castle here.'

'Bless you, sergeant,' said Beatrix. 'You are really looking after us.'

'You'd better make the most of it. When we join the rest of the troops coming up from Genoa, you may find yourselves working for a different company altogether. We'll have to see.'

'We'll miss serving you men,' said Susana. 'You aren't a bad lot. I haven't had a bad experience with one of you!'

'Nor me,' said Beatrix. 'And after you saved us from those pirates we have a special relationship with you. All of you.'

'I hope you think that in the morning. We are having a big party in the great hall tonight and you may be asked to entertain us there.'

'We will want to know exactly what will be expected of us before we agree to anything. I hope I've made that clear, sergeant,' I said.

'I'll ask the lieutenant to come up and have a word with you. I hope you like these rooms.'

Sure enough, within a matter of minutes the lieutenant appeared and knocked on my door. 'I have a special request, Esmeralda.'

'Oh yes.' I kept the upper hand.

'We want to invite you to a party in the great hall of the castle.'

'Go on. Tell me what you really want us to do.'

'I'll tell you straightway, Esmeralda. I would not dream of asking you to do anything disgusting or degrading. All I want you three to do is to dress up in some men's clothing and sit at the table and eat and drink with us. I'll ask the sergeant to fit you up with some garments in good time. After the cheese course is served I want you to stand on the tables take the clothes off and walk naked up and down your table. A guitarist will be playing an accompaniment. Make a bit of fun of it. But I am asking you for nothing else. There will be five tables and a girl on each. How do you feel about that? ... By the way... I will pay you one *ducat* each, after the dinner. In fact tomorrow morning, before we leave.'

'Just wait outside. I'll ask the others.' I closed the door on him.

I soon opened it again. 'Yes, we'll do that and we'll do it with pleasure and commitment.'

'Thank you, Esmeralda. You are wonderful!'

'Just one small thing. We insist on payment in advance.'

He took a small purse from a pocket in his pantaloons and handed me three shining gold coins. 'I thought you might say that!'

Soon after, there was another, louder knock on my door. I opened it to the sergeant who stood outside smiling all over his ruddy face and next to a large basket which over brimmed with clothes. 'I think you are supposed to choose from these,' said the sergeant, with a cheeky, knowing glint in his eye.

I pushed my hands deep into the basket and lifted some of the items to my nose. 'Um... smell quite fresh.'

'We wouldn't expect you to wear a load of sweaty, dirty stuff, just taken off someone's back. I'll come back in twenty minutes or so... to see if you need more to chose from.'

**

Each of us three, along with Ana Blas and Marina de la Cueva, sat about half way along our designated table. The only *tercios* near me that I already knew were Carlos who sat next to me and the sergeant who sat opposite. The men enjoyed one beer after another, served by waitresses in white hats and full length black dresses, edged in white. The tables were soon running with beer as the women missed the cups they were attempting to pour it into and the men missed their mouths as they attempted to drink it. The smell of the beer teased my nose and it didn't take long before I asked one of the waitresses to pour a cup for me.

A separate team of smiling waitresses served the first course. They carried, on high, trays of steaming, suckling piglets and placed them at each end of the tables. The smell magnified our appetites. Then, virtually in unison, the waitresses set about smashing the tiny roasted animals with the edges of plates, which they wielded with practiced skill, while the men shouted and banged the handles of their knives on the tables. They then served the broken meat.

'More on mine, love,' said one, hitting his plate.

'Same here,' another.

'How do I survive on that,' a third.

The sound of knives and forks on plates substituted for the banter of the men as they set about eating the glistening, tender flesh, shoving it in their mouths as if this was their last supper. Indeed, for one unlucky man, it was. To a further round of drinks induced banter, the waitresses laughed as they cleared away the metal plates and returned with huge trays of local cheeses which they placed on the still wet tables.

A guitarist struck up a saraband. All five of us girls looked at each other. I thought for a moment and decided to take the lead. I went to climb up on the table. Pairs of hands came to help me. I stood there. The others appeared, standing on theirs. Then, to a heaven breaking cheer from the company, we all five of us began to take off our clothes. By an inspired coincidence, we each started with the shirt which we threw to one of the adjacent men, then the vest, thrown to another. Another huge cheer broke out as our newly exposed breasts were illuminated by the chandeliers and the candelabra on the tables. Men stood to look. Others pushed them down to get a better view themselves. Some put fingers to their lips and whistled. Others shouted our names.

Then we removed our pantaloons. The place erupted in an explosion of shouting, whistling and table banging. As instructed by the lieutenant, we paraded up and down the table top, nakedly displaying as much as reasonable, as we went. I almost slipped as I avoided a puddle of beer; almost fell as I put my foot in a plate of cheese; and staggered as I nudged into a candelabrum, almost singeing my bottom. The guitarist played on and on and on. 'When would he stop?' I wondered. 'This could go on all night.' Then he stopped. Thank God. I had had enough. So it seemed had Susana and Beatrix who both promptly climbed off their tables and, like me, sat naked in our chairs. Bless the men who threw us our clothes which we struggled into while sitting there.

The other two, Ana and Marina, continued their strutting. It was as if they had agreed a different arrangement with the lieutenant. While the five of us were displaying ourselves, the waitresses placed large plates of fruit in front of the men. Ana bent her large form over and grabbed a banana. She parted her legs and gradually pushed it into her *vava*. She bent over again and picked up another which she eased into her rear. She picked up another, peeled it and started eating it. The *tercios* were not quite sure how to react. Most laughed and cheered. Some got up and walked away. A few booed and whistled. As they did so, Marina then conducted the identical insertions.

Not to be outdone, Susana, still dressed, climbed back onto the table. She picked up a banana and looked in my direction as she dropped her pantaloons and parted her legs. Some of the men cheered anew. Others looked away. I glared at her with the look of ice. Beatrix scorned at her. Susana understood immediately. She peeled the banana, started to eat it and, with helping hands from the men around her, stood down from the table, and climbed back into her pantaloons. We three at least had preserved most of our dignity.

'I can't believe they did that,' said Beatrix as we three walked, still dressed in the men's clothing, back to our rooms.

'Nor can I,' said Susana.

'You're fooling us,' I said. 'You all but shoved one into yours!'

'No I didn't,' said Susana, 'I never intended to do more than eat it.'

I saw no point in arguing.

'The lieutenant knew what they were to do. He persuaded them to do it,' said Beatrix.

'I bet they didn't get more than a *ducat* either,' I said.

'Probably less,' said Beatrix.

None of us was surprised to see a queue of expectant men outside our cluster of rooms. Whatever we did on those tables, or didn't do, we stimulated much interest that night in the services we had on offer. None of us settled our tired body to rest much before three o'clock in the morning. Our exhaustion delivered us into a deep sleep.

***

Next morning we set out early, considering the indulgences of the night before. Our men walked at a healthy pace and around midday we crossed the city boundary of Turin. If Madrid smelt then this place stank. A mixture of human excrement, horse dung and whatever disgusting material festered in their sewer of a river, the Po. The three of us put our handkerchiefs to our noses.

'Where have you brought us, Carlos? The air cannot be breathed,' said Beatrix, scowling.

'Who would live here?' said Susana.

'I know. Just take in air through your mouths. With any luck we'll be out of the place by nightfall.'

I couldn't see that, somehow. Our company kept in order and, with us following, made its way towards the huge main square. We entered it, well behind the main body of the troops, only to be confronted by a picture of chaos, misery and squalor. Thousands of soldiers, some in uniform, some carrying pikestaffs, some muskets, some with harquebuses slung over their shoulders, formed a disorganised rabble, scattered about the square like a mob about to riot. Some were openly relieving themselves against walls, the side of buildings or just urinating where they stood. Some were making the most of the few hours of civil freedom they possessed and were frantically making love to what could have been a wife, a woman friend or a passing whore. Usually against a wall, in a corner or even, in one case, against the wheel of a wagon. Children were running around, out of control, attempting to escape from whoever was their guardian. Dogs barked, so adding to the din. Women were crying. Some in the face of a sullen soldier. Others wept on the shoulder of another woman, their mother, friend or sister. For these men were walking to war. Hundreds if not thousands would never return. Many who did would be maimed in body or mind or both.

'My God, what are we walking into?' said Beatrix.

'Can we turn around and go back?' said Susana. Surely, she couldn't mean the question.

'No,' I said. 'These soldiers are going to Flanders. We are going with them.'

Still sitting at the front of Carlos's wagon, which rocked us gently to the unevenness of the cobbles, we followed the company to the far side of the square. We climbed off and helped to form a tight group at the hands of the lieutenant who directed us to stand as near to him as possible. He stood on the back of one of the other wagons and addressed us. He shouted over the din the thousands of others there, their children and animals, were creating.

'This is what is going to happen tonight and tomorrow morning. First our ladies. Tonight you will be staying in an inn called the San Marco which is over there, just outside the square. Sergeant Luis de Alvarado will escort you. Second, my men. You will be sleeping in tents in the cathedral park which is in that direction. In the morning, you will take down the tents and pack them, ready to take them with you. There is a wagon and driver who will take them up the road to Flanders.

'In the morning, we will be joined by eighty-three new men. They will take the strength of the company up to two-hundred-and-twelve. I shall, of course command you. We will however be under the overall command of General Ambrosio Spínola, who has recruited over six-thousand troops in Italy. He will lead the march to the Spanish Netherlands. He wears no uniform but a blue plumed helmet and he rides a white horse. Do not cross his path or annoy him. If you do, you will be putting your life and that of you colleagues at risk.

'We will leave this square at nine thirty in the morning and will be the second Spanish company following the Italians. There is no flexibility and we must be assembled in rank and file and ready to leave then.

'Our three ladies, Esmeralda Pechada de Burgos, Susana de Rivera and Beatrix de Mendoza will continue serving us. They will serve the whole of the new company. To comply with the general's requirements of discretion, Esmeralda will assume the identity of a seamstress, Susana a washerwoman and Beatrix a fortune- teller. They will continue to travel in the wagon driven by *tercio* Carlos Pinero de Albuquerque.

'Any questions?' No one uttered a word. 'Company dismiss.'

Then the discussion broke out. 'Led by an Italian general? Don't we have our own anymore?' 'Behind the Italians? We should be leading them'. 'I suppose we'll have to start eating pasta', was greeted by laughter. 'Good we've got the same women. Could do a lot worse'.

While we were walking to the inn, feeling nervous about the whole idea of travelling with such a huge army, the sergeant calmly told us that General Spínola and the companies leading the army to Flanders would be departing from the square at nine o'clock sharp, a good half hour in front of our company, and half an hour before that, beginning to get ready to leave. We were surprised and upset to learn from him that we would not be travelling with the company but in the mass of people, other *putas* among them, who would be following the troops.

'How are the men supposed to protect us if we are so far behind them?' asked Susana.

'Don't worry about that, love. No one is going to harm you. And Carlos will be armed with a pistol.'

'How will we meet up with our men when we stop or at night?' I asked him.

'You'll find them easily enough, or they'll find you. Depends on where you are staying the night and where the men will be billeting.' Not very reassuring, I thought.

We discussed our work as the sergeant walked ahead of us, through the frenzy of the mob, towards our inn. 'How can we cope with over two hundred men? That's over sixty each a day. My poor *vava* will be worn out after one night!' said Susana.

'Don't be ridiculous. No one would expect us to serve every soldier in the company. Not every night,' said Beatrix.

'Beatrix is right. When you think about it, when we were at number seven we were working for every man in Madrid. Ten thousand. Maybe more. So having to work about sixty or so each should not be that bad. Because only a small number will actually want us to serve them. Your pretty *vava* will be fine!'

'You a washerwoman, Susana. Is that a step up or down? It could be promotion!' said Beatrix.

'I'll be the richest washerwoman in Flanders. Their cocks will be so clean before they enter me!'

'Maybe we'll send them all to you before they do us!' said Beatrix.

'Will you tell their fortune before or afterwards?' I asked.

'During!' said Beatrix. 'While holding their crystal balls!'

'That'll make 'em squirm!' said Susana.

'Don't leave me out! I suppose I'll be stitching their clothes! I'll make sure
they've taken everything off first!'

We all giggled at our attempts at basic wit and said our goodnights to the sergeant who left us at the door of the inn.

***

The men trickled over to the park by the cathedral to take up their tents which were allocated to them by one of the sergeants. Five were to occupy each tent. This simple military exercise was going well until a corporal and four of his men approached a tent, close to the cathedral and at the edge of the park. They entered only to see a man and a woman completely naked, about to start or just having finished making love.

'What do you lot want?' said the man.

'This is our tent,' said the corporal. 'Haven't you heard about the soldiers?'

'You're the first I've bloody heard. Get back out. And get your eyes off my woman.' She blushed and went to cover herself with a skirt.

'I'm telling you to get out,' said the corporal.

'I give in. Give us a second to get dressed and we'll go.'

By the time the men had turned to go out, and leave the two in private to dress, the man had taken a short knife from his pantaloon pocket. He dashed over to the corporal, turned him by the shoulder and shouted, 'Take that.' He then plunged the knife into the corporal's stomach. A stream of blood began to flow.

'Help me,' he said through a gurgle of redness. Then he collapsed. Two of his colleagues sprung to his aid while the other three captured and tied up the knife man. They let his shamefaced woman go. The surgeons at the local hospital worked frantically to save the corporal but, despite their efforts, he died later that evening. The city constables arrested the knife man and charged him with murder.

CHAPTER 16

Hunger

We were shocked and distraught to hear from the sergeant, later that evening, about the murder of the corporal. Susana broke into sobs. Beatrix's eyes looked upwards, as if to prevent her tears from running down her cheeks. I felt nausea in my stomach. The thought of a knife going into that man made me shiver.

'This is awful,' said Beatrix. 'I feel so sad. And helpless.'

'What will they do with the killer?' asked Susana.

'Executed by burning at the stake, just as they did to Elvira Delgado,' I said. The memory of those hideous events, not that long ago, made me quake.

'It'll serve him right,' said Susana. She started to cry again and that prompted me and Beatrix to weep.

It came as no surprise to us that the death of the corporal savagely affected the morale of the company. He was a popular family man who left a wife and three children in Madrid. He never once partook of our services. We firmly believed that it was the shock and devastation they felt over the corporal's death that deterred the men from coming to us that night. Not one man in our company wanted our services. So, for a reason which we three also found painful to bear, it was a welcomed change to go to bed for the sole purpose of sleeping. We shared in the company's grief because we felt so close to them.

***

The three of us, completely consumed by curiosity, if still numbed by the death of the corporal, planned to meet for an early breakfast and go to the square to watch the events of the morning progress. We were greeted by a scene that contrasted dramatically to what had shocked us so severely the day before. We saw no open lovemaking or tears of sadness. No celebration, no sobbing, just workmanlike progress in organising for a long journey. Men and women were chatting and laughing as they helped each other to load wagons with water barrels, food and blankets, tents and clothing. Drivers were struggling to hitch their horses to the wagons. It was as if they were fighting with their animals and neither side wanted to give in. Companies of soldiers were, under the direction of their sergeants and corporals, shuffling themselves into formation ready to join the march out of the square. Some were loading weapons on wagons, pikestaffs, harquebuses and muskets, bags labelled 'gunpowder', musket balls and shot. Even the smell differed from the day before. A slightly sweet smell of fresh horse dung permeated the air but none of us found it too unpleasant.

'Looks like they might be ready by nine o'clock,' said Susana.

'It's all so well organised,' said Beatrix. 'Everyone's working together. Seems as if they've done it all before.'

Just as she finished speaking, a fanfare sounded from a gallery above the side of the square where we had stood to listen to the lieutenant the night before. We looked up to see five gold-braided trumpeters standing there, blowing with all their might, their cheeks puffed out and red. As they sounded their final note, a shiny helmeted soldier appeared alongside them. He held a conical-shaped instrument up to his mouth and shouted into it.

'Company number seventeen move to the ready!'

A disciplined formation of about two hundred men, in rows of four, marched to the rhythm of a solitary drummer, to the corner of the square. They stopped. General Spínola appeared, his head held high and sitting astride a frisky white horse, his identity confirmed by his helmet, topped by a bright, blue plume of feathers. The general took up his position at the head of the column, lifted his right arm aloft and thrust it forward. The company followed him from the square. The second company followed the first, then the third, the fourth and so on.

Meanwhile our own company began to form itself into ranks. We were close enough to see their mournful, unhappy faces. They were all so sullen as they gathered quietly. Not many words were exchanged. Our feelings for the dead corporal and his family were reflected in the faces of the company. In other circumstances they would have been laughing joking, fooling around and teasing each other. Not that day. About half an hour after the general had led the first of the companies from the square, our men also joined the military parade. By then, we three girls had positioned ourselves close to the corner by which they were leaving. Their procession from the square, at second company behind the Italians, was a funeral cortege without the body, which the authorities had impounded in Turin. The young flag bearer had changed his banner from the company colours to black. Our men marched from the square with their heads down.

We waved as they departed and then went back to find Carlos. There were hundreds of carts and wagons to chose from, scattered randomly across the square. Hundreds of soldiers were assembling into columns, four deep ready to join the snake of troops still leaving the square. Women were loading their wagons, not only with food and water but with their children and dogs, too, in readiness to join them on the journey.

Then we went to join the throng of jostling individuals who were making their move to follow the troops. Everyone, those on foot and those in wagons and carts, wanted to be as close as they could be to the soldiers. Chaos was reborn. Wheels clattered on cobbles. Horses snorted and shook their heads violently. A dense cloud of dust enveloped us as every wagon, every person, every animal attempted a race to the corner from which the soldiers departed. I screamed out in anger at this maelstrom. Beatrix stood to get a better view. Susana swore at the top of her voice. Horses crashed into each other and wagons banged each other's sides as they funnelled towards the corner. A front wheel came off a wagon which crashed into the ground, spilling the driver onto the pebbles and emptying half the contents onto the floor. The driver of the wagon closest shouted out.

'Stop! Stop! There's a man on the ground! D'you want to kill him? Stop!'

Everyone responded. Everybody stopped. A group of ten or so men went to repair the wagon. Several women helped the shaken driver. About five minutes or so later, a chastened crowd moved carefully and slowly to the corner of the square and joined an ordered succession of vehicles and people leaving.

Carlos held the reins and cajoled the horses towards our place in the parade. Normally laughing, he too was affected by the killing of the innocent corporal. He hardly spoke on the ride out of Turin. Our feelings were the same. They contrasted so strongly with the uninhibited jollity – excepting the outrageous performance of Ana and Marina – of the night in the castle in Moncalieri. Not many words were exchanged between us three either but that didn't prevent us from admiring the view from our seat, high up at the front of the wagon, and discussing what we would be doing on this lengthy journey.

'I'm afraid,' said Susana. 'Now we are so far from our men. It must be half a *milla* or more. And this rabble we are travelling with. Wouldn't be surprised if they robbed or raped us. Or both.' She started to sob.

'For God's sake, Susana! I'm getting fed up with you. Stop feeling so sorry for yourself,' said Beatrix. 'We're all sad because of the killing but let's be sensible. Carlos has a gun. Most of this lot are women. Most of the drivers are women. They aren't going to rape us. If they tried to rob us we'd fight them off.'

'I'm with Beatrix, Susana. Let's not worry too much. Not until we've got something to worry about. I want to talk about how we handle the full company of men. Do we divide them between ourselves or make all of us three available to all of them?'

'No. We let them chose between us. That way they can experience the charms of each of us. They won't want to be doing the same one every the time. Otherwise, they'd feel like they were married!' said Beatrix. The three of us laughed.

'What are you three chuckling at?' asked Carlos, by then a little less mournful and turning to speak to us.

'Just keep your eye on the road,' said Beatrix. We broke out into mirth again and rocked from side to side on our bench seat.

'What do you think Susana? Do you agree with Beatrix?'

'I'm not sure. At least if we had a smaller number each we'd get to know them better and know what kind of thing they wanted.'

'Yes, but we are here to give them as much pleasure as we can. And variety is part of that.'

'All right. Let's do it then,' said Susana. So we all agreed.

'I've got two more thoughts,' I said. 'First, I think we should learn the names of all our men.'

'That'll fill my brain up!' said Susana.

'That's going to be a big job,' said Beatrix. 'But I see advantages.'

'I have an aim, a challenge. It is to give the best possible service we can. And that must include getting to know every one of our men. By name.'

We agreed. That's what we would do. And we would do it with total commitment.

'My second thought is about how the men know us. How they recognise us. Especially the new men, the ones who joined our company today. We need to wear something they will immediately recognise. Let's buy some ribbon next town we stop in. We'd wear it around our necks and get the lieutenant to announce to the men what we are doing.'

'You are a genius, Esmeralda. Great idea. We love you!' said Beatrix, turning to kiss me on the cheek.

'I agree,' said Susana. 'I'll wear mine. It should be pink. The same colour as ... well, you know!'

'Trust you to think of that!' said Beatrix, smiling broadly.

'Pink it is then!' I laughed.

**

It was beginning to get dark and drizzling with rain as we pulled into the little town of Avigliana, not five *leguas* out of Turin. So although not good, progress along the road had not been too bad, considering the chaotic start we had made in joining the procession in the city. No one, except Carlos, seemed to know where we were supposed to go. He took us to the centre and then off towards a large lake to the north. For the first time in the whole of the sojourn, we found ourselves at the door of a large private house.

'We're not staying in there are we?' I asked.

'Yes, Esmeralda, we are. The soldiers ahead of us are camping by the side of the road, about half a *legua* away.'

'How are we supposed to serve them here?'

'You won't. Have a rest tonight.'

'That's two nights in a row with no work,' said Susana. 'How are we supposed to survive?'

'There'll be work tomorrow night, but not here. We'll be stopping at the Abbey of Novelesa. You'll like it there.'

***

We were woken up by a sharp banging on the bedroom door at five o'clock in the morning. It was still dark. I slid out of my side of the bed towards the floor, fearing I might have to hide to protect myself, only to recognise Carlos's voice, instructing the three of us to get up and dressed. He said we had a long journey to the Abbey that day and that the troops were already on the march.

It was drizzling again but Carlos seemed much more cheerful than the day before. He smiled a lot and laughed with us at some of the sights on the road. A plump woman carried a child under one arm and a small, screaming child under the other. A running child overtook our wagon. Ten *varas* behind him, a tall, thin woman in a blue dress and white, floppy hat followed in pursuit, waving a cane and shouting for him to stop. Moments later, we could see the woman beating him as he lay writhing on the ground and laughing at her.

'We'll have to speed up if we're going to reach Novelesa tonight,' said Carlos, turning around to tell us. 'I'm going to speed up a bit so hang on tight. We'll be overtaking a lot of this stuff in front.' He snapped at the reins and shouted at the mares. Suddenly, we were trotting past the varied wagons in this chaotic caravan and eventually made our way to the tail end of the military procession, which comprised a company of Spaniards which joined the march in Genoa.

'We can't overtake the soldiers,' said Carlos.

'Why not?' asked Beatrix. 'They're only walking.'

'There's an unwritten rule when you are riding with the army. You don't let the tail get ahead of the dog.'

'I don't understand,' said Susana. I looked at her, then at Beatrix.

'The soldiers set the pace, not the army followers. So we have to stay back, even if we're on the wagons,' explained Carlos.

We reached the abbey at Novalesa, just as twilight began slowly to envelop us. The rain had stopped some hours before and the abbey stood majestically against the low sun. It overlooked the valley which led down to the little town of Susa in which we had stopped briefly for refreshment and to buy pink ribbon before letting the horses tackle the incline to the abbey.

'I don't understand this,' said Beatrix, leaning out of the front of the wagon to speak to Carlos. 'There are eight thousand troops in this army. Surely they're not all staying here.'

'No. About six hundred are staying in the abbey. Our company and two others, all Spaniards. About another fifteen hundred are billeting in houses in Susa and the rest are doing a night march to the next town. They'll rest there. Then take to the road to get ahead of us. This is where over the next five or six days the Italians go forward and we hold back. We'll be two nights at the abbey.'

'Why didn't we stay in Turin for a couple of days and let the army leave ahead of us?' I said.

'Partly tactics and partly cost. We don't stay longer than necessary in Turin. It's too expensive. And it's a better show of strength if all the troops leave the city in one big procession. It's much cheaper to stay at the monastery. We've known the monks for years. They love us and will love you.'

'O God,' I thought, remembering my previous encounter with a man of the cloth. 'I wonder what that means.'

We followed the troops through the huge, wooden gates of the abbey. A dozen or so Benedictine monks in black habits with their cowls down on their shoulders stood there, their hands outstretched before them. They smiled and waved to welcome our ordered throng. The gates opened into a huge courtyard where the *tercios*, who had reached the abbey before us, were forming a queue to enter the main entrance to the abbey itself. There must have been at least a hundred of them, probably more. They were talking to each other, joking and exchanging stories, presumably about their journey thus far. Their cheerfulness showed that, although they could not have forgotten about the murder of the corporal, it was at least far enough back in their minds to enable a degree of jollity and abandon.

Sergeant Luis de Alvarado must have recognised our wagon as it came to halt in the square and he came over to see us. 'Welcome to the Abbey of Novalesa, ladies. Has Carlos told you that we'll be staying here for two nights? You will be relaxing tomorrow. Maybe a chance to look around the abbey grounds. We'll see.'

'Good evening, sergeant,' I said. 'I take it that we'll be entertaining our company tonight.' I laid the stress on 'our'.

'Yes, Esmeralda. Our company and ours alone. I'll take you to the rooms we've allocated for you. As you will expect, one room each.'

Beatrix grinned and replied. 'You understand well what we working girls need!'

'I'm going to take you into the abbey via a side entrance. I don't want you to have to squeeze past all these men.' A thoughtful, if unnecessary, gesture.

We walked past the crowd of soldiers still outside of the abbey and followed the sergeant. Naturally, we recognised many in our company but there were many unfamiliar faces amongst them, in particular, the eighty or so who had joined in Turin.

As we were about to enter the abbey, my eyes fell upon the eyes of a man I felt sure I recognised from our earlier travels on our journey from Burgos to Madrid. His hatchet-shaped side whiskers half confirmed my suspicions but the large earrings had gone. My heart leapt a beat. I said nothing and looked away, wondering if the young man was whom I thought he was and whether he might have recognised me.

The sergeant showed us into our rooms and left. I then knocked on Susana's door and went in. 'Did you recognise any of the new intake of soldiers?' I blurted out the words.

'Yes. The gypsy, Ion. I'm sure it's him.'

I rushed up to Susana and hugged her. I still don't know why. But that's what the emotion of seeing Ion forced me to do. 'Had we changed our names by then, Esmeralda? I don't remember. I'm not sure that we had.'

Beatrix had heard our excited and rapid talking and came in to see what it was about.

'We've seen a soldier we recognise,' said Susana.

'I should think so,' said Beatrix. 'We've bedded nearly all of them.'

'No,' I said. 'One of the new ones that joined us in Turin.'

'How could you? You've never seen them before! You must have made a mistake.'

'No. We are certain. It's a gypsy who gave us a lift on his wagon when we were on our way to Madrid.'

Between us, we explained to Beatrix how we met Ion at the gypsy camp where we had our fortunes told and that he had taken us from the camp at Buitrago and driven us towards Madrid. We explained the horrors of the kidnap and how the kidnappers forced him to go back to the camp and await a ransom demand.

'That's incredible,' said Beatrix. 'But how can you be so sure?'

'He had these wonderful axe-shaped side whiskers... They went right into his moustache. He hasn't changed a bit,' said Susana.

'You're right but he's no longer wearing those big earrings,' I said.

'That's the army,' said Beatrix. 'They made him take them off.'

'Could be,' said Susana.

'What are we going to do about him,' I asked. 'I'm just thinking out loud. I suppose we treat him like any other customer but we can't because we know him.'

'You will have to give him full access to your bodies, in the same way as any other customer,' said Beatrix. 'But there's no reason why you can't be friendly and let him know you recognise him.'

'I agree,' said Susana. 'But I think he will be shocked to find out what profession we have ended up in. I feel just a bit ashamed.'

'No need,' I said. 'I've done quite a bit of thinking about that. I feel proud to be a *puta*. Why not? We aren't thieves. We are doing a service. And we're doing it well!'

***

Once again, we dined with the soldiers. It was a much more demure occasion than the banquet at Moncalieri. We were not asked to perform any special acts for the troops so we simply used the occasion to talk to them over the relatively modest meal which the monks cooked for us in their kitchen. Ana Blas and Marina de Cuenca were sitting next to each other on an adjacent table and seemed deliberately to ignore our presence. The three of us sat together, with me on one side of the table and the other two opposite.

'I can't see Ion. Can you?' said Susana.

I stood up and looked around the huge room. At least four hundred soldiers had been crammed next to each other on benches along the length of dozens of bare wooden tables. They were tucking into boiled ham, roughly cut pieces of bread, artichokes and cups of wine or beer. The whole place bubbled with chatter and laughter. I could smell the fresh, hot meat on my own plate and would enjoy a few sips of the wine. For one thing, it would help me to slip into the mood for work. A number of the *tercios* cheered as I stood, maybe in the hope and expectation that I would, with the others, climb onto the table and take off my clothes, as we had at Moncalieri. I spent a full minute, maybe more casting my eye along the length of each of these tables but could see not a sign of Ion. Some booed with disappointment as I sat down again.

'He isn't here.'

'I don't believe it,' said Susana.

'Stand and have a look for yourself.'

'Climb up and start undressing. You'll see every face in the hall then,' giggled Beatrix.

'No. Not me. I'll accept Esmeralda's word. But where can he be?'

'We'll find out sooner or later,' I said.

***

Sooner, in fact. We left the troops chatting and swilling wine and beer and went up to our rooms. We had been chatting in Beatrix's room for about five minutes when we heard mutterings outside: a queue of about ten of our men waiting to be served. We welcomed them, individually of course, and launched into an evening of fairly easy work. We were interested in seeing how the new intake of men behaved towards us and whether they wanted anything different from usual. A number thanked us for wearing the pink ribbons around our necks. My fourth man that night stood silently in the doorway for a second or two, before entering the room. I could hardly see him against the flickering wall lights outside in the corridor but those same lights enabled him to see me. I laid on my bed, incompletely dressed.

He then spoke. 'I recognise you, don't I?'

As soon as he uttered these words I knew him.

'Are you María or Esmeralda or both,' he laughed.

'Don't say you don't know,' I chuckled, standing to kiss his cheek.

'Well, you found a job in Madrid all right! And so did Lucía. Or is she Susana? See, I remember the two of you!'

'How could you forget?' The raillery continued.

'Weren't you hungry tonight?'

'I'll get to that.'

'Here we are then. Would you like...' I said, sliding back on the bed.

'Just a minute... Surely, there are other things to say. Questions to answer?'

'No harm in just talking!'

'Is talking free or do I have to pay?'

'For you, señor, no charge. I owe you a favour! Maybe more than one!'

'For chatting or doing?'

'Both!'

'Such generosity!'

'Where do we start?'

'I'll start by asking you! So how did you two become *putas*?'

I told him the story from being dropped off in Madrid by the kidnappers, something he said he knew about, to working for the alchemist he had met on one of his missions to Madrid, to the alchemist's girlfriend, to the party at the army barracks and to our journey across the sea to here.

'How did you know they left us in Madrid?'

'They panicked when we didn't pay. They lost their nerve. They didn't dare harm you for fear of us doing the same, if not worse, to them. You could have been in danger if they just left you by the road. So they decided, against their wishes we think, to take you to where you wanted to go: Madrid. It wasn't that far!'

'How could you have known they'd taken us there?'

'We followed them.'

'You could have got us killed!'

'They didn't know we were there!'

'We wondered why they didn't kill us! They appeared to be so kind!'

'They had to be. Otherwise, they'd have had us to deal with!'

'You could be right, I suppose. I'll explain it to Susana. And what about you? A handsome fellow like you has left a beautiful woman to wait for your return?'

'Not for me, Esmeralda. I do not have a lady friend. Not long ago, I thought I was in love. But I couldn't make her love me. So that all ended. She was the most beautiful girl. Made me sad but that is past now.' He chuckled again.

'And why weren't you at the dinner?'

His whole countenance changed. The laughing sparkle vanished from his face to be replaced by a frowning grimace. 'These soldiers hate gypsies.'

'Does it matter? They can think what they like.'

'Yes. It does matter because they show it by doing things. The men around me were kicking my heels, punching my side and calling me "*gitano*"' all the way from Turin to Avigliana. So then I found a different place in the march to here. But that lot were even worse. Got jabbed by a pikestaff and poked in the neck by an harquebus. It could have blown my head off.'

'I'm disgusted. What a way to treat you,' I said and put my arm around his shoulder.

'So, I decided not to eat with them. By luck, the men in the queue outside your room left me alone. I suppose they were thinking of what you would be doing with them. Otherwise, I would not have made it to you.'

'I think I have the answer. Let us know which ones are annoying you and we'll refuse them.'

'That could make it worse. They'd kill me if I was to blame for you not serving them.'

'I'll talk to the others. I'm sure there's something we can do. Or not do, whatever is the case!'

Ion laughed. 'I can defend myself well. But I don't want trouble.'

At the end of this discussion, he told me he had taken enough of my time but asked if I might serve him on a later occasion. I smiled as I said it would be a pleasure. He kissed me and left me to my next customer.

***

Little did the three of us realise that the two nights at the abbey at Novalesa was to be the most difficult period in our careers as *putas*, well, at least up to then. We thought it must be because our men were resting and had little else to occupy themselves, other than walk the grounds of the abbey, which by all accounts were spectacular. So they steadfastly availed themselves of the services we had on offer. All three of us worked until past two o'clock in the morning of our first night there to clear the queue of hopefuls outside our door. Daylight proved an even better opportunity for them. Maybe by daylight they could see more of what we used to entertain them. So we laboured and laboured during the day and had barely time for meals. We all but created a minor skirmish when we decided on our first night there to leave about fifteen outside on the landing to go for our dinner. And we worked just as hard, if not harder, the second night.

We were, of course, paid handsomely for all this activity. The three of us compared accounts as we left the abbey and worked out that since leaving Madrid and hardly having started our journey from Turin to Brussels, we had each earned in excess of fifty *ducats*. A small fortune, more than a farmer would earn in six months. This did not even include our three *reales* a day allowance, just for being there. We deposited it all with the army cashier, represented in our company by a certain Sergeant Pascual Yañez, who duly filled in our bank books every time we made a payment in, regularly joking that he would use the cash to pay the troops who would use it again to pay for our delights. So not only were we serving the troops, we were helping the King, by lending him our money to pay them! Just as Antonio had explained before we accepted these jobs.

Then came the hardest stages of this journey: the march around the Alps. The road became gradually narrower and the hills became steeper. At the little town of Modane, in Savoy, we were stunned to see, for the first time, the snow covered peaks of the mountains.

'Look at that snow, Susana,' Beatrix said. 'Have you seen anything like it before?'

'Never! And it is so white, whiter than a washed bed sheet. It looks like the mountains have scraped it straight from the sky. We don't have to go up that high, do we?'

'No, Susana,' I said. 'The idea is to walk around the Alps not over them!'

We were compelled to abandon the wagons. Our choice was simple: walk or ride a mule.

'Why can't we stay on the wagon? The roads aren't that bad,' said Susana. 'Anyway, what will we ride on when we reach the other side of the mountains when we've left the wagons here?'

'There is a fleet of wagons waiting in Annecy. We pick them up again there, about thirty *leguas* from here,' said Carlos. 'And I'll be escorting you all the way.'

'You'll have to show me how to ride a mule,' said Beatrix.

'Yes, me too!' said Susana in resignation.

'That's my choice, too, but I may want to do some walking,' I said, showing some willingness to be flexible.

So we took to the mules, as did virtually everybody else following the army. There must have been a thousand of us riding them, probably more, but we could see only what fell before our eyes and not the whole of this mule train travelling in its sections, led by six thousand Italians. Somehow we managed this difficult route. That presented no real problem, but we thought we would die of another.

***

The name Maurienne is burnt into my mind. St Michel-de-Maurienne and St Jean-de-Maurienne. St Jean was a painful two days from Modane. We arrived there sore and exhausted. Poor Susana had not by then mastered riding a mule so was even more tired than Beatrix or me. The three of us and Carlos stayed at a small coach house, right alongside the main road through the town. Our company billeted in houses. Just about everyone in the town took in some of our men. We settled into our separate rooms, expecting to work that night, before we went down for an early dinner.

The problem then became clear. The inn had no food. Not a corner of a cheese, not a scrap of meat, not a single fish, not even a crust of bread. Nothing.

The origin of the problem was glaring incompetence. We discovered a few days later that the coordinating administrator hadn't informed the local officials in St Michel-de-Maurienne or St Jean-de-Maurienne that the army would be organised in three tranches, passing through these towns over a period of three days. By the time the second tranche arrived, virtually all the food had been eaten by the first and no arrangements had been put in place to feed the second or third or, consequently, us camp followers. So we ate nothing that night and nor did the troops.

'When will we be fed?' Susana asked Carlos.

'I wish I could tell you. This is not good. There can be no food in the town... otherwise they would have to give it to us.'

'We'll have a meal tomorrow, I'm sure,' I said, more in hope than certainty.

Missing a meal that day hardly seemed to bother us. Our minds were taken from the lack of food by the intense night of work we had to perform for our men who, we supposed, used our services to distract them from their modest hunger. The next stop was St Jean-de-Maurienne. A second night without food.

'This has all gone badly wrong,' I said to Carlos.

'I know. I've never known anything like it before. Sometimes they don't have enough food to go round but to have no food...Well, that's bad.'

'Is there nothing we can do? Poor Susana is feeling weak. I am coping quite well and so is Beatrix. But we can't go on like this for much longer.'

'If there's no food for the troops, there won't be food for anyone. The commanders won't accept this and they will be doing something about it. I hope!'

Our next stop after St Jean-de-Maurienne was a small hamlet about half way to Aiguebelle. No food there either. The situation was becoming unbearable.

'I can't stand much more of this,' said Susana. 'My stomach is hurting. I feel I could pass out. I can hardly stay on the mule.'

'Me too,' said Beatrix. 'It's a disgrace treating us like this. I'm losing weight. I can feel my ribs sticking out.'

'Yes, I'm about the same. I don't feel like working but we'll just have to get on with it. I spoke to one of the other women this morning. They are worried about their children. At least there's plenty of water.'

Our men were suffering, as well. The number who came to us that night was much smaller. Their raging stomachs took priority over their other needs. One of my evening customers was Ion whom I had not seen since our re-acquaintance three nights before.

'Just hold on, Esmeralda. I think I have the answer. Tell the others. I know that there is a gypsy encampment right here. Not half a *legua* from this village. I'm going there tonight to get some food. They're sure to let me have some.'

'How will you find them? It's night out there!'

'Yes, and a clear sky and half moon. I'll find them all right. I'll knock on your door when I get back. It'll be about one in the morning.' Then he went.

I had to tell the others as soon as I could. I waited outside their rooms. Each was dealing with a customer. I could hear their rhythmic stirrings. I told the few men in the queue that they would have to wait a moment because I had to tell them something.

'What is it, Esmeralda? There are men waiting for service,' said Beatrix, looking angry and drawn at the same time.

'Ion is getting us some food tonight. From a gypsy camp up the road. He's coming back at one o'clock!' In my excitement, I could hardly blurt out the words.

'I don't believe you,' shrieked Susana. 'I'm starving to death. I can hardly work at all.'

'You're not fooling us, are you,' said Beatrix.

'Definitely not. He's coming straight here when he gets back.'

True to his word, Ion arrived not long after midnight. By then the three of us were waiting in my room.

'Got some,' he said. 'Some bread, meat, cheese and some grapes. Enough for now and some to see you through tomorrow!' he said, smiling triumphantly all over his face but shivering with cold.

'I love you,' said Susana, sounding as if she meant it.

'Great,' said Beatrix.

'You are brilliant,' I said. 'But what about the children? We'd feel bad eating before them.'

'Don't worry. I spoke to the gypsy chief. He is going to take as much food as he can to the roadside tomorrow. There will be enough to stave off the hunger for a day, but not much more. They will raid their food store first thing in the morning.'

We were ravenous and filled our mouths, trying to talk to Ion and to each other at the same time.

'God, this is good,' said Susana, laughing. 'I would have been dead of starvation by the morning.'

'I too,' said Beatrix.

'How can we reward you?' I asked Ion.

'I think you have a pretty good idea. But I didn't get you food for that! You can warm me up!'

'Come here,' I said, laughing. 'Take your *pantalones* off.' He did so and cuddled into the heat of my nakedness. I made love to him on my bed while the others looked on.

'That's the first time I've done that,' said Beatrix. 'We never stay in the room while the other is serving. It's against our rules!' She laughed and so did the rest of us.

CHAPTER 17

Sickness

We were taken completely by surprise at dinner that night. About half our company had been allocated rooms in a large inn near the centre of Aiguebelle, a small town in Savoy, to the east of Chambéry. Sergeant Luis de Alvarado banged an empty wine pitcher on the table and shouted out: 'Pray silence for General Spínola!'

The general, wearing an elaborate, embroidered tunic entered the room. He stood at the top table where the sergeants and corporals were dining. The whole company stood so we did, too.

'Please be seated ladies and gentlemen.' So he recognised our presence. 'I have ridden back from the head of our marching army with a message to you all. You have endured great hardship during the past three days. Not only have you suffered the difficult terrain here in the western Alps. You have been inflicted with unbearable hunger. You have borne that hunger with great resilience and I applaud you for doing so.

'Praise though you richly deserve, I have not come to praise you. I am here to apologise. I am to blame for your hunger. I failed to check that the arrangements for your victuals were properly in place. I am deeply, deeply sorry,' he said, bowing his head.

'What I can say with total certainty is that nothing like this will happen again. I have sent an advance party of officers ahead of us. They will ensure that the authorities in each town, through which we will be passing, not only know about our passage, but have more than enough to feed us all, including the many of you who are not troops but who are with us to perform a variety of other functions.

'Please indulge yourselves. I invite you to enjoy a drink, at my expense, tonight and the next four. God save the King!'

This was the first time that we had had any contact with the general. He seemed strong, almost to the point of arrogance, when he directed the troops from the square in Turin. But here was a more human, softer manifestation. He showed himself to be a humble, likeable man, a man who meant it when he said he was sorry, 'deeply, deeply sorry', and not too proud to say so. He could have blamed another. Some anonymous army functionary, some local official, even some faceless soul in Madrid. But no, he blamed himself, even when another individual in or outside of his command was culpable. I suddenly became enchanted by this man and proud to serve his army in one of 'a variety of other functions'. I wondered if I would see him at such close quarters again.

'What did you think of the general?' asked Beatrix, once we were back in my room.

'After that speech, I admire him. I think he is a great yet humble man. There hardly seems a violent bone in his body. Of course, someone else was to blame. Someone who didn't do their job. But he is ultimately responsible and expressed his true regret,' I said.

'He'll hang who was responsible,' said Beatrix.

'Yes, he didn't mean a word he said,' added Susana.

'I just can't agree with either of you. Why come all the way back here to apologise, if he blamed someone else? Why take the blame in such a humble way if he was to punish someone else? He won't do that. If he did, everyone would see what a liar he was. His name would be wrapped in rags, destroyed. And he'd have brought it on himself. So I don't agree with you!'

'The best thing he said was that it would never happen again,' said Beatrix, moving away from the question of his character.

'Didn't he get a cheer from the men when he announced free drinks for five nights? That'll cost him a fortune,' said Susana, following along behind Beatrix. I felt as if I had won my argument, by default if nothing else. Still, we three were good friends and no minor disagreement was about to change that.

***

We were almost at the end of our traverse through the western Alps when we stayed in the ancient town of Coflan, high up on a ridge overlooking the road to Annecy. We stayed in the old Red House. As expected we ate well there and our company took major advantage of the general's offer of drinks on his account. The men, influenced by the excess of drink, felt more than able to use our prodigious services. Alas, their performance lacked its usual vigour and most failed to enable themselves for love. One half drunken soldier was sick in Susana's bed and urinated on her floor. The three of us joked and giggled as we cleared up the mess.

The beautiful town of Annecy, situated at the head of its magnificent lake, signalled our completion of the Alpine phase of this incredible journey. As anticipated, we dismounted our mules and took to wagons for what we expected to be the remainder of this marathon. From this pretty town we journeyed through the lowlands of the Rhone and reached another place we loved, Nantua, with its sloping-floored church overlooking the square and river.

As Beatrix dismounted from the carriage, outside our inn, she fell from the step onto the ground with a deathly, sickening thud. She seemed to land on her bottom but not symmetrically and took the greater part of her fall on her left side.

'Don't worry,' she said. 'I'll be all right.'

'Just you take care,' said Susana. 'That was a bad fall. You must have dropped four *pies* before you hit the ground and you fell so awkwardly.'

She staggered up from the ground and brushed herself down, not that there was much dirt on her anyway, but more as an expected reaction to this quite bad fall. Everything seemed fine. We had dinner where we were staying and started work shortly afterwards. Antonio de Salazar was Beatrix's fourth customer that night. He came out of Beatrix's room shouting for help.

'Come quickly, Esmeralda. Beatrix is bleeding badly. I've made her bleed and she's passed out!'

I was resting on my bed alone at that time and dashed immediately to Beatrix's room. She was lying lifeless on the bed, bleeding badly from the vagina.

'What happened, Antonio? She was fine a half an hour ago.'

'I was on top of her. I was taking all my weight with my shoulders and she suddenly yelled out, "Stop, Antonio. Something's gone wrong. It's hurting me badly. Get off me. Quick."'

'Then what?'

'I got off and could see the blood. "God", I said, "See what I've done!" She looked down, saw the blood and passed out. What have I done to her, Esmeralda? What have I done?'

Beatrix looked pale and was trickling blood. She was motionless on the bed, resting on a red stain, about ten *pulgadas* wide. I went up to her and listened by her nose and mouth. She was breathing but slowly and in shallow breaths. I stroked her forehead and quietly said her name. 'Beatrix, Beatrix, come round. Wake up. Don't sleep! You must wake up.'

She failed to stir so I shook her gently. She opened her eyes. What a relief. 'What's happened? I don't feel well.'

'I don't think you are well, Beatrix. It could be to do with your fall. You are bleeding from the *vava*. I don't think it's your monthly.'

'No. I'm not due for two...' She drifted off into a faint again.

Susana appeared in Beatrix's room. 'What's the matter? What's happening to Beatrix?'

'She started to bleed while Antonio was making love to her. It's not her monthly bleed. It won't stop. It's something to do with that fall. I'm sure.'

Antonio stayed by the door, too worried about Beatrix to go and looking as if he had accidentally killed someone. 'Does she need a doctor?' he asked. 'I'll get one.'

'Be quick,' I said. 'She's still losing blood. And tell him she fell out of the carriage.'

We waited anxiously. Beatrix drifted in and out of consciousness, muttering incoherently about her Italian mother and the uncle who had sold her to the brothel. Susana looked frightened of what might happen to our friend. Meanwhile, a number of customers appeared on the landing, hoping to be served. I explained that we could not help them that night because of Beatrix. We had to admire them for their patience and understanding. About an hour after he went, Antonio appeared with a doctor, a portly, grey haired man wearing a white wig and a black tailed, coat. He carried a leather bag, presumably containing medication or instruments. We showed him straight into Beatrix's room.

'She shouldn't be lying down like this. She should have something underneath her posterior, to keep it up. Get some pillows and some warm water,' he said gruffly.

Susana dashed off for some warm water and I went quickly to my room to get some pillows.

'Will she be alright, doctor?' said Antonio.

'I don't know yet. I'll have to examine her.'

Beatrix was hardly conscious and breathing weakly. 'I'm going to put something under her nose which will make her sleepy. But I need to wake her up first.' He took off his coat then looked in his bag and pulled out a packet which he opened under Beatrix's nose. 'Breath in deeply, young lady. I must have you awake before I do anything else.'

'What a horrible smell,' said Beatrix, coming to. 'Take it away.'

'I'm going to give you something to make you sleepy. Don't worry. You'll soon wake up again.'

He took a jar from inside his bag, uncorked it and took out a sponge. 'Put a little hot water on that,' he told Susana. 'Now get out of the room,' he said, glaring at Antonio who left immediately.

He placed the sponge right up to Beatrix's nose and asked her to take deep breaths. Within a matter of moments her head rolled to one side and she was unconscious. 'I want you two to help me,' he said. 'I want you to help me turn her around so that you can open her legs wide. I need to look inside her.'

All three of us gently eased Beatrix around the bed and the two of us girls held her legs wide apart. The doctor opened his bag again and took out the most frightening object I had ever seen. The instrument looked as if it was made of brass. It had six legs and looked like a large metal spider.

And we three were afraid of spiders. The feet were all closed together and joined by levers to a wide screw-like mechanism. 'This is called a dioptra,' said the doctor, as he carefully inserted the spider's legs inside her. He then turned the screw which projected from the end. The legs gradually opened up as did Beatrix's vagina. It took many turns of the screw to open her sufficiently for the doctor to see right inside. 'Give me that towel,' he directed, sternly and without emotion. I gave him the towel. He took a corner and placed it into Beatrix to soak up the blood.

'That's better,' he said. 'Give me that lamp.' I handed him the oil lamp standing on the chest of drawers.

'Um... not sure.' He took another corner of the towel, and wiped her again. 'Yes, she is bleeding high up. There is a tear near her cervix. She must have twisted herself badly when she fell. And serving these men would have made it worse... a lot worse.'

'Will she be all right, doctor?' I said, feeling hollow in my stomach.

'She's not bleeding too badly now. She's weak because she's lost blood. I'm going to put a swab inside her, on the wound. I'll fix a piece of string to the swab so you or she can pull it out in a few days, when the bleeding has stopped completely. Her natural fluids will flush out any remaining debris,' he said with professional authority. 'Give her plenty to drink. She won't be able to work for at least a week.'

'When will she come round?' I asked.

'Any minute now.'

'One thing I need to tell you, doctor. We will be leaving Nantua tomorrow to travel north. We'll be in a wagon.'

'She should be able to manage that. Just about. Keep her feet up high and make her lie down on blankets. That is essential,' he said, emphasising the 'essential'.

The doctor picked up the blood stained, spider-like instrument and wrapped it in a clean cloth he took from his bag. At that moment, Beatrix came to. 'Where am I? What's he doing here?'

'I'm a doctor. I've stopped your haemorrhage, I hope. Take extreme care when you move. You must see another doctor if it starts again.'

'Thank you, doctor,' I said, as he stepped from the room.

Antonio was waiting outside and came in to see us, still concerned at what he might have done to cause Beatrix her injury. 'Beatrix, I'm so glad you're better. I was worried.' He leant over the bed and kissed her tenderly on the cheek. He looked pale and humbled. 'I think I owe you this,' he said, then half breaking into a smile, and placing a silver *real* in her hand.

That night, after we had settled Beatrix in her bed, Susana and I walked over to the tavern in which Sergeant Luis de Alvarado was staying and asked to see him. We explained what had happened to Beatrix and told him she would not be able to work until she was fully recovered.

'Don't worry. We'll look after her.'

He was truer to what he said than any of us expected. After Beatrix had eaten her breakfast in bed, eight of our *tercios*, including Antonio, appeared outside our room with an army stretcher. Four of them lifted her bodily from her bed and placed her on the stretcher as the other four held it steady. Then, keeping her as horizontal as they could, carried her down the stairs and outside onto our wagon. From somewhere, they had made up a double bed in the back of the wagon and eased her gently from the stretcher onto a mound of blankets in the middle of it.

'I didn't expect this!' said Beatrix, softly, as if still very weak.

'Nor did we,' said Susana.

***

Carlos took great efforts to make the following days on the wagon as comfortable as possible. He dodged the potholes, avoided the ruts and steered around the stones and other debris. Our horses seemed, in their own way, to want to ease the way for their sick passenger. At least the perilous Alpine slopes and narrow tracks were behind us, as was the necessity to ride on mule back. The sad fact was that Beatrix was still seriously unwell. While her haemorrhaging had all but stopped she had lost much blood and looked pale because of it. She did her best to sleep, despite the unavoidable swaying and lurching of the wagon.

'I'm still worried about Beatrix,' said Susana as we pulled out of the village of Thoirette.

'All we can do is to keep her warm, rested and drinking plenty of water. She'll be fine as long as she doesn't start haemorrhaging again,' I said, mainly to comfort Susana. I was only too aware of Beatrix's fragile condition. I remembered well the case of a street *puta* who was found dead off the Calle Atocha. She had fallen off a customer's horse, got up and started work straightaway in a doorway. No one knew how many men she had served but the last one left her there. In a pool of her own blood. There were no signs of violence and it became clear that she died of a vaginal haemorrhage. Between us, we had to prevent that happening to Beatrix but not everything was in our control.

She seemed to recovering well but slowly. We spent frantically busy nights in the hamlets of Arinthod and Orgelet, naturally without her help.

'I don't know how we are going to manage all these men without Beatrix doing her share,' said Susana ruefully, while we were on the road to the next town. 'Now we are away from the Alps the men are more active. I lost count of how many I did last night.'

'Unless she can help out soon, we may need an assistant,' I said. 'I'll have a word with the sergeant when we reach Champagnole.'

I was not surprised that the sergeant showed great sympathy with our plight. After all, he regularly sought our services and, apart from anything else, did not want to be disappointed by our lack of availability. Neither did he want to appear inflexible to his men.

'Let's wait until we reach Besançon,' he said. 'If she is not ready to start work again by then, we will try to engage another to help you.'

Beatrix was in a dreadful state when she woke that morning in Champagnole. This normally fiery and cheerful woman staggered into my room crying and clutching a towel between her legs. 'It's started again, Esmeralda. Would you mind having a look? I don't know what to do.'

I felt that everything was going too well, even if progress was slow. 'Lie down on my bed and open your legs. We'll soon see.' I was shocked to see a mass of blood in her pubic hair.

'Yes, you are bleeding again, but it is only slight. Just a little trickle. Maybe it started when you turned over in bed. There is a lot on your hair but only a tiny drop coming out of you. Go back and lie on your bed with your bottom under a pillow. I'll get a doctor, just in case. And I'll get Susana to come and sit with you.'

I went down stairs to the dining room to see if I could find Antonio. He was sitting in a corner with some friends, joking over some fried eggs and bread for breakfast. I dashed over to him.

'Beatrix is bleeding again. It's not as bad but I think we need a doctor.'

He peered around the room. His anxious eye stopped on another group, at the adjacent corner. There were three men drinking coffee and looking stern.

'See those men', he said nodding in their direction. 'The one nearest the door is an army doctor. He'll probably want to check you girls in a day or two, anyway. Come with me.'

We quickly went over to the men. 'Excuse me,' said Antonio, his eyes wide with worry, and looking straight at the man he believed was the doctor. 'I believe you are one of our army medics, señor. Is that so?'

'Yes. I am. Why do you ask?'

'This lady here is one of the women serving us troops.' In accordance with the wishes of the general, he declined to mention the exact capacity. 'Her colleague has been suffering from a haemorrhage which stopped but has started again. Could you please examine her? She is in a bedroom upstairs.'

'I'll come now.' He picked up a cup and swigged the dregs of his drink. 'I'll follow you.' Antonio led the way back to Beatrix's room. I knocked and entered. Beatrix was lying in a nightshirt, with the pillow under her posterior. 'Could you both wait outside please,' the doctor instructed.

We waited outside for what seemed an age. The doctor eventually emerged looking serious. 'I've spoken to her and examined her. She seems to be haemorrhaging from the same place as before. I think the area has almost repaired itself but she is still losing slightly from the same point. I think it will soon get better, but if not she will need hospital treatment.'

'What do we do, doctor? As you know, we are travelling with the army.'

'I don't want her walking. So she will have to be carried to the wagon and rest when she is on it.'

'We've done that every day until now,' said Antonio. 'Every day.'

'Well, you are going to have to do it for a few days yet. Tonight we will be in Salins les Bains. I want you,' he said looking at me, 'to ensure she bathes in the mineral baths there. If after a good bath she is not better, at least by the following morning, she will have to abandon her job with the army and return to Madrid. I want to see her again, after breakfast tomorrow. I can then make a decision.' What a shock but if we had thought more about Beatrix's predicament, we might have concluded that she would have to return, if she did not improve.

Susana and I had worked hard that night but, despite our tiredness, had to support poor Beatrix the following day. Again, the *tercios* bought her to the wagon and settled her on a makeshift bed in the back. Again, Carlos avoided all but the completely unavoidable obstacles. We arrived at Salins les Bains in pouring rain. It flowed from the gutters in torrents. The canvas on the wagon began to leak. The drops fell on Beatrix who became wetter and wetter.

'We've got to get her off this wagon,' said Susana. 'I'll get the men to move her!' A few minutes later, four of our soldiers, including Antonio and Carlos, took Beatrix from the wagon into the huge inn where we were to stay. It was right next to the building containing the mineral baths. The sergeant, once again, escorted us to our rooms on the first floor.

'When do we try the baths?' asked Susana.

'Right now, if you like,' said the sergeant. 'There are towels on your beds. Just find your way to the bath house, when you are ready.'

By then, Beatrix had brightened up a bit. Her body seemed to have replaced the blood she had lost and this showed through her better colour and cheerfulness.

'Let's go straightaway,' said Susana. 'A hot bath will do me good, too.'

***

We made our way towards the bath house. It was a large stone building with a main entrance which beckoned us into one of two internal doors, one for the men and the other for women.

'Let's go into the men's,' said Susana. 'That'll liven them up!'

'No,' I said, probably taking her too seriously. 'The attendants will only throw us out!'

The air was thick with milky vapour and had a strange sulphurous smell about it, a bit like the alchemist's laboratory. The women's section opened into a narrow chamber with a low ceiling. We walked through and were greeted at the end by a wrinkled faced attendant wearing nothing but a towel around her waist. Her breasts sagged so much her nipples were below her navel. She directed us in French, which none of us understood, to another larger room and pointed to a long wooden bench. She motioned us to undress, not uttering a word. We placed our towels on the bench and took off all our clothes, leaving them in three tidy piles. By then not wearing a thing, she beckoned us to follow her towards the sound of water falling onto something, presumably more water or rocks. We did as instructed, walking with our hands modestly covering our lower charms. She led the way, her sagging breasts swinging from side to side in rhythm with her steps.

'Good God!' shouted Susana, as we entered a huge room, all of fifteen *varas* high with a water spout at one end, shooting up as if to touch the ceiling. The attendant led us down some stone steps into a large round pool of hot water. Already about twenty or so naked women were washing themselves, paddling or even swimming in the slightly cloudy, steaming water. Some were standing under the water spout at the end of the pool, casting the creamy, warm liquid over their wet, shiny bodies with their hands or with earthenware jugs.

'Can we get right down in it?' asked Beatrix, anxiously wanting to wet her whole body in this health giving fluid.

'Don't see why not,' said Susana, immersing herself right up to her neck. 'It's lovely. Like warm silk on my body. Not too hot either.'

Beatrix and I followed Susana's lead. 'It's beautiful,' said Beatrix. 'Just what I needed. It feels refreshing. I could drink it.'

The attendant woman must have understood what Beatrix had said and cupped her hands to her mouth as if to drink. She then pointed to her lower body and shook her head as if to say, 'You must not urinate in the waters.'

I cupped my hands and tasted a little of the solution. I swilled it around my mouth as if to rinse it. The metallic flavour hit my lips. The salt tingled on my tongue and the heat of the water struck my throat. I shook my head in amazement. I quite enjoyed it. It reminded me of a combination of diluted sea water and a dryish wine. 'What a flavour!' I said. The other two tried it.

'Horrible!' said Susana. 'I'm not drinking any more of this. It tastes like hot piss!'

'You've never drunk hot piss,' I said. 'Warm, maybe!'

'I have to try some,' said Beatrix. 'That doctor said so.' She took some to her mouth. Her face grimaced and then she smiled. 'I feel better already. The worse the medicine the better the cure!'

'I don't believe that,' said Susana.

'That doesn't matter. As long as Beatrix believes it, all will be fine!' I said.

'Should I put some in my *vava*?' said Beatrix. 'What do you think?'

'Um... I'm not sure,' said Susana. 'I don't want to be responsible for the consequences.'

'How long since you bled?' I asked.

'Not since last night.'

'I'd risk it but be gentle with yourself. I'll try it first, if you like. I'll give you an idea of what it feels like.' Susana screwed up her nose and looked on. I put my hands in the water and opened my legs. I then carefully let the water in. It felt warm inside me and gave me a slight tingling feeling. It gave me a clean, refreshing rinse which I assisted with my wet fingers.

'I think it will do you good,' I said. 'You will feel clean and refreshed. My only worry is whether it will sting your wound. If I were you, I would be ever so gentle. Open yourself up very gradually so you can see how you feel and what effect it has.'

Beatrix eased herself down into the water and placed her hands towards her pudendum. Her eyebrows stood up, she looked so unsure. She frowned as the water penetrated her and moved her body around in the water to help it find its way into her. A full two minutes went by before she spoke. 'That feels marvellous. It itches a bit, at the top near my wound, but I think it is doing me good. I dare not force it with my fingers. I'm only holding myself open so it gets in.' She smiled with the satisfaction of making herself feel better.

'We've been so gentle with our bodies up to now. So why not try some fooling around a bit, just amongst ourselves,' said Susana. So we stood in a triangle and splashed each other's naked bodies with the soft, warm water, laughing and shrieking out as we did so. What pleasure; what uninhibited enjoyment. We spent at least an hour playing and spoiling ourselves in the luxury of the warm salt water. We were behaving like three of Diana's naughty nymphs. We shouted over the constant sound of the water spout, splashing onto the floor, and water running into the pool. We wished we could stay there an age. Then the droopy-breasted attendant, again swathed in her towel, returned to tell us that it was time to go. Our mouths lengthened with disappointment but we daren't disobey her. Who knew what the consequence would be?

**

As we came out of the bath house, a young man was waiting outside. It was Antonio. He rushed straight up to Beatrix.

'I've been so worried about you. Are you all right?'

'Oh. You shouldn't,' said Beatrix. 'I think I'm fine now. I'm certain the salts in the baths did me good.'

'I'm so pleased,' said Antonio, putting an arm around Beatrix's shoulder. She hesitated for a moment and looked at him straight faced. Then she kissed him firmly on the lips. They said goodbye, left us and walked arm-in-arm back to the inn together.

'She's not in love, is she?' asked Susana. 'That's all we want. She'll have to stop working. If he loves her, he will want to be the only one making love to her. He won't want to be at the back of a queue of fifty.'

'Hm... I did wonder what was going on. He's been very attentive while she's been ill. Even from before that. But he knows full well she is a *puta* and may well be happy for her to carry on.'

'Well, she won't be working anyway for about a week, so we'll see what happens,' Susana astutely observed.

**

'I'm dreading what he will say,' said Beatrix as we were eating some tomatoes and bread dipped in olive oil for our breakfast. I have been awake half the night worrying. I'd hate to have to go back to Madrid... I'd hate it...' She broke down in tears.

Susana went around the table to comfort her. 'Now now, Beatrix. I'm sure everything will be fine. Have you bled since yesterday?'

'No, definitely not.'

'Then the doctor will clear you,' I said, as reassuringly as I could.

Just as I said it, the doctor himself appeared over my shoulder and smiled. 'I hope you are right. Come with me, young lady,' he instructed, beckoning at Beatrix. By then she had stopped sobbing and sheepishly followed the doctor, her head bowed as if expecting the worst.

'It would be terrible if she was sent back,' said Susana. 'What would we do without her?'

'We'd manage somehow,' I said, not wishing to make Susana any more anxious and unsettled. Not many minutes later, a smiling Beatrix appeared at the door of the breakfast room and dashed over to our table.

'I'm clear! I'm clear!' she yelled.

'Careful! Careful!' I said. 'Don't rush about. You'll get it going again! What did he say?'

'He examined me in his own bedroom. That was a surprise! He put me on the edge of his bed and moved an oil lamp up close to me, so close I could feel the heat of it. I looked down his face as he examined me. He looked so serious and anxious. I began to think the worst. But then he smiled and I knew I would be fine.

'"That looks mended," he said. "I will give you a note to say you are well now. I can't even see any scaring. The baths have done their job. But you will not be able to work for at least a week." He said. "I'll tell Sergeant Alvarado that your colleagues will need help for a week or two. We must not overwork them or they'll end up sick too."'

'What a nice man,' said Susana. 'So thoughtful!'

'The main thing is that you are well and have stopped haemorrhaging. It's good that we'll be getting some help, I wonder who that will be.'

***

We soon found out. Shortly after we arrived in Besançon and had settled into an inn overlooking a huge square, the sergeant came up to see us. He stood just in front of a fresh-faced woman of about twenty-five. She wore a red and light brown patterned dress which came down to her ankles and a red, brimmed hat which sat on the side of her head. Her black, thick hair was tied in a bun.

'This is Manuelita Forneau. She will be helping you with the men while Beatrix is getting better.'

He introduced us to this rather stern-faced lady and left. We all went into my room and spent some time with her so we all got to know each other a little.

'I'm so pleased to be helping you,' she said, getting away to a good start. 'I am Spanish too but I have a French husband.'

'A husband?' asked Susana. 'And he lets you do whoring for a living?'

'That is not uncommon in these parts. I shall be travelling with the army right up to Brussels. Then I don't know. My husband is a craftsman here and runs a shop. So he will stay.'

'What if he wants serving while you are away?' asked Beatrix, impertinently.

'There are some very reasonable ladies of pleasure in our town and he may use one of them. There is also my mother.'

Susana's eyebrows raised themselves in shock. 'Your mother? He won't be fucking your mother will he?'

'Good Lord! No! She is the madam at one of our *mancebías*. She will provide a good lass for him. That's for sure.'

All three of us were surprised at the lady's openness about her husband and shocked at her condoning his adultery. But each of us liked her and it wasn't long before we worked out a routine by which she would help us. We had to engage Beatrix in some way and agreed that she would act as our assistant, rather in the way that I did while working for the alchemist's mistress, the delightful Angélica de la Torre. We bought some small hand bells and sounded them as each customer finished. Beatrix would come in, clean us up a bit, dab on a little perfume below our navels and bring in our next client. The system worked quite well, at least until our next problem arose.

CHAPTER 18

More Adventure on the Way

While we were on the road from Besançon to a little town called Baume-les-Dames, not more than ten *leguas* away, news percolated back to us that the unsuspecting populace of the town had been reduced to panic over the arrival of the first tranche of *tercios*. No one had informed the authorities there that the troops were coming through or that they needed food and lodgings. A concoction of panic and anger soon turned to action. Local officials, instructed by the army, hastily organised a convoy of wagons and sent them to Besançon so that food could be collected and brought from there to Baume. Needless to say, they were too late to provide an evening meal but most of the troops enjoyed a hearty breakfast the following morning.

Solving the problem of the victuals did nothing about the issue of billeting. No preparations had been made and most of that first tranche spent the night sleeping under roadside hedges. A small but lucky contingent slept on the floor of the church of San Martín. We were still two days behind these soldiers who were of course Italian. The kind landlady of an inn where we stayed, near the church, told the four of us – Manuelita included – about the problems in Baume. She was called Felipina and Manuelita did her best to translate the landlady's utterances for us.

'We couldn't believe our eyes when we saw all these soldiers marching into the town,' she said. 'I'd gone to the market just inside the town gate to buy some bread and vegetables. Imagine my shock when I heard the soldiers marching in. I first thought they were German and that they had come to lay siege to the town. People ran into their houses. Just to get out of sight of them.'

'Bit of a panic, then,' said Susana. Manuelita passed her meaning to Felipina.

'Yes, I'll say. They were led by a commander in a plumed hat, riding a white charger. He looked so proud and purposeful. Then there were hundreds of soldiers following him. Hundreds. Most were marching, carrying their pikestaffs on their shoulders. Hundreds more carried harquebuses. Lots were on horseback. I tell you, we were terrified.'

'Then what happened?' I asked.

'I'd already bought my things at the market and wanted to get back here. I didn't think they'd harm an old lady like me so I walked along beside them.'

'How far did you go?' asked Beatrix.

'Well, that was the strange thing. It was as if the commander knew something was wrong. He stopped by the town hall, got off his horse and went in. I thought I'd stop to see what happened. It wasn't until about a quarter of an hour later that he came out again. He looked angry and said something to two other senior looking officers who stayed outside. I half expected him to shout but he spoke in a very calming tone. You could tell from the look on the senior men's faces that things had gone wrong.

'Then about ten men came out of the town hall to speak to the commander who was already back on his horse. They said something about getting the priest to open up the church and getting food from Besançon. Then it dawned on me. This was another of the armies from Spain, passing through on their way to the Netherlands. And no one had told us they were staying the night here. What a mistake. What would we do? I had one idea. I'd tell the commander I had twelve vacant rooms in my inn that night. And that I'd go around to the other innkeepers to let them know what was going on.

'Anyway, I said that straightaway to the commander who thanked me for helping and said he was very grateful. He even asked me if he and some officers could stay in my inn for the night. Of course, I said they could.

'Just before I went to speak to the other landlords, I stopped there and listened for a minute or two at what they were all saying. The commander explained it all to the group of ten men, some of whom I recognised. One was a retired constable who had a job there collecting land taxes. Another was an alderman on the council. Anyway, the commander told them that they had had trouble in San Michelle de Maurienne a few weeks ago. There was no food there for days and some of his men and the followers nearly died of hunger. Is that true?'

'Yes,' said Beatrix. 'It's true to the letter. If it wasn't for some gypsies who fed the children, some would have died, for sure.' Manuelita translated again. 'The general... the commander you saw... is General Ambrosio Spínola. He came back after to apologise and tell us nothing like it would happen again because everything ahead would be checked.'

'That didn't happen, then. Did it?' said Felipina.

'Well, not here,' said Susana.

'Anyway, the general asked these men, in the politest words you could imagine, to organise themselves to get plenty of food from towns nearby, to let the people of our town and the innkeepers know that the rest of the army and the followers were no more than two days away and that they would have to put them up, feed and water them. He also said he wanted plenty of beer and wine for his men to drink, not just water.'

'He made sure they knew what he needed, then,' I said. 'He didn't leave much out.'

'He said just before I went, that he wanted a written report by nine o'clock in the morning from one of these officers on what had gone wrong, who was to blame and what they could all learn from "this dreadful, unwanted debacle", as he put it. He spoke lovely French and went from Spanish to Italian to French again, depending who he was talking to. What an educated man. He was the only one there who knew what was going on.'

The old innkeeper lady became quite emotional during her explanation, especially at the point where she reported that the general accepted her offer of rooms at her inn. The man had a kind of overpowering presence, which I felt deeply when he came to the inn at Aiguebelle and apologised so humbly to us all.

All four of us liked and admired the innkeeper. Unlike some we had encountered before, this one treated us *putas* with touching respect. Whether it was due to Manuelita speaking fluent French and the lady feeling a kind of identity with us because of it we'd never know. She was almost in tears as she bade us goodbye the following morning. It made me wonder if she had been one of us, a *puta* herself, at some time and retired to become an innkeeper.

***

The route we marched on, the Spanish Road as they called it, took a strange and unexpected path. The way from Besançon via Baume les Dames seemed deliberately to avoid any large towns. We stopped at places with odd or romantic sounding names like: Rambervillers, Luxeuil-les-Bains, Remiremont, Blamont, Lagarde, Épinal and Villersexel. There must have been a good reason for avoiding large towns like Nancy, Mulhouse and Strasbourg but none of us girls could work out what it could be. We came up with several possibilities.

'Perhaps the locals won't want an army passing through. They might feel threatened,' said Beatrix.

'These towns stink of shit anyway and I wouldn't want to stay in them,' said Susana.

'Maybe they want us to stay near the rivers. The water is fresh and drinkable. And there are plenty of fish in most of them. We've eaten some of the fish ourselves. We wash in them, too,' said Beatrix.

'I don't know,' said Manuelita. 'Maybe the road we take is the straightest!'

***

Beatrix had no more haemorrhages, thank God, but as a wise precaution the army doctor said she should not go with the men for a full two weeks. This meant, naturally, that Manuelita would continue serving our company of men, along with Susana and me, at least for the full fortnight. It was during that time that a tricky problem emerged. Beatrix and I began to lose money, quite a large proportion of our daily earnings. Neither Susana nor Manuelita's money went missing so each of them automatically became suspects, along with any number of our company. I was first to discover the loss. We were by then right up in Franche Comte and staying overnight in Baccarat, which is about ten *leguas* from Nancy and on the river Meurthe. The inn we stayed in faced the road on one side and the river on the other and for our dinner that night we ate fresh brown trout and bread made by our landlord, a plumpish, smiling fellow who delighted in serving our table of four himself. We felt sure he knew what business we were in and probably thought he could take advantage of the fact while his pretty little wife slumbered.

We worked ourselves to the point of collapse that night. No sooner had we dealt with one customer and rang our little hand bell for Beatrix, the next customer was stripping off and ready. Between us, we must have satisfied at least three dozen men. It turned out to be fairly routine work, that is, as we discovered when we compared notes, the men wanted nothing especially unusual from us. But the work tired us out and we went to sleep utterly exhausted.

After each customer of mine finished, I habitually put the money in a small leather purse which I kept under my pillow. After the last customer of the day left my room, I would empty the cash into a much larger purse I kept at the bottom of my bag, the same one that I brought from Burgos. I felt so tired that night that, after working my body so hard on about a dozen of our men, I put my small purse straight in the bag, without transferring my earnings to the other purse. I put it more or less on top of the bag, locked my bedroom door, got into my bed and went to sleep. I slept so soundly that night that I didn't wake up until daylight. Before I went down and joined the others for breakfast, I went to transfer my night's earning to my larger purse. I opened the small purse only and counted its contents: five *reales*. But I had served about a dozen men so about seven *reales* was missing.

I searched the room for it. I got down on my knees and peered under the bed; I pulled back the bedclothes and looked in the bed; then I scanned the windowsill and the chest of drawers. I could not see the money. I looked in my larger purse which I had deliberately hidden at the bottom of my bag. I knew I had a total of five *ducats* and five *reales* but no *maravedís*. It was an interesting coincidence of fives so I remembered it well. Sure enough, the large purse was sitting there at the bottom. I counted my money: exactly what I expected. So I sadly concluded that I had been robbed in my sleep.

I walked over to the door. It had been left unlocked. I knew for certain that I had locked it the night before. I remember turning the key, taking it out of the lock and placing it on the dressing table. So someone had unlocked my door, entered the room, robbed me and left. As I reached this hideous conclusion, a hollow emptiness formed in my stomach and I began to shake. I felt horrible and molested. Seven *reales* was not a lot of money but I had been robbed while I slept and that is what hurt me.

I needed to work out what to do. Would I tell the others? Could it be one of them? Should I tell the sergeant? I sat on the bed with my head in my hands, feeling almost as if I had been raped. For a few minutes, the shock of this awful happening numbed me so much I just could not think at all. Then I came up with the answer. I would tell the sergeant but ask him to do nothing until I could tell him more. I walked over to his table while he was having breakfast alone.

'No, Esmeralda. There have been no reported thefts. Needless to say, we've had a number of complaints about troops robbing some of the places we've been through but none in relation to our company. I'll tell the paymaster, in case any of the women pay in more than he might expect.'

'Are you sure you want to go that far. I'd rather keep it between you and me for now.'

'That would be unwise, Esmeralda. It is always better if, once a theft has been reported, that at least two of those with some authority know about it. So if you...'

'That's fine, Luis. I understand.'

I found it quite hard that day to be cheerful while we sat behind Carlos on the wagon but I did try. Susana, however, detected that something could be troubling me.

'What's the matter, Esmeralda?' she asked. 'You are not your usual self today.'

'I'm fine,' I said. 'I still feel exhausted, giving my all to about a dozen men last night. I'm still a bit sore,' I lied.

'Yes, that was a hard night's work. I'd really like a sleep during the day, if I can,' said Manuelita.

'You'll never sleep up here,' said Beatrix. 'Not unless we stop somewhere quiet for half an hour and there's not much chance of that.'

All four of us laughed. I was not sure at what but it lightened up the atmosphere and that could only be to the good. As usual, we made a mid-morning stop after about two *leguas* and stopped at a square in a tiny village. The people there greeted us at the roadside. They gave us fresh water and some tasty French cake. Between mouthfuls, Beatrix came over to where I stood, away from the others, and said, 'There is something wrong, Esmeralda. I know it. It could be the same problem I have.'

'Really? What's that?'

'I'm not sure how to put this, Esmeralda, but last night, someone came into my room and stole some money from me. From on top of the chest of drawers.'

'How can you be sure?'

'I counted my money last night and left it in my purse. More than half of it had gone by the morning.'

'How could anyone see what to take?'

'It's light early now and I slept so well.'

'The same happened to me, Beatrix. We have a thief in our midst.'

She hugged me tight and whispered. 'It's bad and sad. What do we do about it?'

'I've told Sergeant Luis de Alvarado. And he said he'd tell the paymaster. I think you should find a quiet opportunity to tell him you've been robbed and that you've told me.'

'Fine. I'll do that. What do we do about telling Susana and Manuelita?'

'Nothing for now. I cannot believe it's Susana. I'll have a quiet word with her.'

'I have something else to tell you, Esmeralda. I've told no one else. You are the first.'

'What is it?'

'I think I am in love. With Antonio.' She said it with pride but her eyes filled as if she could cry. 'I don't know what to do, Esmeralda. I feel so bad. He says he's in love with me and I believe him.'

'Susana and I thought you were falling in love. I can't see a problem. Unless you decide to stop working for the troops. That would be difficult, mainly because the sergeant would have to find someone to replace you. But if Manuelita carried on instead that may not be so bad.'

'I've talked to Antonio and he doesn't mind me carrying on working for the troops. I'm surprised at his reaction but...'

'So am I. If I were him, I'm sure I wouldn't want that.'

'That's why I'm not as happy as I feel I should be. If I were just one of the general's fortune-tellers, I would not have a problem with his attitude. But as a *puta*... He should want me to stop working.'

'If you are asking for my advice, I should just wait and see what happens. He does seem very loving towards you. Especially, when you had the haemorrhage.'

Beatrix hugged me again. 'You are such a good friend, Esmeralda, and so wise.'

***

We made steady progress for the next few days and, at least from my point of view, spent a surprisingly interesting night in Sierck-les-Bains, which is not far from The Grande Duchy of Luxembourg. We stopped at the old Duke of Lorraine's castle which overlooks the river Mosel. I took my bag and various things up to my room and began to unpack the clothes I would need for that evening and the following day. As I was about to finish this routine exercise, a loud knocking on the door took me by surprise. It sounded like the knock of a strong man. I opened the door cautiously to see our sergeant standing there with a strange look on his face. I wondered for a brief moment whether he had come to arrest me on suspicion of theft.

'I have an unusual request, Esmeralda. You will know that your little group of ladies has gained an excellent reputation... for the work you so assiduously perform for our company.' So he wanted us to do something really outrageous. And my 'little group'? He had put me in charge. He paused, presumably expecting a comment.

'We only do our best, Luis. Our job is to serve.'

'Well, your reputation has spread through the whole of the Spanish *Tercio*. To the extent that one of the most senior officers, a *maestro de campo*, who reports direct to General Ambrosio Spínola himself, has asked that you personally work for him tonight. He will be your exclusive customer and he will pay you one *ducat*. Plus of course any gratuity.'

'I feel deeply honoured,' I said, not really knowing whether I meant it or not. Probably not. I wondered what outlandish acts this man would expect of me, to keep me and indeed himself occupied for as many hours as he felt he wanted me.

'He will be arriving at your room at 8 o'clock. You may serve no other until then. Is that all clear?'

'Yes, completely. But before you go, have you made any progress in catching the thief?'

'No, except to say that I have been told of two other thefts, one of which I believe you are aware of. The paymaster and I have a few ideas for catching the offender, and I will discuss them with you later. Maybe tomorrow.'

I couldn't wait to discuss this incredible assignment with the others. 'You are fooling us!' said Susana.

'What's so special about you?' asked Manuelita, looking down her nose and her eyebrows raised.

'Well done, Esmeralda!' said Beatrix. 'You were always the leader of our little group.'

'I'm not so sure about that!' said Manuelita. We all chose to ignore her.

'I'll give you a special dash of perfume before you start!' said Beatrix, laughing.

'I've an idea,' I said. 'When I ring the bell – if I ring the bell – you come in and give me a wipe and a touch of your perfume!'

'I can do that,' giggled Beatrix.

I waited for a further knock on my door. Then, as expected, it occurred, at what I imagined was 8 o'clock. 'Come in,' I said. The door knob slowly turned and one of the most handsome men I had ever seen entered and looked straight at me as I lay on my bed.

'Are you Esmeralda Pechada de Burgos?' asked the man, not quite smiling, in fact looking surprisingly nervous for someone who had specifically asked for me.

'Indeed, I am, señor,' I said, looking as relaxed and welcoming as I knew how, considering the military seniority of this rare individual whom I was about to entertain. 'By all means come in, señor. And sit on the bed. May I say how honoured I am that you selected me among the hundred women serving the *tercios* to serve you tonight.'

'I'm sure that will be my singular pleasure, Esmeralda, if I may call you by your first name.'

'By all means, señor.'

'Then you may call me, Régulo.'

I'd never heard of that name before. 'I am entirely in your hands, Régulo. I can do whatever you ask or would you prefer me to set the agenda? I can tease you with some undressing or we can both take off our clothes and caress each other. Whatever you want.'

'Thank you. What if I lie on the bed and you tease me while undressing?'

'Do you want to remove some of your clothes before you start, maybe your pantaloons?'

'No. I am perfectly happy, just to lie here with my clothes on.'

I didn't expect that. Most of the men I had previously teased while undressing had lain naked on the bed or at least without their pantaloons, so that they could touch themselves during my little act. So I started with him fully dressed. I wore only seven items of clothing, my shoes, pink stockings, to halfway up my thighs, a blouse, a bolero top and a skirt which reached almost down to my ankles. I performed this fairly familiar act with as much erotic feeling as I could. Even as I removed my shoes, I rubbed my hands high up my thighs but not as high as to display the ultimate treasure which I imagined he was shortly to find. I removed my stockings, one at a time smiling intently at him as I did so and making the most provocative movements I could, still keeping that special secret out of sight. I then took off my bolero, stroking the outside of my camisole so that I was casually caressing my breasts, giving my nipples additional and welcomed attention. I quite enjoyed this self-touching, despite the field marshal's apparent, if not actual indifference.

I then slowly undid the individual buttons on my blouse so that my not insubstantial, firm, youthful breasts were exposed but facing away from him. I turned back towards him and smiled as I swung them from side to side. He smiled in an awkward way. It seemed as if he felt embarrassed at my gyrations. 'Happy with this?' I asked.

'Yes! Please continue. I like your shapely breasts.'

'Fine, then. I'll go on!' I was unsure about him and felt uneasy and awkward. His words were that he was enjoying me; but his expression betrayed something else. I wasn't sure what. But he was one of the most senior officers on this march so I dare not challenge him. Not even Susana, in her most cheeky moment would have done that. So I continued. Only one item of clothing clung to my form, my skirt, the only item which concealed my secret place. Should I remove it slowly and erotically or quickly and violently like an impassioned dancer? I stripped it in a trice but, as I did so, I faced away from him, only to reveal my bottom. I stood naked and vulnerable. So I turned towards him. I could see from the direction of his gaze what had taken his attention.

'I've never seen anything like that before,' he said pointing and smiling what seemed a genuine smile for a change.

'Seems that mine are larger than most!' I said. 'Shall I open them up for you?'

'Not now,' he said. 'Maybe later. Should we start now?'

'Making love?'

'What else?' he said, sounding only vaguely interested.

'That'll be fine,' I said. 'Want to take your clothes off?'

'Why not?' he said, indifferently. He eased off his boots, shirt and pantaloons, revealing his manhood. I half imagined that after my teasing him with my undressing he would at least be in a state of half preparedness; if not fully ready. But there was not a glimmer of life in the thing. It sat there between his legs, as limp as a wet dish rag.

'We'll need to work on that,' I said, not venturing humour, in case he didn't appreciate joking at this juncture.

'I suppose we will,' he said, almost without interest.

I clambered on top of his handsome torso and started rubbing him with my lower body. I must have done so for a full five minutes but still could not feel a flicker in his limpid member, not the merest spark of excitement, hardly a sign of life. 'Could we try something different?' I asked.

'What have you in mind?'

'I could take you in my mouth. That would really help. But I'll have to wash it first.' I poured a small amount of water from a jug on my chest of drawers onto a corner of a towel. I then gently wiped him with the wetness on the towel.

'That'll be fine,' I said and lowered myself onto him taking him between my lips. From seeing him as an easy, if prolonged, assignment, I now regarded him as something of a challenge. I suppose I must have spent ten minutes manipulating his manhood with my tongue as he, at my invitation, fondled me wherever he chose to do so. But all this effort failed to have the effect we both sought. His member remained in its sorry state of limpness. I hesitated to say anything and just worked away, leaving him to speak first as eventually he did.

'My dear Esmeralda, whatever we do has no effect on him. Perhaps we should stop there. I feel that he is sleeping tonight and that nothing we can do will wake him.'

'What a pity, señor. I was looking forward to making love to you. Indeed you are a very handsome man. Perhaps you should return tomorrow and we can try again to make him ready. In the meantime, I will think of other things we can do to arouse him from his slumbers. And I will take no payment for tonight's efforts.'

'It is vitally important that I pay you for tonight. I have a gold *ducat* at the ready.'

'It cannot be that important, señor. Surely not.'

'I can assure you it is. Please don't ask me why. I will not see you tomorrow but the day after,' he said, with authority. He then quickly dressed, took a *ducat* from a pocket in his pantaloons, placed it in my hand and went. I felt perplexed and disappointed because of my failure to arouse this handsome man and because of my own, unsatisfied desires. This was not a routine assignment and, for once, I was looking forward with some anticipation to enjoying my encounter with the most important person to whom I would ever have made love.

I found his insistence on paying oddly puzzling. It was as if some someone senior had instructed him and he dare not disobey. I felt I had to respect the field marshal's position and decided to say nothing to the others about his failure to ready himself for love.

'Did you get your *ducat*?' asked Susana as we all met up before retiring to bed.

'Yes,' I said as I took it from my small purse in front of her, Beatrix and Manuelita. I bit the edge of it, as if to test whether it was solid gold, not that I could tell. I then slipped it back and thought nothing of it. I worried more about how I could cure the field marshal of his little problem.

***

The following morning, the four of us sat together at breakfast, and continued comparing stories from our labours of the night before.

'Ion came to see me again. He's very fond of me,' said Susana.

'We don't want you falling in love as well,' I said, just a bit mockingly. We all chuckled.

'Who is this Ion?' asked Manuelita. Never heard of him myself.' Susana and I explained in some detail and, in particular, how we had spotted him at the abbey at Novelesa and his surprise explanation of our arrival in Madrid.

We continued chatting until, suddenly, Sergeant Luis de Alvarado appeared at our table, accompanied by another man I recognised as the paymaster.

'Please remain seated ladies. I have come here on a mission. Susana, please take your purse from your bag.' Susana did as instructed. 'Put all of its contents on the table.' She poured about two and a half *ducats* in change on the table, spilling a few *maravedís* and a *real* on the floor. She bent over to the floor and picked them up, one at a time. Among her change lurked a solitary gold *ducat*. The sergeant picked it up and examined its edge.

'No, that's not it,' he said. At that point, Manuelita moved as if to stand.

'Stay where you are, señorita,' said the other man.

Susana put her money back in her purse. 'Now you, señorita, empty yours on the table,' said the sergeant, looking intently at Manuelita.

'Why should I?' she asked.

'I am here on behalf of the judge-advocate. He has instructed me to investigate a crime of theft. So, señorita, I'd be grateful if you complied with my wishes.' Then in a slightly louder, firmer voice, 'Empty your purse.'

Manuelita blushed and looked scared but she complied. Her coins tinkled on the table. There were two gold ducats amongst them. The sergeant retrieved the first. 'No, this isn't it,' he said and went to the second. He held it up and closely examined the edge. 'Señorita, you are under arrest. I charge you on at least three counts of theft. Anything you say will be written down and could be used against you.'

She went again to stand and seemed angry and embarrassed at the same time. The rest of us looked on, our eyebrows raised in amazement, but said nothing. 'Stay there,' said the sergeant. Then he spoke again. 'I am going to give you a choice. You can either give me the money you have stolen and I will return it to its owners or I will submit a report to the advocate who will arrange for you to be summoned to court on the charge of theft.'

'I'll give the money back,' she said, her anger having dissipated and by then hanging her head in shame. She delved into the bag from which she retrieved her purse and took out another small purse. 'It's all in there,' she said, placing it on the table in front of the sergeant. He opened it and counted. 'Five *ducats* and seven *reales*. Sounds about right. And you've provided us with a witnessed confession, señorita,' he said without a hint of emotion.

There ended our acquaintance with Manuelita. Just after her 'confession', the sergeant explained to her that he summarily dismissed her from service of the army and that she would have to find her own way back to Besançon, presuming that she chose to return there. She had been found out by a very simple device. The field marshal had paid me a gold *ducat* which had a small amount of its edge filed away. The sergeant and he had assumed that, knowing I would be paid a good sum for my night's work, she would almost certainly break into my room to steal from me, while I slept. Before she left, the sergeant and an assistant searched her room and things and found a skeleton key. She admitted that it was hers and said that it was made by her brother-in-law who was a locksmith. They also found some spare keys to a number of rooms in the inn which she must have taken from the key cupboard near the entrance. She had taken these in case her brother-in-law's key didn't work.

The following night, after a moderately hard day's travel, we stayed in a lavishly appointed inn, right in the centre of the Grand Duchy of Luxembourg. On the way there we talked a lot about Manuelita and her unprovoked crimes. We all admired the paymaster for the clever solution he'd put in place for finding her out.

CHAPTER 19

Journey's End

By good fortune, Beatrix's fortnight of acting only as our assistant expired the day Manuelita was dismissed so she was, once again, fit and delighted to serve the troops. The three of us were saddened by Manuelita's behaviour but none of us was that surprised. Beatrix and I were two of her three victims – we never did discover the third – and Susana could not possibly have even contemplated stealing from anyone, let alone her closest friends. Living in such close proximity to Manuelita made us her most obvious victims. The three of us concluded that she had attempted to throw suspicion on Susana by not stealing from her. We wondered why Manuelita hadn't claimed that someone had robbed her. She may, however, have thought that the losses resulting from her thieving may just go undiscovered. So why draw attention to herself by falsely claiming that she was a victim? We agreed that that would have made little sense.

'We should take more care of our money in future,' said Beatrix.

'Good thinking,' said Susana. 'I intend to sleep with mine under my pillow.'

'That's a very good idea,' I said. 'I also think we should make more frequent payment into our accounts, via the paymaster. Maybe every three or four days.'

'Let's do that,' said Beatrix. Susana concurred.

***

As we had agreed at our previous meeting, the field marshal visited me that night. He reserved two hours this time and, according to the sergeant, would again pay me a *ducat*, even though I would be free to service other men, after he left.

'Good evening, Esmeralda, how are you today?'

'I am well, señor. And yourself?'

'I feel good and think I'll do better tonight. Would you like to start your undressing routine, the one you did for me the last time?'

'It will be a pleasure, señor!' I said cheerfully, giving him the impression that I was relaxed and looking forward to this session with him. 'Why not take your clothes off. You may like to touch yourself while I undress. That may just increase the pleasure.' I put it this way rather than say that he might find it easier to arouse himself while I teased and displayed myself to him. So I went through the same act again, with slight variations. This time I touched my breasts more frequently and erotically than before, through my bolero and through my blouse as well as when they were showing and, as it were, looking at him. I also put my hand under my skirt, appearing to touch my secret place while he looked on smiling.

Progress on his part appeared not to be good. Despite my writhing, wriggling and touching, it remained as limp and uninterested as it was two nights before. Although he did not say as much, his facial expression made it quite clear that he was becoming extremely frustrated with himself.

'I have an idea, señor. I'm not sure how to put this. To such a senior person, that is.'

'Go on, Esmeralda. Say it. I promise not to be offended or cross with you in any way.'

'Are you married, señor? I ask only because you may feel guilty, having me when away from your lady wife.'

'No, Esmeralda. I'm not married and have no sense of guilt whatsoever.'

'That's good. That may make it easier.'

'What will it make easier, Esmeralda?'

'What I'm going to suggest may or may not work. I don't know. But I've been thinking over this last couple of days how we might be able to solve your problem, if you have a problem that is.'

'So what are you suggesting, Esmeralda?'

'That we try to change what is going on in your mind. What you are thinking about is getting yourself ready to do me. Maybe we forget about actually making love but just taking pleasure without you having to do that. So what we work on is getting you ready. But nothing else. I refuse to let him in! So you can relax and just enjoy my body without that! And I won't charge you.'

'Esmeralda, if that works, I'll give you ten *ducats*. I am so desperate!'

'Señor, that is more than I can earn in a week! But we'll see what we can do!' I said. 'But don't forget. Whatever happens to your sleeping fellow, you don't enter me tonight, right?'

'Let's do it! Or not do it, I should say!'

'You relax while I get dressed again. Then we'll start with me doing my teasing routine.' I said, still naked and standing before him. He smiled and laughed optimistically.

I turned away from him and dressed, even putting my shoes back on. Facing away from him, I said, confidently, 'You dress if you want to do so. If not, just remain naked on the bed. You decide whether you want to touch yourself. Do what feels right for you.'

By the time I had fully dressed and turned to face him, he had replaced all of his clothes, except his breeches. 'I'm not going to touch myself. Not yet,' he said.

I performed the most erotic undressing routine I possibly could. I touched myself under my skirt, even while taking my shoes off. I took my skirt off before I took off my bolero, blouse or stockings. At every chance, I touched and displayed myself. 'Aren't I just beautiful there?' I said. 'Isn't it the most beautiful thing?' Then I turned my bottom towards him and touched the floor in front of me, thus revealing myself from a very different perspective. I wiggled my bottom in front of him. I had showed him every detail of my body. I had nothing more to show and knew no means of being more erotic, even though I wondered whether there was more I could do to make him ready.

Then I looked around. The state of him shocked but delighted me. He had aroused himself to a state of rampant rigidity. He looked intent on having me. 'No, señor. You are not doing it tonight!'

'Esmeralda, look at it. I'm so happy! You did that! What am I to do?' he said, beaming in a way that I had never seen before.

'We tease it until it can stand no more,' I said, with no consideration to whether what I said actually meant anything. It thrilled me that my tactic in making him firm had worked so well. I anxiously asked myself whether it would work again, when the intention was to insert it. 'Let's meet again tomorrow?' I said.

'Definitely,' he said pushing ten gold *ducats* into my hand and turning to go. I felt sure I saw a tear run down his cheek as he did so.

***

Life is never as simple as it sometimes appears. The complications in our lives were that both Susana and Beatrix thought they were falling in love. I had no such problem and had no wish for love. Not at that point, anyway. For one thing, I had no interest in a long-term relationship with a young soldier who could be maimed or killed in battle because battles, bloody and many, were sure to confront us. Beatrix and Antonio were entwined in what I saw as a passionate friendship. He did not object, for a moment it seemed, to her being gainfully employed as a *puta*. Indeed, he seemed to take a vicarious pride in it. They would meet when each was free and spend time in each other's company. The kind of relationship they enjoyed betrayed itself in the way they treated each other. While always gentle and kind, open demonstrations of love and passion did not occur, at least before my eyes. She claimed he always paid for the pleasure of her body. The full price at that! But why not have such a handsome male just as a friend?

Susana, on the other hand had problems coping with the evident fact that Ion was madly in love with her. He was unhappy with her working as a *puta* and made her promise that she would give it up at some, as yet to be agreed, time in the future, at least that is what she consistently told us.

All three of us discussed her love problems at breakfast the night after my second assignment with the field marshal.

'But you signed a contract to work for the army on the road to Flanders and when we got there. They'll charge you to get out of it,' said Beatrix.

'And you'd be letting us down. We are relying on you to help us. If you weren't part of our team we'd be in the same mess as we were when Beatrix was ill. And we don't want another Manuelita!'

'I know! I know! But he says he won't marry a *puta*. I'm not sure what I want.' She broke into a flood of tears and Beatrix went round to her side of the table to comfort her.

'Don't worry, Susana. Everything will work out well.'

'If he really loves you,' I said, 'he'll realise that you've commitments. To the army. Not us. Maybe tell him that you will go back with him when he returns to Buitrago and give up work a good time before that.'

'Go back to Buitrago?'

'Yes,' I said. 'He won't want to leave the gypsies and go with you to Madrid, will he?'

'I hadn't thought about that, Esmeralda. I was thinking of him coming back to Madrid with me.'

'That's something you will need to discuss,' said Beatrix. 'But you will have plenty of time. We will be away from Madrid for a few years yet. And Ion is in the army.'

'Well, you've both given me something to think about,' said Susana. 'And plenty to talk about with Ion.'

'Does he join the queue to make love to you?' I asked.

'Yes. And I never charge him. Should I?'

Neither Beatrix nor I was prepared to answer that question.

***

The field marshal arrived outside of my room that night. He ignored the queue of our customers and knocked firmly on the door. Naturally, I asked him in.

'What are we to do with you tonight?' I said.

'I'm not quite sure. You should set the agenda.'

'We do exactly what we did last night. Nothing more and nothing less!' I had something different in mind but decided not to tell him what it was.

'Whatever we do, I will pay you the same as last night.'

'I really don't want to discuss charges. You were so magnanimous last night. I didn't expect you to pay that much and I'm not asking for that again. I have to do a hundred men to earn that much and we didn't even go the whole way.'

'But you made everything work so well. If we get that far again, I shall give you ten *ducats*. I'd like to pay you even more but I don't want you to have so much so quickly that you decide to resign from your job!'

'Thank you for your willingness to pay me so well, señor. You are so generous. But we should not speak of rewards. I suggest I start my work. With you! I will go through the same teasing game as I did last night. And you can do what you want to do, while just watching me.'

'I'll just take some clothes off,' he said while undoing the buckle on his belt.

'Please, señor, just sit on the edge of the bed. I'll tell you why later, if I may.' So I started to undress, again in the provocative manner I had the night before. As I did so, I glanced at him while he was gently stroking himself. Not much seemed to be happening and I was disappointed but tried not to show it. I kept moving and teasing. Then suddenly, as I revealed more to him, he stiffened. His member became as solid as a gun barrel.

'There! I knew you could do it!'

'You did it yourself, señor!'

'But what do we do now, Esmeralda. I can't stand much more of this self-induced frustration.'

'Then you will see why I asked you to sit on the edge of the bed.' By then I was wearing only my stockings and my blouse. I backed myself towards him and slid myself bodily onto him. He entered with audacious ease. 'What do you think of that, señor?'

'I feel triumphant, Esmeralda. Triumphant! It is almost as if I have won a battle. Between us we are victorious!'

'Make the most of it, señor. All that built up frustration. The reason I am sitting on you is to make it last as long as we can. I am limiting your movements and that will hold it!' My tactic worked well. I moved my bottom up and down on him but slowly and in short strokes.

'This is beautiful, Esmeralda. Beautiful. I could cry with joy. You are a master of your profession. I cannot thank you enough. And this is ecstasy,' he said.

'I am thrilled that we have succeeded, Régulo,' I said, daring to use his first name for only the second time. 'It is a great triumph for both of us. So we are both pleased with ourselves. Now I want you to bring me to a climax. When I climb off you, I want you to lie in the centre of the bed with your head on the pillow and I will climb on top of you. Then let me do all the moving.'

I was soon moving rhythmically on top of him as he held my bottom with both of his hands. We were both naked and both enjoying each other. As I moved on him I wondered whether, at some future time, this man of serious rank could help me achieve my ambition: could he help me meet the king? Could he know the relevant people? Surely, he would think I deserved something more than a cash payment for changing his life. He had hinted as much, the night before. Then I lost all sense of reality as my body convulsed into a shaking orgasm which was so violent he had no choice but to release himself, too. We quaked together.

'Esmeralda, I cannot tell you what pleasure and joy you have brought me. You are truly an angel. I cannot reward you enough.'

'You are so kind, Régulo. But it has been a great pleasure for me, too. It is rare indeed that one of my customers gives me so much pleasure that I end in a climax. Think I have nearly drowned you! Shall we start again?'

So we did it again and both enjoyed each other again. I wondered while doing so whether I could fall in love with this handsome, now virile, senior officer. I answered my own question: love was the last thing I wanted, so no.

'Thank you, Esmeralda. So much. I don't know what I would have done without you.'

'You don't have to worry about that now!' I assumed we had completely cured his affliction.

'Somehow we should keep in touch. I trust you will serve me again?'

'Of course, Régulo. I'd be delighted. You should ask the sergeant if you don't want to queue. I'm sure he will oblige!'

'You have helped me so if you need my help at any time, here or back in Madrid, you only have to let me know.'

With that he placed another ten gold *ducats* in my hand and went. I felt honoured to have served this man and wondered if, sometime in the future, I might dare to call on him for a favour.

***

Not many days up the road, we entered the beautiful city of Namur. We could not be more than four or five days from Brussels, so nearing the end of our journey. It was pay day and the soldiers were anticipating receiving and spending some, if not all, of their wages. They were paid forty *reales* a month, so many were down to their last *real* or had nothing left at all. With their new found wealth, many would want to indulge themselves in our services as well as spend some drinking in the bars of this pretty, enticing town. The first we knew of a problem was when the paymaster and Sergeant Alvarado came anxiously towards us as we were sitting and chatting outside the inn where we would be staying for the night.

'This sounds a ridiculous question to be asking you ladies and I'm sorry to have to ask it, but have you any money for payment into your accounts?' asked the paymaster.

'Yes, I have about thirty *ducats* or so.' Susana and Beatrix looked at me in astonishment.

'Thirty *ducats*. My God! What did you have to do for that?'

'I'll tell you later! I don't think the sergeant... or the paymaster... is concerned about what we do for our money. They are asking how much we've got!'

'I've got about five *ducats*, maybe a bit less,' said Beatrix.

'Yes, about the same,' said Susana.

'Why are you asking?' I said.

'We have a serious problem in paying the troops. We've nowhere near enough money. So we are asking our women followers for loans or bank deposits to see us through today. If we don't pay the men there could be trouble.'

'When you say trouble, what exactly do you mean?' I said.

'Our soldiers are badly prone to mutiny,' said the sergeant. 'They are past masters at it. There must be four thousand mutinous troops in Flanders already and we don't want to swell their numbers any further.'

'I can't believe our men would want a mutiny,' said Susana. 'Our men are nice men.'

'They may be nice to you because you've got something they want. But no pay and they are trouble. Not long ago, I spent two years up here sorting out a mutiny. And that was just about pay. So I know what I'm talking about.'

'If you haven't got enough, why not pay all of them something on account?' asked Beatrix. 'I can see a problem if some are paid and others are not!'

'We've thought of that but we only need another hundred *ducats* – enough to pay twenty five men – and we can pay all of ours in full. We were expecting a cash delivery from the Treasury in Brussels but it hasn't arrived and won't. They've had serious problems with money. The king assured the Governor of the Netherlands that a million *escudos* would be delivered in Brussels the week before last. The delivery came but it was only enough to pay off some debts. So no one has come with cash for the troops.

'The other companies are in a bigger mess than us. Because we are at the tail end of the march, we've got access to the camp followers. So the sergeant and I are asking you girls and the others for any spare cash.'

'Well, you'll get over thirty *ducats* from us, by the sound of it,' said Susana. 'But if you give it to the troops how will we get it back?'

'Have you got your bank books?'

'Yes,' said Beatrix.

'I'll sign the amounts into your books and you can draw it out again when you need it. Not just after I've paid the men because I won't have any money. You can use a bank anywhere in The Netherlands. But they may pay you in *pattards* and *florins*! Or even *escudos*. You've probably never heard of *pattards*.'

'Tell us about this Netherlands money!'

'It's pretty easy. There are ten *reales* to the *escudo*. And two and a half *florins* to the *escudo*. So there are four *reales* to a *florin*. There are fifty *pattards* to the *escudo*. So there are five *pattards* to the *real*. We pay the troops in *escudos* and they get four a month. An *escudo* is about the same as a *ducat*. Is that clear?'

'No! I'll have to write it down to remember all that!' said Susana.

'I think I can manage,' said Beatrix.

We wished the sergeant and the paymaster good luck in finding more money and stayed outside of the inn chatting.

'I hope they get all the money they need,' said Susana. 'There will be trouble if they don't.'

'I don't believe they will,' I said. 'If they only need a hundred *ducats*, they must have nigh on a thousand anyway. So all of our men will get everything owed them, except about a tenth. No one is going to be daft enough to mutiny for that.' Beatrix agreed and we went on to something else.

'It's all very well for these soldiers,' said Susana, 'but how are we expected to protect ourselves when the men are fighting the Dutch?'

'What made you think of that?' I said.

'We are near to Brussels now and I'm just worried about the battles they will be fighting. I'm also worried about their safety. I'd die if anything happened to Ion.'

'You've hardly mentioned him for days,' said Beatrix.

'I know. But only because I'm worried about him. The troops hate gypsies and he will be in danger from our own men let alone theirs. Remember what he said about being treated badly when we met him at Novalesa? Well imagine what it will be like in battle. They'll shove him right to the front.' She began to sob in the typical Susana way, obviously looking for sympathy.

Beatrix consoled her. 'You mustn't worry about Ion. He is a professional soldier and will know how to defend himself. Gypsies are men of the world. They are survivors.'

'I agree with Beatrix,' I said. 'Ion is a very strong man and I would bet on him to win a fight with any of the others, with the possible exception of Carlos. The thing about Ion is that he knows of gypsy ways and they can fell a man by a single punch,' I said with as much authority as I could generate.

***

Whether it was because we were approaching the end of this difficult journey or for some other reason, in the last few nights of the march from Savona, only a few of our men wanted to avail themselves of our services. For example, in the town of Nivelles, which was less than ten *leguas* from Brussels, we served only a dozen men between us. We were puzzled and wondered if we had upset some of them.

'I don't understand,' said Susana. 'Have they had enough of us? Is it something we've done?'

'It's hard to say,' said Beatrix. 'We haven't changed what we have on offer. Except that when Manuelita was with us, I used to come in and perfume you between customers. I can't imagine it's that. They seem to have wanted us just as much since. Except in these last few days.'

'I'll tell you what I think,' I said. 'There are several things happening. First, the troops have all but completed a backbreaking journey of two hundred and more *leguas*. Unlike us, the great majority have marched. Carrying pike-staffs, muskets or harquebuses. And they've had to carry personal possessions as well. And they've had to sleep in ditches and suffer billeting. Apart from that, they've had to survive on a few pounds of bread a day and not much more.

'Second, their real job as fighting soldiers begins once we get to Brussels. Many are new and have never been to war before. So they will be frightened. Frightened for their lives. Maybe half will never return to their homes. Many will be maimed for life. So there is genuine fear among them and while marching this would be so distant that it wouldn't have troubled them. But now they are approaching Brussels and a battle assignment will be more in their thinking. And they will be scared all right.'

'You are clever, Esmeralda. I would never have thought of that!' said Susana. 'Maybe we should be scared as well!'

'I think Esmeralda could well be right. They will be talking about battles to come and what the Dutch could do to them. What does Ion think, Susana?'

'He is completely fearless. Nothing could frighten him!'

'What about Antonio?' I said.

'Well, he is an experienced soldier and won't show fear. Not when talking to me, anyway.'

We could only speculate about why most of the *tercios* didn't want us to serve them, at least not during those last few nights.

***

The people of Brussels gave us the welcome usually reserved for victors returning from battle. We had spent the previous night in Halle, risen for an early breakfast and started the last leg of our journey before daybreak. This was designed to ensure our arrival in the centre of Brussels by mid-afternoon. As we entered the gate through the city walls, we were astonished by the sight which greeted us. Wooden barriers, running down both sides of the road, contained the shouting, flag waving crowds. The Habsburg crossed, red laurel branches adorned the white background of their banners. We rode over yellow straw which had been scattered through the streets to absorb the horse dung and urine.

'What a reception,' said Beatrix, as our wagon rumbled over the cobbles. 'Who could have expected this?'

'Imagine what a welcome the troops will have received when they arrived before us!' said Beatrix.

'Tumultuous!' I said. 'It goes to show how important the Spanish army is to the people of Flanders. We are their defenders. Keeping them safe from the Dutch.'

'Don't forget, six thousand are Italians!' said Susana.

'It's still an army under the King of Spain,' chuckled Beatrix.

As we approached the centre of the city, we could hear trumpets and drums over the noise of the cheering crowd.

'What's that?' asked Susana.

'Don't say all that's for us,' said Beatrix. 'I don't understand. Most of the troops will have gone through two days ago.'

Carlos turned around to interrupt. 'No. The troops will be assembling in the square. The whole army closed ranks at Halle. All eight thousand billeted there ready for the march to Brussels.'

'What's the point of that?' asked Beatrix.

'It's a major event when an army arrives in Brussels. There's always a huge welcome. Just seems an excuse for the people here to get drunk. You'll see soon enough.'

As we entered the huge square we imagined to be at the city centre, the most incredible array of soldiery met our eyes. The whole of the army, four or five *Tercios* of them stood in a huge array of columns and rows in front of an impressive building we later learned was the King's House. They looked up expectantly at a balcony two floors above. We, the army followers, arranged ourselves behind this massive display of military strength, still on our cart, and stood up to watch. After the whole parade had assembled inside the square, which was lined with noisy onlookers, a trumpet fanfare blasted out from a balcony in a building facing the King's House. Then three men and a woman, all four ornately and formally dressed, appeared on the main balcony of the House. I recognised one of the men as General Spínola himself. Then one of the other two men shouted at the top of his voice: 'Pray silence for The Archdukes, Albert and Isabella.'

The crowd instantly quietened and the Archduke Albert addressed us all. 'General Ambrosio Spínola, your commanders, your men and everyone who has accompanied you on your arduous route from Genoa. Welcome to the great Flemish city of Brussels!' He shouted these latter words as loudly as his voice would permit.

'We have been awaiting your arrival here with great anticipation. Flanders is under constant attack from its enemies, the French, the English, but most fearsomely, the Dutch. These, our neighbours to the north, are encroaching on His Majesty the King's territory here and we will engage you in their repulsion. They have captured several of our towns and your army will recover them. And defend us from any further attacks by the French and English.

'You will have a well-earned rest in our famous city. Enjoy yourselves and make merry. For in two days you will be heading towards our border with the Dutch where your real work will begin. Thank you again for coming here. I thank you individually, each man and woman of you and I thank you collectively as an army under your great leader, General Ambrosio Spinola... God save the King!'

'Well, that wasn't much of a speech,' said Susana. 'And I could hardly hear him!'

'A welcome is a welcome,' I said. 'The main thing is he meant it. All three of us need to prepare for a few nights' hard work. The Archduke instructed us all to make merry. Pay day was only a few days ago so the men will still be able to afford us.'

Work hard we did, long into the night. We were in Brussels. The army celebrated. They celebrated with us. The next stage of our adventure was about to begin.

PART III

CHAPTER 20

Mutiny

What was going on? What was happening? We had been in Brussels for more than a week and no one had an idea where we would go next. Or what we would be doing. Would we be going to war? Would we be defending this city or another? How true were the words so profoundly uttered by the Archduke as his plump little wife looked on?

We had travelled with such haste from Madrid to this albeit beautiful city. And stopped here. And waited. Eight thousand troops and their attendant wives, helpers, hangers on and us, their serving *putas*, always ready to entertain and pleasure our men. And pleasure them we did. Not only did we serve our company, Susana, Beatrix and I made the most of our presumably scheduled stop and, after about three nights, made ourselves available to the men of Flanders. Everybody we met seemed to have money and plenty of it. So we made it our business to relieve them of as much of it as we could. The sergeant ensured that we were housed in comfort and put us in a hostelry not far away from the central square. We flirted with the local men and escorted the willing ones back to our rooms to indulge them in our delectable services. We smiled at them, lifted a skirt, exposed a little cleavage or touched them as we passed. It hardly ever failed!

'Like to try something Spanish, señor, just like you did at home?'

'How about a naughty lady from Madrid, señor?'

'Could you do with some service, young man? And only half a *florin* a go!' Yes, we charged the locals half a *florin* a piece, twice what we charged our own men. But no one objected. Quite the opposite, they seemed only too willing to pay. We would jump out on them from doorways or go up to them and touch them on the shoulder. But we only took to the streets when we were free and none of our men seemed in need of serving. So we always gave our boys priority.

'Esmeralda, you naughty girl! I saw you yesterday, accosting a rich-looking, gentleman in the main square! And you took his hand and brought him back here!' said Felipe Sanz, whom I had hardly set eyes on since his heroic action on board *El Crisantemo*.

'Are you complaining, Señor Sanz, or merely relating back to me your acute observations?' I said, removing my bodice for him.

'But we are your masters, not the burghers of Brussels,' he laughed.

'It's all very well for you. You've come here to face the enemy and take your chances against their gunfire. So the longer you wait before you go to war, the happier you must be. You can't earn an extra *florin* in the town by pulling out a musket. Or by lifting a skirt. But why shouldn't we make the most of the opportunities walking by?'

'I can't say I blame you. But watch your step. There's no one to protect you while you roam this evil city. You could be dragged from the street, into some backstreet den and never seen again.'

Not many days later, his words seemed ominously prophetic. Susana decided she would look for work in the Cornmarket, just a few streets away from the hostel and to the north of the main square. She told us where she was going and we expected her to return within an hour or so, either on her own or with some innocent lad on her arm. But she didn't.

Beatrix came into my room after she heard my door close behind my latest customer, a short pikeman who visited me several times while we were marooned in Brussels. He loved to make love in the afternoon, after a beer or two. 'Esmeralda, Susana hasn't come back yet. Did she say how long she would be?'

'No. But she should be back by now.'

'She said she was going up to the Cornmarket to find a customer,' she said with a pained look on her face. 'She's been gone about three hours. I'm really worried.'

'Come in, Beatrix. Something's happened. What do you think we should do?' Beatrix sat on my bed as we wondered whether to wait there or go to the Cornmarket to look for her.

'I know,' I said. 'Let's ask some of the men to help us find her. She could be in danger. The sort of danger it needs a man to get her out of.'

'Do you know which rooms any are staying in? We could go and knock.'

'I saw Carlos yesterday, coming out of room 52, I'm sure.'

'Let's go and get him.'

We explained to Carlos our predicament. 'I'll come with you. And we'll get Felipe. He's next door to me.'

'Where's Antonio, Beatrix?' I asked.

'Not here. In an inn near the King's House.'

'The four of us should be able to find her,' said Felipe. 'Put a note under her door in case she gets back before we do. She can read, can't she?'

'Yes,' I said. 'Better than she can write. I'll quickly do a note.' The four of us, divided into two couples: Felipe and me; and Beatrix and Carlos. Within a matter of minutes we were out hunting for her.

'You two take the north side of the market and we'll do the south,' said Felipe.

We walked urgently along the cobbled street, looking in every direction. We went into shops, peered around market stalls, dived into dingy side streets, even stepped into open doors to glimpse around the murky inside. She had vanished. We tested three beer houses before we challenged the fourth and nearest to our hostelry. The stench assaulted our noses. An unwholesome combination of stale beer, sweat and rotten food. I took a handkerchief from my purse and put it over my nose. 'Take that away from your face or you'll never get used to the smell,' said Felipe, as we struggled past clumps of animated drinkers, some of whom could barely stand and others who had so much to say and so loudly that they seemed to be making royal proclamations.

An old woman, holding a pot of beer, whose front teeth had long since gone and whose breath smelt like dog faeces, glared at me and muttered something in French or Walloon, I couldn't tell which. Her tone and expression said, 'Don't fuckin' push past me, love.'

'I'm sorry,' said Felipe, in Spanish and on my behalf.

She replied in Spanish, 'Why the hurry? What do you want?'

'We are looking for a friend who could be in trouble,' said Felipe.

'What does he look like?'

'It's a woman friend. She's got long brown hair, is fairly thin and is wearing a maroon coloured dress down to her ankles. She's about sixteen and not very tall,' I said.

'There was a young woman who looked like that in here about two hours ago. I thought she seemed like a *puta* looking for business so she's unlikely to be your friend.'

'No. That's her,' I said. 'We are both *putas* serving the army. This is one of our soldier friends.'

'I was a *puta* until ten years ago. I worked these streets until ...'

'Where did she go? In what direction?' asked Felipe.

'She left with three men. An old fellow I'd seen in here before and two younger men, both about twenty-five.'

'Any idea where they could have gone?' asked Felipe. 'Could she be in any harm?'

'Now you're asking me. I recognised the oldest of 'em. He owns the leather shop on the opposite side of the square. Can't miss it. There's always a lot of skins hanging outside. Only when he's open, of course.'

We left and quickly made our way across the crowded square in the direction the retired, toothless *puta* was pointing. There were no skins hanging outside any of the shops. 'Have we come the right way?' I asked Felipe.

'No. Look over there,' he said pointing to a shop on the side of the square adjacent to an inn. 'There are cow hides hanging outside that one. Let's go.'

We dashed towards the shop and went to open the door. Someone had locked it, even though a sign that looked like 'open' was still in the door. 'This has got to be it,' I said. 'I bet she's in there.'

'Let's knock and see what happens,' said Felipe, as he hammered his fist loudly on the wooden door. A moment or two later, a young, querulous looking man opened it, let it swing towards the wall and faced us while, at the same time, doing up the belt on his pantaloons.

'Good afternoon,' said Felipe, in Spanish. 'We've come to buy some leathers. Why aren't you open?'

The man muttered something in a guttural language and left us standing at the open door. A few moments later, a much older looking man appeared and spoke to us in Spanish. 'What did you say you wanted?'

'We make leather coats and need to buy some leather.'

'Never seen you before. Why are you coming here and not to where you'd usually go?'

I could feel things going badly wrong but tried not to betray my thoughts to the man who seemed to be the owner. I wondered how the redoubtable Felipe would deal with the question.

'We're looking for some soft pigskin for a special order.' It would have been the end of our meeting if the man said 'no' but he replied with another question.

'How much d'you want?'

'Enough for five jackets.'

He looked at Felipe as if to say, 'You don't want leather at all.' So we were surprised when he asked us in. He closed the shop door behind us. 'Now tell me what you really want?'

Felipe pulled a pistol from under his leather jacket. The man looked at him in horror and put his hands above his head. 'Don't shoot me! Don't shoot me!' he blurted, his eyes almost leaping from their sockets.

'We are looking for a woman friend called Susana. We are sure she is here. Take us to her. Now!'

'There are no women here. Just me and my two friends.' There were two others, so the toothless old crone was right. I looked at Felipe and he looked back, not taking half an eye off the man.

'Take us to the woman or I'll shoot you in the kneecap.'

'Follow me, señor and señorita.'

We followed the man through the back of the shop and up two flights of stairs to the second floor. We rounded the top banister and walked along the landing towards a closed door. As we did so, a voice from behind us uttered the words, 'Not so fast.' Felipe and I turned round to be faced by a red-headed man, also carrying a pistol, which he was pointing straight at the gap between my eyes.

'Down!' shouted Felipe. I fell to the floor as a shot rang out above my head. I thought I had been struck. I felt my painful breast. It was damp. 'Blood,' I thought, terrified and about to cry out. 'I'm dying.'

'Get up, Esmeralda,' said Felipe. 'You hit the banister rail as you crashed down. You're not hurt, just perspiring with fear!'

I climbed to my feet. On the floor at the top of the stairs lay a man's body with a red stain, about two *pulgadas* across on his chest. By his right hand, on the floor, his pistol pointed awkwardly towards him. The door ahead of us suddenly opened and a young man appeared. Felipe spoke first. 'We want the woman you've got in there. Bring her out now.'

The man turned and shouted, 'Wake up! They've come to get you.'

'Where in hell am I?' We immediately recognised Susana's surprised voice. I rushed into the room to see her. She lay stark naked on a filthy, unmade bed. I went to hug her. 'Susana, we've been looking for you. How did you get here?'

'Christ only knows... Haven't got a clue!' As I approached her, I could smell liquor on her breath. Brandy. There was no doubt about it.

'You're drunk, Susana. What have you been up to?'

'Can't really remember. I was chatting to these three men in an inn... next thing I knew I was fucking them on this bed. God knows how many times. Then I nodded off and you turned up. Haven't had time to be scared.'

Felipe kept an eye on the other two men during this peremptory exchange. He waved his gun around as a healthy reminder of our invulnerability. 'Come with us, Susana,' I said. 'Where's your purse?'

'Over here. Here it is.'

'Have they paid you?' asked Felipe.

'What are we supposed to pay for?' asked the older one.

'Come on! You know!' Felipe said.

'You owe her about a dozen *florins* by the sound of it,' I said.

'Here you are. Take this,' the old man said, passing Susana a handful of coins from his pocket.

'Give it here,' I said. I quickly counted it. Fifteen *florins*. 'For what she's been through that's hardly enough.'

As Felipe waved his gun in the old man's direction, the younger one spoke up. 'You'd better have this, too'. He placed a further pile of coins in my hand. I hadn't the gall to count it, but it felt like another dozen or so.

'Let's go,' said Felipe. 'And any more bother from you and you'll get a taste of this.' As we passed along the landing, Felipe picked up the dead man's gun and pushed the barrel between his belt and his trousers. The three of us ran back down the two flights of stairs towards the door of the shop. Felipe kept looking back up the stairs and aiming his gun in that direction, just in case. Outside a small crowd had gathered, we assumed because they had heard a gunshot from within. A crown constable broke his way through to the front and spoke angrily to Felipe, as I held Susana, doing my utmost to prevent her from collapsing in the street.

'What's happened, mate? What's all the fuss?'

'There's a body in there. I had to shoot a man to stop him killing her,' he said, nodding in my direction.

'That's true,' I said.

'There are two witnesses on the second floor. They'll tell you what happened. My name is Felipe Sanz. I'm an harquebusier. I'm staying at the hostelry by the square.'

'If I need to see you, señor, I'll be right there. If you're lying, it'll be to arrest you!'

The brandy Susana had drunk, voluntarily or by force, affected her badly. No sooner had we turned out of the square, she held her head towards the pavement and vomitted. As she did so, Beatrix shouted in our direction. 'So there you are! What a relief!'

So this frightening diversion came to a happy conclusion, except of course, for the young man whom Felipe had to kill. As Felipe reminded me, more than once, we were lucky to have survived without being shot, maybe even shot dead. Susana collected an extraordinary twenty five *florins* for her afternoon exploit. The key thing was that she had survived, even if her pride suffered. But knowing Susana, it would hardly have been dented.

***

Something like a week later, all three of us were surprised to hear from Sergeant Luis de Alvarado that the lieutenant had summoned his troops and their followers to a meeting which would take place in the square, beneath the balcony the Archduke used to welcome us to Flanders.

'What's this all about, sergeant?' said Susana, then fully recovered from her ordeal and in a daring, happy mood.

'You'll find out soon enough. I've been sworn to secrecy so can't tell you anything.'

'Really?' said Beatrix, 'Not even us?'

'Truly, I cannot say a thing.'

The three of us attended along with the whole of our company of men. No one seemed to be bothered whether we were separated from the troops or not, so we stood with Carlos, Antonio, Felipe and Ion, who held Susana's hand tightly the whole time. It was as if the frightening incident above the leather shop had made Ion more protective of her. The lieutenant, with the aid of a few men, climbed up onto the top of a large wine barrel and spoke.

'Gentleman and ladies, I have an important announcement for you. We have been over two weeks in Brussels since our arrival here and you will doubtless be wondering why. Well, I can tell you now. The high command has been prioritising what issues in this war are most important against a changing canvas of problems. One major difficulty is prominent. It is the incidence of mutiny. Our immediate concern is the mutiny in Weert.

'Most of the mutineers are Italian. We cannot fight Italian against Italian. That would be like civil war. So we are joining forces with all Spaniards who accompanied us here from Genoa to go to Weert. Our aim is simple: to use all of our resources to quell that mutiny. In effect we will be two regiments of *Tercios*. Field Marshal Régulo de Aracena will command our forces. I will be his deputy. At seven o'clock tomorrow morning, we will assemble here, under this balcony, and leave for Weert. God save the King.' He shouted his last sentence at the top of his voice.

'So my customer, Régulo would be in charge. How interesting,' I thought but said nothing to the others.

'Weert? Is that a town or what?' said Susana, still surprisingly voluble and firmly attached to Ion.

'I think it's a town to the east of Brussels, near the border with the Dutch,' said Carlos.

'No, it's near Antwerp, to the north,' said Antonio.

'Well, I hope whoever leads the march there knows which way to go!' said Felipe. Our whole group burst into laughter. The lieutenant frowned in our direction.

***

A week later, over two thousand odd troops and some five hundred of us camp followers were approaching the outskirts of the walled town of Weert. Apart from farm houses which dotted the landscape, we were struck by how featureless and flat the area seemed. The road itself emerged, straight and constant, above the level of the surrounding fields and drove through an avenue of tall narrow trees, probably poplars. People using the road moved to one side as we closed in on the town. A local driver put his wagon into a ditch as we passed. A number of our men stopped to rescue and untether his terrified horses, heave the wagon out and right it. Our rambling procession came to a gradual halt between about four hundred and seven hundred *varas* from the main gate. We stopped too far from the front to hear any bellowed orders but, after a penetrating, distant bugle call and indistinct shouting, we could see the troops flanking off to each side of the road into the green fields of grass.

We stood on the front of our wagon driven by Carlos, of course, and anxiously watched this sequence of events. Never before had we been close to a battle. Never before had we stood in cannon range of an aggressor. We were well behind the army so our men were in more obvious danger than we were.

'What happens now?' asked Beatrix, directing her question to Carlos.

'Not sure,' he said while still looking into the distance. 'It looks like the *tercios* are digging themselves in. Wouldn't be surprised. If that's the case, we could be here a long time.'

'How can you tell that,' I said.

'If they are, as I think they are, beginning to dig trenches, that means the commanders have either decided to draw up battle lines here or to put the town under siege, at least until they kick out the mutineers. It's all a matter of tactics. The one thing that is clear is that we are not going to force an attack on the town. Not yet, at least.'

'What happens to us?' asked Beatrix. 'We can't stay in the wagon all night.'

'Well, you can but you're not going to! My next job is to drive you to one of the farm houses. Back down the road about a *milla*. One of the things the army fixed while we were in Brussels.'

'Did we pass it on the way?' I asked.

'Yes, but they instructed me to go as far as the army, to give the town the biggest show of force.'

Well before night closed in, Carlos and virtually all the other drivers turned their wagons around and made off back along the tree lined road. Many took to narrow side tracks, barely wide enough to take them. As we gradually retrod our path, I couldn't help wondering how we were supposed to serve our men while they were so far away. I'm sure the other two would have thought the same. Then we turned off down a steep slope to our left on to a track lined with tall grass and bushes. The track wound and curved as if it was following a river but there was no river, not even a dried up riverbed. I completely lost my sense of direction while we traversed this winding, twisting path, turning to avoid tree roots and lurching away from deep ruts and hollows.

'I think that's the farm, over there,' said Carlos, as we turned yet another bend. About two hundred *varas* ahead of us on the left of the road a pretty farm house stood out from the flat fields behind it. Its sloping tiled roof, a balcony about a *pie* from the ground, and a large wooden door beneath a sloping canopy gave it an embracing feel, even before we stepped from the wagon.

Carlos halted right outside, climbed off and knocked at the front door. A man with a smouldering pipe of tobacco in his hand opened it and looked questioningly into Carlos's eyes.

'Have you an army billeting chitty?' asked Carlos. The man said nothing, closed the door round, leaving it slightly ajar, and went back into the house. Then a woman appeared dressed all in white from her tiny, wooden clogs to her large white bonnet.

'Welcome to the Riverside Farm, señor. Here is the chit you asked my husband for,' she said, in perfect Spanish with a strange clicking accent. 'Bring your señoritas in. I will welcome them too!'

Carlos beckoned us out of the wagon so we climbed gingerly down and walked towards the lady standing in her doorway. She kissed each of us on both cheeks in the most effusive welcome. It felt as if we were her daughters and we'd returned home from a long and arduous journey.

'I have been so looking forward to you coming to stay with us. You are going to be here for a very long time, I think. Maybe, even for a few years,' she said, as if she knew much more than we did.

Susana looked at me and I glanced at Beatrix. 'Two years?' Beatrix said.

'Well, that's what it says in the petition: for up to two years,' said the woman in white. 'But it's not a convent and we are not expecting you to behave like nuns!' she said smiling, as if she'd been told of our profession but didn't want to mention it for fear of causing embarrassment, either for herself or us.

'They told me to put you in separate rooms so that's what you've got'.

'I must go now. I'm billeted away from here,' said Carlos. We told him not to forget to unload our things from the wagon and bade him farewell. He went to leave.

'Just a minute,' I said, stepping back with him and moving to the side of the wagon away from the house so the farmer's wife couldn't hear me. 'How do the soldiers reach us for service?' I said in a half whisper.

'Sorry, I should have told you. We've been round in a big circle and the soldiers are over the other side of those fields, less than half a *milla* away. But don't worry. You are out of range of enemy fire. Our company will be told where you are. When they need you to service them, they will come here. You must not go to them.' He put heavy emphasis on the 'not'.

'And what if we need you, Carlos?'

'You should not ask me to take you anywhere. That is against army rules. You are to stay here until I or someone else collects you to take you to our next military assignment. But as your landlady said, that could be quite some time in the future. I will come to you for service, Esmeralda, and look forward to that!' he said, breaking into a naughty smile and climbing back onto the wagon. 'See you soon.' He cracked his whip and pulled off.

I stepped into the large hall of the farm. Susana and Beatrix were talking to the farmer's wife.

'Oh! There you are,' she said looking in my direction. 'As I was saying to the others, you girls should treat me like a mother. I want this to seem like your home. I'm looking forward to your stay here and you must ask me for anything you want. My husband is a lovely man but only speaks Walloon so won't be able to speak to you. Unless you learn Walloon! His name is Gerlach Zoot. You can call him Gerlach but I don't know if he will reply.

'My name is Alisa del Montero. Please call me Alisa. My mother was a *puta* in Madrid, just like you, and I came here in '67 with the first army to use the Spanish road. I met the Duke of Alba.' So she knew about the business we were in and wanted to help us in ours. At least that was how I interpreted her friendly words.

We introduced ourselves to her. She then showed us to our rooms which were along a short corridor, off the hall and out towards the fields at the back of the house. Each room glowed with that freshly prepared welcome that comes only when great effort has been spent on it.

'I'm so happy with this!' said Susana, beaming at her pretty bed and a carpet fit for a queen's bedchamber. 'I don't care if we are here for two years. We could do much worse.'

'I'm not so sure,' said Beatrix. 'We can hardly do our job on a farm.' The landlady's cordial smile evaporated.

'Come on, Beatrix,' I said. 'We must give it a try. It could work well. It's comfortable and clean.'

'I'm not convinced,' she said, as the landlady coolly showed Beatrix her comfortable looking abode.

'I will like being here,' I said, flopping on to the bed in my equally homely room as the landlady vanished and the other two followed me in. 'I'm just concerned abut our lack of freedom. We could be marooned here at the mercy of these two for months and months. This place is so isolated.'

'Good thing we're on a farm. Shouldn't go hungry should we?' said Susana.

Days, weeks and months passed in this quaint but friendly lodging. In effect, we had turned Gerlach and Alisa's home into a *burdel*. At first, and as Beatrix had predicted, we felt awkward, entertaining our men in their house. Although they never asked about the varying stream of men that came to see us or what we did with them, they made the men as much at home in their house as they made us. They even gave them cups of beer Gerlach brewed in one of the distant outhouses and offered them sugar decorated cakes which Alisa made in her ample kitchen. The couple had never had their own children so they seemed to be making up for that by treating us and our men uncommonly well. They were especially welcoming to Ion and Antonio after they discovered that they had close relationships with Susana and Beatrix respectively.

Despite Beatrix' misgivings, we soon fitted well into Gerlach and Alisa's household. We wondered why they gave us all our meals and became quite upset when we suggested that we should pay. Carlos explained. The army had made clear in the terms of the billeting contract that they had to provide a minimum level of sustenance, which they almost always exceeded. Apparently, the papers said nothing about provision for our customers so presumably the army did not compensate them for that.

Our customers willingly explained to us what progress the army was making in quelling the mutiny. In short, for more than six months, they failed to make any. It was winter by then, a severe one, and the troops were becoming exhausted and miserable. No one wanted to relieve them from living in the filth of the trenches they had dug. They lived in their own excrement. Few ventured from the protection of the trench, even to do what they had to do. Food and drink was short as was warm clothing. In effect the army itself was under siege while the mutineers enjoyed the riches of the land. The mutineers had taken control of this vulnerable little town and their leader had had the audacity to write to the field marshal, threatening him with attack, if our army was to enter the town. The letter infuriated the field marshal who dreamt up a plan. Antonio played a part in its execution and explained what happened.

'It was amazing. Ten of us were armed with ropes and grapple hooks. We knew the gates of the town and the nearby walls were under guard. Heavy guard. So in almost total darkness we crept along the base of the wall, until we were about halfway to the second gate. The walls at the point we chose made a "vee" shape. We took a chance and one of the men threw a grapple hook clean over the top. No one heard it. He climbed up the wall, making the most of his position in the "vee".

'We threw two more grapple hooks over the wall and within minutes all ten of us were inside the town. A paid informer, a woman, told us a week ago where four mutineers were living. We found the house, broke in and fought the men. We injured one so badly we had no choice but to leave him there. We tied up the other three and made our way to the main gate. We surprised the guards, knocked them cold and took our three hostages back to the camp.'

'Then what happened?' asked Beatrix.

'We manhandled them into a shed we built behind the trenches and put them under guard. They are going to be tried for treason.'

'When?' I said. 'There is no court out there.'

'You can set up a military court in a trench, if you want to. Anywhere. We have a company *barrachel* and the means to punish those he finds guilty.'

***

One morning, quite early and not long after we heard about the captured mutineers, Alisa knocked on my bedroom door. 'Esmeralda, I have a visitor for you.' I was resting at the time from a hard night's work and climbed off the bed, still half asleep. I opened my door and smiled broadly at my visitor. There, returning the smile, stood Field Marshal Régulo de Aracena. Nothing he wore revealed the elevated rank of this distinguished soldier. Quite the opposite: he wore no hat and his hair was tied modestly at the back of his head. His heavy, belted jacket covered the top of his breeches which he had tucked into the top of his knee length leather boots.

'Esmeralda, it's lovely to see you,' he said, coming towards me with his arms outstretched, as Alisa dissolved away from us, along the narrow corridor.

'Do come in, Régulo. I know you are the commander and I just didn't expect to see you here. I haven't seen you since our wonderful night in The Grand Duchy of Luxembourg, months and months ago! I trust you are well.'

'You're right. I am busy. Things are happening in the background to this stupid mutiny that I have no control over. It's ridiculous. But we have some ideas up our sleeves.'

'I'm sure you won't want to talk about them, señor. You can if you so wish!' I chided. 'But I'm sure that is not the reason you are here...'

'You know why I'm here, Esmeralda. I cannot wait. I am bursting with need,' he laughed, with a wanting, almost anxious look on his face.

'I've been dreaming of your beautiful body, your shining eyes and those slender legs and I want to see you undressed and love you again!' His words were on the verge of poetry and I felt flattered by them.

'You shall, then, señor Régulo! Right now! Take your clothes off and I'll do the same. In seconds he was naked and parading his half erect member before me. 'Not a bad start,' I thought. 'I've seen it almost dead!' I took off my blouse, smiled at him and used my shoulders to move my breasts teasingly from side to side. He chuckled gleefully.

'You have the most delightful breasts, Esmeralda, but...'

'Yes, it is this you want...' I said lifting my dress so that he could see my secret place.

'Get on the bed, Esmeralda. I want to kiss you there!'

'Go on, señor!'

I kept my skirt over my chest as he did so. I wondered then which of us was enjoying this the most. This warm tingling pleasure was mine. He said nothing, nothing to interrupt our mutual pleasure. I thought then that I would allow him to do anything he wanted, to any part of my body with any part of his. I savoured his masculine aroma as he moved his head while kissing me. This man would be the key to the gypsy fortune-teller's third prediction: he would help me to meet the king!

After this glorious and shared indulgence, Régulo climbed off the bed. I looked with pride and anticipation at his readiness. 'Now, Esmeralda?'

'Now!' I said.

We came together in the most ecstatic climax. 'My God, Esmeralda, you are so good for me. You have made this soldier a man! I could fall for you forever!'

'Please señor, Régulo, don't even think of that. A man in your position and with the potential to be a captain general... you shouldn't get too close to a whore. If you know what I mean! But I enjoy being done by you, more than any other man I know. And you can return to do anything you like with me at any time. I can show you some good tricks whenever you want.'

'You are too kind, young lady! I will come back to you, for certain. There's a lot for me to do right now... but I'll be back. Sooner than you might think!'

'Before you go Régulo, can I ask you a question?'

'Of course. And I'll do my best to answer, Esmeralda, but there are things which are confidential or secret that I cannot tell you. Or I will be shot at dawn! What exactly do you want to know?'

'Those three men which your men captured the other night. What will happen to them? Will you use them to negotiate the end of the mutiny?'

'I cannot say,' he said, in a quiet, lowered tone. 'But what I can tell you is that they are to be put on trial for treason. They appear before the company *barrachel* in two days time. If they're found guilty they may well be hanged.'

CHAPTER 21

The Hanging

Just a few days later, the three captive mutineers were tried at a court martial. We three girls could not attend nor did we want to do so but we were curious and asked Antonio about it. He had of course participated in the men's capture and had been a key witness in the court.

'Yes, I was there all right,' he told us. 'They held it in a big tent. I've no idea where they got it from but it appeared one morning. Out of nowhere. As if they'd put it up at night. It stood on the grassy field on your side of the trenches. Looked like a big white whale.

'All ten of us who captured the three men were there. The way the judge questioned us, you'd have thought we were the ones on trial. I had to say what we did and how we caught the men. How we tied up the guards and got the men out. Where we put them when we got back to camp. What state they were in when we got them back. I thought the judge would never stop asking questions.

'Then he questioned the three men. All through an interpreter.

'"Give me your name and rank," said the judge to the first man.

'"I am Favio Gambalota, corporal in the *Tercio* of Milan."

'"Do you live in Milan? Are you married?"

'"No, Your Honour. I live in Genoa. And I'm single."

'"Do you understand that you are charged with the offence of mutiny?"

'"Yes, I understand the charge, Your Honour."

'"Do you plead guilty or not guilty?"

'"Guilty, of course, Your Honour. I am a mutineer and proud of it. If more of our troops had the balls to mutiny we'd all be better off!"

'"Would you mind explaining yourself, corporal? I for one don't understand you. And moderate your language."

'"It's simple when you think about it, Your Honour. We haven't been paid for twenty months. I am a musketeer and His Majesty the King owes me 320 *florins*. How am I expected to support my poor widowed mother if His damned Majesty won't pay me?"

'"I told you to control your language, corporal," the judge shouted. "I'll charge you with contempt of court if you won't behave."

'"I can't say I'd give a shit for that, Your Honour. I reckon I'm in enough trouble with a charge of mutiny on my head. Let alone contempt."

'"If we all took the action you've taken, we'd have no serving army here at all. What do you say to that?"

'"If the King can't be bothered to pay us or can't afford to pay us, he doesn't deserve an army. So it would serve him right if everybody mutinied."

'"Step down corporal. Call the next of the accused."

'Then a younger man stepped into the dock. His eyes were looking here and there and just about everywhere. You could see the fear in his glance.

'"What's your name and rank?" asked the judge.

'"I'm a pikeman in the *Tercio* of Milan and my name is Julio Belmerardo."

'"Do you understand the charge against you?"

'"Yes, señor. I am charged with mutiny."

'"How do you plead?" said the judge coldly.

'"I have to plead guilty, señor, because I am guilty. I mutinied for two reasons. I have not been paid for nearly two years, señor. And I am one of the Milanese *Tercio*. All my company mutinied, señor, and I wasn't going to be the one left out."

'"Where do you live, Señor Belmerado?"

'"I live in Brussels. With my wife and three children," he said, fearing for their futures without him.

'"Where did you join the *Tercio* of Milan?"

'"In Brussels. I was a volunteer, señor, and being Italian had no trouble getting in."

'"Do you realise you could be hanged for your offence?"

'"I do, señor." He then broke down and cried uncontrollably.

'"Take him off the stand," said the judge. "And bring in the next of the charged."

'The next man limped to the stand and heaved himself up on to it.'

'Didn't you know he was crippled when you took him prisoner?' asked Susana. 'You should have left him and brought one of the others instead.'

'We hadn't an idea at the time. We just grabbed them and manhandled them out through the town gates. Don't forget it was as dark as the pit of hell.

'Anyway, the judge asked him his name and went through the same questioning as the others. The only thing is he made a different plea.

'"My name is Lorenzo Arrivaldi. Not guilty, my Lord. Not guilty."

'"I heard you the first time."

'"Ay?" Laughter erupted at the impertinence of the question. An usher called for silence.

'"I told you. I heard you say, 'Not guilty' the first time you said it."

'"I only said it once, My Lord!" Then muffled laughter from the witnesses.

'"You... Oh, never mind... What have you to say in your defence?"

'"It's like this, My Lord. Nearly the whole *Tercio* decided to mutiny because of no pay. But I didn't want to mutiny and wanted to stay in Maastricht. Couple of others did too. Anyway, the *electo* suggested a vote and said that we'd all have to go with the majority. I voted against, My Lord. But they brought me here at gunpoint, along with the others who voted against. So I had no choice but to join the mutineers. That's why I'm not guilty."

'"A likely story, my man. Is there any one here who can corroborate that? No. Of course there isn't! Take all three back to the cell. I shall reach my verdict this afternoon, after lunch."

'After lunch came and we all paraded back in. The army officials, us witnesses and the accused. It was grim. You'd have thought it was a tribunal of the Inquisition... trying some poor souls charged with heresy. But in a way it was even worse. The judge sat at his desk, let everyone there settle and stood up. In a flat, disinterested tone he said, "Favio Gambalota, Julio Belmerardo and Lorenzo Arrivaldi this court finds you guilty as charged. You will hang by the neck until dead."

'Señor Belmerardo exploded into passionate crying then shouted out aloud, "What about my wife and children? How will they be able to live without me?" He collapsed in tears on the floor with the others still standing erect beside him.

'"Call this a court?" said Señor Gambalota. "You'd decided we were guilty before you begun. This wasn't a trial at all! God save the King but not bastards like you who work for him."

'"I've had all I can take from you. One more word and it's a charge of contempt!" the judge bawled. "Take all three down. They will be hung in five days."

'The field marshal looked angry. He left the court first, dashing out as if somebody had called him to some emergency. But no one had spoken to him. He left at such speed, he almost knocked over one of the ushers, but at least had the manners to turn and apologise.'

'Typical of my man,' I thought. 'Polite in any situation, even in bed.'

'Will we be allowed to see the hanging?' asked Susana, seeming quite excited at the prospect.

'Don't know,' said Antonio. 'We'll have to see about that.'

'I don't get you, Susana,' said Beatrix. 'How could you want to see these poor men hanged?'

'I don't know really. Maybe, I don't want to see it. I said it to sound strong when I'm quite weak really.'

'Don't worry, Susana. Sometimes you just don't think before you speak!' I said.

***

We three talked about the hanging a lot and decided we definitely didn't want to see this hideous and distressing event. None of us could think of anything worse than three men being hanged, whatever their crime. During our time in Madrid, there had been several executions of heretics and each of us had, unlike many of the population, avoided being witness to such upsetting and cruel happenings.

However, we had no choice but to be witnesses. The *barrachel* who conducted the trial issued an injunction, instructing everyone over the age of fourteen years to attend. 'Couldn't we say we were fourteen?' said Susana.

'No, definitely not,' I said. 'You should know that we could not legally trade as *putas* unless we were fifteen. If we try to make out we're fourteen they could sack us and where would we be then?'

We all laughed but the sadness of realising that we would have to witness this hideous event, whether we wanted to or not, struck us like a bolting horse.

'I feel sick,' said Beatrix, when I told her about the injunction. Ion had brought it to the farmhouse and had decided to show it to me before telling Susana.

'I feel the same,' I said. 'I know it's a man only doing his work, but I do not understand how a hangman can do that. It's inhuman. Barbaric.'

'I suppose if no one would do the deed, there would not be a death penalty. Because it could not be carried out. Do you agree, Esmeralda?'

'Too many "ifs", Beatrix,' I said. 'There is always someone who will do something, however disgusting, cruel or mean. Especially in the name of doing their job.'

'You are right, Esmeralda. Look at some of the things we are expected to do for a living.' She laughed. I could not resist joining in so we looked each other in the eyes and laughed out loud. But that three men were to lose their lives was far from being a laughing matter.

***

That grim day arrived with inexorable certainty. We left the farmhouse as late as we could. We asked Gerlach and Alisa if they wanted to come with us but, not surprisingly, they politely refused. 'Sorry, girls, you have to go. We are the lucky ones who don't.'

So we walked quietly across the field along the same path as our men would come, but in the opposite direction. Their needs were the last things on our minds during this melancholy sojourn. Then Susana broke the dreary silence. 'I never understand things, I know. I'm not as clever as you two. But why are we expected to attend the hangings? We've done nothing wrong?'

'It's the *barrachel*, Susana,' I said. 'He's decided that the hangings should be an example to all. It's supposed to make us so horrified we'd be scared of doing anything wrong ourselves. And apart from that, it will draw attention to him.'

We could see that we were nearing the site of the executions. The soldiers had built and erected three gallows. They loomed ever larger as we approached. They reminded me of the three crucifixes at Calvary, which the nuns at the convent told us about repeatedly. Who would be as Christ in the middle? Who would be crowned in thorns? These thoughts overcame me. I could not speak them.

As we crept ever closer, we could see and hear the crowds which had gathered there, on this flat land, before us. Their vacant chatting punctuated the dismal air of certainty of what we were about to witness. We had no interest in a forward position so we stayed together at the back, mingling with other women and a sullen soldier, his arm around the shoulder of the lady he accompanied. We waited a few minutes before a hollow drum beat sounded. *Boom... boom... boom... boom*. Its regular monotony totally fitted the sobriety of the occasion. I felt revulsion at the thought of men dying at the hands of other men. And of my part in being here. This was not war. It was nothing but naked inhumanity. Susana took out a handkerchief to wipe her eyes. Beatrix wiped her tears on the corner of her apron.

To a bugle call, three men appeared to the right of the gallows. They wore black pantaloons and black shirts. We imagined they were the accused. In a black mask and black overcoat appeared the executioner followed, as Ion later told us, by the *barrachel* himself. He looked sickeningly triumphant, straight backed and proud, as if this despicable event was some momentous career achievement, of his own making, and his alone. This grim parade stopped short of the scaffold. The executioner directed the men to their positions on the stand. He went up to each in turn and placed a small coarse sack over the man's head and a rope around his neck.

As he finished tying the third knot, we could hear the rapid, urgent sound of a galloping horse. In a cloud of dust, the rider pulled at the sweating black beast's reins and heaved it to a halt, right at the foot of the gallows. Field Marshal Régulo de Aracena shouted from the saddle, 'Stop! Stop!' He frantically waved a parchment scroll at the *barrachel*. 'I have here a Royal Pardon! Get them down!'

To a man and woman, the assembled crowd cheered and shouted. All there transformed rapidly from being grim bystanders to ecstatic celebrators of the gift of life, life that was but seconds from being taken away, broken and rejected. Tears flowed as never before, the tears of uninhibited joy. The three of us kissed each other and gasped with relief. We exchanged not a word: the looks on our happy faces sufficed. The three accused, now innocent, now untied, hugged each other. Their tears flowed in measure. Pikemen threw their hats in the air. Musketeers fired their muskets as they aimed them at the sky. The place erupted. Women clasped each other and danced around in frantic circles, laughing and shouting as they did so. Men jumped into the air, kicked their legs high, roared out and laughed. All, except the *barrachel*.

The *barrachel*'s expression suddenly changed from a look of triumph to one of misery and disaster. What had happened? What had gone wrong? His face told it all. His previously proud, straight back, bent forwards as he looked to the ground, consumed by the shame of it. He could stand no more of this celebration of his decision reversed so he sneaked away, out of view, like a chastened dog cowering under a table.

***

The five days after the trial were five days of misery. The morale of our men fell to its lowest level. Our business dried up to a mere trickle. We may have serviced two men, maybe three each in a day. But that night the queue of our smiling customers stretched twice around the hall and out of the front door. We had so many, all from our company, apart from the occasional interloper, that we had to work well into the night to satisfy them. And Alisa, bless her, delighted in helping us by ushering the next man into one of our rooms, after the previous customer had left it.

'I can't take much more of this,' said Susana, during a few minutes break at about midnight. 'I'm doing it in my sleep. I almost have to ask them to wake me up before they go.'

'Don't be selfish,' snapped Beatrix. 'We've done without them for a week so we've got to finish them off tonight.'

'Beatrix is right,' I said. 'Imagine the trouble we'd be in with the lieutenant if we stopped now and sent the rest back to the trenches without doing them. We'd be the next to be charged with mutiny!'

'Let's get back to work then,' said Susana anxiously, fully appreciating the seriousness of our comments but seemingly failing to understand my attempt at humour.

The senior officers seemed to anticipate that there would be many of the junior ranks who would wish to celebrate the pardoning of the accused by enjoying themselves in our delectable company. So just for a few days, they generously held themselves back from such indulgence. Eventually Régulo made to see me, exercising, as he said, his privilege of bypassing the little queue and going straight to the front of it. He knocked a few moments after the customer before him had left.

'Good evening Régulo, señor. I thought you'd be here soon enough,' I said, holding the door open. I was wearing a cream camisole and my yellow skirt.

'I'm delighted to see you, Esmeralda. You are looking as pretty as ever and so well.'

'You flatter me, Régulo. Not many of my customers call me pretty!' I said, smiling modestly at his compliment.

'Then they don't know a good looking woman when they see one,' he said continuing his praise.

'There's a motive behind your charm, señor! You want to put me in the mood for mutual pleasure. Not just pleasure for you!'

'You have seen straight through me, señorita! The pleasure for one is by far the greater when it is pleasure for two!'

'I wish more of the men would think that way. Most are so quick, I hardly know they've touched me, let alone felt any pleasure myself.'

'Then how can I charm you tonight?'

'I'll leave you to guess,' I teased.

'In that case, I will kiss you.'

I lay on the bed and began to lift up my skirt.

'No! Not there!' I pulled my skirt back in place and lay on my side to give him room to get onto the bed beside me. He let his fingers touch my face and pass up to stroke my hair. I felt a lovely tingle.

'I should be paying you,' I laughed. He planted a kiss on my lips to silence me. I responded. What pleasure! I had never kissed or been kissed like this before. He rotated his head to and fro as if to make the kiss a permanent feature. He then took his mouth away from mine.

'How did you like that, Esmeralda? From a man so much older than you?'

'You are a lovely kisser! Who taught you? Not me!'

'No one taught me. But, when I was a young lieutenant, I was walking through our town and saw a young couple standing off the street in an alley. They were kissing just like that and so wrapped up in each other they didn't see me watching.'

'You stopped to watch them? You're not meant to do that!'

'I cannot be ashamed. I lingered for a few moments, rather than stopping, and moved on. But I remember them well. And you have just enjoyed the benefits!'

'And where is your town?'

'Burgos.'

I felt a shiver down my spine and paused. I wondered whether he knew of the killing. Should I chance saying I was from there, too. I took the risk. 'Are you really? I'm from Burgos, too!'

'We must talk about the town and see if we knew any of the same people. But perhaps this is not the time!'

'You are right, señor Régulo. We should continue with our mutual pleasure, now that I'm in a loving mood. Would you like to converse while we are making love?' I asked. 'But perhaps on a different subject.'

'Thanks to you, I now have the confidence to do that,' he said.

'In which case we can talk. May I start with a question?'

'I don't see why not, but I will answer only if I will not be in breach of state law.'

'I understand. Then tell me, if you can, why were the three mutineers pardoned?'

'You have struck a sensitive nerve,' he said, still moving gently and looking down and directly into my eyes. 'But I can answer that. Even though I command the *Tercio*, I have no power over the *barrachel*. He could try me, if he had reason to do so and I could not object. Do you understand that?'

'Yes, I do.'

'Well, I watched the trial and was struck by its unfairness. The *barrachel* gave no opportunity for witnesses to speak on their behalf. He dismissed all of what they said in their defence and mocked them cruelly. It was as if he had decided in advance that they must be guilty. He took no account of the fact that they had not been paid and that in itself struck me as grossly unfair. He had the power to imprison or fine them but...' Régulo then lost control of himself. 'Oh. I'm sorry, Esmeralda, I didn't mean to do that. Not yet...'

'Don't worry,' I said. 'You did well. You pleasured both of us!' He paused for a moment and slid off to my side.

'I decided that I had to get the *barrachel*'s decision reversed. So immediately after the trial, I rode to Brussels for an audience with the Archdukes.'

'Archdukes?'

'Yes, the Archduke and his wife the Infanta Isabella... Once they realised the urgency of what I wanted, they saw me. I cannot tell you any more of the details. But on behalf of the king they issued me with a pardon. As you know, I arrived at the scaffold with a matter of moments to spare,' he said, closing with emotion in his voice. He almost shed tears.

'You are a great man,' I said, 'as well as an improving lover!'

'Now who is doing the flattering, Esmeralda?' he chuckled. 'I'd better go now. You have a queue outside and I have taken enough of your time.'

'You can love me again and I won't charge you!' I said, as he placed two gold *ducats* in my hand.

'Thank you but I must go. Really.'

'Just tell me one thing? How much of your visit to Brussels can I tell others?'

'All of it. All I've told you! That will amuse. The men learning from a woman! And we must speak about Burgos next time!'

***

'How do you know that, Esmeralda?' asked Ion as he, Antonio and we three girls relaxed one quiet afternoon, a little more than a week later, in one of our rooms at the farmhouse.

'Can't tell you, but it's true. The field marshal rode all the way to Brussels and the Archdukes, both of them, signed the pardon,' I said, confidently.

'I still don't believe you,' said Susana.

'Believe what you like!' I said.

The story did not end there. The fact is that the army had two thousand mutineers in the little town of Weert. How were they to punish them if the result of a conviction was a pardon? A month or so later, Antonio and Ion explained it all to us.

'It's hard to understand this but the Archdukes have recognised the facts of the mutineers' case. It is that they have mutinied because of no pay. Some haven't been paid for two years. So the Archdukes have put a case to the king to pay them their arrears in full,' said Antonio.

'The only condition will be that they will have to settle all their debts,' added Ion, twisting his sidewhiskers. 'That's what the Archdukes want. Any who don't immediately pay off their loans would be expelled from the army and have thirty days to leave the country.'

'What happens to their families if they are with them in Weert?' asked Beatrix.

'I imagine they will have to go with them,' said Ion. 'But who knows?'

Not long after, a matter of days after our conversation with Ion and Antonio, the mutineers were all pardoned and the king agreed to pay their arrears in full. Anyone would believe that that would have been the end of the matter but, as with many issues to do with our king and the Treasury, by the time the cash to pay the settlement - some 175,000 escudos - arrived in Weert via Barcelona, Genoa, the Spanish road and Brussels, several more months passed. The army command did not waste this time but gainfully used it to issue individual pardons to the mutineers and organise their readmission to the corps of *Tercios*. Because, in effect, the town of Weert was under siege when occupied by the mutineers, a huge amount of damage had been inflicted on the town, including to the church, not only by the mutineers but also by our *tercios* during attacks in the six hundred days of the mutiny. Field Marshal Régulo de Aracena directed the reparations. Our men Carlos and Antonio worked on this and complained to us that they hadn't joined the army to be builders mates or to dig out sewer lines. I formed the view that their grousing stopped at us and didn't reach their superiors. Ion, on the other hand, seemed much more reconciled to doing what the people of Weert needed to restore the place.

Eventually, and under military escort, the back pay arrived in Weert.

The former mutineers were jubilant. We were less than thrilled.

'We are going to be worked to death by these men,' said Susana. 'We've got enough to do to keep our own men happy, let alone fuck a load of ex-deserters.'

'I'm not too sure either,' said Beatrix, while we were sitting in Alisa's kitchen having breakfast the morning after the day we heard that the money had arrived.

'I don't know what to expect,' I said. 'There are all but two thousand of them. And we've agreed with the lieutenant that we'll take our fair share. Let's hope they decide to spend most of it on drink. Any who come here will be drunk and we can charge them for next to nothing!'

'Trust you to say that,' said Beatrix.

The sheer bureaucracy of dishing out about two hundred *escudos* to each of them played to our advantage. The paymaster had so few clerks that his office could cope with only about two hundred or so payments a day, all to be made in alphabetical order. What with half of these poor souls being unable to spell their own names and barely able to sign for what the clerks gave them, this two hundred fell to less than a hundred. So the number of men we serviced per day rose quite gradually and by the time the last of them were paid, the ones who were at the front of the queue had settled themselves from having to do one of us two or three times a day to making love two or three times a week. We were happy and so were they.

Many of these men were given the option to leave and, as we learned later, many did. They collected their back pay and made their way back to Italy, down the Spanish road. Naturally, they were accompanied by their family members living in Flanders. Many were attacked by highway robbers and relieved of their back pay. No one could say they deserved such a fate but the cynical amongst us suggested that they may have had it coming. After many more months, many occupied by the field marshal's reparations, including the rebuilding of the church tower, the army's job in Weert concluded, as did ours.

Alisa's prediction was not far out. In all we spent almost two years, in the pretty little farmhouse as her guests and that of the quiet Gerlach. We got to know them well. True to what she said when we first arrived at the house, Alisa did everything she could to make us welcomed and comfortable. She cooked us a fried egg breakfast, not every day, but several times a week; she made our beds and tidied our rooms, even put vases of flowers in them; she escorted our customers into our rooms when there were a lot of them and we had difficulty managing them all. We often wondered if she would help us out by serving them herself, if so many turned up at once that we may have been overstretched to do them all ourselves. But we indulged ourselves in this nonsensical sort of chat simply to pass the time of day. Doubtless, despite her mother having served as a *puta*, she remained faithful to her husband throughout her married life. While she would chat to us about many things, including the progress of the army in dealing with the mutiny, she never once discussed our work, what we did, what the *tercios* did with us or anything close to that subject. Even so, she treated us like a mother. Not that any of us really knew a mother so we could only speculate.

Gerlach did not treat us like a father only because work consumed his life. He assiduously farmed his land, from first thing in the morning to late into the night. So we hardly ever saw him. When at home, he treated us with respect. He never touched one of us, tempting though that may have been. You could not have wished for a more decent host.

The fact that they were so good to us made our departure from their home sad and regretful. We just didn't want to go.

'I'm so sad,' said Susana as the day arrived. 'You have been so kind.'

'You have been lovely guests. Just like having three busy daughters staying here!' said Alisa, with tears running down her face. 'If you are ever near Weert, you must stay with us again.'

'I hardly knew my mother,' said Beatrix, also sobbing. 'But you are the mother among mothers. We'll never forget how kind you have been.'

'You are wonderful,' I said, equally full of emotion. 'Likewise, if you ever come to Spain, come and see us in Madrid. We don't know where we will be when we return, but the place to ask for us is a street called the Arganzuela.'

'We'll never come to Spain,' said Alisa, sobbing frantically and hugging me. 'It's a world away.'

We loaded up our things and climbed aboard the same cart which brought us here, with Carlos at the reins. 'We are going but I don't know where. Back down the road towards Brussels. That's all I know,' he said.

CHAPTER 22

Hoogstraten

If Carlos didn't know where we were going, nor did we. But not knowing affected us. Apart from the most basic and obvious, there are certain other things that the fragile human mind needs in order to be satisfied. One of them is that when you start out on a journey, however long or short, you need to know your destination. If only the name of the town, even though you have no idea where it is or even how to get there. Little is more disturbing to the mind than being in a state of knowing ignorance. We felt like water flowing in the gullies down a mountainside, never knowing where it would end up. Why indeed are we travelling at all if we don't know where we are going? We could hardly say we knew our way around Flanders but, although we were not exactly frightened, we were apprehensive about this trip because we could not engage our minds on where we would be, say, in two days' time a week's time or a month's time. We wondered if anyone knew where we would be. We were on the move from Weert and understood that we had finished there but knew no more than that. Surely someone must know.

Carlos took us back to the main road and we turned back down the poplar lined route we used to get here. Our cart plodded along on its own. It looked as if we were the only ones on the move. However, within a *milla* or two we joined up with other wagons which emerged from other exits on to this pretty avenue in the same manner that we had. And within a few more *millas*, there was so much dust raised by the cavalcade of horse drawn wagons that it made us cough and splutter.

'Can't see a damned soldier yet. Not one,' said Susana.

'At this rate we'll have no work tonight,' said Beatrix.

'After the last few nights of celebration my *vava* could do with a night off,' I responded.

Within a few more hours we had caught up our marching army colleagues and Carlos had to slow down for fear of overtaking them.

'Look! There are the soldiers!' said Susana.

'Good!' said Beatrix. 'We may not know where we are going but I'm much less bothered about not knowing, now that I know that the soldiers are with us.'

'I don't know why you are so worried,' said Susana.

'I know,' I said.

'Now we've caught up with them, we'll have to work tonight, whether we like it or not,' said Beatrix.

'I'm so glad to see them, I don't really care,' I said.

***

That night, the three of us, along with our company, stayed in a newly built castle close to the village of Heeze which was to the north west of Weert. The red brick construction stood dominantly above the surrounding fields and at the end of a long, winding track. It looked quite different from any other castle I'd seen or knew about. It seemed more like a homely mansion. It didn't threaten like some crenelated citadel with cannons aimed at the absent enemy outside.

We entered over a drawbridge through a pair of huge oak doors into a magnificent hall, draped in red damask. The walls were panelled in bright, newly polished oak. Sure enough, Sergeant Luis stood just inside the threshold, anxious to greet us. 'You must be quick. There are things to prepare for and I need to settle you into your rooms.'

'What will we be doing?' asked Beatrix.

'You will be joining a group of senior officers at dinner and watching a pageant with them.'

'Go on,' said Susana. 'You'll be expecting us to perform some disgusting act or other in front of them.'

'That's where you're wrong,' he said. 'We want you to sit with the senior officers and be available to serve them, if they want you to. After the meal and pageant.'

'You do surprise me, Luis,' I said. 'The lieutenant usually wants us to do something special on this sort of occasion.'

'Not this time.'

'Why not?' I said.

'You'll soon learn!'

The rooms were the most spectacular we had stayed in. The walls were decorated in carved oak panels about a *pie* square, set between cross members and equally wide verticals. We could smell the newness and extravagance. Whatever had someone paid the carpenters to carve each panel into a symmetrical scroll? A four-poster bed, which reached right up to the cavernous ceiling, dominated each room. The same pattern of damask, which adorned the entrance hall below, draped each of these massive constructions.

'My God, Esmeralda. What are they expecting us to do on these?'

'Our best and no more. We know we're having the senior ones whom we are dining with. I don't know what they'll expect. What do you think, Beatrix?'

'I'm not so sure. We may have to do more for these men. Mind you, they may pay us more into the bargain!'

'So we could be in for a good night!' I said.

***

Sergeant Luis escorted us to the dining hall. We were stunned by our reception. Lieutenant Jorge Castillo, held out his arms to welcome us and, to a lively tune played by a small orchestra of smiling musicians, he escorted the three of us to a table at the end of the hall. The company stood as we approached and applauded us. Between them, the sergeant and lieutenant took us to our seats on this, the top table. They sat me next to Field Marshal Régulo de Aracena himself. He greeted me with the most eloquent smile as I grinned and chuckled, slightly embarrassed, back at him. The lieutenant sat Susana next to the sergeant who sat opposite me. A captain with the most enormous moustache and a paunch of equally generous proportions sat next to the field marshal and Beatrix next to him. The lieutenant took his place last and, as he sat down, signalled the orchestra to cease playing.

The field marshal rose and raised his arms aloft, as the lieutenant settled himself on his chair. 'Gentleman and ladies,' he said, loudly so all there could hear. He paused. The chatting between the men stopped immediately. 'We are here to enjoy a hearty meal and to be entertained. These ladies have served your company so well during the last few years that I decided to put them in this place of honour tonight. Long may they continue to deliver their utmost to you. God save the King!'

A huge cheer and applause filled the hall. The three of us glanced at each other and glowed with a sense of pride. How wonderful to be acclaimed by this heroic soldier. Precisely at the moment the field marshal sat and, as if prompted by his doing so, a dozen or more pretty, young waitresses began to serve the meal.

'That surprised you, didn't it?' the field marshal said. 'You didn't bargain for that!'

'You could have bowled me over with an acorn!' said Susana.

'It's so good to be appreciated,' I said, smiling and still warm with the embers of self-satisfaction.

'No. It's true. You all three deserve it. I know what effort you have put into pleasing these men. All right. I know you have been paid but you three have got to know your men, even by name. That's much more than they'd normally expect!'

Beatrix leant over to join the discussion. 'We merely serve, field marshal. Our men are willing customers and without their enthusiastic participation, we would have no business at all!'

'Let's not talk of work. Maybe later,' said the field marshal. 'I'd like to carry on talking where we left off last time, Esmeralda.'

I had a horrible feeling that he would want to talk about Burgos and that feeling must have shown on my face. I tried not to look fearful but somehow couldn't help it.

'You look worried, as if I've touched a nerve! But I'd rather talk about something else than upset you. I was going to talk about our town. Where we are both from?'

'There are things that happened in Burgos that I would hesitate to talk about. Same with Susana. I certainly would not want them discussed with anyone else, away from this table,' I said, speaking for my friend as confidently as I felt able. She said nothing but glanced vacantly at me and the field marshal, not sure whether to say anything or not.

'I will do a deal with you then. Anything you say about Burgos will go no further than here, we four and you three. None of us will mention anything you tell, once this night is over.'

'How can you speak for the captain here, Lieutenant Castillo and Sergeant Alvarado?' I said.

'How rude of me. How ignorant. I haven't even introduced you to the captain. Please stand, captain. Introduce yourself to my ladies!'

Captain Vicenzo Bota struggled to his feet and, after putting his hands to his moustache and twisting the ends, bowed to each of us in turn, modestly uttered the word, '*Encantado*' and sat down again.

'Yes, I can speak for all four of us,' the field marshal said, 'can't I? This conversation will be about Burgos and will be treated as confidential. We all respect that. Agreed?' Each of the other three nodded, the look in their eyes anticipating scandalous revelations.

'Well, where should we start? Maybe I will. I was born in Burgos and christened in the cathedral,' said the field marshal.

'Yes, where we hid,' I thought.

He continued. 'I was a demon as a child. I remember, at about ten years old, stealing from the till at the bakery in the market square and being chased by a crown constable. I hid under a vegetable stall. I stayed there for ages! He never caught me! I did quite a few other bad things. I used to fight other kids and get into all sorts of trouble. One day, I got angry with a kid who wanted to fight me so picked him up and pushed him into a rubbish pile. He came out stinking of rotten fish! It all seems so distant now and quite amusing to look back on. Anyway, my behaviour used to infuriate my father and he made me join the army. I was glad to get away! I suppose my aggressive streak made me a reasonably good soldier. The army promoted me a few times and here I am! What about you Esmeralda? I've confessed. Now it's your turn!'

I didn't know what to say, whether to tell them of the killing or not. But this was a secret meeting: I could say what I wanted. And I knew something about the field marshal that he wouldn't want anyone else to know about. That would surely be something he would not want discussed, not at any price. To hell with it: knowing that Susana would also be protected by the promise, I would tell them.

I looked him in the eye and said it, calmly and in a clear and confident tone. 'I killed a man in Burgos. He was an *hidalgo*. When I left the orphanage I got a job as his housekeeper. I kept the place clean and tidy and used to cook for him and run errands. In return he paid me a *real* a week and let me have a room in his house. He started by being very nice and quite protective towards me. But within a few weeks he expected me to do other things for him. Things I didn't want to do. He tried, many times, to rape me but failed because he was drunk and I fought him off. He would come at me with his stiff penis in his hand and demand that I satisfy him. I would fight him off. More times than I want to remember. I hated him. I thought he would kill me. But I could not fight him for ever. I thought unless I killed him, he'd kill me. I couldn't see a way out. If I escaped he'd chase after me. So I dreamt up a plan. I'd push a paving slab onto his head from a window above the front door. I'd kill him and flee to Madrid. And that's exactly what I did.'

'My God! It was you, Esmeralda! It was you!' he said, beaming all over his face.

'How do you know about it?'

'My father knew him! They used to play cards together at a tavern in the Plaza Mayor. He used to annoy my father by cheating. Father reckoned he swindled him out of tens of *ducats*. When he realised what was going on, he stopped playing with him. What finished my father was when my mother told Father that the *hidalgo* made a serious pass at her. He came to our house while my father was at work and asked her for oral sex. He got out his penis in front of her, as he did to you. Mother refused and screamed out so he went. Father was furious when she told him. He exploded with anger. He took a pistol and that night went around to the *hidalgo*'s house with the sole intention of killing him.

'As Father reached the house, he slipped on a pool of blood and urine outside. The ground was strewn with pieces of stone. He realised that something was wrong. He knocked on the door and waited. And waited.

No one answered. He put his ear to the door and heard nothing. So he called a constable. They broke into the house and found the *hidalgo*, dead. Not a sign of life in him.

'Apparently, Father cheered out aloud. "He's already dead! Someone's killed him!" He even confessed to the constable that he had come to kill him. At first, the constable didn't believe him. So Father took out his gun and showed it to him. Then the constable thought Father had killed the *hidalgo* and was about to arrest him. But Father showed that his gun had not been fired. The constable whistled up a colleague and they both interviewed my father, on the spot. There and then. They saw that the *hidalgo*'s head was caved in and he had no gunshot wounds.

'Eventually, they convinced themselves that the *hidalgo* had been killed before my father arrived. So he was never charged with anything because he had not committed a crime, not even intent to kill. You cannot mean to kill someone who is already dead! You, Esmeralda, had already done it for him! Amazing, Esmeralda! Incredible! What a revelation!'

The shock of what he said stunned me like an unexpected smack in the face. I retained my composure and within a second was able to continue this amazing discussion. 'I had no idea that your father was going to kill him! I wish I'd known beforehand. I'd have left it to your father! Anyway, I knew if I stayed in Burgos, I'd be caught, so I went to tell my friend, Susana, here. She wouldn't let me go alone. So we fled together. The two of us.'

'The body was still warm so you must have killed him not long before they found him. Maybe only minutes before! There was no one in the house so you must have left soon after.'

'I didn't spend long there. I can tell you.'

'Yes, the constabulary tried to follow you and catch you. But you outwitted them and escaped. But the girls they were looking for were called María and Lucía. I think they were the names. You are telling the truth Esmeralda, aren't you? Something isn't right,' he said, looking at each of us quizzically.

'We changed our names!'

'You clever girls! So you vanished?' he said, the doubt falling from his face.

'Just that,' I said, smiling back at him.

'What a story. And you saved my father from being a killer. I'll be indebted to you forever. And for more than one reason!' he let slip.

The ponderous captain, sitting between the field marshal and Beatrix, stirred himself to speak. 'And what is the other reason for being so grateful?' he said in his slow, resonant voice.

'Ah! Now you are asking me something,' said Régulo. 'But it would be ungallant of me to discuss what happens between a man and a woman in private.'

'I was right,' I thought. 'He doesn't want to admit to his own impotence. Even if it was in the past.'

**

As we were consuming our last mouthfuls and drinking the dregs of the wine, an indoor firecracker exploded at the side of the hall. Surprised and shaken by the bang, we all looked at each other wondering what was to happen. As the smoke began to clear, the little orchestra started up and two cheery-looking performers appeared from the smoke. Each was laughing and juggling with four or five bright yellow balls. Just about everyone burst into applause.

'What skill,' said the field marshal.

'I've never seen anything as clever,' said Beatrix.

'Nor me,' I said. Susana looked on in wide-eyed amazement.

Then one of the jugglers dropped a ball and then another. Balls fell across the floor, one under the foot of the other juggler who fell and scattered his. The whole audience exploded into laughter. In an effort to regain their credibility, the distraught jugglers quickly picked up their balls, launched them into the air again and continued with their act. Within a few minutes they finished, bowed in unison to their audience and vanished through a door. A mixed round of applause and laughter marked their shamefaced departure.

The little orchestra stopped playing, flicked through the music on their stands and started up again with a romping jig. This cued the entry of a team of five acrobats made up of a male and a female dwarf, another woman and two large, strong-looking men. The men, including the dwarf, were dressed only in bright red pantaloons and all three women wore boleros and pantaloons of the same gaudy colour. They came in holding hands, dancing and singing, I supposed in Walloon, to the lively tune the orchestra were playing. Again we laughed and welcomed our new entertainers with noisy applause. They each followed the leading man in cartwheeling around the stage.

'What a great display,' said Susana. 'I wish I could do that!'

'I'm glad you can't,' said Beatrix. 'You'd never lay flat on your back if you could!'

Then one of the men picked up the man dwarf and threw him across to the other man who caught him in his arms and threw him up in the air, back to the other man. The second man picked up the woman dwarf and threw her into the air and caught her in his arms. He then kissed her and threw her up into the air again. As she landed in his arms he lost grip of her and, but for the other woman in the troop who outstretched her arms to save her, she would have fallen flat on the floor. We all gasped an 'Oooo' at the unscheduled incident. The troupe reassembled in a line facing us, took a bow and left through the door.

The orchestra paused for a minute or two, shuffled their music again and resumed their playing with a daring, erotic *chacona*. Each of us on the table recognised this tune and glanced at each other, wondering what spectacle it would accompany. Our erstwhile colleagues, Ana Blas and Marina de la Cueva, each daringly stripped to the waist, appeared at the door with two of the men – but not the dwarf – from the acrobat troupe. The two women peered across at us and scowled. We did our best to ignore them. Each of the two acrobats was by then totally naked, smiling and cavorting to the audience. Ana and Marina moved towards the front and began to turn their bodies, so as to swing and jiggle their breasts. The men in the audience roared and cheered their approval. The field marshal smiled knowingly at me and at Susana, sitting opposite. I cringed as I wondered what would happen next. Nothing, however shocking, seemed outside the repertoire of these two repugnant *putas*.

'You don't have to watch this if you don't want to. Perhaps it wouldn't look good if you went out so maybe look the other way,' he said to me and Beatrix, bending over the table so Susana could also hear. He obviously knew what 'delights' would follow.

'No. I'm all right,' said Susana. 'May learn something!' The other two of us nodded to indicate we'd watch, contemplating something gross and obscene, if the past performances of these two aggressors were anything to go by.

Their act began. With a calculated flourish, Ana Blas removed her skirt from her plump frame to expose her ample rear and luxuriant growth of pubic hair. She faced the audience so that the men could see her in all her wobbling glory. She then turned to the side and, to the rhythm of the *chacona*, now sounding louder and more fiery, awoke the penises of the two acrobats, one in each hand. She rubbed them against her body and soon stiffened them to penetrating readiness. Marina de la Cueva then, with the same painful flourish, removed her skirt to reveal her total, rather more compact, bareness. She stood on a short stool and faced the other three, leaning back slightly. Ana pulled one of the laughing men, clutching only at his penis, towards Marina and appeared to ease his member into Marina's vagina. The man moved within her to the dance. Ana then dragged the second man round to Marina's rear and seemed to ease him into her anus. He soon adopted the same rhythm, as if he was doing her in time with the man apparently occupying her vagina. Ana raised her arms above her head and swung them and her breasts in time with the music, signalling to the audience to join the applause and clamour. The whole dining hall erupted in shouting, clapping and stamping of feet. The men at the back stood up and some moved to the back for a better view.

'Get back or get down! We can't damn well see,' several shouted from halfway.

'I wish I could make it last that long,' the field marshal whispered to me.

'I'm glad you can't,' I replied. 'I'd never get rid of you!'

'But think what I'd have to pay!'

Not many minutes later the two acrobats ejaculated together in a shaking spasm, or appeared to do so, inside the woman. She let out a piercing cry, as if enjoying a breathtaking climax. The audience's applause deafened us.

'My God,' said Beatrix, stunned. 'I wasn't expecting that. I wouldn't have thought it would be possible. Not to have a man in each orifice at the same time.'

'I'm not sure what to make of that. I suppose I should be disgusted but I'm not. Was that an act or did those men actually get inside her? I couldn't really see. Trust those two to put on an exhibition like that! At least they didn't involve an animal this time and no one got hurt. We certainly won't be advertising that as a service,' I said. 'You'd need to be an acrobat to do it!'

'That Marina's no acrobat,' said Susana. 'She'd do anything for a few maravedís. I can't say they get the best jobs. I wouldn't want to perform in public, not like that!'

***

This unwholesome display marked the end of this grotesque pageant. The sight of the men cavorting with Marina had its effect on our men. They needed urgent attention. The problem, however, was that the senior officers would have first call on us and the rest would have to wait or avail themselves of other ladies and their services. Many couldn't wait and pursued the latter course. The sergeant decided that he was too tired and wanted an early night. The result was that Susana went off with the lieutenant, Beatrix with the moustached Captain Vicenzo Bota, and I was to bed the field marshal.

He couldn't stop talking. 'Sorry to bring the subject up again, but I still can't get over you killing the hidalgo,' he said while undressing in my ornate bedroom. 'You could have saved my father from being executed for murder! You did our family a great service. '

'I'm not sure what to think, señor Régulo. I'm still in shock! I could not have known that I was first in the queue to kill him. Otherwise, I may have made sure I was second. But then, I would not be here. Susana and I would still be poor orphans, struggling to survive in Burgos. Life would have been completely different from what it is now. I suppose, when I think about it, I have no regrets. It took my killing of the *hidalgo* to make us leave Burgos. I doubt that anything less drastic would have made us go.'

'The fact is, my father and I are greatly in your debt. I shall always be grateful to you. You showed great courage in killing that man and no one can blame you.'

'I'm sorry Régulo, you are wrong. The authorities were after me – and Susana – and I could have been hanged if they found me guilty. Please, let's talk about something else. We've come up to my room for me to entertain you, not to speculate on the past. How can I please you tonight? Anything you like!'

'Um... after that display... I'm so tempted to try something quite different. May I? Just the once!'

***

They still didn't tell us where we were heading. Not for two more days. But we could tell that we were heading in a vaguely north westerly direction.

Near lunchtime, on the second day after our preposterous night at Heeze Castle, we stopped by an inn with a huge water trough outside.

'Ideal for the horses, girls. Let's stop here for a while.'

'I could do with a drink,' said Beatrix. Suddenly we all felt thirsty and trailed into the tavern for a cup of beer. Carlos paid. Susana decided to use the room near the rear to relieve herself but no sooner had she gone than she returned.

'I've never smelt anything like it. God it stinks! I'm going for a piss outside. I'll see you later. Oh for fresh air!'

As we came out of the inn, Susana was walking back to the wagon from a small thicket. 'Look what I've found,' she said, waving what was apparently a piece of fabric in the air.

'What's that?' asked Beatrix.

'I'm not really sure. There are lines all over it and what looks like place names.' She offered it to me.

'It's a map. A map of Flanders. It's wet. Let's put it on the floor of the wagon. We may be able to work out where we're going! Or at least where we're heading.'

The three of us and Carlos cleared a space in the back of the wagon. 'Here's Heeze,' said Carlos, 'and we are heading this way. We've been through here – Tilburg – and heading there. They're taking us to Breda. That's where we're going!'

'What so special about Breda?' I asked.

'It's always being fought over. One minute it's Dutch. The next it's Spanish. That's where we're going. For sure!'

'We could be heading for Antwerp,' said Beatrix. 'Look. It's only down there!'

'No. It's too far south. We'd have gone through Turnout if that's where we were heading. No Breda. Definitely!'

I had to admit, the ever dependable Carlos had to be right. This map had shown us the way. There could be little room for doubt. There seemed to be nowhere else we could be heading.

'Well done, Susana,' said Carlos. 'I'm glad you peed outside!'

'I wonder what's happened in Breda?' said Beatrix. 'They wouldn't be sending us there for a rest!'

'It's got back into the hands of the Dutch and we're going to get it back off them. Just wait and see!' said Carlos as he clambered onto the driver's seat and got ready to pull away.

Susana took possession of the map and followed our route with her finger.

There could be no doubt that we were heading for Breda. Carlos had the horses trotting along nicely but when we were within two *leguas* of Breda we had to stop. We had no choice. We were staggered by the sight before us. Troops were marching straight towards us from the direction of Breda. Instead of running into us, they turned off along the road to our left onto a route which headed south.

'My God! Look at that lot! We are here,' said Susana, pointing her finger at a barely discernible crossroads on the map. 'They are heading down here. I'm not sure how to pronounce the name of the place but it's the only town for *millas* down there. It looks like... Hoog... Hoogstra... Hoogstraten.'

'Never heard of it,' said Carlos.

'We've only heard of places like Brussels and Antwerp. So that's new to us, too!' said Beatrix.

We stood up on the wagon seat to get a better view of this cavalcade of soldiers, eight or ten abreast, marching through in waves. The pikemen's polished halberds glistened in the sunlight. Their leather boots kicked up the dust as they hit the ground in a grinding rhythm. Then followed the harquebusiers and musketeers, all shouldering their weapons and driven along by the shouting from brigades of cavalry. 'I suppose they are all ours, are they?' asked Beatrix.

'Yes, they're ours all right. The red sash gives them away,' said Carlos.

We must have waited an hour or more, watching this grand army pass. Thousands came pouring through to the incessant beat of a grim-faced young soldier, standing at the crossroads banging a side drum. Our own men had merged into this procession. 'There's the lieutenant,' said Susana. 'Give him a shout!'

He rode over to greet us. 'What's happening? Where are we going, señor?' said Carlos.

'Heading for Hoogstraten,' he said as his horse tugged at its reins. 'Another mutiny. We're going to drive out the mutineers. By force this time. A huge force. We are an army of thirteen thousand men. We can't lose. There are three thousand mutineers holed up in the castle there.'

Suddenly, fear climbed into my heart. I started to shake.

'What's the matter, Esmeralda? You look pale. A minute ago you were fine,' said Beatrix.

'I don't know. I am afraid, all of a sudden. The sheer number of troops. There is going to be an almighty battle. Thousands will be killed. Our men among them. And we'll be in the midst of it...' I verged on tears but managed to hold their wetness at my eyes.

'You are usually the calmest of the three of us,' said Susana, speaking to me. 'I feel protected by all of these men!'

'I think I know what Esmeralda is saying,' said Beatrix. 'There is going to be a big battle and who knows how many and who will die.'

'Let's not make too much of it,' I said, trying too late to reassure my friends and settle myself. 'We go along as usual. Maybe things will work out better than my fears are telling me.'

***

Hoogstraten was a small town. As we approached it, we could see the castle, a dogged looking stronghold that stood proudly above the flat land surrounding it. As we got nearer we could appreciate even more the size of our massive army. Thousands of troops, mostly infantry, but hundreds on horseback, were positioning themselves in readiness for attack. From where we stopped to watch, it looked like an army of busy worker ants frantically clambering on a corpse and devouring it piecemeal. The men had positioned at least fifty cannons, to threaten the castle ramparts. With the infantry at the front and cavalry to the rear, it looked as if a raging battle was about to begin.

'This is going to be a bloodbath,' said Carlos, speaking with a note of fear in his voice. He seemed to be echoing the anxiety I had expressed five or six hours earlier.

'I've never seen anything like this before,' said Beatrix. 'They're all arranged like hordes of toy soldiers, ready to attack.'

'Where will we be staying tonight? Has anyone thought that far ahead?' asked Susana.

'Not good news on that,' said Carlos. 'Either we put up a tent or you sleep on the wagon. There are so few houses near this town that they couldn't arrange billeting for anyone except some of the followers with children.'

'That's ridiculous. How can we be expected to work in a tent... or even worse, on the wagon?' I said

'There is no work tonight, ladies. All the men are at arms and that means they have to stay in their positions until told otherwise. There's a big enough tent for the three of you in the back. Either we put up the tent and I sleep in the wagon or you sleep in the wagon and I sleep underneath.'

'I can't see why we can't all sleep in the wagon!' said Susana.

'In that case, nor can I,' I said.

'So we'll have to fight for our only customer tonight,' said Beatrix.

'I'm not fighting with anybody,' said Susana.

So the four of us slept in the wagon. Carlos slept at the front and the three of us near the back. It was a mild August night so we made the blankets into a heap and slept on top of them. Susana insisted in sleeping in a nightgown but Beatrix and I slept in nothing but our dresses. 'I'd sleep naked but for giving Carlos a free show!' joked Beatrix.

I woke up only a few hours after I had dropped off to sleep. With over twelve thousand soldiers within a few hundred *pies* of our wagon there were the inevitable sounds of sentries changing guard and ammunition being moved as well as other battleground noises: horses chomping at hay and clicking their hooves, flags fluttering in the mild breeze and the occasional dog barking or owl hooting. I decided to step out of the wagon just to give freedom to my curiosity. I was amazed at what I could see. I could easily make out the castle. So as to make it a visible night target, our men had surrounded it, at least to the extent which I could see, with braziers and bonfires. Detachments of men were moving between these little conflagrations topping up the braziers with tar and piling tree branches on the wood fires. It would have been possible to see the town and the castle from miles away, let alone from where I stood. I cast my eye around the area in front of the castle, expecting to be able to see troops in their thousands but the light from the front of the castle ramparts prevented me from seeing anything but murky shadows. All I could imagine was that our men, quietly lurking in the darkness, were awake and ready to unleash their weapons at the least sign of danger. The fact that they had illuminated the castle so completely made it an unmissable target. The cannons I had seen the day before would surely destroy it.

***

Three days later, we were still in the same place, bored, uncomfortable on the wagon and hot in the summer air. And the army hadn't fired a shot.

'I know. I'm as fed up with this as you, girls. I'm going down to the front line. Someone down there is sure to know what's happening.'

'Pretty obvious, if you ask me,' said Susana. 'Nothing. Nothing at all. And I'm thirsty.'

'And I'm hungry,' I said.

'Don't worry. I'll bring back some food and water.'

Carlos had been gone so long, we were beginning to worry. It was late and getting dark and he still hadn't appeared. Our mouths cracked with the dryness of our thirst and our stomachs groaned with hunger. Then we heard voices and laughter outside.

'Come in and meet my girls,' we heard him say. His voice slurred as he spoke. He'd been drinking and in all likelihood so had the men he was with. He came in through the canvas flaps at the front bringing his friends with him. They all stank of cheap beer.

'These are my new friends,' he said. 'They've brought you food and water.'

'Thanks be to God! Well done,' said Beatrix.

'Where have you been?' I said, as Susana poured out some water for each of us.

'I had to wait for the commander's men... to come back from the castle,' he could just about say. 'He'd sent a captain and two lieutenants. Doing some bargaining... my mates here helped me carry the stuff back.'

'You're drunk!' shouted Susana. 'And what do these men really want. We don't work, except in private.'

'No. They're not expecting business. I told them you weren't available. Did I do right?'

'You did well,' I said. 'Thank you, men. Very good of you to help us. We're starving and parched!'

'What have you all been drinking?' asked Beatrix.

'Flanders' beer. It goes down a treat!' said one of the men.

'Strong as an ox's hind leg,' said another.

'No wonder you're all gone,' said Susana. 'I only hope you can find your way back. It's damned near black out there!' We all laughed heartily and Carlos's helpers, still chuckling at Susana's comments, climbed out of the wagon and left.

'So what's really happening,' I said to Carlos. 'Tell us.'

'The commander in charge of these *Tercios* is a Francisco de Mendoza. I've never heard of him before but they say he is number two in the Flanders army. He is the Admiral of Aragon, apparently, and a clever soldier. It was his idea to beat out the mutineers with a huge army. Well, he can't do anything now. The Dutch have sided with the mutineers and have got just as big an army to the north ready to attack ours. They want the mutineers in their army and it looks like they're going to get them. The Admiral will decide tomorrow what we do. We either take on the Dutch and the mutineers or we withdraw.'

'So this massive army could have come here for nothing,' said Beatrix.

'You could say that,' said Carlos, now beginning to sober up.

'The one good thing is that if he has to back down he will save many lives, maybe ours included,' I added.

Three hot days later, the Admiral made his decision. We would leave Hoogstraten to the Dutch. Not a shot was fired. Not a lance was thrown. Not a pike was thrust. No one died and no one was injured.

'So where next?' I asked Carlos.

'Ostende.'

'Ostende? Wherever's that?' asked Susana.

'No idea,' said Beatrix.

'Think I've heard of it but no idea where it is,' I said.

'It's on the coast, it's Dutch and it's under siege,' said Carlos.

CHAPTER 23

The Siege

Ten days later, in the bright summer mid-morning, we were approaching the outskirts of Ostende. For some reason, I felt more confident in my bones than ever I could be in Hoogstraten. I hated that place, the fear I could never dispel, the discomfort and the tension on the battlefield which never saw battle but even so spilled over on to us. The safest I felt was when Carlos drove us out of there.

We realised only when we were near Ostende that our company of men had rejoined the two Spanish *Tercios* which, more than two years before, had accompanied us up the road from Milan to Brussels. The lieutenant, whom we last saw on the road to Hoogstraten, came to tell us what would happen outside this beleaguered town.

'Ladies, you have all but reached Ostende. This is going to be a different kind of assignment for our men and it will affect you. The town has been under siege for more than two years. The Archduke has failed to break it. Rumour has it that he will step aside in favour of General Ambrosio Spinóla whom the king will engage... no... command... to finish it. To take the town for Flanders... whether the Archduke likes it or not.'

'So how will that affect us?' asked Beatrix. 'You will put us up somewhere and we'll be serving the men. Just like we did in Weert?'

'I agree,' I said. 'You know how our business works. We need a room each, a bed to sleep and work on, food and drink... and off we go.'

'You will, I promise you, have all of that but...,' he paused.

'Come on. Out with it,' said Susana.

'Well... it's not going to be the same here. There has been so much destruction around Ostende since the siege began, there are no comfortable houses or farms we can billet you in. Or any of the other girls.'

'Really? So what is that supposed to mean?' shouted Beatrix. 'Go on. Tell us!'

'Less of the loudness! We are going to put you in a disused fort, not far from the town and on its west side.'

'I'll tell you something straight away, Jorge. We are not going to live like tramps or street whores in some derelict pile of rubble you call a disused fort,' I said.

'You are jumping to conclusions, Esmeralda. The fort we have in mind for you is disused only because we have made advances towards

Ostende over the last year or so and have built a ring of new forts to house our troops and ammunition. The newer ones are closer to Ostende so in better strategic positions. You will be staying in one with the pretty name of "Sand Dunes". It is not unpleasant at all and we will help you make it comfortable.'

'Which means it's not comfortable now,' said Beatrix.

'I have to confess... Yes. You are right. The fort is derelict but it's in good order, at least according to a memorandum I've received from Brussels. We were thinking of using it for troops but we need somewhere reasonably close for you girls to live and work.'

'A memorandum from Brussels?' I said, fearlessly challenging the lieutenant. 'Surely you wouldn't have had anything as important as a memorandum from Brussels just about where you were going to put us three? Either you are lying to us, Jorge, or there is more to what you are saying than you've been telling us.'

'Of course I wouldn't lie to you. Why would I? No. But you haven't given me chance to explain it all. Not yet. It's like this.'

We listened in silence, anticipating things we wouldn't want to hear. 'We need to accommodate something like seventy five of you to serve the troops on this side of the town. There will be just as big a number on the other side, to the east.'

'Whatever's going on? We've never had this before? We've always had a separate billet, except when we had to share with Ana Blas and Marina de la Cueva,' said Beatrix, glaring sharply at him.

'Things are different here. To start with, this is a long-term campaign. It's going to be bloody and vicious. And the general wants his men to be happy. Satisfied troops make the best warriors. And you women will satisfy them all right!'

'But why do we all have to be in the same place? How do we know we'll be only serving our own men?' said Beatrix.

'There is going to be a "master"...'

'So it's a brothel then!' said Susana.

'No. The "master" will be a soldier, a corporal, in fact. He will allocate the men to the girls. And you'll only get your men, your company. And there's nowhere else for you to go.'

'We could go back to Madrid,' said Beatrix.

'I'd think twice about that,' I said. 'We must give this a try. It may work out better than we think.'

'Thank you, girls. I'm relieved.' So we'd eventually pleased the lieutenant, even if we remained sceptical ourselves.

***

We were shocked at the state of the fort. It was the wreck we first imagined it to be. The name 'Sand Dunes' fitted perfectly. As we approached it, on foot because Carlos simply could not drive the wagon on the sand, we could see what a hideous mess it was in. Sand was piled up against the walls. The wind picked it up from the ground and blew it in our faces. We climbed in up some steps. The smell hit us as we walked inside.

'It smells like someone's died in here,' said Susana. 'What a stink.'

'Vile,' said Beatrix, taking a handkerchief and putting it to her nose.

We explored the place, climbing from floor to floor on the stone stairs. Sand covered everything and filled every corner of every room. The smell permeated every space in it.

'What do we make of this?' asked Beatrix.

'It's terrible. Disgusting. And that stench. I could cry. It's the worst we've had to put up with. Worse than sleeping on the wagon at Hoogstraten,' said Susana.

'The lieutenant said they were going to clean it up. Make it more comfortable,' I said.

'We'll see,' said Beatrix.

As we turned at the top of the uppermost staircase, we could see three women with twig brooms sweeping the sand towards the stairs, towards us. Each wore a stained, white skirt and yellowish, dirty blouse, as if it was some kind of uniform. One looked as if she could be pregnant. We recognised them as *putas* we had seen before but didn't know.

'Who are you?' asked one, in a tone that was hardly friendly.

I thought I would answer before Susana or Beatrix, mainly to prepare for what I hoped would be a good relationship with these women, each of whom appeared older than us. 'We're *putas*, serving a company of *tercios* from Madrid. We followed them up the Spanish Road to Brussels. We spent two years at Weert, where there was a mutiny and then to Hoogstraten. We were only there a week, if that. Now we're here. Looks like we'll be living with you girls and I'm sure we'll all get on well together. What about you?'

'We've been everywhere General Spínola has been. Don't ask me the names of the places. But we've been in all manner of battles and seen some bad things. Mainly dead and wounded soldiers.'

'Smells like there's a corpse in here,' said Beatrix. 'The stench is disgusting.'

'Yes, it's awful. We're sweeping out the sand. To clean the place up. And to try and find what's causing the smell.'

'Any more brooms and we'll help you,' said Susana.

'We haven't got any more brooms but there are some shovels on the floor below.'

Beatrix soon fetched them and we were shovelling sand through the windows as our three new housemates kept up with the sweeping. We laboured several hours and into the afternoon. It was so hot and we were perspiring so badly that we decided we would work naked. All six of us piled our clothes on the floor of a room we had finished and carried on.

'This is one way to get to know each other,' said one of the others, a dark haired woman of about thirty with enlarged breasts and distended abdomen. 'My name is Ursula. As you can see, I am expecting a customer's child. I've no idea whose. It's due in about four months now. There's already a limit to what work I can do.'

Thankfully, and to our great relief, we three had each avoided becoming pregnant, at least up to then. I wondered what would happen to the baby but the-mother-to-be didn't seem too concerned. It would probably be looked after by nuns, like me and Susana. God help the child if that was so.

'I am Sancha,' said the second, a tall blonde shy-sounding woman with what sounded like a Portuguese accent.

'And I am Olalla, the oldest of the three of us.' Her drooping breasts and wrinkled bottom commiserated with her age.

We introduced ourselves to them and carried on working. The bedrooms on the first floor were smaller than on the second and smaller still on the third. The large drawing room on the first floor accounted for a lot of the space there. We split into three groups to continue our work. Susana went with Olalla, Beatrix with Sancha and I with Ursula. We took a floor each, leaving the ground floor until later.

We had worked for about an hour when I recognised a piercing scream as Susana's. I thought at first that she had been stabbed by an intruder. It was that kind of death embracing shriek. All of us descended to the room where Susana and Olalla laboured. Olalla, too terrified and stunned to talk, pointed to an amorphous entity which Susana had uncovered with her shovel. Susana had withdrawn herself so far from the thing that her back was pressed against the wall. I could feel my heart thumping in my breast as I recognised with terror this gruesome object, confronting us in our nakedness. It was a disembodied, human arm.

I had to examine it more closely. I could see flies crawling over it and flicked my hands to scare away those flying near it and me. I held my nose at the stench and crept towards it. I felt a strange vulnerability in my nakedness, afraid that it would jump up and touch me, while knowing that it could not. A finger had been stripped of flesh to the yellowy brownness of the bone. The other fingers and thumb were almost completely black and bloated so the skin was separate from the flesh. The skin on the forearm and above the elbow was mottled from black and brown to a yellowing white where the skin had not yet decayed. Where there were breaks in the skin, the flesh was being consumed by wriggling maggots. From the state of the flesh near the shoulder joint, the arm had been torn from the body. This thought drove a violent shudder through me as I realised the agony the human soul who experienced this amputation must have suffered. An arm severed from the shoulder socket. The result could be nothing but death. No human being could survive such intensity of pain and bleeding. How could it have happened? I could not touch it with my hand so I gently slid it with my shovel, only to provoke an erupting cloud of flies. I could see then that the main bones had been shattered. Some had broken through the flesh into the air. Then a frightening thought. A cannon ball may have taken off this arm: ripped it from its body; divided what should never be divided; separated the inseparable. How the arm had found its way into the corner of this room and when exactly it did so remained a mystery. Could it have been taken there by an animal, a fox perhaps? Could it have been left there by some sick individual, hoping to frighten anyone who stumbled across it? Or, worst of all, had the victim suffered the removal of his smashed arm in this room and the arm left there by his torturers? We would, I imagined, never know.

These terrible thoughts occupied me for a full minute, if not more. I shrank back from the arm, suddenly consumed in an odd kind of fear. I looked behind me and the other five had gone, left me there with it. As I emerged from this room of unquenchable agony, the rest were all looking at me in horror.

'How could you, Esmeralda? How could you? You went right up to it,' said Beatrix.

'I had to. Something inside me compelled me. I could not turn my back on it and go. However bad the smell. However horrific. Despite the flies. I knew it couldn't hurt me.'

'You are brave, Esmeralda,' said Olalla. 'I was so shocked to see it in the first place. My body went stiff. I had to get out.'

'I didn't have the shock you had,' I said. 'My first reaction was relief. Relief that my friend was not hurt. I thought she had been stabbed by some insane *tercio*!'

'What do we do now?' asked Sancha.

'Get out of here,' said Susana.

'No,' I said. 'We get one of the men to take it out and bury it. We shut the door on it and leave it until then.'

'I'm not having that room,' said Susana.

'Don't be precious,' said Beatrix. 'Time it's cleaned out it'll be fine. We're among the first here so can have any room we like.'

Something struck all of us about being naked in front of the dead arm. We all felt uncomfortable at being undressed in front of it, even guilt at being bare before we discovered it. So we all went back up to the room where we had left our clothes and sheepishly put them on again.

'That's good. I feel much better now,' said Ursula.

'We all do, I think,' said Beatrix.

I decided there and then to find a soldier to take the arm away and give it to whoever was responsible for disposing of these sacred parts of human bodies. A man was standing at the gate of the fort as I reached it. He turned round on seeing me. It was Carlos. Breaking down in tears at his smiling face, I rushed up to him and hugged him.

'Am I pleased to see you?' I said and, wiping my eyes while he held my hand, explained our grim discovery.

'I imagine it's a common occurrence around here. A siege it may be but battlefield it certainly is,' said Carlos. He took a sack out of the wagon and followed me into the fort.

It took the six of us and a further contingent of ten or so *putas* three days to clear the fort of sand and other extraneous material. Thankfully, we found no more human remains and once Carlos had removed the decaying arm – we never did ask him what he did with it – the obnoxious smell soon dispersed. True to Lieutenant Jorge Castillo's word, a convoy of wagons arrived outside the fort with carpets, furniture and various other homely pieces but all were worn and in a state of dilapidation. We and some of our company, all too anxious to make the fort suitable for us to conduct business, soon had the place habitable and, indeed, surprisingly comfortable, despite the battered condition of the furnishings. There were no arguments about which rooms we would occupy. Susana, Beatrix and I had, as among the first there, set up in adjacent rooms on the first floor. Ursula, Sancha and Olalla joined us.

'We're better off on the first floor,' Beatrix assured us. 'If the tide comes in we'll be safe.'

'Yes, even if one of the dykes gives way and sea water starts to break through,' said Olalla.

***

The true horrors of this siege soon became apparent. The Archdukes Albert and Isabella remained in control while the king decided whether or not General Ambrosio Spínola should take over. Archduke Albert's approach to sending troops into battle was reckless and ruthless. We had been staying in the sparsely furnished 'Sand Dunes' for only a few weeks, when one of the bloodiest battles of the siege took place. The Archduke sent a huge contingent of men to attack one of the Dutch held forts nearer to the town. The first we knew about it was the constant sound of muskets being fired and cannons being discharged.

'My God,' said Susana, as we were relaxing that morning in the large dining room on the ground floor. 'All those explosions. They sound as if they're right outside. I'm scared.'

'It's the worst I've heard,' said Olalla. 'But there's nothing we need do. These walls are two *pies* thick. We're as safe as we can be in here. Just don't go outside! And don't lean out of a window.' Olalla seemed a sensible if hard woman, hardened by a long career as a *puta*. But she found it easy to be friendly with us and seemed to have adopted the role of leader of the three of them.

'There's nothing we can do,' said Beatrix. 'I suppose we'll just have to wait to see what the troops say when they come here tonight.'

And find out we did. Antonio arrived in a dreadful state. His right leg had been burnt in an explosion and his pantaloons were in shreds. He went straight to see Beatrix and the two of them came into my room where Susana and I were sitting and chatting.

'Give me something to put on my leg,' he said, limping and with a hand on his knee.

'We'll tear up a sheet,' said Susana so we did.

'I've never seen anything like it. I reckon five hundred men died out there today. It was hideous. Blood, limbs and bodies everywhere. Not just the men, the horses were mangled, too.'

'What about Ion,' shrieked Susana.

'I haven't seen him but I imagine he's all right. It was mainly the Italians who suffered and a few like me who got caught up in it all.'

'I'm going to find him,' said Susana, breaking into tears.

'I wouldn't do that, if I were you,' said Antonio. 'You could easily be wounded or at worse killed.'

'I agree with Antonio,' I said.

'So do I,' said Olalla.

'Well, tell us what happened out there,' I said.

'The Archduke had this idea that we would take one of their forts. His intelligence had informed him that it would be an easy ride. So we all took up our positions. The pikemen were in front with the harquebusiers and us musketeers behind them, backing them up. The cavalry took up the rear. The Archduke decided that we would attack from each side so the flanks made the first move towards the fort. That's where the Italians were. We held back to be the second force of attack. There must have been three or four thousand of us.

'It was an amazing sight to see the waves of pikemen, weapons pointing before them, heading to the fort. Two drummers, one at each flank, banged out a rhythm which seemed to excite and inspire the men. They were ready for battle. Ready for a fight. They shouted to the beat as they moved forwards. Flag bearers, their heads held high, carried the banner of the Spanish Netherlands, you know, two red laurel branches on a white background. I felt a sense of pride to be part of this. A sense of the rightness of what we were doing.

'Then it happened. Hundreds of heads appeared over the ramparts. Dutch troops with guns. Hundreds of them. Their muskets and cannons were aimed at our troops. The pikemen stopped in their tracks. No one expected to see this huge force defending their fort. It was clear that our men would have to retreat. Our own artillery turned as if to retrace their steps. But the commander of the cavalry signalled the charge. The cavalry on each flank drove into the pikemen, harquebusiers and musketeers, pushing them towards the onslaught of musket and cannon balls raining on them. It was horrific. I felt helpless as I watched powerless at this massacre. Happening right there in front of me. I daren't fire for fear of hitting our men. The smell of burning gunpowder choked us. Men fell on top of men. They screamed in their agony. It was like a hideous dream but I was awake and there. Blood poured...'

'Stop,' said Ursula. 'I can't take any more of this. It's horrible. I can't bear it.'

The other five looked at me for some guidance or inspiration. I didn't know what to say. I somehow knew that Antonio would have to continue with his emotional account of this bloodbath. He had to tell somebody. Then it occurred to me. I at least would listen to him. 'I can understand you, Ursula. What we are listening to is the worst account I have heard of anything, let alone of something that happened not two hours ago... only a few hundred *varas* from where we are now. But unless I am wrong, Antonio feels he must tell someone about it, don't you, Antonio? So if anyone doesn't want to hear him finish, just leave us here and go to another room.'

By then Antonio was not actually crying but tears were running down his cheeks. 'Thank you, Esmeralda. I just have to tell it. I have to get it out. Otherwise I'll never rest again.' Ursula and Susana, still anxious about Ion, left but the others of us stayed and looked to Antonio.

'Well, the next thing was that the cavalry started getting a pounding. I saw a cannon ball rip the head off a grey mare which kept on for five strides before collapsing dead with its rider still on its back. The horses began trampling over the men, dead men wounded men and men just trying to stand upright to hold their ground. I couldn't tell which happened first, whether the cavalry decided to a man that they had had enough or whether the commanders gave the order first. I think the order to retreat came after the retreat began. Then the horses turned back into horses coming at them. What chaos. Horses crashing into horses. Eventually, they were all heading back, many riderless. Leaving their riders dead on the ground or running after them. Then the men still standing in front turned and started back. The Dutch could have finished us but as soon as they saw we were running they ceased fire. My God, what a relief. What mercy they showed.'

Antonio, a regular soldier, had never seen anything as horrific as this before. He had never until then witnessed anything so fearsome that it would bring him to tears. At that moment it became clear, at least to me, that we were caught up in something so bloody and hideous that it would need strength of mind and courage, even on the part of us *putas* to cope with it. We would have to learn to contend with what was likely to unfold at Ostende.

***

Not many days before General Ambrosio Spínola arrived here with another nine thousand Italian troops, we witnessed the most bizarre spectacle. The night before it, and much to Susana's relief, expressed in a downpour of tears, Ion came to see Susana. He hadn't met up with her for many weeks, not since we left Hoogstraten. She told us what he said, naturally, after they had spent an emotional time reacquainting themselves with each other.

'Have you seen the Infanta Isabella aiming and firing the cannon at the town?' he asked her.

'What? The Archduke's wife? Firing a cannon? Not over the walls of Ostende?'

'Just that,' he laughed. 'She'd hardly be firing at us! She thinks it's a joke. I cannot see what she gets out of it. But she's done it dozens of times. Must have. At least.'

'How do you know?' asked Susana.

'I've seen it. Only once mind. But they're all saying she's going to have another go tomorrow.'

At that time, our days were spent tidying up 'Sand Dunes' and preparing ourselves for the night's work ahead. The fact that the surroundings at the fort were not that comfortable seemed not to put off the men who needed our services there just as much as they had anywhere else, if not more. So when Susana told us about the Infanta and her showing off with the cannon, we decided to leave the tidying and go and see for ourselves. Just as Ion had said, at just before midday, the Infanta arrived. With a bewigged attendant holding the door, her lady-in-waiting stepped down from the carriage in front of her. Then the Infanta, girded in a plain maroon dress that barely stretched over her ample rear and her hair piled high over her head, gently put her heavy foot on the wet, sandy soil and eased her portly frame to the floor. As she did so, half a dozen musketeers stood to attention, close to a large black cannon, chained to some heavy metal stays, set into the ground.

The Infanta mumbled some words to one of the musketeers who went to the far side of the cannon and quickly returned with a burning, yellow flamed spill. He handed it to her with a bow. She nodded in return. The musketeer shouted at the top of his voice: 'Hands over your ears!'

She placed the lighted spill on the breach of the cannon. A second later the ground shook at the almighty explosion. The cannon flashed and leapt a *pie* into the air, against the restraining chains. The deed was done.

The Infanta appeared out of the cloud of gunpowder smoke and looked around at the small crowd that had gathered to watch, expecting a round of applause. She smiled and laughed. No one responded.

'How patronising,' said Beatrix as we walked back to 'Sand Dunes'. 'She's come all the way here from God knows where just to do that. What a show of arrogance. As if she's qualified to fire a cannon!'

'I know,' I said. 'I can hardly believe it. How humiliating for the soldiers who had to set up this charade. I can't imagine Spínola putting up with that. I'm amazed. And ashamed that she is Spanish, too.'

***

The new commander brought many changes and made many of them over the savage autumn and winter that we all had to endure. We working girls had no direct contact with this great but humble man but gleaned our knowledge of him and his works from our company which, mainly by luck, had survived virtually intact, at least up to his arrival. Thousands of others had been unlucky enough to be on the receiving end of a musket ball, a cannon shot, an exploding mine or the wrong end of a pikestaff.

'He wants us to dig trenches,' said Ion in one of his love encounters with Susana.

'What? Does he expect you to grow vegetables or something? Bit cold for that isn't it,' said Susana.

'No,' said Ion. 'It's to give us protection as we advance on the town. At least we'll be protected from most of the direct fire. Not only that, we've got to dig tunnels as well!'

None of us could understand how these 'trenches' or 'tunnels' would work. It seemed a hard way to capture Ostende, by digging our way there. But that is what they did. The men dug a network of trenches and tunnels right across the polder, beginning only a few hundred *varas* from our fort.

Not many weeks after all this digging began, Carlos appeared one night to join the queue outside my bedroom. He couldn't wait to tell me what had happened that day. While taking off his clothes, he told me.

'You'll never believe this, Esmeralda. About ten of us had just finished digging a new trench about fifty *varas* long towards the south east, perpendicular to the direction of the town. Me and an infantryman were holding one of the pine posts we were using to prop up the side of the trench and another was hammering the top, banging it into the ground. Then a man with a neatly trimmed beard appears from nowhere. All on his own he was and not very tall. You could tell from his accent he wasn't Spanish and he wasn't from Flanders either. He sounded Italian. "Let me give you men a hand," he said. "You've come to the right place to work," said one of our gang. "Here, take this shovel and dig some of that sand out over there."

'The man climbed down into the trench and started shovelling out the sand. He didn't say anything but just worked his way for about ten *varas* along the bottom and came back to us. "I've tidied it up a bit along there," he said. "Do you want a hand hammering in these posts?" Well, not to turn away willing help, we got him hammering away at another post or two as we worked our way along the side of the trench.

'Anyway, I decided to ask him who he was. Seemed an innocent enough question. You could have knocked me over with a feather quill when he told me: "My name is Ambrosio Spínola," he said. Yes, he came right out with it. "I'm in charge of the army in Flanders."'

'"You're making this up," I said, laughing at him as he got himself ready.

'"Not one word is a lie," he said. Just for a moment, none of us could accept it but he spoke with such authority, I for one had to believe him. "You don't mind getting your hands dirty, sir," I said.

'"Not in the least," he said. "The only way to lead an army is by example and that means by doing. Not by just sitting on a horse and giving commands, even though you do have to give them. Let me tell you, men, the eyes of the world are on this miserable stretch of sand. And we are going to liberate it. It will be the bloodiest, hardest fought war there has ever been. But we will grind down the enemy, little by little and see him into the ground. Triumph will be ours, however many we send to glory." And with that he handed his mallet to one of the others and went.'

'What a speech,' I said, 'those words prove it was him. No one else could have said that. No one.'

***

Our nights were nearly always busy. It seemed that our men could not fight without us! Somehow the smell of the sea and maybe the excitement of the battle made them more attracted to our services there than they were earlier, either at Weert or Hoogstraten, which after all were situations of mutiny rather than battle. We were never sure who gave the order but the lieutenant came to see Susana, Beatrix and me just as we were beginning to witness the emerging buds of spring.

'I'm afraid I've been sent to tell you that we want you to change your mode of working. Up until now, you've conducted you work in the comfort of the fort...'

'Call that comfort?' broke in Susana. 'Yes, the place is furnished but with the oldest and scruffiest furniture you could find! And the carpets are threadbare!'

'No need for that. It's the best we could do... As I was saying, we want you to change your method of working.'

'Out with it,' I said. 'Give it to us straight and we'll tell you what we think.' The lieutenant always spoke politely to us but could never command respect, not from the moment we first met him at the Madrid *Tercio* barracks. 'We want you to serve the men in the trenches and in the tunnels.'

'Out of the question,' said Beatrix. 'It's either in our beds or not at all.'

'Let me explain. There are good operational reasons for this change. We are very close to the enemy. So close that even at night, from the light of their torches, they can see what we're doing. So if a thousand men decide they need the services of you women, they will notice that they've deserted their positions and we'll be vulnerable to attack.'

'For once, I can see what you're saying,' I said. 'But what will the conditions be like? We want an honest answer.'

'Not as good as you might hope. But not too bad. The trenches, most of them anyway, are so well established that the men have built beds down there and sleep there. In the open or with awnings over their heads. The trenches are two *varas* deep. That's the specification.'

'So we may be doing them in beds then, or whatever?' said Susana.

'Yes. The one thing the men will want is privacy and you'll have to rely on them for that. Have any of you been down the trenches?' We all said, no.

'Then I will take you there tomorrow. You will see where the company's quartered.'

Oddly enough, we were quite excited at the idea of visiting the trenches and tunnels. At first, we were worried about the dangers but the lieutenant reassured us, saying that these constructions extended so far back from the enemy that only the most powerful of their cannons could possibly reach us. And none were then trained on us.

***

We could not believe what work the men had put into these constructions. They looked like a network of narrow streets that had been sunk into the sand. The sides were held up either by posts that had been inserted into the ground next to each other or by planks placed on top of each other and held in place by posts. On the sides closest to the town, the men had tunnelled into the sides of the trenches to make rooms big enough to live in.

'Come into this one,' said the lieutenant. 'What do you think?'

Inside a soldier was laying down on a bed against the far wall, his arms cradling the back of his head. He stood up as soon as we entered.

'Don't mind me showing our ladies around do you?'

'Not at all, sir. Good to see our lovely ladies,' he said, with a knowing grin.

'I know you, don't I?' said Susana. 'I think you've been a customer of mine. More than once!'

The man flushed with embarrassment. 'I'm not sure, señorita. I can't remember, to tell the truth,' he said, definitely not telling the truth. 'Anyway, come in.'

'We call these places "the caves" and the men who live here "the troglodytes",' said the lieutenant. We were quite taken by the level of comfort, if primitive, the soldier had created in his subterranean home. The floors were rough sand and the walls were posts, banged into the ground. The ceilings, planks, held up by posts. There was a bed with a mattress, a little wardrobe, a small table with a jug, a plate, some cutlery and an armchair leaning against the wall.

'I'm so surprised at what you've got here. Don't you feel vulnerable in these little caves?' I asked.

'Not at all. We face away from Ostende so if a cannon ball lands anywhere near us, it will hit the opposite side of the trench. So won't do us any harm!'

The lieutenant then took us to a tunnel. A wooden ladder protruded from a narrow hole in the ground, just wide enough to allow a man to descend into the darkness below. He took a torch from a rack and lit it from an oil lamp. 'I'll go down first and one of you can follow me. Wait until I get to the bottom or the heat from the torch will burn you.'

'I'm not going down there. What if the sides collapse?' said Susana.

'They won't. They're held up by this wood,' he said, pointing to a complicated arrangement of posts and planks which retained the sand.

'What if the dyke is breached and the water gets in?' asked Beatrix.

'Then we're in trouble and we have to start again!'

With some trepidation, I followed the lieutenant down the ladder. I didn't know what to expect when I got to the bottom. Again, the amount of work the men had done astounded me. The tunnel was made tall enough for men to crawl through. It was not wide but two men going in opposite directions could easily pass each other.

'These tunnels will enable us to capture Ostende,' said the lieutenant.

None of the others wanted to come down the rickety ladder. I made my way back up, followed by the lieutenant.

'We won't be expected to work in the tunnels, will we?' asked Beatrix. Then, after a pause. 'I'm not going to work down there whatever you say.'

'No. I was just showing you what the men had built here. Nothing more. But we'll expect you to work in the trenches. That's why I showed you over here.'

CHAPTER 24

Death in the Dunes

By the beginning of the summer of 1604, we had been living and working in the fort or in the trenches for nearly ten months. By then, General Spínola had made tangible progress in his aim of winning Ostende for the Spanish Netherlands and for King Philip III of Spain. But the price had been high. He had lost five thousand men, many of whom were Italians who, like us, had reached Flanders by walking the Spanish Road. Thousands of civilians had died, some blown to pieces by our weapons. Looting of property and bodies took place after every attack on the town. One of our spies, and there were plenty of them, told our men that a greengrocer was standing in his shop serving customers when a cannon ball struck him in the chest. By the time his tearful wife returned from reporting his death to the authorities, his body had been stripped of his shoes, his rings and a gold necklace and his broken, bloodied body lay there, dressed only in his pantaloons. Every item of produce had been stripped from the shop, the stalls were gone from outside and every penny had been stolen from the till. Three days later she drowned herself in a bath of water.

We shed many tears at the suffering and the deaths of our own men. We were lucky, in that our main soldier friends had survived. Ion, Carlos, Antonio, Régulo de Aracena and the lieutenant, had escaped serious injury. But the ever helpful Sergeant Luis de Alvarado was killed by a short range musket shot which hit him in the neck. We attended his simple burial and that helped us in our mourning. He was among many of our regular customers who died. Over a third of the company lost their lives there.

One of the most tragic cases, that of a front line pikeman, upset us terribly and me in particular. His name was Paulo. He had been fighting hand to hand with the Dutch in a failed assault on a fort called 'The Porcupine'. One of the enemy, standing on a parapet, threw a lance which struck him in the chest. He fell to the ground bleeding badly but one of his colleagues quickly staunched the flow and saved him from dying on the spot. However, the wound did not heal and he started to deteriorate. After two weeks, it was clear that he had little longer left to live. Even so he made a last wish. He wanted to make love to me and only me. Ion and he were friends and he came to tell me of Paulo's last wish.

'What do I do, Ion? Why me? I feel sad about him. I really do. But if he's almost dead, how will he be able to?'

'Please Esmeralda, do go to him. He may only have a few days. He's got some strength left. All you can do is your best to help him.'

Paulo was one of the troglodytes, so I went with Ion who showed me where he lived. He looked pale and lay motionless on his bed, almost as if we were too late.

'Wake up, Paulo,' shouted Ion. 'Esmeralda is here. She wants to grant your request.' He didn't say 'last request', even though it was evident that it could be nothing else. He slowly turned his legs off the bed and sat up.

'That took some doing,' he said, not quite breathless. Ion put a flask of drink to Paulo's mouth. 'What's that?' he said.

'A drop of brandy,' said Ion. 'It'll help you wake yourself up.' Paulo took a deep swig and swallowed. He smiled and started chatting, asking me how I was and where the others were. Ion looked at me and winked. 'I'm only next door,' he said, nodding towards the adjacent cave. 'I'll go now.'

'I'll start to take my clothes off,' I said, slowly undoing the buttons on my blue patterned blouse.

'I've always loved your firm, youthful breasts,' said Paulo, still sitting on the bed. 'Can I touch them?'

'Of course you can,' I said and knelt on the sandy floor in front of him.

'I didn't realise they were so firm and your skin is so warm and smooth,' he said, still smiling and stroking me. 'Lean over and let me kiss you.'

'He planted a single, firm kiss squarely on my lips. I could feel the soft hair of his beard and moustache touch my face. He then sat back a little on his bed and looked longingly at my breasts, still with that contemplative smile.

'Would you like to see some more?' I said, slightly fearful of causing him too much sudden excitement, but anxious to start more intimate contact.

'Yes, that would be nice,' he said. 'Shall I take off my clothes, too?'

I dropped my skirt to the ground and stepped out of it, keeping my legs modestly together. 'Honestly, Esmeralda, you have a beautiful body. Everything is so firm. Now show me more!'

Smiling my best and most willing smile, I did just as he had asked. I couldn't see what his eyes had lit upon but could see his member gradually stiffening.

'May I touch you there, Esmeralda? I'd love to do that, love to.'

'Yes, go on. Touch me, if you'd like to,' I said, giving him every encouragement.

'You are so beautiful, Esmeralda. God gave you a wonderful gift when he made your gorgeous body. Not many women are so pretty there.'

'I'm glad you appreciate me as much as you obviously do! I'm rather proud of my body myself!' I said. I was standing with one foot on the floor and his face was only *pulgadas* from my body.

'My goodness, you are quite wet,' he said, gently exploring me. By then he had stroked himself to an amazing firmness, amazing in the sense that in his sadly weak state I had wondered if he could fully prepare himself. Somehow he looked paler than before as if it had drained him of the blood which had previously coloured his cheeks. 'Shall we make love now?'

'You are completely ready,' I said, laughing. 'I'll lie on the bed and you can start.'

Within a few moments he was within me. 'Esmeralda, my dear, you've made a dying man so happy...'

Those were this poor man's last words and I would never forget them as long as I lived. As he uttered the last syllable of 'happy', he collapsed on me, still firm and engaged with me. The force of him dropping his full weight on my body took the air from my chest and it took me a minute to recover. The bed was curved badly and with his body on top of me I simply could not move. I did not know then whether he was dead or whether he had suffered some form of collapse. He had made no shaking movements or croaking noises that the dying are said to make but I could not detect him breathing. My thoughts flooded back to the *hidalgo*. I felt a sudden sense of guilt that, had I not brought this man into such a state of driving excitement, he may still be alive, if indeed he was dead. I felt scared that his body might suddenly explode or do some unexpected thing. I could feel his dead penis, if dead it was, remaining solid and within me. I didn't want to touch it but I could not expel it. The more I thought about lying beneath a corpse the more scared I became. Terror struck me hard. I shouted out.

'Ion, help. Help me!'

'I'm there!'

Ion appeared as if he was standing outside and half expecting some kind of disaster, perhaps even Paulo's death. 'Can I come in?'

'Of course! Help to get him off me. I can hardly breathe!'

'He's dead, I'm sure.'

'Well, get him off me!'

Ion pulled at Paulo's body. 'Don't do that. It hurts. He's stuck inside me and it's agony when you move him.'

'Don't worry. I'll try to ease him out.'

I could feel Ion's hand touching me as he tried to disconnect Paulo. 'It's no good. I can't get him out either!'

I was beginning to panic. I could feel my heart beating faster. 'What can we do?'

'We are in luck. The surgeon barber is only a trench or two away, cutting off the leg of some badly injured soul. I'll see if I can get him. Just lie there and breathe normally, Esmeralda. We'll sort this out, I'm sure,' said Ion, showing the calmness of a typical Spanish gypsy.

A few minutes later, which seemed an age, with me still impaled on this indefatigable object, the surgeon barber arrived. He had a noticeably large, white haired head and wore a bloodied apron. Ion explained the problem.

'That shouldn't be too difficult to remove. Just a moment. I need to check that he's dead.'

The surgeon barber put his head right down, until he made contact with Paulo's back. He listened closely. 'Dead as a pickled partridge,' He said. 'But I'm going to have to make sure before I can get him out.' He then took a sharp, very narrow knife from the pocket in his apron front and stabbed it with an upward thrust under Paulo's left shoulder. 'Yes, he's dead alright.'

I didn't see exactly what the surgeon then did. All I know was that he let a certain amount of blood and that blood did not belong to me. He gently washed it off my lower parts. 'Give me a hand with the body,' he instructed Ion. 'There. All done, señorita. You can get up now!'

What a relief. I bade my farewells to Ion who kissed me tenderly on the cheek and I went back to 'Sand Dunes'. 'How did it go?' asked Beatrix. She could see I was upset. I tearfully explained what happened.

'Well his life ended in a similar way to how it started. The first ten minutes of his life coming out and the last ten minutes... Well...' said Beatrix. My torment dissolved as we all laughed together.

**

Serving our men in the trenches became a routine method of working. Sometimes, in the summer months, it was so hot in the fort, even at night, that we actually preferred working in the trenches. At least the wet sand gave them a welcomed coolness that we could often not find in the fort. We would even work outside, if the circumstances allowed. On a blazingly hot August day, one of the men and I were engaged in a languid session of lovemaking in his cave when we heard an anguished voice from outside. It was Antonio's.

'Esmeralda, are you in there. Something terrible has happened. It's Susana.'

Susana willingly obliged our men and would carry out little shows for them. She would sit up by the side of a trench, lift up her skirt and display herself while the men would stimulate themselves as they looked on. She loved to do it and would smile and chat to them while doing so. They would persuade her to do all manner of things as part of her exhibiting. These performances usually climaxed in some form of physical contact between Susana and her customers for which they amply paid her, especially as the men loved to watch as another did what he wanted to the gladly obliging Susana.

'Get off me now, please. I must go.'

'Prepare yourself for something horrific, terrible,' said Antonio. 'Susana has been hit by a cannon ball.'

My heart almost beat its way through my rib cage, it thumped so hard. 'Is she dead?' I asked, as we hurried to the spot.

'Yes,' said Antonio, almost in tears. 'Maybe it is better if you don't see her.'

'I must,' I said, now sobbing uncontrollably.

We rounded a corner from one trench into another and there it lay. The cannon ball had smashed her head into a shapeless pulp. An eye hung loose outside its socket. I screamed out loud. Out of control. 'My dear friend! I love you. This cannot be happening. It is not true! I must get away but I cannot leave you here.' A hideous, black wave of guilt smothered me like a death shroud. My thoughts were jagged and broken. I had brought this poor innocent from Burgos. I should have left her there. But for me, she'd still be alive. What had I done to her? Brought her to face the enemy cannon. I felt myself give way and fall into an abyss. I collapsed on the ground at Antonio's feet.

I never knew how long I lay there but eventually heard the soothing words of Antonio as he brought me back out of the faint. 'Esmeralda, you will be fine. I understand your grief. It's a terrible shock for all of us. She was a great friend and we loved her.'

I hoped I had been asleep and tortured by some demonic nightmare but the reality was the nightmare, the nightmare the reality. I did not know how to respond. Some force within me drove me to kiss her misshapen head. My lips touched what I believed, in that broken face, were her lips. They moved inwards, away from mine, as I touched them, as if the bones in her head had shattered and could not sustain them. Her blood and brains smeared my face. I could taste them.

I looked around for the rest of her body. It was not her, still sitting there naked, parading herself. I cried out again but managed to remain on my feet, despite a calling from within to collapse again. I went to close her legs together, to give her body at least some dignity. Then my bitter tears of sadness tuned to tears of anger. My eyes fell on the redness of her anus. I could see a white fluid dripping from it. I took some on my finger and put it to my nose: semen. She'd been buggered, dead or alive.

'Who did this?' I said, more composed in fury and staring hard at Antonio.

'They all sat there toying with themselves when it happened. One of them in cold blood went to her corpse and stuck himself into her rear. I know who it was.'

The one thing we would not agree was to have anal penetration. I had, of course, succumbed the once, to the field marshal, but we generally left such things to the likes of the Mule at the Arganzuela, Ana Blas or Marina de la Cueva. We were all (but me), until this brutal intrusion, anal virgins. Fingers and *consoladores*, maybe but penises no. So I boiled in anger at the desecration of Susana's dead body and became determined to avenge it.

'You must tell me, Antonio. But not now. Take me to see Beatrix.'

***

'What do you two want? What's happened? You've been crying, Esmeralda. There's blood on your face. It's Susana, isn't it?'

My tears flowed uncontrollably. I could hardly speak. I opened my mouth but I could not say those words. Beatrix rushed to hug me, pleading to know what had happened. I steadied myself enough to say it. I couldn't hold it back from Beatrix any longer. 'She's been killed,' I said, my voice shaking as I cried. 'A cannon ball took off her head.'

'No! No! It cannot be. Tell me it's not true. She is a child. Everything to live for.' Beatrix dropped to the floor and banged her hands on the ground, crying and shrieking as she did so. Antonio crouched down and put his arms around her shoulders.

'Yes, my love. It's true. I was close by and got there straight after. She could not have suffered. It happened in a moment. An explosion from a distant cannon. We looked around and Susana had been struck.' Poor Antonio. His tears streamed down to his chin.

I got down on the ground with them and hugged them. I felt a desperate need to be holding Beatrix. Antonio gave both of us strength. Eventually we recovered a degree of composure.

Then Antonio spoke again. 'We all need to be strong. We loved Susana. She was best friend to each of us. We enjoyed her cheeky remarks and her misunderstandings which we never knew were deliberate or not.

But we have to accept that we will have to live without her. We will all treasure her memory in different ways but now she is a memory.'

Then a terrible thought struck me like a thunder flash. Ion. He could not know. Who would tell him? His love had been killed. Our discussion moved to him.

'I'll go and find him now,' said Antonio. 'It is too much to expect one of you to do it. He will be heartbroken, poor man. He loved her so much.'

The news of Susana's death almost destroyed Ion. He hardly spoke for days. Wherever he went he looked sullen and would look down at the ground, as if deliberately to avoid having to look at or talk to anyone. Our problem was whether to involve him in Susana's burial. It could cause him even greater stress. We agreed that we had to ask him because they had been so much in love. So, on the second day after she died, I found enough courage to talk to him about it.

'Yes, I have to come. She is my wife after all.'

'Ion, are you sure?' I said, wondering if he had been affected in the head by losing her in such a hideous way.

'Yes. We were married in secret, in Brussels, just after Susana frightened us all the day she disappeared. We persuaded a priest in the cathedral to marry us. We explained it all to him. That Susana was a *puta* and I a gypsy *tercio*. He managed to find some witnesses and five days after seeing him, we went back and he married us, right up by the altar. Poor Susana wept as I put a ring on her finger. She soon recovered though. Enough to pay the priest. I had no money because I hadn't been paid. If you're in any doubt, I've got the certificate to prove it.'

'Don't be silly, Ion. We all believe you. We feel bad because Susana didn't tell us. Married in secret? Why? Where is the ring?' I asked.

'We agreed that Susana would continue working as a *puta*. But if we were eventually to marry at a gypsy wedding, she should be a virgin. We discussed this and decided to marry in Brussels. I think I was happier about it than Susana. I didn't like the fact that she was serving all these men but I loved her enough to put up with it. She said she would stop at the end of the siege when we would start a new life in Madrid or Buitrago. We hadn't decided which. She said she dreaded what you and Beatrix would say. The ring is at the bottom of her bag. When we are together she takes it out and puts it on.' He then looked back at the ground.

The same day that Susana died, and still sobbing, the five of us, Beatrix, Ion, Carlos, Antonio and I, went back to the trenches to recover Susana's body. Ion broke into tears when he saw her and knelt down to hug and squeeze her. We thought he would never let go but we eventually persuaded him to release her. All of us were devastated to discover that her head had gone. Someone or something had taken it. We cried again, even more intensely because of this added layer of agonising misery. Ion had to look away while Antonio and Carlos put her bloodied remains into a large hessian sack. Beatrix and I hugged each other for comfort. Ion looked on as if in a trance. We did not find Susana's head.

Of the thousands who died at Ostende, nearly every man was buried where he fell. His colleagues dug a hole in the sandy earth and buried him. No priest attended; no prayers were said; few if any tears were shed. But because Susana served the army, and was not a member of it, the chaplain made an exception. Ion, Carlos and Antonio dug a grave not far away from the trench line. We couldn't understand a word of the short ceremony which was conducted in Latin and Walloon. We just stood there and sobbed for our departed friend, as others looked on. We would always miss her. We each cried again as we put a handful of sand in the hole, then Carlos filled it in as the other four of stood and watched.

'You must have this, Esmeralda,' said Ion, recovering. 'It's yours now, to remember her by.' He placed their wedding ring in the palm of my hand. My tears welled up again. I could not speak.

***

I had to do it. An inner compulsion drove me. I could not let Susana rest in my mind or in her grave before I did. I had to punish the evil man who buggered her body and I had a plan. The day after Susana's burial – soon enough for my anger still to be boiling – I crept into Carlos's makeshift bedroom and took his loaded pistol. What I would do with it, I had not decided. But I planned to use it in some way, if only to protect myself. I would certainly use it to forestall an act of buggery. Antonio had told me who this monster was and where he lived. So I paraded myself up and down, outside his cave. I felt awkward and strange in this role as street whore because I and the others did not work this way. Eventually, he came out.

'Looking for business, my dear?'

'Well, I'd just love to oblige you, señor. If you have the means and inclination, I have the time and something you may enjoy.'

He furtively glanced each way up the trench before he spoke. 'Come in now. I'm bursting for you.'

He performed one of the most urgent acts of copulation I had ever experienced. He took off his breeches with such speed he almost ripped them. Then he started to stimulate himself. 'Get your skirt off, señorita. You couldn't have turned up at a better time. I'm desperate!'

I placed my bag on the floor and dropped my skirt to the ground. 'There you are, señor. All yours. On the bed or against the wall?'

'Let's do it against the wall!'

Within a few seconds he was thrusting at me with all his energy and making quite a noise. 'Less of the animal sounds, señor. Or all your mates will turn up! Good for me but could be embarrassing for you!'

It lasted less than a minute and he withdrew as soon as he had expended himself. 'I have an idea for you,' I said. 'Let me get to my bag. I've got this special thing. I'll put it in your rear. I'll give you such pleasure; you may want to do me again.'

'What have you got, then?'

'A *consolador* we call it. I've got a drop of oil, too. Look. I'll put some on it, like this,' I said, uncorking the top of a small bottle. 'If you lie face down on your bed, I'll ease it in.'

No sooner than I had said so, he was sprawled on his front and I was working the *consolador* into him. 'Is that good? Are you enjoying it?'

'Yes, put it in further. It's very nice!' I moved it in further and in and out. Then I made the ultimate suggestion. 'I've got a slightly wider one, if you want to try that. It'll be so good you'll wonder why we hadn't tried it before!'

'Go on!' he said, in eager anticipation. I took Carlos's flintlock from my bag and warmed the barrel in my hand.

'What are you doing,' he said. 'Can't you just put it in?'

'Right now,' I said. My heart beat hard and fast as I pushed the oiled barrel into him.

'God, that's really nice. What a feeling.'

I asked myself the question: 'Should I do it or not? If I did, I would fully avenge the death of Susana. If not, I would regret it for the rest of my life.' As I contemplated my choices, there were several bursts of gunfire outside. The shots sounded as if they were close, not more than twenty *varas* away. What God given cover!

'It's a pity to stop, right in the middle of me enjoying this, to see what's going on out there,' he murmured, his head still facing the pillow. 'But I ought to go, really. We can start again on my return!'

Then I pulled the trigger. An almighty explosion added to the random blasts happening outside. The gun almost broke my wrist as it recoiled out of his anus, out of my hand and hit the improvised wall opposite. 'You bitch,' he shouted, and fell off the bed in a heap on the floor, bleeding from his rear. His eyes stared vacantly at me. I moved from their gaze but they remained staring at the spot from which I had moved. I placed my hand on his chest. He'd stopped breathing. I'd killed him. My heart started to beat even stronger and I felt a great sense of elation and excitement. It was almost like an orgasm. I'd avenged his act of brutality on my friend and could feel no happier. Now I could let my dear partner rest in death and peace.

I waited for a few minutes until he stopped bleeding. I thought about cleaning him up but decided to leave him there untouched. I didn't want to smear his blood. That would be to leave evidence that he'd been handled after death. I slipped back into my clothes and put the *consolador*, the bottle of olive oil and Carlos's still smoking gun into my bag. I then slung it over my shoulder. I went to the door, looked in each direction and left. Not a soul saw me leave. So I walked calmly back to 'Sand Dunes'.

'Where have you been?' asked Beatrix, as I walked towards my room. She was chatting to Olalla whom she liked more than the other two, maybe because she was older and seemed to be like the mother she hardly knew. I didn't want to speak about the dead man in front of the others so I made an excuse to go straight to my room but signalled Beatrix to follow me.

'What's this about,' said Beatrix as she sat on my bed and looked at me, puzzled.

'I'm not sure whether to tell you this,' I said. 'I will but only if you swear to me not to tell a soul.'

'For all I know, you may have committed some dreadful crime and I may have to report you,' she said, laughing all over her face.

'Well, do you swear? On pain of death? For I'll kill you if you tell!' I made a laugh but felt quite serious, but not of course with the threat.

'All right. I swear, but I may not keep my promise,' Beatrix chuckled.

'I've killed that man who buggered Susana.'

'I knew you would!' she said, excitedly. 'You were so angry! But if you hadn't I would have!' She hugged me tightly. We both broke into tears. 'We can live our lives now, Esmeralda. So let's get on with them.'

Luck blessed me with her fortune. To my way of thinking, justice prevailed. The lieutenant interviewed me about the death of the man because someone reported that they had seen me go into his cave. I admitted giving him service and to using a *consolador* on him but said that he was fine when I left him. The lieutenant believed me. No one suspected that his death had been caused by a gun shot. There were no signs of an entry wound. Apparently, no one discovered an exit wound either. The flintlock ball must have come to rest somewhere inside his body. The surgeon barber said he died of a massive haemorrhage.

Another factor contributed to my fortune. It diverted all attention from the death. The siege of Ostende concluded the day after the killing. After a final, deathly onslaught led by General Spínola, our men could freely enter the town. Hardly a building had survived. The town was a total ruin. No cause for celebration could be found. We went to watch the plump Archduchess Isabella survey the wreckage. She cried and we wept with her. Could this mess be worth the death of Susana? And tens of thousands of others?

***

The night the siege ended, I entertained a welcomed but unexpected visitor, Field Marshal Régulo de Aracena. I felt so pleased to see him, I hugged him tightly.

'Esmeralda, why all the emotion? It's unlike you!'

I just could not hold back my tears as I told him about the hideous death of Susana. He put his arm around my shoulders as I gave my account and wondered what he could do to ease the pain which Beatrix and I felt.

'I have an idea for you, Esmeralda.'

'Go on!'

'I have been called back to Madrid. There is still much work to be done here in Flanders but now the siege is over, the army here has to be rationalised and I am returning to lead our troops in Spain. You need to get away from this place. My idea is for you to come back with me. Beatrix could come, too.'

'Thank you. You are kind. But we'll have to think about it. The death of Susana has shocked and frightened me. I would dearly love to escape from Flanders. I'm less sure about Beatrix.'

Beatrix really struggled with the thought of going back to Madrid. She loved Antonio so much she just did not want to leave him. 'I don't know what to do, Esmeralda. I am in a quandary. I now hate Flanders. The death of Susana has done that. But I want to be with Antonio.'

Antonio himself solved the problem for her. He insisted that she should return to Madrid, if for no other reason than her own safety. He realised what a great tragedy it would be for her to be killed or maimed in some pointless battle in Flanders. They agreed to write to each other, once a week, until Antonio returned to Madrid. He also encouraged her to continue working as a *puta* but not to work the streets or some back lane brothel, if she could avoid it. It surprised me that he thought that way but he had always accepted her working for the army and told her as much many times when she herself had doubts. I wondered whether he actually was in love with her or whether they were merely good friends. Time would tell.

The field marshal never knew the other three, Olalla, Sancha and Ursula who had all become close friends of ours, the more so after the terrible death of our dear friend. Nothing could bring her back but Ursula, bless her, renamed her baby daughter Susana in her memory. We admired her for deciding to bring the baby up herself while continuing to work and not to give her up to some foreign orphanage or convent. Beatrix and I wondered about asking the field marshal about taking them back, too. But we decided not to do so. And while we didn't discuss even the possibility of them returning with us, they seemed more than content to stay in Flanders and continue serving the troops there.

Two days after Beatrix's discussion with Antonio, we were all but ready to leave. The emotional farewells almost made us change our minds and stay. We five friends, Beatrix, Antonio, Carlos, Ion and I hugged each other endlessly. We girls hugged, kissed and cried with the other three. The men were braver and managed to control their feelings. Ion also promised to write to us. We all vowed to meet in Madrid when the men returned. If they ever did. Our Susana stayed in Ostende but the rich memories of her came with us. They would never fade.

PART IV

CHAPTER 25

Back in Madrid

The return by land and sea almost broke us. The field marshal's men took us back at speed. Even the galley from Genoa to Barcelona travelled as fast as sail would permit. It seemed to be more urgent to get back than it was to reach Flanders in the first place. But we were not travelling with an army. Not more than two dozen of us journeyed in that select group. We arrived in Madrid exhausted. I wondered whether Pedro could be in Madrid and whether I would find him there. I wasn't sure why but after we reached the town I felt a strange closeness to him which I couldn't explain.

'We must find somewhere to live,' said Beatrix as we came through the Puerta de Alcalá.

'No,' I said. 'We want somewhere to stay. We can look for somewhere to live later. And there are other things we must do. We have to go to the bank and examine our accounts. We have to sort out Susana's will. We need to stay in an inn for a few weeks. We should do these things and decide later where we want to live. And what to do for work.'

'So we need to stay near the centre then?'

'Yes.'

'Is there anyone we know who could give us a room for a few days?' asked Beatrix. 'What about Madam Isabel? She always promised to look after us when we returned?'

'Good idea. Let's try her.'

Our little convoy stopped in the square of the barracks near the Calle de San Nicolás. We both said our goodbyes to Régulo de Aracena. 'Listen, Esmeralda, I want to stay in touch with you. You have been good to me... and for me... and I want to continue to see you. So you must let me know where you end up living. My house is in the Calle de San Salvador. Near the Plazuela de la Villa. It's the fourth on the right, going north.' He hugged me and planted a kiss on my lips before disappearing inside the officers' quarters.

Our driver realised that we did not want to stop in the barracks so we asked him to take us to the Calle de Arganzuela. He drove at a trot down the Calle de Toledo and turned left into the road. We peered out of the canvas wagon cover to show him where to stop. What a shock: Number seven had gone. No building stood there and nothing stood on either side of where it once was. We looked at each other with wide open eyes.

'My God. What has happened?' said Beatrix.

'There could have been a fire. Maybe property agents have bought the places and knocked them down.'

'Shall we find an inn or something?'

'Not yet. Let's stop outside one of the other houses and ask someone where Madam Isabel is working or living. Someone is sure to know.'

The driver stopped the wagon outside of a prosperous looking house about four or five doors further down the street, on the same side as number seven. I knocked at the door and stood there until a man in a tricorn hat and dressed to go out appeared at the door.

'Excuse me,' I said. 'I wonder if you can tell me where Isabel Jiménez is living. She was at number seven, but the house has been destroyed.'

'I've no idea, my dear. I'm only a customer here. I'm on my way. Knock on the door again.' The man looked embarrassed, not expecting my question, and as if he was leaving after indulging in the pleasures of some lady in residence.

A pretty, middle-aged woman answered my knocking. 'How can I help you, señorita?'

'I'm looking for Señora Isabel Jiménez. She was the madam at number seven.'

'I'm afraid I have bad news. Señora Jiménez was badly burned in the fire.'

'The fire?'

'Yes. A mad priest thought he could purify the Arganzuela by destroying the *mancebías*. So, one night, he came down to our street and set alight to the brothels up there at the end,' she said, pointing to the Calle de Toledo. 'What he didn't realise was that several women lived there. One died in number five and several others were injured. Señora Jiménez had to have an arm amputated or she would have died. I know her well. She's living three doors down on the other side of the road. You can't miss it. It's got a black front door.'

'Thank you, señora. You've been so helpful,' I said, vacantly and thinking of our poor madam at number seven. We were stunned and saddened to hear of her awful injury. I could not help but wonder what other bad news we might encounter before we had been here for much longer.

'What do you think, Beatrix? Shall we go to Isabel's or find an inn somewhere? How can we expect Isabel to put us up? She is so badly injured, it seems.'

'We should go there. We must see Isabel. If she can accommodate us for a time, so well and good. If not, then we go to an inn.'

Isabel recognised us as soon as she opened the door. 'Esmeralda, Beatrix. You are back. Oh, we have missed you.' She put her left arm around me, then Beatrix; and then burst into tears. The empty arm of her dress betrayed her terrible injuries, as did a large burn scar on her right cheek.

Each of us hugged her and we were almost in tears ourselves. Our driver stayed outside during these exchanges but Isabel saw immediately our dilemma.

'Have you just arrived back from Flanders? Please stay with me. I have three empty bedrooms here so you can stay as long as you like!' She welcomed us like a mother and soon persuaded us to accept her offer.

'We will have to pay you,' I said.

'Don't talk about money. Just get your things and come in!'

***

Madam Isabel gave us the full story of the reopening of number seven, the arsonist priest and her injuries and we told her all about our adventures in Flanders. She almost died in the fire. One of the customers took her to the General Hospital on his wagon and that saved her but her arm was burnt almost to the bone and she was in agony. The surgeon anaesthetised her with brandy and sawed it off above the elbow. She felt every saw stroke. The thought of it reminded me of the arm we found rotting in the fort. In my mind, I could smell its decaying stench, as if it were there in Isabel's lounge, not lying in that corner, in that room in 'Sand Dunes'. We sobbed as we told her about the death of Susana. Poor Isabel burst into tears the moment I told her about the decapitation. All three of us cried together.

'I'll get some drinks,' said Isabel, through her tears. 'We can't just sit here bawling our eyes out.' She vanished into her kitchen and came back smiling anew with three glasses of wine on a tray she held with her solitary hand and steadied against her hip.

We talked and talked until the early hours. We told her about Antonio and Ion, about Field Marshal Régulo de Aracena, the mutinies, the battles in Ostende and our encounters with Ana Blas and Marina de la Cueva whom, of course, we first met in the Madrid *Tercio* barracks before we went to Flanders. She told us about the woman who died in the fire. She was no one we knew but subject to a hideous and painful death, of the kind with which we were all too familiar. Isabel had done her best to comfort the poor girl as she screamed in the agony of her last moments. She told us that the errant priest had killed himself rather than face execution by burning at the stake.

We ended by talking about what we would do, now that we were back in Madrid. 'I don't want to work in a brothel,' said Beatrix. 'Antonio has asked me not to do that or to work the streets.'

'I don't either,' I said. 'Ideally, I would like to buy a house and set myself up to serve the upper end of the market. A bit like Angélica de la Torre, the alchemist's lady friend. We've earned so much in Flanders we should be able to buy a house each.'

'Don't believe it. Houses have become so expensive here. Mind you, you might be able to share!'

'We hadn't thought of that, had we Esmeralda?'

'That's an idea, you know. There's no reason why we couldn't work together. In the same house.'

***

The following day we walked to the bank in the Calle de Tenerías, on the corner of San Pedro. We soon discovered how well off we were. Beatrix's account contained 787 *ducats* and some change and mine a colossal 1105, which reflected the many extra payments Régulo de Aracena had made to me. So between us we had all but two thousand ducats, more than enough to buy a house in a decent part of the town. We told the bank clerk about the death of our friend and about the wills we signed before we journeyed to Flanders. I gave the clerk a copy of Susana's death certificate which he studied minutely. 'Death by cannon ball? Where was she when it happened?'

'On the battlefield of Flanders, working for our troops,' I said, avoiding any display of emotion, despite the rawness of my feelings. This seemed to satisfy him so he went to the vaults to retrieve Susana's will.

'Yes, you are each beneficiaries under the testimony. There are six hundred and ninety six *ducats* in her account. That's three hundred and forty eight *ducats* each.'

'No, she was a married woman and her husband should at least take a share,' I said. Beatrix nodded. The clerk agreed to arrange for half of Susana's inheritance to be placed in a holding account for Ion. Beatrix said she would write to him to tell him of the money, albeit given as a consequence of the hideous death of his wife. Beatrix and I embraced each other as we left the bank and the slightly bemused clerk.

'We're rich,' said Beatrix. 'We can do what we like.'

'Yes. We can do who we like, too! We can be choosy. Not any stinking *hombre* who comes through the door. Lawyers, doctors, playwrights, architects, engineers. They'll all be ours. So will the dukes, barons, knights and marquises! We'll have them all!'

'And they'll pay us for the pleasure!'

'I suppose we should calm ourselves a bit. But one thing is clear. Our four years in Flanders has earned us enough to work at a higher level, with more select customers. Shall we do as Isabel suggests, buy a house between us?'

'Let's do that, Esmeralda. Let's do it.' We embraced again. We would be friends and partners. So we worked on finding ourselves a house.

***

After several weeks of fruitless searching, an excited property agent came to see us at Madam Isabel's.

'Ladies, I've found you the most beautiful house. You'll love it!'

'How much do you want for it?'

'Two thousand two hundred and fifty *ducats*. It's a bargain.'

'It maybe to some but that's about all we've got. We can't afford it,' I said.

'I agree,' said Beatrix. 'We must have money left for furnishing. We'll have to look elsewhere.'

'Before you refuse it completely, I'd like you to come to see it,' he said.

'Where is it?' I said.

'In the Calle de Santa Clara, overlooking the Plazuela de Santiago.'

'I know where it is,' said Beatrix. 'I had a customer who lived in that street. It's a very good area. What do you think, Esmeralda?'

'Let's go to see it. We can't lose. If we like it we can make an offer. If not we'll look for something else.'

The agent took us in his carriage up Calle Toledo, across the Plaza Mayor and through the Calle Nueva then up through the Calle de Santiago. As we passed through the Calle Nueva, I pointed out the ham seller's house to Beatrix, and told her about this strange couple Susana and I worked for. I described Susana's reaction the day he became such an ardent customer. Beatrix laughed at the thought.

The property agent took us around the house. He first showed us the two magnificent downstairs drawing rooms which dominated the ground floor area and overlooked the pretty Plazuela where busy people were going to and fro about their daily chores. He then stood by the kitchen door and opened his hand to invite us in. The stove facing the door, the rack suspended from the ceiling for kitchen utensils and the pantry with shelves for food and storing drinks impressed us. 'You haven't seen the dining area yet.' He smiled as he showed us this elegant room which overlooked the garden. At its centre, stood a magnificent, polished mahogany table that could seat a dozen. Then, ahead of us, he climbed the stairs and showed us the four large bedrooms and a huge drawing room on the first floor.

'We have to buy this,' said Beatrix. 'It's like two houses in one. We could each set ourselves up to entertain our customers and live like queens in a palace!'

'But if we bought it we'd have hardly any money for furnishings. It will cost five hundred *ducats* to do it in a way which will attract good clientele and then we need to furnish ourselves. We'll have to buy some nice clothes, fit for a pair of high class *putas*!'

'I can take an offer,' said the agent.

'Two thousand!' I said.

'That's just rude!' he said.

'All right. Two thousand and fifty,' said Beatrix.

'Can't you go higher?'

'No,' I said, closing the argument.

'It's yours!'

We hugged each other for joy. We owned a property, a magnificent house almost in the centre of Madrid, near the Plaza Mayor, the palace and in the most prosperous part of the city. What a contrast to living in a fort in a swamp by Ostende.

That thought alone took us to our tears.

'Susana would have loved this,' said Beatrix, gently sobbing for our friend.

I put my arms around her. 'I know,' I said, trying to wipe my eyes. 'But her memory will be here with us. We'll never forget her.'

***

It didn't take us long to purchase and furnish our beautiful house. We absolutely loved it and owning it gave us an amazing sense of pride. We spent as much as we could afford on the house and, by the time we had finished, each room glowed with a newness and freshness of its own. We soon realised that we had an urgent need to find customers and discussed how we should approach that.

'We can't trawl the streets. That just won't work. All we'd get are the sort of customers we want to leave behind. For the street workers or the *burdels*,' I said.

'I suppose we could go to the barracks. I'm sure we'd pick up some officers there. After all, we know some already.'

'That would be a start but what about this? I will go to Angélica de la Torre. She may have some ideas. After all, she got Susana and me to start working as *putas*.'

'Why don't we both go?' asked Beatrix.

'I suppose we could but I'm not sure if she'd be as open if we both went along. She may feel that we are pressing her when we wouldn't be of course but you never know. I knew her well and I think she'd do her best to help me.'

So I went alone to see Señora Angélica de la Torre. I knocked on the frog shaped knocker which adorned the centre of her front door and stood there. A young woman with a long, bottle like neck and wearing a daringly short skirt appeared. I imagined she did the job of assistant to the señora, the same job as I did before becoming a *puta*.

'Good afternoon,' she said politely. 'Can I help you?' It felt that she was expecting a customer for the señora and that I had surprised her by my presence there instead.

'My name is Esmeralda Pechada de Burgos. I am known to Señora Angélica de la Torre and have come to see her.'

'Do you have an appointment?'

'No, but would be willing to return later, if she is unavailable?'

'I'll ask her. Do come in.' I waited in the sumptuous entrance hall as the woman disappeared for a few moments. 'Yes, she is awaiting another caller but can see you now, as long as you are quick.'

The señora rushed towards me and hugged me as I entered her pretty drawing room.

'Esmeralda! What a surprise. I thought you were still in Flanders. I heard all about you going! I hope you made a fortune!'

She looked happy and well and smiled all over her face as she spoke. I explained as concisely as I could what had happened in Flanders, that Beatrix and I were staying with Madam Isabel and why I had come to see her. She listened intently and silently. We both cried when I told her about Susana. Then she spoke.

'Allow me to correct you, Esmeralda. Madam Isabel was tortured by the priest who set fire to the brothels. He drugged her and burnt her arm over a fire. What he did to the other girl was even worse. He set fire to her while she slept. I knew her well, poor child, because she worked for me, just like you did,' she said, touching the bridge of her nose with her hand as if to retain new tears.

'But you didn't come here to learn about what happened at number seven. In fact you could not have come at a better time. I am about to leave Madrid to become courtesan to an earl in Mantua. He visited me while he was in Madrid a year ago and has invited me back with him. So I am looking for someone to look after my current clientele. You would be ideal, especially working with your friend Beatrix. What is she like? Does she perform well? Has she any specialities?'

'She is a beautiful, shapely girl with a lovely personality. We helped each other to come to terms with Susana's death. She is completely uninhibited and while I haven't seen her at work – except once – I'm certain she'll be good with your men. She enjoys her job and loves doing it. She loves to do it standing up,' I lied because I didn't know, but thought I'd better say something in answer to her final question.

'That's all good, Esmeralda. One other thing. I will have to charge you to take over my clients. It would be a sign of your commitment. I am thinking of, say, three *ducats* a man. How does that sound? It's only reasonable because I'm saving you a lot of work and, in effect, selling you my business!'

'Let me ask Beatrix and I'll get back to you. I'm not so sure about paying you, but I'll discuss that with Beatrix.'

'I'm certain we'll agree something,' she said, smiling as if she had secured a deal. 'By the way, when we spoke about you, before you went to number seven, you told me about your lost brother. Did you ever find him or hear from him?'

'I constantly think of him. When I wake up he is the first person I think of. Every day. And I miss him. Every day. But sadly, no, I have not even glimpsed him and have heard nothing of him. I sometimes think I can see a figure that looks so much like what I imagine him to be. And I hurry along the street. But it is never him.' I could feel the tears welling up in my eyes and troubled to control them in front of her.

'You never know. He may turn up when you least expect him. I hope I haven't upset you by mentioning him.'

The idea of taking over the señora's clients delighted Beatrix. But she did not want to pay for them. She argued that Angélica de la Torre would lose them anyway when she left for Mantua so was not in a position to charge us. I could see both sides of the argument. On the one hand, the señora would be leaving and where her customers went would be up to them. But on the other, she may have someone else in mind who might want to buy them from her. We agreed that we'd both visit the señora and agree something with her, if we could. We left it a few days – so as not to sound too anxious to take them – before we went to see her. Once again, we made no appointment but just arrived on her doorstep. She opened the door herself and let us in.

'I was beginning to think you'd abandoned the whole idea, Esmeralda,' she said as she showed us both into her opulent drawing room. 'I was wondering about asking someone else if they wanted my customers!' So a useful start: she clearly had no one definite in mind to whom she would pass them.

'We'd love to take over your clients,' I said. 'We are just concerned about paying so much for them.'

'I agree,' said Beatrix, clearly pleased to be part of the negotiation. 'We just can't afford to pay you that much, especially if you have more than fifty.'

'I've got about eighty!'

'There's no way we can afford more than two hundred and odd *ducats*! We did well in Flanders but not that well. I suppose that is the end of it then,' I said, if provocatively. Beatrix and I stood as if ready to depart.

'Don't go!' said the señora. 'How about a hundred *ducats*?'

'Call it seventy five!' said Beatrix.

'They're yours!' she said and hugged each of us, relieved to have made some kind of deal, however disadvantageous.

'We'll have to sort out the details,' I said. 'We'll need a list of who your customers are and we'll want to tell them that we've taken over. Is that all right?'

'I know! Why not have a party to introduce yourselves to them?'

'Surely, they won't all want to come to such an event,' I said. 'I'd have thought they wouldn't want to let the others see them!'

'In which case I'll let them all know by letter. I'll be leaving with the earl in just over a week so had better get things moving! When will you be able to start?'

'Any time,' said Beatrix, as if she was just dying to start this new line of work. 'Our house is all set up for business.'

'May I ask just a small favour? Could you take over my maid, Dulcina? She's trained for the job, very efficient and would serve you well. She's a lovely girl and will love working with two younger girls. She was born in Vigo and her parents brought her to Madrid when she was only four years old. Her father was a soldier. They came to Madrid to find work but after doing some badly paid, menial jobs her father became a *tercio*. I am telling you this because her father died in tragic circumstances in Flanders only about three months ago. She's still very upset and I beg you not to mention her father in case you upset her. May I ask her in?'

We spoke to the crane necked Dulcina. She was younger than either of us, about fourteen or fifteen. She spoke with a slight accent. The main point in her favour was that she expressed great enthusiasm to join our new venture. We asked her how she felt about having to douche and perfume us. After all, we were strangers to her and wondered if at worst she would find it objectionable to touch us so intimately or whether she might be embarrassed. She laughed as she told us that she couldn't see a problem. After our informal little interview with her, we asked the señora if we could leave the room a moment for a private discussion.

'Thank you so much,' said the young girl as we told her and Señora Angélica that we would be delighted to take her on as our assistant and pay her the same as she earned working with the señora. 'I can't tell you how pleased I am!' she said as she hugged us. So we agreed that the day the señora stopped work, the day we took over, Dulcina would come to work with us.

Within a few days of settling on the terms of the transfer, Angélica de la Torre sent us a complete list of her eighty four customers, annotated to betray some of their special requests and tell us about their personalities. We were amazed and amused at their idiosyncrasies and excited to see the range of their jobs and social positions in our town. The most senior official was an assistant to the Inquisitor General. Apparently, he would never visit the señora who entertained him in a private room attached to his offices. She said she sometimes served another official there but didn't know his name. Another was a judge at the royal courts who had some odd predilections. Before making love to the señora she would strip off naked and he would watch her urinate into a chamber pot. He'd pour some of it onto some brandy in a glass and drink it straight down. This peculiar ritual seemed to excite him so much, he was ready to perform the instant he swallowed this weird concoction. 'Make sure you're full of pee before he arrives,' the relevant note concluded.

'Good God! Listen to this one!' said Beatrix, reading aloud this extraordinary missive. '"The Marquis of Montequebrado. A regular visitor, at least once a week. Fill a bath with water at body temperature and let him watch you bathe yourself. Stand in the bath and wash yourself, making sure he can see everything. You climb out and he climbs in. Still naked and wet, you bathe him. Ensure you clean his penis thoroughly. Then help each other to dry off and powder. Take as long as you like because he is always ready after his bath and copulation is over and done within no more than two minutes." We're in for some entertaining times with this lot, Esmeralda. Some real fun!'

'We've struck lucky, Beatrix. It has to be said. And there are people here we know! Look! The alchemist, Benito Ortiz de Navarette, he's still a customer. He must have recovered after the explosion in his laboratory. I used to work for him. I'll tell you more later. "He's always telling me he loves me. You sometimes need to work hard to get him up. Don't worry if you can't. Happy to chat and tips well. Occasionally have to visit him at home in the Calle de la Luna." I think I'll have to leave him to you, Beatrix. I just can't be doing my old boss!'

'You're a coward, Esmeralda. He'd love it. You'd fulfil his naughty fantasies. I bet he lusted after you like mad when you worked for him!'

'Never touched me. I'd have killed him if he did! And here's another one I remember! The gunsmith! The señora would always say how long it took to get him ready. Then he'd never finish! "I'd work him and squeeze him and lift my bottom up and down and eventually he'd reach the end. Then he'd break into laughter as if it was some kind of expensive joke." And he'd leave the place with a smile on his face and give me half a dozen *maravedís*.'

The señora had flattered us by taking so much trouble to tell us about her customers. She had produced a document of nearly thirty pages, setting out who they were, where they lived, what they wanted and what they were like. It must have taken her several days of thought and writing. And she had written well and clearly. We could not have wished for a better introduction to our new enterprise. We were in business!

CHAPTER 26

The Marquis

We met with several surprises after our return to Madrid, not least the awful effects of the arson attack on the Arganzuela and the horrific injuries suffered by Isabel Jiménez. We also learned that Josefina Ramírez had been imprisoned for the attempted murder of her husband, Juan. Apparently, while making an urgent, special delivery to one of the few 'respectable' houses in the Arganzuela, she had met her husband coming out of one of the brothels. He attempted to lie his way out of the situation but, as soon as they arrived home at the ham shop, she attacked him with a meat cleaver. He almost bled to death but managed to crawl from the house onto the street to attract a passer-by who called for help and managed to save him. Had her husband not pleaded for his wife's life, there was little doubt that she would have been hanged for the offence or even burned at the stake.

The most pleasant surprise by far was the fact that Señora Angélica de la Torre was willing to sell us the customers in her high class brothel before she journeyed to Mantua as courtesan to her earl. (She never did give us his full title.) The seventy five *ducats* we paid turned out to be the best investment we could have made. Within a few months, just about all of our new customers had visited us and most had partaken of our services. I say 'most' because quite a number made appointments simply to visit and chat with us, presumably expecting to be fully served at a later date. Maybe they just wanted to look us over and see what we were like before committing themselves to paying for the delights we could offer. After all, we were new and a change from the rounded and familiar voluptuousness of Angélica, for some at least, may not have been particularly welcomed. A number made appointments for a later time, some later the same day. The way we conducted business was quite different from the way things worked in the Arganzuela. Everything was more formal and precise. We conducted all of our business on the basis of appointments only. None of those queues of embarrassed faces formed outside, which we were compelled to serve until the last man there was satisfied.

We were amused by some of the means our new customers used to make their engagements with us. The simplest and most convenient was to decide on a new date immediately after completing their business of the day. Dulcina kept an accurate diary. But many of the most senior ranking of our customers sent one of their junior, sometimes embarrassed, staff around to arrange something. One of the lawyers sent a woman. That really surprised us, especially when she made it clear to Dulcina that he 'just wants the usual. Nothing special and no extras.' It sounded as if she had been given instructions to make an appointment at his barbers!

***

All three of us worked well together. Dulcina turned out to be a great asset who fully justified the señora recommending her to us. We loved her and her long neck. She showed no inhibition in doing what she had to after each customer had completed his session with us. Although we offered her the possibility of living with us, she decided, not surprisingly, that she preferred to live with her recently widowed mother. Neither of us could fault her for that.

Deciding who, of the two of us, should serve any particular customer raised some interesting discussion and activity. Very few of our customers had consorted with either of us before, so most could not express a real preference. Generally, the way we dealt with the issue was to ask Dulcina to identify to the potential customer who was the next one of us available. We told her to balance up the number of customers, as best she could, for any given date in the diary and not to expect either of us to perform for more than six a day. After all, we were no longer common *putas* but sophisticated *señoras de placeres* who charged up to a *ducat* a time, depending on what particular service we were asked to undertake. Nonetheless, a number of our clients were less than thrilled at being offered one of us in particular. I remember being in bed naked with a very active cotton seller when I heard this commotion in the hall. Dulcina was doing her best to stay calm. I suggested we stop in mid-session and listen for a moment. He willingly obliged.

'Listen to me, young lady. I'm not being told which of them I want to do. I want to see them both and then decide. I may not fancy the one you've picked! In fact, I might not fancy either!'

'Well, señor. Each of them is engaged with a customer at this moment. Perhaps you'd care to wait in the drawing room until they are both available. It'll be in about fifteen minutes.'

'Fifteen minutes! I haven't got that long! I've a meeting at the Weights and Measures House in ten and it'll take that long to walk there!'

'In that case, señor, may I suggest that you come back again later? I can arrange for both Esmeralda and Beatrix to meet you later today?' she said, responding quietly and calmly to his shouting. Her approach seemed to work.

'I'm available after four o'clock.'

'Let's say four-thirty then, señor.'

The man duly arrived as Beatrix and I were teasing each other in the downstairs drawing room. 'This is Señor Losada. He would like to see you both.'

'Good afternoon, Señor Losada. How can we help you?' I said.

'I merely wanted to meet you both before I decided to whom I would make love.'

'Should we strip or would you prefer to decide with our clothes on?' asked Beatrix, naughtily and smiling with her whole face. She could see the amusing side of this arrogant request.

'No. You can keep your clothes on. I'd prefer the slightly older one, Esmeralda.'

'I'm the older!' said Beatrix, still smiling.

'All right. I'll have you then,' he said, embarrassed by her response. He just seemed to want to escape. 'I'll fix an appointment with your assistant.'

As he left we both burst into uncontrolled laughter, hoping he hadn't heard our explosion of mirth. 'God, that was funny,' said Beatrix, with tears of laughter rolling down her face. 'Next time we have a request like that, we won't ask but take all our clothes off straightaway and stand there naked. Just to see how the customer makes his decision!'

***

As we had earlier agreed, we decided to let the *Tercio* barracks near the Calle de San Nicolás know that our services were available and it was not that long before my frequent and welcomed customer in Flanders, Field Marshal Régulo de Aracena, came to visit me. I'd been expecting him after the fond farewell he gave me, on our arrival back in Madrid

'My dear and lovely Esmeralda, I'm so pleased to see you. I've really missed you. In more ways than one!'

'You always were a flatterer and you haven't changed by one *maravedí*,' I laughed.

'You won't be talking small change working in this palace of luxury!' he said, eyes wide open and glancing around our exquisitely furnished drawing room.

'And depravity!' I chanced.

'The more of that the better!'

'Just because you did my rear the last time you had me!'

'I don't remember that!'

'I do! So does my bottom!' I retorted, enjoying the teasing exchange.

'Chase me!' I said, getting up from the sofa and dashing for the door. I ran up the stairs with him in hasty pursuit. Dulcina saw us and stood in the hall, locked to the spot and totally bemused. Beatrix gave us her surprised and not particularly approving look as she peered up the stairs to see what was happening.

'I've been dying to see you, Esmeralda. I really have!'

'I thought you'd be among the first from the barracks to try out our new business.' I gave him an account of how we stayed with Madam Isabel, what the priest had done to her arm in the fire, our experiences in buying this lovely property in the Calle de Santa Clara and, of course, our incredible fortune in being invited to take over Señora de la Torre's business, along with all of her customers.

'You deserve it, Esmeralda,' he said as he was undressing and getting ready to enjoy me. 'The three of you did so much for our troops, not only when we journeyed up the Spanish Road but also while in Flanders. None of us could praise you enough. It's good that you are no longer relying on work in the Arganzuela and can be choosier about whom you serve. I'm surprised that you allowed your pretty young assistant to let me through the door!' Evidently, the problems he experienced when we first met and I had helped him solve had been long forgotten.

'Go on!' I said. 'But we do like a bit of rough work occasionally!'

After he had finished and was about to bid me farewell he looked at me quizzically. 'How open would you be to a business suggestion, Esmeralda?'

'Tell me!'

'I was just thinking of some of our other senior people. There are quite a number of what you might call the higher class ladies of pleasure, such as you and Beatrix, who are working discreetly in our town. This means that these men do have a choice about where they go to be serviced. If you could attract them with a discounted rate, you and they may benefit.'

'Interesting! I'll try the idea on Beatrix.' We did not want to serve any soldier below the rank of captain, so we decided on applying a ten percent discount to officers that rank or above. By then we were a good few months into the operation of the business and not looking to increase the number of customers, not by many at any rate. And we had an idea that there were relatively few of these more senior of the senior ranks at the barracks. I dreaded the field marshal's response and worried that it might affect our future business with him. But he was surprisingly sanguine about it and accepted what we had decided without any discussion at all. In an odd way he seemed quite pleased. It was as if he didn't think much of his original idea either. Maybe he didn't want to be greeted by some slovenly sergeant as he was leaving through our front door.

**

Over the following months, and eventually years, our business went from strength to strength. We couldn't go wrong. The three of us, Dulcina included, worked so well together we made it obvious to all we served that we operated closely and smoothly as a team. Nothing could divide us. We became renowned for providing the best service of its kind anywhere in or near our town. Our reputation even became international: dignitaries visiting government offices, including the palace, would make our premises an essential port of call. We served prelates, officials from the Vatican, dukes, princes from the Maghreb, war weary Italian generals, viscounts and earls from Genoa and Mantua – perhaps even Angélica de la Torre's earl when he visited Madrid. Who knows? We enjoyed our work and put our bodies and souls into it. And made a fortune out of it. Could this outrageous success last forever?

Needless to say, our success brought us a degree of wealth, if not the kind enjoyed by the richest in our town, certainly enough to enable us two to indulge in a range of whims which we willingly shared with Dulcina. We would treat ourselves to new and exuberant clothing, going to the best shops in Madrid to make our purchases. We bought jewellery in The Platería. But most of all we loved to go out to be entertained And why shouldn't we? We spent most of our time in pleasuring others so why not be entertained ourselves? We would close for the weekend and hire a carriage to take us to a nearby town, Pedraza or Aranjuez. We'd laugh and joke the whole way and just enjoy the ride. We'd always hire an armed escort: I'd been held up once at gunpoint and didn't want that again.

Most of all we would go to the theatre. The Príncipe was our favourite and we went many times to see the timeless plays of Lope de Vega who often appeared on stage himself. We loved his clever plots which twisted and turned their way to the most unexpected of endings. We'd sit in the *cazuela* and, along with the other women there, torment the men with lascivious action or by bombarding them with random missiles. Nothing had changed since the Alchemist sent me and Susana to the theatre, not that many years before. After the performance we would go to the Mentidero and mingle and chat with the musicians and actors, nearly all of whom met there after the curtain fell. The actors, still draped in the costumes they played in, smelt of face paint and make up. We'd tease them about how ridiculous they looked, how badly they'd performed and the wrong notes we'd accuse them of playing. In turn, they would tease us about our work and what our customers might expect for their money.

***

It was around the time that the three of us achieved such wide recognition, and even acclaim for our work, that the King, Philip III, made a proclamation. He declared that the converts from Islam to Christianity, the *moriscos*, were to be repatriated to their Muslim roots in North Africa. Every *morisco* in the land would be notified of their fate and of the exact date and arrangements for their repatriation. The proclamation, and its hideous consequences for the half a million of our citizens it would affect, passed right over our heads. It could surely mean nothing to us, unless of course, some of our customers were among the victims of this terrible scourge. Then, one morning, a matter of a fews years or so after the King had issued his decree, Dulcina burst into tears the moment she saw me in the hall.

'Whatever's the matter, Dulcina? What's happened? Is it your mother?'

'No. It's both of us. We're being sent to Africa. I'm terrified. They've got it all wrong.' She continued crying as I ushered her into one of the drawing rooms and got her to sit down.

'Tell me. I want to know!' By then Beatrix had heard Dulcina crying and had come in to see what was troubling her.

'We've just had a letter from the palace. I've brought it to show you. Here it is. It says:

"By command of His Majesty the King, you and your mother, as registered moriscas, will be repatriated to the city of Tunis. You will leave the Plaza del Palacio, Madrid at 3 pm on 16th June, 1611 to travel by road to Cartagena where you will be put on a galley bound for Africa. You may take sufficient items of clothing for the journey which will take nine days and take with you up to fifteen ducats each in cash. You will pay ten ducats each for your passage. God save the King."

So we've got two months to pack up and go,' she said, tearfully.

'I didn't know you were *moriscas*,' said Beatrix, putting an arm around her.

'That's the problem. We're not,' said Dulcina, by then sobbing and wiping her eyes in the hem of her dress. 'We may be a little dark in skin colour but we are Spanish, through and through.'

'We'll get you out of this,' I said, 'including your mother.' I had no idea how we could achieve that but felt I should at least say as much and sound committed to doing so.

'The problem is that we think my father took our family documents, proving we are purely Spanish, with him to Flanders. In case he had to prove his origins.'

'Exactly how did he die?' Beatrix said, asking an innocent enough but sensitive question.

'It was about six years ago now, maybe a little more, and the agony of it for me and my mother has partly healed. They say time is a great healer. But I always feel sad to think of it, the circumstances of his death. If I can tell you two, my friends, that will help me, I'm sure.'

'You tell us,' I said. 'If that will help.'

'It's quite embarrassing, really... I'm not sure how to start...'

'Just say it how you want to. Don't think of us. We can't be embarrassed. I promise you,' said Beatrix.

'It was the day before the siege... the siege of Ostende... finished. Apparently, because he was away from my mother, he had been... well... having some *puta*. They had made love quite normally. Then the woman suggested something different. She suggested he would enjoy having something pushed into his anus.' Dulcina started to cry and Beatrix put an arm around her shoulder. My heart leapt in my chest: I felt awful. I could feel where this was going.

'Whatever the woman did, no one seems to know. And no one knew who she was. If they did, they weren't going to say. Anyway, whatever the woman did caused a huge haemorrhage and he bled to death.'

I had never felt worse and could not prevent the tears from rolling down my cheeks. I somehow prevented myself from total collapse because I needed to shield Dulcina from my guilt. I would have to explain any excess of emotion to her. She'd never forgive me if she knew what I had done to her father, however well I thought I was justified in doing so at the time. Nor could I tell her what he had done to Susana's torso. I was trapped in my own mind. The sense of guilt overpowered me: I had killed our friend's father and taken him from her and her loving mother. The nameless, faceless man I had killed in Flanders was no longer either faceless or nameless, even though I still didn't know his name. I felt disgusted with myself, despite the justification I believed I had for killing him when I did. Beatrix, whom I had of course told, came to my rescue.

'Whatever your father did with those documents, there must be copies somewhere. Some justification for their content. Don't worry, Dulcina. We will find the copies or the evidence. We have sixty days.'

'Thank you, you two. You have made me feel better already. Thank you for listening to me. I'll go and start my work,' said Dulcina, leaving Beatrix and me looking at each other in amazement and despair.

'What a nightmare of a coincidence,' I said. 'How was I to know that the man was Dulcina's father? I've never felt more disgusted with myself.'

'I can't believe it either, Esmeralda. I have to admit: I hoped it was someone else but the timing of his death and the haemorrhage. It all fits together. But it is just possible there was a similar death. If not, and likely not, you are the victim of the worst kind of misfortune. It's terrible. But, I told you at the time. I'd have killed him myself, if you hadn't.'

From that moment, that discussion with Dulcina, I became badly unsettled, to the extent that I could not shake from my mind the image of that soldier dying after I had shot him. It had taken all these years – six years, coming up to seven – and the knowledge that it was her father that I had killed – in fact, murdered – to stir those intense feelings of guilt. At the time I killed him, I was outraged at what he had done to Susana. I felt that I had to kill him. But now, I felt so different. I had deliberately killed our assistant and friend's father. My only thought of mitigation, which gave little comfort, was that, at that time, in the depths of the siege of Ostende, I had never heard of Dulcina, and nor could I know either that she was working for Señora Angélica or, in the future, that she would be working for Beatrix and me. And that, in committing the killing, I had acted like a battle worn animal.

These intense feelings of guilt and self-disgust affected my whole approach to life. I could not sleep for thinking about the incident. I became burdened with hideous nightmares. I dreamt that Antonio handed me over to the authorities. That I was tried, found guilty and burned at the stake. Worst of all, I dreamt that Pedro had somehow discovered my crime and came to our house and shot me through the head. Those nightmares were so real, that I could feel the agony of the flames on my feet and smell my own flesh burning. I woke up screaming and terrified at the thought of an enraged Pedro killing me. Being awake and carrying the guilt was even worse. I would cry at any minor provocation.

I knew in my heart that I had to find a way of taking control of what was going on in my mind. To quell the incredible feelings of self disgust. To let them take over my thoughts would lead to insanity. If I didn't dispel them, I could end up chained to a wall in an asylum. I had to do something. So I made two decisions: I would somehow take control of my guilt; and I would never let Dulcina know that I killed her father, assuming the extreme likelihood that I had. But overcoming the guilt and getting this dreadful feeling of self-loathing out of my head took time and was far from easy. I would pretend to be happy in my work and in my relationships. And I would look for distractions to take my mind off, or as far away as possible from, these hideous thoughts.

Beatrix and I had another worry: the question of Dulcina's future. I felt strongly that if we could help her and her mother avoid the punishment of repatriation, for punishment it would be, then I would to some extent, absolve myself of murdering her father. So we made every effort to prove Dulcina's pure Spanish origins. We could not go to Vigo where she was born but Beatrix wrote to the church where Dulcina was christened to ask them to confirm her origins, either from the baptismal record or from a copy of any certificate they kept of the event. We had to move quickly so we wrote the day Dulcina told us.

'Here's a letter from San Pedro's in Vigo,' said Dulcina as she took it from the delivery man. 'Read it to me please!'

I quickly scanned the reply which had arrived nearly five weeks after we had written. 'Not good news. Their birth and marriage records were destroyed ten years ago when an Atlantic storm tore the roof off the vestry of the church. They cannot help,' I said. Poor Dulcina cried her heart away.

'What will my mother say? How can we escape being sent to Africa? There are not many more days left.' Dulcina began to weep and I put my arm around her shoulders.

'I wish I knew,' said Beatrix, looking desperate to help poor Dulcina.

'We'll think of something,' I said. 'If the day comes and we still haven't been able to prove your origins, we'll have to hide you and your mother here. We just won't let them take you.'

'You are kind, Esmeralda. I cannot thank you enough. Can I tell my mother what you said? She is so worried she can't sleep or think of anything else.'

'Yes, tell her. But not to tell another soul.'

***

It was during the time that we were doing our utmost to prevent Dulcina from being deported, that one of señora Angélica's best customers, the Marquis of Montequebrado, took to asking specifically for me to serve him, not just once a week, but nearly every day. He was an amazingly ordinary man, considering that he was a titled gentleman and he just loved to make love to me. I have to admit enjoying him and, as I've said before, there cannot be anything wrong with a lady enjoying her work.

As the señora had anticipated in her elaborate and detailed report about her customers, he would watch me bathe myself before any physical contact took place. He'd either sit on a wooden chair or stand on the kitchen floor which was the only room we could use for bathing because the stove, our only means for heating water, stood there, next to the wall. He'd be fully dressed while I washed myself all over, except my hair. He'd pay special attention while I washed my charms and would regularly say what a lucky lady I was to be endowed with such beautiful attributes.

'Go on, Esmeralda! No need to be modest! Let me see more,' he would say, laughing as he enjoyed my body. Needless to say, I would regard this as an instruction and tease him with my lower body in every way I could, facing him with my legs closed, then suddenly open them, then turn away from him and bend over, with my rear towards him and put my hands in the water, so he could see my attractions from every angle. We both laughed as I did so. I was proud of my body and enjoyed showing it off, but only in the right circumstances, of course. It was hardly something I'd do for passers-by, standing by the front door.

'Now my turn, young lady!' he would say. Then I'd get out of the wooden bath and he, by then undressed, would step in, right into the bath water I had already bathed in. Dulcina would be waiting and ready outside and I'd call her to put some fresh water in. By then the slabs on the kitchen floor would be slopping wet but that didn't matter.

'God, you're nearly ready now!' I would say, washing him as gently as I knew how. There were occasions on which we'd lock the kitchen door and finish off there and then both soaking with water and sliding all over each other as we stood against the stone wall or lay on the soaking floor. He'd love the naughtiness of doing it in the room we shouldn't do it in and be joking and teasing me as we did so. We'd finish in the kitchen by drying and powdering each other, dressing and making our innocent exit into the hall. We'd go to my bedroom, more times than not, and he'd enjoy finishing the job on or in my bed. As the señora said, he'd not linger and he'd pump his way to a conclusion in never more than twenty seconds flat.

I couldn't help but like this man. Unlike some of the more surreptitious participants of our services, who would glance each way up the street after they'd done with us, to make sure there was no one there they recognised, the marquis showed no such inhibitions and brazenly stepped into the daylight, regardless. He enjoyed other manly pleasures, too.

'I'm sorry I'm in such a sweat,' he said as he greeted me, one particularly memorable day. 'I've just returned from boar hunting with the king. He likes to give the impression that he's a stern and formal person. But you should have seen him galloping his horse, after these fat, ferocious boars. He got so excited, charging around and taking shots at them. I know what they'll be feasting on at the palace tonight!'

Could this man be the key to that prediction by the gypsy fortune-teller, made all those years ago? He suddenly re-awoke my interest in the future and his very words sharpened up my memory of her other forecast, namely that I would someday meet my brother, Pedro. I'd love to meet the king but I would sacrifice this in a trice if I could cast an eye on my brother again, not just in some ghastly nightmare, and know he was still alive. I would have to accept that I had killed Dulcina's father and live with the guilt. And 'live' should mean live, not cower under a cloud of self denigration. I resolved from the moment he mentioned the king that that is how I would live my life. I felt elated and grateful to this man for making my thoughts take this welcomed turn, even though he could not be aware of the effect his words had had on me.

'How do you know the king?' I ventured to ask him.

'I am an advisor to one of his councils, the Council of War.'

'But you are not a soldier, are you?'

'No, not now. But I am a so-called "expert" on military tactics and I know how foreign powers tend to use their armies.'

'How did you find your way into learning about those subjects?'

'It's a long story and I won't labour you with the detail, but I did military studies when I was a student at the University of Salamanca. I then took a commission and served with the Duke of Alba in the Netherlands. Before the Archdukes took over.'

'Do you see the king very often?'

'Depends. If there is some crisis to deal with: every day. If it's routine business: about once a fortnight, maybe not that often.'

We shared the delights of each other's bodies and, once we had finished, he sat on my bed. 'There is something I want to ask you, Esmeralda. I have a proposal for you to think about. It may shock you. It may concern you. But I'd like you to give it serious and careful consideration. My idea is this: I want you to serve me alone and no other. I want you to be available for me whenever I want to make love to you. And I want to make all this very worthwhile to you. I am a rich man and can pay you, within reason, whatever you want... You look shocked at what I'm saying.'

'I am, My Lord... I'm very flattered... I don't know what to say. I need time to think about it. My first reaction is to say I would like to accept. But I can see problems. I run a business here with Beatrix and Dulcina and I don't really want to give it up.'

'You wouldn't have to, Esmeralda. You'd still run the business. You'd still be in charge. But you would share your beautiful body with no one... Except me.'

'I will respect your proposal My Lord, but I will have to discuss it with my colleagues before I can decide. I'm sure you will understand that.'

I agreed to reach a decision within two weeks and let the marquis know the result. He accepted that my decision would be final.

***

Two days later, just after I had put the marquis's idea to Beatrix and Dulcina, a thought struck me about Dulcina and her mother's plight. There were only five days left to find a solution and poor Dulcina was beside herself with anxiety. I wondered if anyone at the army barracks near the Calle de San Nicolás possessed any information about their origins. So, without telling Dulcina, I walked to the barracks and asked to speak to Field Marshal Régulo de Aracena who still continued to visit, as one of our most valued customers.

'He is not available today,' said the soldier at the guard post.

'Could I make an appointment to see him tomorrow? It's really urgent.'

'I'll find out.'

He came back with an appointment for me to see the field marshal the following day. The field marshal showed great concern about my seeing him in the barracks.

'What ever brings you here, Esmeralda? It must be something very urgent.'

'It is, Señor Régulo. A very serious matter.' I explained the problem that Dulcina and her mother could be deported to Africa within the next three days.

'Just sit here for a few minutes,' he said. Looking very intent, he left his office and closed the door behind him. After a few minutes, I stood up and wandered around his sparsely furnished but large office. From his window, I could see right across the parade ground to what I thought was the Plaza del Palacio and the Alcazar Palace and beyond. In my quiet reverie, I wondered whether I would ever meet its principal occupant. The field marshal seemed to be gone an age and looked stern and troubled when he returned.

'I've looked at our records and they are clear, Esmeralda. In his signing on papers, Señor Perdigon said he was Spanish and of Spanish blood. But, for all I know, he could have been lying. There is no record of our checking what he said when interviewed. The only thing I have found is a list of his effects handed to his widow when she was informed, now nearly six years ago, of his death. One item says, "a file of documents". I wonder if the certificates Dulcina says he took with him to Flanders are in that file.'

'Surely she'd have looked in the file.'

'She may have been so distressed to learn of his death, she put them somewhere and forgot about them. Who knows?'

At least we now had something to go on. If necessary, the four of us, Dulcina and her mother, Beatrix and I would search the house from top to bottom. So that's what we did. The three of us girls went round there early the very next morning.

'Nothing will come of this,' said her mother. 'I've looked everywhere. And I don't remember seeing any file with documents in it.'

'We'll look everywhere again,' said Dulcina. 'Even if we have to take the house down, brick by brick!'

We allocated two rooms to each other. And Dulcina's mother did the hall as well. About an hour after we started, Beatrix shouted from a bedroom. 'What's all this?'

We almost collided with each other as the rest of us entered. Beatrix stood facing us, holding a shabby, buff file.

'Someone must have put it there. I've never seen that before. Let me open it!'

Dulcina's mother didn't know whether to laugh or cry. Her face lit up like the morning star. 'They're here! They're here!' she yelled. 'The birth certificates and everything!'

Dulcina couldn't contain herself and exploded into tears. 'I'm so happy, *Mamá*, so happy!'

'But I'd looked in those drawers dozens of times before! And I never saw a thing!'

'Ah!' said Beatrix. 'I bet you didn't take all the drawers out of the chest. The papers weren't in a drawer at all. They'd slid over the back and were right at the bottom of the chest, under the drawer at the bottom!'

'Amazing,' said Dulcina's mother. 'I don't even remember putting the papers in there!'

Dulcina's mother took the papers straight to the judicial office and showed them to one of the managing officials. He fully accepted that there had been an error and issued her with a document which cancelled the repatriation order. So that solved that little problem. She had one more day left before the two months' notice expired. We were all delighted with our success. I felt especially good about it, having thought of seeing the field marshal and following up his idea of searching the house. My killing of Dulcina's father seemed to slide further towards the back of my mind. But then, we had another issue to settle.

CHAPTER 27

Fit for a Prince

'I know,' said Beatrix with a serious, concerned look. 'We'll ask Melchora Cabello.'

'She didn't enjoy the work,' I said, with a chuckle. 'She'll be no use.'

'Who's Melchora Cabello?' said Dulcina.

'She used to work at number seven, the Arganzuela, with the rest of us, until the three murders that is. Then she went to sing in a theatre company,' said Beatrix.

'I don't remember any murders.'

'You couldn't have been nine years old then. We'll tell you more another time,' I said. 'She'd be a possibility, now we're working for a better class of client. I'm sure it was some of those dirty, smelly customers that put her off. We could always ask Madam Isabel who she'd recommend.'

'Anyone else we can ask?' said Beatrix. 'At least we know where Isabel lives. We want someone who really loves the work... and would do anything... as long as it didn't hurt!'

'What about María Nuñez. She'd do anything. Whether it hurt or not! Provided the money was good,' I laughed.

'Now that's a brilliant idea,' said Beatrix.

'I'm lost. I don't know these people,' said Dulcina.

'María also worked with us in the Arganzuela. We called her the Mule because she'd take any load off the rest of us! I sent many odd characters to her who wanted to do things to me that I just couldn't contemplate. There are games I wouldn't play that María would!' I said.

'We could do with a specialist!' said Beatrix. 'So we've got a few ideas.'

It was on the very last day of the fortnight the marquis and I had agreed upon that we appointed a girl to replace me, or rather, take over my customer portfolio. We had just solved Dulcina's problem with a day to spare and hadn't even that long left when we closed in on this one. We chose María Nuñez. She was thrilled. We'd taken her from the stinking streets of the night.

***

There were still problems to overcome. I felt I had to tell the field marshal about my decision. I arranged to meet him at the barracks. At first he glared across his desk at me. His eyes stared straight through mine. Then he stood up and went to the window. I imagine he cast his eye across that parade ground towards the palace in the near distance. He then came back to his desk, sat down and interlocked his hands behind his head as he looked up at the ceiling. He paused, frozen in this pose for a full two minutes. He then spoke.

'My dear Esmeralda.' It looked and sounded as if he was dictating a letter. 'I am so grateful that you came to see me about your decision. You are the one who made it and I shall, for as long as you keep to it, miss you and your beautiful body. More than that, I shall miss our conversations and the enjoyment that I think we've brought to each other... since we first met on the road to Flanders... when you cured me of a certain ailment. And I'll always be grateful to you for that. But I support you and you have my blessing. Your career comes first. I shall continue visiting your house of pleasure! Good luck to you!'

With that he stood, therefore indicating that I should go. So I stood, too, and made my way to the door. I had the feeling that my relationship with the field marshal would not end there.

**

The marquis proved himself to be a difficult, interesting but enigmatic customer. Before our agreement – which he documented carefully and gave me the original, signed copy – he would visit at least four times a week and we would almost always indulge in the bathing ritual before making love. After we signed the contract, I hardly saw him for nine months, maybe longer. It seemed to me that he wanted to reach our agreement solely to prevent me from serving others. We hardly communicated. I had no idea where he was and he showed no interest in me, apart from the odd visit for a brief talk and perhaps a drink. He did, however, ensure regular transfers of three hundred *ducats* a month from his bank account to mine. Three thousand six hundred *ducats* a year, more than three times what a reasonably successful farmer could earn, twice as much as a commercial lawyer would squeeze from his customers and five times as much as a middle ranking civil servant would exact from the state.

He may, of course, have realised that I needed time to reshape the business, to bed in our new partner, María Nuñez, and to manage the *mancebía*'s finances. Beatrix came up with that theory but I seriously doubted it. I held the view that, as a member of the king's Council of War, he spent many hours working in the palace, writing briefings for the king, meeting other officials and arguing his corner. In times as troubled as those we lived in, he would certainly be in demand. We were, after all, still having problems with the Dutch, despite the agreement reached after Ostende; the French who fought us at their jealously protected borders; and the English who would attack our ships on the high seas at every opportunity that presented itself.

Then after that nine months or whatever it was, he needed me much more in his life. Not just for physical pleasure but as his companion at a number of public and private functions. It surprised me to be in such sudden demand. He came in one day and told me that I would be going to the palace with him, that night.

'Are you serious, My Lord? What is the function? What would I be expected to do?' I half imagined that I would be expected to perform some bizarre sexual act in front of the others attending.

'Yes, deadly serious. You would come as my consort. I've been invited, with a lady, to attend a supper and concert in the palace. It would be a public manifestation of our relationship. Nothing else. What others might think is up to them. But you need show no shame. No contrition. You would hold yourself high. You would act the part of a princess,' he said, his head held back, mimicking the proud pose he would expect of me.

'But I have nothing to wear.'

'I thought as much and have prepared for that. I've made an appointment for you at the dress shop on the corner of the Calle Príncipe and the Calle de Pardo. You know the one.'

'Yes, I know it. The best in the town. For when?'

'In half an hour.'

'You've got a nerve! I'd better get ready to go.'

'No hurry. My carriage is outside.'

The shop looked quite sorry for itself as it stood at the corner. Its peeling green paint on the door and the shabby display window gave it the appearance of a cheap trinket stall rather than the purveyor of fine and expensive attire. The lady assistant, well into her fifties and with a grey, undernourished look, screwed her hands together as she asked, quite obligingly, if we wanted anything in particular. It staggered me that the marquis helped me chose the dress. Or rather, he chose it. He could not resist a beautiful red creation that left my shoulders bare, showed off my narrow waist and was full down to my ankles. It fitted me as if it had been made especially for me. 'You are more than a princess in that. You are a goddess,' he said. 'I've never seen you look so beautiful.'

'It fits me perfectly,' I said with tears forming in my eyes. The underfed assistant nodded her agreement. Here I stood, a not quite common *puta*, in a dress fit for a queen. That pride he wanted me to feel began to pour into my veins like a friendly, mulled wine.

'We'll have it then,' he said in a way that betrayed little emotion other than a strength of purpose. The shop lady took it and wrapped it carefully in what seemed at least ten *varas* of fine white paper.

We arrived at the Alcazar Palace in the marquis's carriage, drawn, as he said, by his favourite pair of horses. The white mares threw their heads from side to side as the driver stopped outside. Two flunkies opened the carriage doors and ushered us out. As we walked through to the hall in the West Wing where the event was to be held, the marquis pointed out the door to his own office. I wondered what lurked inside, what scandals were discussed, what plotting took place and what intrigue festered there. 'What are you thinking?' he said with a suspecting look in his eye.

'Just imagining how big your room must be inside,' I lied with a smile.

A bewigged gentleman in a long coat and white silks over shiny black shoes, standing at the door of the hall, introduced us to those already within.

'Who are you, señor? And your señora?' he whispered in the marquis's ear. I only just heard him.

'The Marquis of Montequebrado and his consort, Señora Esmeralda Pechada de Burgos,' the marquis whispered back.

'Please welcome The Marquis of Montequebrado and his consort, Señora Esmeralda Pechada de Burgos,' shouted the bewigged gentleman, so loudly that our names reverberated around the high ceilinged hall. I could detect a hundred pairs of eyes staring at me like hungry predators. I glimpsed at my bare shoulders. Terror welled up within me. I became the focus of attention, the point where all stares merge together. Then that self-conscious feeling abated somewhat as, to my astonishment, I recognised a few of the faces in that sea of strangers. There stood Field Marshal Régulo de Aracena, next to General Ambrosio Spínola. The field marshal smiled and looked knowingly in my direction as he uttered a few words to the general. The marquis saw me return the smile.

'Do you know these people?' he said, with a pained edge to his voice.

'Yes... um... but only professionally.' He knew full well what that meant. I half expected him to remind me of the terms of our agreement but, if he considered doing so, he must have thought better of it. 'I imagine you must know them, too?'

'Yes, the general is my boss and the field marshal's boss, too. Let's go and speak to them.'

'Please don't get upset if they refer to my past work with the army of Flanders,' I said, meekly.

'The past is the past, Esmeralda. The past only informs the present. It cannot dictate to it.'

'Esmeralda! How are you?' asked the field marshal. 'You are a lucky man, Bernardo, to have such a beautiful woman on your arm. Even more beautiful in that dress!'

I stepped in before the marquis had taken breath. 'I'm well, field marshal. Thank you for the compliment. The marquis gave it to me as a gift.'

'You are the lucky one, in that case,' said the general. Wisely and discreetly, he did not acknowledge our previous acquaintance, even though I had never bedded him. The three of them then launched into a conversation about some military exercise they were planning to take place in the north. I took advantage of the moment to look around the hall at the others present and to admire their finery. I had never before seen such opulence expressed in clothing. The women looked their very best, with their hair up in knots or wearing expensive, heavily curled wigs. The colour cream had won supremacy with many ladies wearing it, trimmed often in gold brocade. Their perfume, a blend of jasmine, cedarwood, rose and orange petal gave the air a lofty richness. I held my head back, and felt proud and then at ease, especially after my initial attack of the horrors. Then an unwelcomed announcement from the door.

'Señoras and señores, I have received a note from the king's private office to the effect that, sadly, he is indisposed. His Majesty apologises profusely. Your host for the evening will be General Ambrosio Spínola.' So I would not be meeting the king, at least not then. Anxious talking followed. 'What's wrong with him'; 'Is it the Queen?'; 'Must be serious'; 'I hope he's all right.' Then the announcer spoke again.

'Please take your allocated places for the meal!' I could not believe that mine was next to the field marshal, with the marquis to my left. It reminded me of the shocking pageant at Heeze, on our way to Hoogstraten, the night the field marshal and I confessed our sins to each other and when I discovered to my utter confusion that I could have waited for his father to kill the *hidalgo*. The field marshal had noticed the coincidence, if that is what it was.

'Well, here we are, dining together again. Different from the company in Heeze, all those years ago.'

'And a different subject for conversation, I hope!'

'I wonder what ails His Majesty.'

'You will know better than I!'

'Truly, I have no idea. He seemed well yesterday when the general and I spoke to him.'

The marquis spoke softly to the general as I engaged in banal chatter with the field marshal. The marquis and I hardly exchanged a word during the whole supper, or afterwards when a small band of Royal Chapel players and some singers entertained us. I enjoyed their lilting refrains as did many others, at least as measured by the by enthusiastic applause.

The atmosphere in the carriage on the way back to our house in the Calle de Santa Clara was frosty.

'I hadn't appreciated that you were so well known as a *puta* in Flanders and on the Spanish Road,' said the marquis, his eyebrows raised. 'At least, that's what the general indicated.'

I took a chance. 'The general is right. There were few in our company who I didn't serve, many more than a hundred times, I'd say, over that period of well, five years. That's how we came to afford our lovely house in this street,' I said, as his carriage and white mounts pulled up outside. 'Who was it said something about the past not dictating the future?'

'Quite right, Esmeralda. There is not a problem!' but I wondered if there was.

Beatrix and Dulcina chuckled as I told them about the supper and recital at the palace, especially Beatrix, when I told her about my meeting the field marshal and General Spínola and how his praise of our serving the troops in Flanders had shaken the marquis.

'I thought he was going to ask me for an account of the service I had given to each *tercio*! I could feel his jealousy burning my face!'

'You had so many of them, so many times, you'd have never remembered anyway.'

'Now, now, Breatrix. But I think you are teasing me. I'm sure I can remember every time I served the field marshal, but luckily the marquis didn't touch on that one! And I'd never before heard him called Bernardo!'

***

This supper and recital gave me my first introduction to the partying of our higher echelons. The marquis's helpful suggestions about how I should deport myself and my confident conversations with the general and field marshal, as well as the beautiful dress, which itself attracted compliments, meant that I felt well equipped even at the tender age of around twenty six to participate with some assurance on these occasions.

Many more followed. Only few were at the palace. Some were at our local theatres when the marquis would expect me to accompany him to a *comedia*. I never did admit that I'd seen some of Lope de Vega's before with Beatrix and Dulcina. Some were in towns near us, in Toledo, Segovia or Guadalajara. And, on one occasion, he took me to see his brother who was the King's Constable in Seville.

I wondered and laboured for many years about his poor wife, the marchioness, and eventually plucked up the courage to ask him. 'Don't worry about her,' he said, dismissively. 'We have a relationship on paper only. She lives in Aranjuez, on an estate she inherited from her father. She makes a substantial and regular income from the farm which occupies most of it. And she lives with a woman friend of about her age. It is rumoured that they occupy the matrimonial bed. But I've no evidence for that. Anyway, why should that concern me?'

I remembered then the intense pleasure that I and a marchioness from my previous existence had experienced when she had paid me handsomely to indulge her in the most illicit of pleasures. And I subsequently and shamelessly pleasured those other women. I shook inside with the excitement recalled.

'Well, I don't think you are asking for my opinion but, I suppose it shouldn't. Not when I will do anything to please you!'

'You reassure me, Esmeralda. But I do feel guilty at times. I go there once a year, on her birthday, but she usually greets me by looking into my eye and asking me when I intend to return to Madrid. I feel under a duty to go there once a year – no more – to see her and check that she is in good health.'

'She's lucky you go there at all.'

'That's the least I can do and the most I want to do.'

So that peremptory, if mildly emotional, exchange solved the mystery of his wife. Up to then, I'd judged him as an unfaithful philanderer. But what he said put paid to that view, assuming he told me the truth.

***

Although the marquis and I visited the palace many times, over the years, we never saw the king. At least we never more than glimpsed him, scurrying along a corridor swathed within a coterie of babbling officials who were seemingly guiding him to some important but anonymous meeting. When the time approached, I expected it to be at a party, a dinner or at a concert of Royal Chapel musicians to which the marquis 'and his lady' had been invited and where we would hardly be noticeable among the other dignitaries also present, not that I counted myself as a dignitary. However, our first meeting with His Majesty turned out to be a surprisingly intimate occasion.

Three days before it, the marquis came to see me at the house in the Calle de Santa Clara to tell me that we'd been summoned to see the king.

'What have I done?' I said trembling, and in fear that my past crimes had caught up with me.

'You have absolutely nothing to worry about, Esmeralda. The king wants to see you. He wants something of you. I have spoken to him about you, in the kindest and most praiseworthy terms.'

'What does he want? Are you coming with me?'

'I cannot tell you what he wants. But, yes, I will be with you the whole time, if that makes you feel better.'

I went to hug him and he put his arms around me. Despite his reassurance, I felt extremely nervous about meeting the king in this direct and personal way. It puzzled me that the king wanted some special favour which the marquis could not describe. His reputation as a man of great purity and piety precluded even a remote chance that he wanted to make love to me or even admire my full or partial nakedness. I spent almost the whole of the three days wondering what 'wants something of you' meant. Would he offer me some kind of post in the palace? Did he want me to participate in some form of entertainment? I could not imagine what he wanted and it annoyed me that I was being kept out of what he needed when the marquis knew so well in advance.

Then the day arrived. I dressed in one of my prettiest dresses and looked, according to the marquis, 'at my most beautiful'. Those comforting words made me feel as confident as I could be at the prospect of a meeting with the king. In fact, I was determined to face up to anything the king wanted of me. The marquis called in his carriage to take me to the palace. Hardly a word was exchanged between us during the short ride.

The meeting was to take place in a small office in the West Wing, about four doors further along the corridor from the marquis's own office. An escort took us there from the main entrance. He ushered us in. I felt nervous and at the same time fairly confident that everything would work out all right. Knowing that I looked my best helped. I expected the king to be there, waiting by the door to see us or sitting behind the bare wooden desk below the large, open window. But there was no one there. The usher pointed to two chairs in front of the desk.

'Please be seated.' He then stood by the door.

About five minutes later, we heard voices in the corridor, two or three men in conversation. They entered the room. The man in the lead came over towards us. His eyes were brown, sharp and penetrating. He wore a brown shirt, brown pantaloons and brightly polished brown shoes. His hair was cut short. It seemed odd that he had donned a fresh, white ruff which seemed to push his head back on his shoulders. We stood. 'Good morning, My Lord. Good morning, señora,' he said, looking straight at me. 'I am Philip the Third. You are here at my specific request. This is my Chief Minister, The Duke of Lerma. He is my main political adviser and this is the Duke of Olivares, who has responsibilities which relate to my son, The Infante Philip, my heir apparent.'

So this could be something political, to do with The Infante. But for the life of me, I couldn't imagine what. Then I wondered if the king wanted me to be The Infante's escort, on some as yet undefined mission, either in Spain or abroad. After all, this would need trust, and I imagined the marquis had told the king I could be trusted on such an assignment. I would have to be patient and wait to see. I sensed a warm glow of being needed, for whatever reason, and felt more at ease, helped by the presence of the king himself who had so modestly introduced himself to me. I glanced at the marquis who looked back approvingly.

'I've had a number of discussions about you with the marquis,' said the king, as the two distinguished looking dukes looked at me. 'He has a great respect for you and you serve him well.'

I could not know whether the marquis has revealed the intimate details of our relationship to the king but could do no more than hope not.

'Thank you, Your Majesty,' I dared to utter.

'I understand you run a very successful business in our town. In the Calle de Santa Clara, I believe. And that you accompanied our troops up the Spanish Road to Flanders and served them with distinction there. You and your colleagues have been much praised by one of my imperial proconsuls, General Ambrosio Spínola, whom I think you have met on several occasions. Field Marshal Régulo de Aracena has also spoken well of you.'

I smiled at the king and purred inside at these lavish compliments but I still could not work out where this was leading. I could not imagine giving The Infante instruction in running a business. And thought his knowledge of geography would more than cover the road to Flanders and the disposition of the Spanish Netherlands.

'But I judge than your most important quality is that we can trust you.' – So I was right about trust – 'Trust is what we need. No. Insist upon. And before I go further in this discussion, I want you to swear to me that you will discuss my specific request with no one. Not your colleagues, not your friends nor anyone else.'

I had to make an important point. 'But please forgive me, Your Majesty. The three ladies who work with me' – I hesitated to say 'for' – 'know that I am seeing you. And I would not know what to say to them. I suppose I shall say, simply that I cannot say.'

'No. We have thought about that and have a solution. We will get to that later.'

'In which case, Your Majesty, I swear to say nothing about your specific request. I am longing to know what it is!' I could not hold back from saying so.

'It is a simple request. And I shall put it in simple terms. I want you to show my son, The Infante, how to make love,' he said, emphatically, as if this was an instruction rather than a wish or desire. 'You will show him, not only the mechanics of lovemaking, that is the conjugation of man and woman, but you will demonstrate to him the female functions in particular and show him the detailed structure of the female body. Do you have any questions, at this stage?'

His demand, clearly what it was, sent my mind into a spin. I felt flattered, confused, delighted and dubious, all at the same time. Not to say staggered at what the king had said. Any lessons I gave The Infante could affect the birth of future monarchs. If I failed there may be none! Then, after a second or two, which probably seemed longer to the king, I regained my composure. 'No, Your Majesty, except one.'

'That is?'

'I have a written contract with the marquis here which prevents me from having intimate physical contact with any man, except him.'

'We have dealt with that in prior discussion. The marquis has agreed to make an exception in this case. It will apply to this case only but my request may mean more than one, shall we say, educational, meeting with The Infante.'

'I fully understand and accept, Your Majesty.' Not that I had a choice in the matter or needed one. 'May I ask another question?'

'Please do.'

'When would you like me to start this course of instruction?'

'As soon as you are ready. You can start tomorrow, if you wish.'

'Yes, if the marquis is happy, Your Majesty,' I said turning in his direction.

'Of course,' he said, not showing the least concern that his rights to me would be shared, if only temporarily.

'Now to the subterfuge,' said the king. 'You will tell your colleagues that you are coming to the palace to advise on the planning of a ball that the marquis is organising in honour of those who fought in Flanders. In future, I want you to deal with the Duke of Olivares here on the issue of educating The Infante. He will arrange for a carriage to meet you outside of your house at, say ten o'clock tomorrow morning.'

Beatrix, Dulcina and María were all but waiting at the door when I entered our house in the Santa Clara. I had no choice but to lie so lie I did.

I told them that I would be picked up the following day and taken to the palace to begin organising a ball. The fact is they didn't believe me. Beatrix constantly showed herself to be a perceptive lady and when we were first alone let me know what she thought this was all about.

'You are in a difficult position, Esmeralda, and I can understand that you have been told not to say what your mission is. I think it's something to do with The Infante. But I respect what you said and you need not say more!'

So I didn't. I stayed true to my word. I feared the worst if I did otherwise.

***

With clockwork precision, the king's carriage arrived outside. It was a fresh, sunny day and the smell of the night soil had all but dispersed. The Duke of Olivares looked out of the side window as his carriage driver stood by the door to let him out.

'Good morning, Señora Pechada de Burgos. We are going to meet The Infante at a place outside the town, not far away and it will take half an hour or so to get there.' The driver closed the door after me and set off towards the Puerta de la Vegva, at the western edge of the town. Then, after crossing the river, he started down the Camino de Mostoles. Fifteen minutes or so later, we took a path off to the left and followed it through the forest for about five hundred *varas* to a small hut in a clearing. Another, more ornate carriage drawn by a pair of horses had stopped outside of the hut. Two men with muskets slung across their shoulders were standing guard. The Duke then spoke for the first time since greeting me at the front door.

'The Infante is waiting for you inside the hut. You will knock at the door, walk in and introduce yourself to him. The hut is fully equipped for you to instruct The Infante, as you have been requested. I and these men will retire to a point a discreet distance from the hut and the clearing. Once your period of instruction has finished, The Infante will sound a horn. We will then collect each of you and return you, respectively, to the palace and your house.'

I stepped out of the carriage, knocked the door and waited. The door opened and a tall, gangly young man with curly hair and a distinctive plump, lower lip opened the door. He looked nervous and it was as much as he could do to raise but a limp smile. He was dressed in a white shirt and brown pantaloons and had short wavy hair.

'Good morning,' he said as the carriage slowly drove off behind me. 'Do come in. I believe your name is Esmeralda?' He spoke softly and quietly but with precision while he looked me straight in the eye.

'Thank you,' I said. 'Yes, I am Esmeralda. And you are The Infante Philip?'

'Yes, indeed,' he said, suddenly smiling widely.

'I imagine you know why I am here.'

'Yes, of course. You have come to give me instruction in lovemaking. I'm looking forward to it.' His nerves began to vanish as he beckoned me to sit on a wooden sofa while he sat on another. A large bed with a white cover had been placed against the wall opposite the door and windows.

'There are some things I need to know before we start, Your Royal Highness.'

'Oh please, let's be on informal terms. I am Philip and you call me that. I will call you Esmeralda, if I may?'

'Of course, Your Roy... I mean Philip.' He broke into laughter and I promptly followed.

'I think we will like each other, Esmeralda,' he said, still laughing. I was beginning to enjoy this friendly encounter and was determined to give him as much pleasure as I could with the lesson.

'Can you tell me, Philip?' I said. I could not believe what was happening. I was talking to the heir apparent and on first name terms with him. 'This is a sensitive question. Please forgive me for asking it. I need to know whether you have made love to a woman before. Your father thinks not! And I will not tell him otherwise if otherwise it is!'

'I have no problem telling you, Esmeralda. I am of course married to Elisabeth and have been for four years but the marriage has not yet been consummated. Up to now, I have been kept away from her bed. But, yes, I have. About six months ago, I was working in the palace stables and one of the stable maids and I took each other's fancy. We exchanged a few seductive words and the next thing was we were making frantic love in a hay cart! I so enjoyed it... and so did she, I believe! That's when I lost my virginity! We were lucky that no one saw us!'

'It's good to know you're not a complete beginner. But there is still a lot to be learned. I'm going to start by showing you around my body and letting you touch me. I'll undress first and get on the bed. You may want to take some of your clothes off later and we'll make love.' He stood and listened as I took control and led the lesson. I unbuttoned my blouse, slipped out of my skirt and climbed onto the bed. I had bathed and perfumed myself earlier and could smell the subtleness of the gentle aromas as they released themselves from my body.

'Come on, you climb on, too!'

Still fully clothed, he climbed on and sat on my right hand side. 'You smell lovely, Esmeralda. Your perfumes are beautiful. And you have a lovely body. Such pretty breasts!'

'Thank you,' I smiled, running my hand over my light covering of hair. 'This area is called the 'vulva'. It's a strange word, don't you agree? A bit like *vulgo*,' I giggled, 'but with a completely different meaning! I will show you everything there is to see down here and what to touch to excite a woman. To make her want to make love to you.' I then introduced him to my labia, another new word, and invited him to touch them and move them from side to side.

'I don't remember seeing anything like this on the stable lass. They are so pretty and flexible and quite large, too.'

'Yes. You are right. Not many women have been blessed with labia as meaty as these and you mustn't be disappointed if the Infanta Elizabeth's are smaller. The size of the labia only affects the appearance; not the performance. Now I want you to part them and look inside. Start at the top. Do you see that little round button just inside the little hood? Just there.' I touched it.

'Oh, yes. It is pinkish red! I can feel my manhood responding to this! I'm getting quite excited.'

'Keep yourself covered and concentrate on touching me! That tiny button is so, so sensitive. Not many men know about it but most women do, even the nuns! It gives me great pleasure when you stroke it. Wet your finger on your tongue and touch it again. Oh...that's lovely!' I smiled joyfully. This whole experience made me feel very proud to be of such service to our next king and at the same time quite humble.

'Now open my labia further down. You will see a little hole in the centre. Touch it. That's it. You're on it! That's where my pee comes out. Now, just below that is my vagina – you must have heard that one before – where your member goes in. I'll let you see inside.' He nodded with a look of total concentration. I couldn't tell whether he was showing that he did know it or was simply agreeing to further exploration. I daren't say 'cock'; and 'penis' would have sounded far too formal.

I used the forefinger and second finger of each hand to open myself as far as I could without it hurting.

'There you are. Look in!'

The Infante beamed with fascination at my parts. He hadn't expected anything quite as interesting or complicated. 'This is fascinating, Esmeralda. I feel really excited now. Can I undress and try it?'

'Do it, but not too quickly!'

He undressed in a trice. He needed no stimulation and I lay back as, on my instruction, he took his weight on his arms and slid himself into me. 'Now keep to a slow steady rhythm and think of something else, like what you will have for your next meal or the next boar hunt. That will keep you from finishing too quickly.'

He managed to hold himself for about three minutes. 'Well done, Philip,' I said, as he released himself. 'You'll make a good lover.' He eased himself off me and I took a towel that was hanging from the bed post and wiped myself gently. 'There is just one more thing I want to show you today, Philip. But we need to meet again. Let's quickly dress and we'll go outside.'

We looked to make sure none of the guards were there and crept out. About five *varas* from the door of the hut a tree stump stood about a *pie* and a half above the floor of the clearing. 'Have you ever seen a woman peeing before?'

'I don't think so, not from close quarters anyway.'

'I'm going to sit on the edge of this stump. I'll then put my skirt around my waist and let my pee go. You can get as close as you like but don't let me pee on you!' He crouched in front of me and looked up as I peed. The look of amazement showed across his whole face. I peed and peed and couldn't stop. Then, eventually the last few squeezes and I did.

'I think I'm empty, now!' I said, pulling my skirt back down and chuckling at my new acquaintance. 'That's all!'

'Esmeralda, you've been wonderful. Wonderful. What is there left to show me?'

'You'll see! When can we meet again?'

'In two days? I'm busy tomorrow.'

'In two days, then. I can show you the rest at my house, in the Calle de Santa Clara. Ten o'clock, as before?'

'I'll be there.' We sneaked back into the hut. The Infante took a silver horn from his bag, put it to his lips and blew.

CHAPTER 28

Lorraine

I told the girls that I was expecting a visitor at ten o'clock that morning. Dulcina opened the door, ushered him into the drawing room and shouted upstairs for me. I stopped brushing my hair and went down to meet him.

A priest wearing a wide brimmed hat, so wide I could hardly see his face, stood with his hands crossed in front of him in the middle of the room. His head was lowered as if he had come to deliver bad news. I closed the door behind me.

'I wasn't expecting you, Father. Has something bad happened to The Infante? He should have been here half an hour ago. I do hope he is all right,' I said, genuinely anxious about him.

The priest removed his hat. 'I am The Infante!' he whispered and laughed into his hand.

'My God, Philip! You really made me worried! You fooled me!'

'I hope I fooled your assistant. What a pretty girl.'

'Keep your eyes away from her. It's me who's giving you the lessons!'

'I've been longing to see you again. Just itching to know what's in the next instalment.'

'Follow me upstairs but keep your hat in place. If you don't want to be recognised!'

The Infante stayed right behind me as we dashed up the stairs and crossed the landing into my boudoir. 'What a beautiful room. Do you do all your work in here? Shall we start now?' he said, keen to enter the next phase of his education. 'Shall I take my clothes off?'

'No. Please be patient, Philip. Keep them on and I'll tell you what we are going to do,' I said, keeping the lead, even though instructing our future king. I still could not believe that the king himself had put me in this privileged position and I simply glowed with pride.

'You are going to be an actor today. The part you are playing is that of a lover, seducing a reluctant mistress! I will be the resistant one but will instruct you on how to overcome my resistance. For now, I'll keep my clothes on. We'll start by cuddling up to each other on my bed. You will then hug and kiss me.'

He climbed awkwardly onto the covers and moved up next to me. 'That's no good. Closer... I need to feel the warmth of your body... Now kiss me on the lips... Don't pull yours away like that... Stay in contact. Make the kiss linger... That's better. I enjoyed that! Now take your hand

and touch my face... and gradually move it down my neck... Lovely. Gently, as if you are touching the feathers on a gosling's back. Slowly and softly. Now slide your hand further down... slowly... and touch my breasts over my blouse... now try fondling my nipples... slowly and gently, but meaning to give me pleasure!'

'You have such sweet, firm breasts, Esmeralda. I could do this all day.'

'Thank you and excellent. A woman loves to hear compliments from a lover. Especially about her body as he is enjoying it. Can you feel the stiffness in my nipple?'

'Oh yes. It's really firm.'

'That feels nice to me, too, and it's what your stroking it has done. Good! Now undo the buttons on my blouse. Then stroke the skin on my breasts. Beautiful. Like a good lover. You've really put me in the mood to love you well.'

'That was so easy, Esmeralda, with your instruction.'

'Now we go further. Take off your shirt, slowly as if to tease me... That's right... You have strong shoulders... Now slide off your breeches and face me... Your member is ready again, just like last time... Just a moment and I'll slide out of my skirt. There you are! What next do you think?'

'I'll climb up over you and start?'

'No! Go down on me with your head, as I showed you the other day, and put your tongue there.'

'You are soaking wet. And your perfume is lovely! Do we have to stop this?'

'Stay as long as you like. The pleasure for me is as good as you being inside me, if not better!' I laughed.

'Well, I'll stay here all day then. It tastes like a warm, light wine.' He chuckled.

'That's enough. Oh! Oh! You've given me such a climax,' I shrieked. 'God. I must control myself or they'll all hear me!'

'What was that?' he said, anxiously as if he had injured me.

'A woman's body shakes with pleasure when you bring her to a climax. It's a wonderful feeling and that one gave me huge pleasure. And you did that with your tongue, young man,' I dared say. 'I'm still shaking! Now put yourself within me... Perfect. The wetness has made it easy... now keep going as long as you can.'

He looked into my eyes as he did so. His eyes shone with the intensity of his new pleasure. After about five minutes he came, in full flood and let out a pleasing moan.

'Esmeralda, my beauty, how can I thank you? That was so enjoyable. Now I need to practice on my Elisabeth.'

'I'm pleased that you're pleased. There's nothing as satisfying as a satisfied customer. Now get dressed and put that hat back over your eyes. Then we'll smuggle you out!'

'I imagine that is the end of the course. Thank you for being so patient and showing me so much.'

'There is just one other thing I must teach you. But the timing is critical. Can I let you know, by say, delivering a message to the palace?'

'Could you tell me more?'

'No, I'd rather not! I'll tell you on the day, in about three weeks?'

'Fine.'

The Infante took a small leather purse from a pocket in his surplice. 'I want you to have this, Esmeralda. A small token of my thanks.'

'I cannot take it Philip! The pleasure has been mine. You have honoured me!'

'You have no choice,' he said, smiling broadly. 'I am the heir apparent and am demanding that you take it, in the name of the king!'

He left the purse and its contents on my dressing table and walked to the door.

'I cannot thank you enough,' he said as he went out of the house and climbed into his awaiting carriage. I could not be more pleased with my two encounters with The Infante. I felt I had really been helpful to him. I had given my very best and couldn't see how I could have done any better. It was a pleasure to get to know this charming young man. He would become a good king. And he'd left me 100 *ducats*!

***

Three weeks passed and I sent a message to The Infante, inviting him back for his final lesson. In his reply, he said he'd visit at midday the following day. Dulcina panicked when I told her I was expecting the priest again.

'But I've booked our banker to speak to you then! You said you wanted to discuss our finances!'

'You will have to change his appointment, Dulcina. I have made a promise. I cannot go back on it.'

The enterprising Dulcina accepted my difficulty and even took the trouble to go to the bank, the same one in the Calle de Tenerías, on the corner of San Pedro, that we had used for years. She arranged for me to see the official after the 'priest'.

'What excitement are you offering me today, Esmeralda?' asked The Infante, as he followed me, still wearing his disguise, into my boudoir.

'Not so quickly, Your Highness,' I hesitated to use his first name. 'Come and sit in my chair. The one by the dressing table. Your father gave me very precise instructions when he commissioned me. He told me to demonstrate to you "the female functions in particular and the detailed structure of the female body". I well remember his words. So I have to show you something that you may or may not want to see and you must not get excited. Do you know about a woman's bleed?'

'No, I've never heard of it. Tell me more.'

'Better still, I'll show you.' I walked over to my dressing table and took a small basket from a drawer, placed it on my bed and sat next to the little basket, facing The Infante. I then lifted my skirt and opened my legs a little. 'I'm not sure if you can see this, Philip, but there is a little piece of towel showing from my vagina. See it?'

'Yes, it's white.' I could see a quizzical look on his face. He looked serious as if he couldn't work out what would happen next.

'Now you are going to see something that is so intimate that hardly any woman has shown it to a man. So watch carefully.' I then placed my thumb and forefinger on the corner of the piece of towel and gently removed it. 'You will see before I do whether there is any blood on it. Is there?'

'Yes, Esmeralda, a large smear on the innermost part.'

'Well, that is a lady's bleed. You have now seen it.'

I placed the used towelling in the little basket and took out a small cloth which I had previously dampened. 'I now clean myself down there and, here we go, I insert a clean piece of towel, making sure a small corner is just showing.'

'Goodness, Esmeralda, you are so gentle with yourself.'

'Yes, I need to be. You already know how sensitive it is and during the bleed my tummy hurts, up here.' I touched myself in the area of my womb. 'There,' I said. 'It's all done now,' and lifted myself up from the bed enough to pull my skirt back down.

'May I ask some questions, Esmeralda?' He looked truly puzzled.

'Of course.'

'How long does your bleed last and what is it for?'

'It lasts for no more than five days or so. It's to do with conceiving a baby. A woman cannot conceive during her bleed and her man should let her rest from lovemaking. You should be able to manage that. It's only a week! And it happens every month.'

'That often?' he said, with a hint of disappointment.

'I'm afraid so. There's nothing anyone can do about it.'

'Well, you have taught me something today. I didn't expect this. You are an excellent teacher. I had no idea how ignorant I was about these things. I cannot thank you enough.'

'It's a pleasure, Philip. If at any time you want to ask me anything to do with a man and a woman, you only have to let me know and I will tell you. Or even show you!'

'I am grateful. Should I go now?'

'Not before you have donned you hat and pulled it over your face!'

He stood up to leave, kissed me on the cheek and handed me another small purse. I thanked him profusely, put it on my bed and escorted him to the front door.

'Good bye, Esmeralda.'

'Good bye, Father.'

The generous Infante had left me another one hundred *ducats*.

***

I had been pondering, in these last few days, about that meeting with the gypsy, when she had read my fortune in the crystal ball. I clearly remembered her saying that I would meet the king and that I would become close to him, even a friend of his. I had met him and had enjoyed intimate contact with his son. But, to me, the king seemed a remote figure and, but for him giving me a special assignment, I could not see how I could become his friend. I thought it wise to keep these thoughts from Beatrix and the others.

Then the position became tragically clear. A town crier walked the streets on that unforgettable day and announced what fate had delivered. I saw and heard him from my bedroom window. 'The King is dead. Long live the king!' he shouted to his clanging bell of proclamation. It saddened me immensely to hear of Philip III's sudden, tragic and early death. While we had not developed a relationship that could be called friendly, he had brought me into the ambit of his court and given me the unique opportunity to educate The Infante. For that I would be forever grateful. From that moment, my ambition became to befriend the new king, Philip IV.

I rushed downstairs to tell Beatrix and the others. 'Have you heard the news? Did you hear the town crier?'

'What a terrible, terrible tragedy,' said Beatrix. 'It's such a shock. What could have killed him? It's so sudden?'

'I've no idea,' I said. 'But all will become clear.' It never did. No one could explain the mystery of the poor man's death, not even the best doctors in the land. They concluded that it was by 'natural causes'.

***

I never could satisfactorily explain my breaking with the marquis. For many years we were regarded in our town, in particular in the higher social circles which centred on social events at the palace, as man and wife. We were not, of course, because his wife lived a separate existence with a lady friend in Aranjuez. That being so, I accompanied him to every function at which a female companion was demanded by the etiquette of the day. To my knowledge, no other woman took that role for him. And, of course, he continued to enjoy the delights I regularly and frequently paraded before him.

It was on a calm summer's day that Field Marshal Régulo de Aracena paid a visit to our house in the Santa Clara. He knew perfectly well, because of my ongoing relationship with the marquis, that my charms were prohibited from his indulgence. Nonetheless, he paid me a social call and I entertained him in one of the downstairs drawing rooms before he was to be served by one of the others, probably María. As we were chatting and laughing, exchanging reminiscences about our times in Flanders and back in Madrid, we heard an excessively loud knock on the front door.

Moments later an anxious looking Dulcina opened the drawing room door and the marquis burst in. He went straight up to the field marshal, who was sitting with me on a sofa, and glared down on him. The field marshal immediately stood.

'You dishonourable swine. I knew you were here. The two of you have been playing... behind my back. Don't try to lie your way out of it. I would have thought better of you, Esmeralda, but not of him.' He drew a ceremonial sword and aimed it at the field marshal's throat.

The field marshal stepped back in surprise, his eyes straining in an attempt to escape their sockets. 'My God, Bernardo! What the hell are you talking about? This is merely a social call and Esmeralda and I are just having a chat. Have you gone mad? Put that damned thing away before I smash it over your head!'

My heart thumped with fear. I stayed motionless on the sofa, looking anxiously at the two combatants. I could not believe that the marquis had suddenly had this fit of jealousy. He rushed at the field marshal who grabbed the blade of the sword to save his neck. He tried to wrench it from the marquis. Blood ran from the field marshal's hand and splashed on the carpet. He shouted at the marquis. 'Look, you've almost cut my finger off, you idiot!'

The field marshal backed himself into the corner, staring at his injury. The marquis attempted again to thrust the sword at him but missed as the field marshal ducked to one side. I grabbed a metal vase that stood on a table by the sofa. I dashed up behind the marquis and brought it down on his head, as hard as I possibly could. He collapsed to the floor in a dishevelled heap. The field marshal took the sword from his hand and stood over the marquis with the point of the sword touching the soft skin on his neck.

'Well done, Esmeralda. You've saved my life. This crazy idiot almost killed me! Go and get a constable. We'll have this one arrested.'

The three of us, Beatrix, Dulcina and myself rushed into the street and down towards the Plaza Mayor. There was almost always a constable somewhere in the square and we were doubly lucky. There were two. Within moments, they had arrested the marquis and marched him off to the judicial offices in the Puerta de Guadalajara.

That day marked the end of my strange, many year relationship with the marquis. He never came near our house again. The crown constables charged him with committing an assault against the person. But the field marshal, whose injuries, but not his pride, soon healed, refused to act as a witness against his colleague on the Council of War so the courts dropped the charge. I never forgave the marquis for his unprovoked attack on my innocent friend and vowed that I would, as long as I lived, never be a consort again.

***

The events of that dreadful day and the consequential cutting off of the marquis' regular monthly payments into my account meant that I was compelled to revert to my previous work as a lady of pleasure. There were, however, already two of us in the house working as such, along with the indefatigable Dulcina, our assistant. Nonetheless, business was booming and soon picked up to the level where all three of us were serving six or even seven customers a day, a surprising number of whom said that sources at the palace had recommended they visit our establishment.

Naturally, the fact that the Marquis of Montequebrado had unjustly banished me as his consort meant that my opportunities to visit the palace, certainly as a guest, completely vanished. My hopes of befriending the king, as foreseen by that distant fortune-teller, vanished with them. I was therefore quite surprised one cold January day to receive a summons from the palace demanding that I attend a meeting with the king. The missive simply gave the time and date but revealed nothing about what purpose this meeting would serve. A carriage, it said, would arrive outside our house at half an hour before the meeting to collect me and take me there.

The king stood up from his desk as his principal private secretary ushered me into his office. He looked troubled as he came round and planted a kiss firmly on my lips. 'My dear Esmeralda, I am delighted to see you. After such a long time. Much has happened to each of us since we last met... at your house... and you gave me those crucial lessons. Everyone knows that I have consummated my marriage. Tragically, the first two of our offspring passed away within moments of their birth, sad though it is for both Elisabeth and me. But this was not a consequence of what you showed or told me. Turning to you and your business: you, I understand, were rejected by the Marquis of Montequebrado and rumour is that you, and my colleague Field Marshal Reguló de Aracena, were treated unjustly by him. And more widely, much is happening in our Empire, in Europe and in the Americas. And we will get to that.'

He then paused and looked towards an official. 'You are dismissed, Private Secretary. There is no need for a note of this meeting.' The man stood and left the room, gently closing the door behind him.

'That's better, Esmeralda. We can be totally free and open with each other now. There is much to speak about. In fact there are two major issues I want to discuss with you.

'I am now going to tell you about something which you must regard as confidential. You must not tell another about what I am about to say. Would you have a problem with that?'

'No, Your Majesty,' I said, quietly and humbly. The start of this conversation had similarities with the one with his father. It could not go down the same path. I dared not revert to calling him by his first name, as I did when he was The Infante. And I dreaded to think what secret existed that he was about to share with me.

'Then I will begin. You will not know, I think, that I am responsible for a cadre of individuals, most of whom live here in Madrid, and whom I call my special agents. Their main, routine function is to inform us of anything they could construe as a plot or attempt to usurp me or overthrow me as king. In effect, my special agents are spies. And by accepting the position as a special agent, he or she can be given an assignment which they may decline, only on the assumption that they are dismissed, from the moment of refusal, from that office. My council responsible for overseeing and reporting to me about this cadre of agents is the Council for State Security. Its head official is Señor Alvaro Gutierro de Marchena. All current special agents, and there are fifty nine of them, are men. I hope to tell you who some of them are but not yet.

'My proposal is this, Esmeralda, and you have probably guessed where this discussion is leading. I am offering you the post of my sixtieth agent. That will complete the cadre for there cannot be one more than sixty... No. I will reword that. I am not just offering it to you. I seriously want you to accept it.

'Before you decide, and I want you decide before you leave here, I will tell you about the second issue because the two issues are closely linked. If you accept my proposal, I want you to go to France to obtain some extremely important information. You would not go there alone. You would be accompanied by Monsieur Marcel Montpassant who is a spy for King Louis XIII of France. He is also a spy for me so he is what we call in the business a double agent.' He paused and laughed, I presumed at his joke about 'the business' or perhaps his cleverness at appointing a double agent, but I could not be sure either way. Then he resumed.

'He has come to Spain on a diplomatic mission but we are sending him back to Paris with some credible but erroneous information about the strength of our armies in the Spanish Netherlands, an area with which you are painfully familiar.' I imagined his use of 'painful' could refer to our tragic loss of Susana. Surely, the king could not be aware of such a small event in the context of the war in Flanders.

'He will be returning to Paris in one month's time. You would go back with him. The exact relationship with you would be as follows. In that month he will pretend to fall in love with you. You and he will become passionate lovers and you would agree to his proposal – his, not mine – to return to France with him. So you would become an actress! You gave me an acting role at our second, educational meeting and I am offering you one now!' He stopped speaking, looked at me with those soft but penetrating eyes and stroked his chin. I thought he wanted me to say something, to react in some way to the startling offer he had made.

'Well, Your Majesty. I am staggered at what you are saying. I'm flattered that you have chosen me to become one of your special agents... and to undertake this rather crucial mission. What important information would I be expected to obtain in France?' I refrained from asking what kind of reward I might expect for this serious disruption to my daily life for fear of appearing ungrateful.

'Therein lies a minor problem. One of trust. You must appear totally unaware of the nature of that information until you receive it. You will be placed in a position to obtain it. From a man or men. You will recognise its importance immediately. But I cannot elucidate further. You will have to trust me on that.

'There are some other details. The mission will take between four and six months to complete. You will travel with an armed escort, in one of our most luxurious carriages. You will stay in the best quality inns and we will provide you with a full wardrobe of clothing to meet every eventuality. You will be given five hundred *ducats* for any expenses you incur... And you will be paid ten thousand *ducats*, on your return. Finally, you will be armed with a small pistol for any necessary self protection. And you will be trained to use it.'

'If you are to arm me, Your Majesty, you must believe I could be putting myself in danger. What do you regard as the risk, exactly?'

'I perceive only the very slightest of risk and the pistol is a precautionary measure. I don't expect you to use it. You must, of course, tell no other of the information you will receive and you will have to commit it to memory. On no account write it down.

'There is one other thing. As soon as you return, you will come to the palace and say one word to the guard. That word is: "Lorraine". You will then be escorted direct to my office... Well, what do you think?'

He then sat back in his chair to await my response. Whether he was prepared to admit it or not, I could perceive a definite risk, however small, to my well-being. Someone could realise that I had been given this vital information, to whatever it related, and kill me rather than endanger the country of France or its population. So I would have to accept the king's judgement on the level of risk: only the very slightest. I would have to leave the house in the Santa Clara and the business in the care of the other girls but could not see a particular difficulty in that. So my mind was made up: what an adventure I could see unfolding before me: A French lover; a journey to a foreign land on a mission directed by the king; to be treated so well and given everything I could conceivably need. And ten thousand *ducats* into the bargain. I need never work again.

'Yes, Your Majesty. I'll go!'

The king stood and came round to my side of his desk so I stood, too. 'My dear Esmeralda. You are a heroine. I shall love you forever. I cannot explain to you how grateful I am. And I am proud to know you!' He hugged me firmly and planted another kiss on my lips. He looked as if he wanted to make love to me, there and then, but perhaps thought that I might not appreciate that form of thanks.

'I said I wanted you to meet some other of my special agents. We'll do that now.' He went to the door to his outer office. 'Come in,' he beckoned and two men entered, one a dark haired man of about my age with an upwardly curled moustache. The other looked a few years older, was clean-shaven and had his hair tied at the back.

'This is Diego Velázquez,' he said, his hand outstretched towards the younger man. 'He is the royal portrait painter. He hasn't been here long and I already have a mission planned for him! I haven't told him about it yet! And this is Antonio Hidalgo, an itinerant musician. He travels the towns around Madrid and tells me of any trouble he sees brewing! So he is a regular spy! This lady, my men, is Esmeralda Pechada de Burgos, my latest recruit to the cadre and our only lady member. I cannot tell you what she will be doing or the Count Duke will shoot me dead.'

We all laughed at the king's frivolity. The meeting with the king adjourned at that point with the painter inviting Hidalgo and myself to his office for a short chat. The three of us exchanged addresses and the two men instructed me firmly to contact them if I had any questions about being a special agent. The friendly and welcoming discussion covered a narrow ground, confined to working in this role for the king. Hidalgo took me by surprise by mentioning payments. 'Not much is it. Three *ducats* a month! You won't make your fortune!'

'The king didn't even mention that!'

'Did he mention the tattoo?' asked Velázquez.

'Tattoo? No. Not at all.'

'You will have to go to the tattooist near the Platería to have the Habsburg coat of arms put on your shoulder!'

'Are you serious?'

'Yes. It's so you don't forget you are in this club!' said the musician.

***

The Monsieur, as we affectionately referred to him, turned out to be what I had expected of a French lover. Passionate, selfless and generous. He differed so much from the marquis who had an underlying streak of jealousy which would reveal itself at the least provocation; and the marquis wasn't such a good lover. The Monsieur arrived at the Santa Clara over a week after my meeting with the king, thus giving himself only three weeks to 'fall in love' with me. I could not, of course, reveal to the others what was about to happen; nor did I want to upset their morale. So I had to think very carefully about what to tell them. Then an idea dawned on me. I would say that he had invited me to Paris to help his sister set up an establishment similar to ours. I couldn't see how that could fail, especially as I would show him the accounts of the business and tell him about other aspects of its operation. So there would be two stories. As far as my immediate colleagues were concerned the one about a new *burdel* in Paris; and as far as the French and the palace knew, he had fallen in love with me. He could fall in love with me anyway and I would not stand in his path!

The day of our departure arrived with inexorable certainty. A carriage turned up, at the exact time specified, at the front door of our house. The Monsieur stepped out to greet me with his usual kiss on both cheeks. Beatrix, Dulcina and María came to the door to wish me 'bon voyage' and they, too, in mimicry of the Monsieur, kissed me on each cheek.

'Whatever you do in France, promise us that you will return,' said Beatrix, a tear running down her face.

'I shall be back. Fear not,' I said. 'If only to see how the business has expanded while I've been away!' The last thing I wanted was an excessively emotional farewell so I thought a little humour would help.

As we approached the Puerta de Santa Barbara, we could hear the rhythm of hooves from behind us. Two horses, ridden by the king's promised armed guards, joined us and led us on our way. As we passed through the Puerta, I glimpsed a bearded man in a heavy coat standing there looking straight at me. It couldn't be. Or could it? My brother Pedro? I had to be imagining it so dared not ask the Monsieur to stop.

'Are you all right, Esmeralda? You suddenly look shocked, as if you have seen a ghost!'

'No, Monsieur. I just thought a man back there was someone I knew. But it cannot be so.' But the image of that man stayed with me.

We hadn't travelled far up the road to the north before the Monsieur said he had something important to say. 'Esmeralda, my dear, we are not going to Paris.'

'Let me guess... We are going to Lorraine.'

'How could you possibly know? Up to now, only three of us have known and one is the king.' I explained that the king had given 'Lorraine' as the code word I should use when I returned to see him.

'That was careless,' said the Monsieur. 'He could have thought of something else! We're heading for Nancy, my home town.' Two weeks later, we arrived there. The carriage driver who had accompanied us the whole time had no idea where the Monsieur lived so with the Monsieur himself directing from next to the driver, we arrived outside the man's beautiful house, just off the central square of the town. The Monsieur took me in and, after he had given me a drink of cloudy French beer, took me on a tour of the property. The house was not as large as ours in the Santa Clara but it was exquisitely furnished with the most expensive looking carpets and furniture so ornate it could only be French.

'This is my bedroom, Esmeralda. I hope you like it. The one I would like you to use is further down the landing.' What a relief. I had never shared a bed with a man, unless he was a night customer, and I didn't want to start in these circumstances where, if anything, I was to a degree vulnerable and therefore would struggle against a suggestion with which I disagreed. He then threw open the door to my room and, with a flourish, said, 'Here you are. It's all yours. I hope you will be comfortable here.' The room looked to me as if it had been put together by a woman; such was the softness of the furnishings and delicacy of the rich, predominantly light green, colour scheme.

'I love it already,' I said, smiling at the Monsieur. He left me to unpack and settle in. It was on occasions such as these, while alone, that my mind threw at me the image of that man in the overcoat standing at the Puerta de Santa Barbara. Could he be my brother? If so, what was he doing in Madrid? I could do nothing here to satisfy my curiosity but that did not stop the recurrence of these images. I combed my hair and went downstairs.

'I am going to cook you a typically French meal. Then we will explore the town. We will look out for some friends of mine, in an inn not far from here. But don't worry about the king's mission. I will tell you more about that in a day or two. But we must start the pretence that we are passionately in love. I will introduce you as my bride to be.'

'This is going to be such fun, Marcel. I'm looking forward to the whole thing!'

I had never tried wine as tasty as the rich fruity red which the Monsieur served me at dinner. It was truly delicious. And not cloudy like his beer. The only problem was that I drank a little too much of it and by the time we left the house to go to the inn, I was quite tipsy. Fortunately, the Monsieur had also had plenty to drink: we rolled around the streets as we went on our merry way, arm in arm, giggling and laughing like children at play. We crashed through the door of the inn still holding on to each other and laughing even more raucously. A man's voice called out in French. I had no idea what he said but he laughed as he shouted so he could even be welcoming us into the drinking house. The Monsieur explained to me what the man said.

'That is François. He's an old friend. I will introduce him to you.' We staggered over to François who got up from a table where he sat with another man and a woman. The Monsieur put his arms around François who almost pulled him over on top of him.

'François is a civil servant, like me. He is an administrator at the town hall. He is responsible for collecting taxes. He's an honest, kind fellow and you will love him. This is Antoine. He is a farmer and this is Monique, his lovely wife. His main crop is grapes and he made the wine we drank at dinner.'

The two men smiled as they greeted me but the woman looked stern and frowned as she looked in my direction. She saw something in me that she did not appreciate. It could be that I seemed too close to Marcel for her liking and she harboured some degree of jealousy. So my acting appeared to be working well. I couldn't possibly drink more or I would be totally out of control. So when François offered me a glass of wine I politely refused. Marcel, however, accepted and carried on drinking with the three of them, as I looked on. Naturally, they spoke in French and apart from the odd translation which Marcel uttered in my direction, I had not much idea of what they were discussing. However, at a point not far, as it turned out, from the end of this conversation, he told me not to listen there for the information I would take back to Madrid.

The encounter with Marcel's three friends concluded around midnight. By then, he had consumed an unhealthy amount of wine the result of which was that I had great difficulty in manoeuvring him back to his house. Eventually, we stumbled through the front door and I somehow managed to lever him up the stairs and onto his bed where I left him fully dressed.

'Esmeralda, I am so sorry about last night,' he said the following morning, his head lowered, as he entered the kitchen where I was agitating a frying pan on the stove, cooking some eggs and mushrooms for breakfast. I laughed at his embarrassment.

'How's your head, Marcel? You were too drunk to undress yourself last night, let alone do anything else!'

'I know. I apologise. I'll not do it again.'

'We'll see,' I said waggling my finger at him and giggling.

'I need to explain something to you,' he said. 'For much of the day on most days, I will be working and you will have to stay here. You are an independent lady and I'm sure you will not find that difficult. I don't expect you to be my servant, but if you can buy our food from the market I can cook us a meal in the evenings. Then we can go out. To the inn or maybe to the town theatre. The play will be in French so the sooner you learn it the better!'

'That'll not be a problem, Marcel, except learning French!'

The routine of the Monsieur working and my staying in the house during the day continued for about three months before it was suddenly and unexpectedly broken. That day the Monsieur failed to arrive home. He usually came in at about six o'clock so when he had not arrived by nine, I became quite anxious. I realised then, if I didn't before, that the Monsieur was the key to my well-being while I was in France. I spoke virtually no French so could hardly survive without him. But I still had the pistol the king had promised me and almost all of his five hundred *ducats*. Then at about midnight the Monsieur crashed through the front door and slammed the door behind him. I rushed into the hall, hugged him and kissed him firmly on the lips.

'Where have you been? I've been frantic with worry!' I said, as I let some tears of relief.

'Get away from the door. Quickly. Someone's following me. God knows who!'

We ran down the hall, into the kitchen, shut ourselves in and waited in silence. Nothing happened. 'Did you recognise whoever it was?'

'No. But I would if I saw him again. Swarthy looking man with big sidewhiskers. I'm sure he carried a gun.'

'Do you think they've discovered that you're a double agent?'

'Doubt it. But I can't be sure. But I can tell you that tomorrow is the day. The day you will find out what the king wants to know, if the subject is raised.'

'Where will that be and what will be discussed?'

'We are going to the town hall in the morning to see François. The meeting is at ten thirty. We will be talking about supplies to the army.'

'What army?'

'The army in Lorraine. I'll say no more.'

'How will I know what the king needs?'

'You'll find out tomorrow.'

We decided to retire to our beds. The Monsieur took a gun with him and I put my pistol under my pillow. I lay there in bed, trying to work out what this meeting could reveal which could help the king. It would not be what the troops would be eating or drinking or even what they would be paid. Then it struck me. It was so obvious. It would be about the numbers: how many troops there would be. If the king knew the numbers, and especially the kind of troops they were, he would be better prepared to defend any army of his, passing along the Spanish Road, which of course went via Lorraine. Sleep then came easily, despite the mystery of the Monsieur's shadowy follower. Maybe it was as innocent as a beggar or one of those unfortunate lunatics who frightened the anxious Monsieur all the way to his house. Maybe, we'd never know.

After a tense breakfast, before which the Monsieur cautiously opened the front door to check whether his 'assailant' lurked outside, we made our way to the town hall. 'Why are you involved in this meeting and why take me?'

'Good questions, my dear Esmeralda. My interest is in supplying food to the troops. I am a diplomat only when spying for the king of France. My regular job in the civil service is feeding and watering our troops, wherever they may be: in France, on the high seas or defending French assets, anywhere in the world. I'm taking you because you are an agent for the king. You will learn what you need to know, I hope. François doesn't know what you are, other than my betrothed. And we are lunching with him after the meeting so you are coming along. Quite convenient, eh?'

'Why didn't you tell me this before? I could have embarrassed you and myself if one of our neighbours or friends had asked what you did and

I told them you were doing something you weren't!' I said, genuinely annoyed with his unnecessary secrecy.

'The fact is I am a civil servant. The detail of what I do is irrelevant. Neither of us could be embarrassed whatever you said.'

I couldn't see any advantage in arguing further and anyway we were about to reach the town hall. François escorted us to his office. He always seemed to be smiling, especially during our encounters at the inn where I first met him, and lit up his familiar smile here, at his work.

'Come in, you two. Still content for lunch? This won't take more than an hour or so. We will be discussing some very sensitive facts but Esmeralda hardly speaks any French so won't understand much of what we are discussing. True?'

'Yes and yes. Still fine for lunch and yes, she won't understand us. Except when I translate for her!' as indeed he did for this short exchange.

The Monsieur and François began to discuss the items on their imaginary agenda. At times they argued and the discussion became quite heated. François' smile evaporated and returned. They drew some figures on a large sheet of paper. It seemed as if they were positioning platoons of troops on a map. Then they would cross out some of their scribblings and replace them. Then they talked about numbers.

'Three thousand infantry. Did you get that, Esmeralda. Two thousand five hundred cavalry and one thousand two hundred harquebusiers. All twenty *millas* to the west of Metz. From the tenth of May,' said the Monsieur, in Spanish.

'What are you telling her? She doesn't need to know those figures!'

'I know. I'm just teasing you, François. She's not a spy for the king of Spain, you know.' The Monsieur laughed as did François and so did I. After about another half an hour of exchanges, exclusively in French, François rolled up the sheet of paper, tied it with a length of thin red ribbon and placed it at one end of a long shelf. We then adjourned to lunch in a tavern next to the town hall. After a few beers, some bread and cheese, and a glass of wine for me, the Monsieur and I left the inn with François still sitting at a table with a lady colleague who joined him too late to meet us. We started to walk back to the house. I had difficulty containing my joy at discovering and retaining the information the Monsieur had given me, through translation.

'I cannot thank you enough, Marcel. I must...'

He interrupted me. 'Don't look around. It's the man who followed me last night.'

'What should we do?'

'Keep walking to the next corner. I'll kiss you and turn off. You go straight back to the house and I'll see you there. Don't worry. He'll soon lose me around these streets. I know them well.' A deep sense of trepidation struck. From the elation of gaining that crucial information, the urgent need for survival, mine and the Monsieur's, overcame me. I dashed back to the house, occasionally glancing behind to see if the man was pursuing me. I didn't see him. He had to be following the Monsieur. I went in and closed the door behind me. And waited. And waited. Then I heard the sound. A knock on the door. I didn't know what to do. My mind stopped working. I stood firmly to the spot I occupied when I heard it. Should I answer it? Or leave it. Then I decided. I would go to the door carrying my bag. It held the pistol. I opened the door. Then a thunderbolt struck me as I saw the man standing there, complete with his sideburns. It was Ion. He looked straight into my eyes and for several seconds said nothing. Then he spoke.

'Esmeralda. All this time has passed. And it's you. It is you, isn't it?' The passing years had been kind to him. He possessed the same trim figure I remembered courting our darling Susana. Only his hair had changed. His sideburns were tinged with grey but still joined to his luxuriant moustache.

'Yes, Ion. It's me all right. Why are you following my beloved?'

'Your beloved? I think you are lying, Esmeralda.'

'Come in. We have much to discuss.' I dared invite him through the doorway. I trembled at the thought of what had happened to the Monsieur and whether Ion had played any part in his fate, whatever that could be. Although I suspected the worst, I could not believe that Ion would want to harm me.

'Well, it's a long story, Esmeralda, but I'll keep it short. After Susana died and you girls went back to Madrid, life... My life... became unbearable. My fellow *tercios* constantly insulted... and assaulted... me for being a gypsy. So I deserted. I decided to change sides and went to Paris to enlist in the French army. I knew I had to tell them I'd been a *tercio*, so I did. They decided it was too dangerous to let me enlist and made me a spy instead. At first they tested me because, I guessed, they questioned my loyalty. But then they gave me bigger, more important work. My Spanish helped me and, of course, I now speak fluent French. Spies are good at spying on fellow spies. So they made me spy on my colleagues, to test their loyalty. I followed hundreds of them and most were loyal. Some however were in the pay of others. The greedy and the self-seeking. They became double agents.

'The latest in this line of the not to be trusted was Monsieur Marcel Montpassant. I have been following him for almost a year now, on and off. Shortly after his return from his mission to Spain he reported some Spanish troop movements near the Spanish Road. We knew they were wrong and that confirmed our suspicions. We knew that he had brought a woman with him from Spain – I had no idea, until today, that it was you – with the promise of marriage. But we've carried out detailed checks which prove that, unless he is to marry outside of France, this was all a pretext. Unfortunately, he was today given some crucial information about our troop movements near Metz. So I had to execute him. He is lying dead in a derelict house about a *milla* from here...'

I trembled with fear. Would I be Ion's next victim? He must know that I also knew these dangerous details. How could he not know if he had seen me coming back here with the Monsieur. The fool. He had warned me: He'd killed the Monsieur so I would be his next victim. An inevitability. Unless I acted first. But how could I bring myself to kill this man, our friend and helper on the road to Madrid, our coincidental encounter on the Spanish Road, Susana's friend, lover and husband, the one who mourned the most over her loss? And the man who gave me her wedding ring which still rested at the bottom of my bag. Perhaps he was thinking the same: how could he kill me? But it would be nothing more than his duty to King Louis XIII. No. I would act first.

'Ion, I have something to show you. Come here,' I beckoned him toward me. I took my pistol from my bag, aimed it at his heart and fired.

CHAPTER 29

Truly a Lady

I uttered the word 'Lorraine' to the guard. He silently signalled that I follow him. He led me into the West Wing, past civil servants, lawyers, flunkies, messengers and escorts. The palace palpitated with the morning's activity. 'Wait here for a minute,' he said as he led met into an ante-room. I sat in a shabby, well-worn chair as he shut the door behind me. After I had sat there for about a quarter of an hour, wondering what was happening, the door opened again and a man with short black hair, dressed in an ornate braided jacket, whom I imagined was a private secretary, asked me to follow him to the king's private office. Then another wait in his outer room. Then the king appeared.

'Good morning, Esmeralda. Do come in!' he smiled. I followed him in. 'Sit down! How are you?'

I could not help myself and exploded into tears.

'Whatever is the matter?' he said. He stood up, came around to my side of the desk and put his arm around me. I wiped my eyes in a handkerchief and, still sobbing, apologised.

'Tell me, do. But, first, do you have what I sent you for? Just say yes or no.'

'Yes, Your Majesty. I have it in my head. I have remembered what I learned.'

'Excellent. More of that later. Now, tell me what happened.'

I spared the king much of the detail. I didn't tell him how I panicked when I could not find the soldiers or carriage to bring me back. Nor that the Monsieur had forgotten to tell me that they had moved to the west side of Nancy after a neighbour had become too inquisitive. I didn't tell him about meeting the Monsieur's friends, François, Antoine and his unwelcoming wife, Monique. Nor about the many evenings we shared with them, drinking our way to obscurity in the tavern near where the Monsieur lived. Nor did I mention the prowess and generosity of the Monsieur as a lover.

'Your Majesty, I shall keep it brief. The crucial meeting took place on my last but one day in Nancy. That day, Monsieur Marcel Montpassant took me to the town hall. He explained to me that he and a gentleman I knew only as François were going to discuss provisions for the troops near Metz. The Monsieur's clever pretext was that I was attending only because the three of us were going to lunch at a nearby tavern, after the meeting.

And, of course, because the exchanges between the men were in French, I would not understand, anyway, what they were saying. They put a complicated map on the table and sketched various things on it. I could vaguely follow what they were doing. Then the Monsieur spoke to me in Spanish. He said, "Three thousand infantry. Two thousand five hundred cavalry and a thousand two hundred harquebusiers. All twenty *millas* to the west of Metz. From the tenth of May." Then he joked about me being a spy. Me a spy? I ask you?'

The king leapt up from his over ornate chair and again came around to my side of the table. 'Esmeralda, you are a great spy. You are the only one of my special agents I love! You've succeeded. You got what I wanted! Excellent!' He placed a kiss in the centre of my lips.

'Then something terrible happened, Your Majesty, and I haven't recovered from it. That is why I cried when I saw you. I'm sorry about that. Truly sorry...'

'Don't worry. But tell me. If you cry in the telling of it, I will forgive you, you lovely lady!'

'We were walking back to the Monsieur's house and he thought there was someone following us. He told me to go ahead so I did. I went into the house and shut the door behind me. Shortly after, there was a knock. I took my bag to the door with your pistol hidden inside. Your Majesty, I almost collapsed with surprise. I recognised the man standing there. It was a gypsy *tercio* I had known since before I came to Madrid. Not only did I know him, he was a close friend and espoused to my beloved friend who died in Flanders.

'I asked him in. He said he'd deserted and become a spy for Louis XIII. Within minutes he'd confessed to killing the Monsieur.'

'You are not serious, Esmeralda. My double agents are the cleverest, most skilful spies I have. He cannot be dead, surely?' he said, beginning in a confident tone but suddenly realising what I was saying.

'Every word is true, Your Majesty. I swear. He killed him because he'd discovered he was your double agent and that he knew about the troop movements. He knew that the Monsieur had come to France with a woman who could be a spy. But he didn't know it was me. So it was obvious. He would have to kill me, too. So I pulled the gun and shot him dead, in the heart. I'm sorry, Your Majesty,' I said as I began to cry again. 'I cannot believe that I killed my old, lost friend Ion.'

'You did right, Esmeralda. Doubly right. You killed a French spy. Well done for that. And you saved your own life. Unless you did, you'd never have brought this information back. You are a true special agent! But I owe you an apology. I had no idea that your life would be at such risk. I am truly sorry.' He sounded genuinely upset at putting me through this dreadful ordeal.

'I would do anything for you, Your Majesty. You know that.'

'I do know that and I want to give you a special gift for suffering this awful mission... and succeeding. I am going to ask my portrait painter, Velázquez, to paint you. Something you can take and hang on your wall!'

***

I had to work out what I would say to Beatrix, Dulcina and María when I told them where I had been and what had happened. In fact, it was easy. I told them before I went that the Monsieur had asked me to set up a brothel in Paris. So that was the line I'd take. They were completely fooled, even the intelligent and mature Beatrix. I felt bad having to lie to them but as a special agent for the king I had absolutely no choice. The worst aspect by far was concealing my fateful encounter with Ion whom Beatrix had known so well. I could imagine that she would be completely devastated to learn of his death, especially at my hands. Needless to say, they welcomed me back to our house as if I'd always been with them and been their constant friend as well as colleague. I soon learned that the business thrived in my absence. I could not be surprised, especially as each was so committed to its success.

***

A week after my meeting with the king, the field marshal came to see me.

'Esmeralda, I'm not sure how to put this but I feel I should tell you before you learn from another.' He looked sullen and sad. I anticipated that he was priming me for my arrest. Some investigation, initiated by the king, had found that I was wanted in Burgos for the killing of the *hidalgo*. Or had Carlos or Antonio been killed or maimed? I felt the colour vanish from my face.

'The Marquis of Montequebrado is dead. We have suspected for some time that he was acting in some way for the French. The king commissioned me and one of my captains to investigate him. We discovered some coded messages in a cabinet in his office. They were decoded and showed that he was acting as a spy for Louis XIII. He was found yesterday, hanging by the neck from a meat hook in his kitchen. Those who were instructed to kill him made his death appear to be a suicide.

'Another thing. Monsier Marcel Monpassant's body has been discovered in Nancy. He had been shot twice, once in the head and once through the heart. He would have died instantly. He is to be buried in Nancy. The constabulary in the town found his body in a derelict house and are investigating his death. Needless to say, we have told them nothing.

'I am telling you all this on the express instruction of the king. As you are one of his special agents, he is relying on you to treat this as confidential.'

He could see I was shaken and planted a gentle kiss on my cheek. I didn't know how to react. I already knew, in my heart, that the Monsieur was dead. So this confirmed what Ion had told me. Somehow I was not surprised that the marquis had been found out as a spy. He must have spent all that time away from me on various spying missions. So I doubted that he had been as many times as he had said to meetings with the king, his councils and officials.

'Thank you, Régulo, for telling me. At least I know now. I shall tell no one.'

'I'd love to stay, Esmeralda, but I must go now. I have a meeting at the palace at ten.'

With that he kissed me again and went. In a way, I felt quite satisfied with what he had told me. It proved that what I'd told the king about the death of the Monsieur was true, sad though it was. And the marquis and I did not part on the best of terms. If he wanted to live he should not have chosen to spy.

***

Diego Velázquez charmed me as his sitter. I loved him. I pretended to seduce him but his eyes were, he insisted, only for his beloved wife, Juana Pacheco. He did, however, enjoy flirting so, once he'd made the limits clear, we spent our time teasing each other with daring banter and giggling provocation.

'If you sit like that, Esmeralda, the last place anyone will look is at your eyes!' he laughed.

So I would ease up my dress and even further. 'You naughty girl, Esma, what are you trying to do to me? You are breaking my concentration.' I'd never had a shortened name before and, at first, the corruption upset me but I never complained. There was however a sense in which it made our sittings even more delightfully intimate.

'As long as I don't break your heart!' I said.

'That's the danger!' he mildly admonished. So I carried on teasing.

My first visit to his studio, which was a haven for about fifty finished and incomplete canvases, overwhelmed me. Here stood the anvil of his genius. I trespassed in the sanctuary of his creation. The huge room scintillated with colour, the yellows of the ripe corn and the dry plains, the reds and deep purples of the fabrics, the myriad shades of green of the grasses and the trees, the blues of the sunny skies and golds and silvers of the jewels, all captured by this master craftsman in his gallery of images. Faces, frozen in oils, stared from every canvas, some sad, some happy, some querulous, some in disdain, looked at me from all corners. The sight dazzled my eyes. The smell of half-dried paint tickled my nostrils. I was dwarfed by the sheer size of some, the tops of which almost reached the ceiling and for which he must need a ladder to reach.

'Don't be shy, Esmeralda. Do come in.'

'I can't believe what I am seeing. It's too much for a simple girl like me to take in.'

'Let me show you this,' he said, his back proudly straight and already walking between some pictures, precariously standing on old, wooden easels, towards the rear of the thirty *pies* workshop. He had thought of some means to settle me. 'Here. What do you think?' He was pointing to a picture in which a young woman with a headscarf poured wine from a jug into an earthenware cup.

'It looks real. If I touched that wine, it would wet my fingers. It's flowing and you've captured the movement. It's perfect. And the look on the woman's face. She's determined not to spill even one drop!'

'So you like it?' he said, his thin eyebrows raised expectantly.

'It's beautiful. I think they call paintings like that masterpieces.' I smiled into his glowing eyes.

'You are too kind, Esma. And you are an intelligent admirer of my work. You have understood exactly what I am trying to convey. Now we must talk about what we should show the world in my portrait of you.'

'I just sit in a chair and you paint me... Don't you?'

'No, no, no,' he chuckled. 'It's nothing like as simple as that! But I do have an idea for a composition. Something I've wanted to do for a long time and you'd be the perfect subject. Let me explain! Have you heard of a sibyl?'

'No, I've no idea. The word is new to me.'

His eyes lit up with excitement. 'It is, would you believe, a woman prophet?'

'Not a fortune-teller,' I said, remembering the gypsy soothsayer.

'No. Not at all. Much more powerful. The most famous is the sibyl of Cumae who guided Aeneas on his journey through the underworld. He wanted to meet his dead father, Anchises. She was of course a mythical woman but the story goes that she predicted the birth of Christ. I think you would make a wonderful sibyl. You have that strength of personality and the beauty which she surely had. What do you think?'

'I cannot argue with you, Diego. I cannot say no because I have no grounds to do so. And I must trust your judgement. The more I think about it, I like the idea of a sibyl hanging on a wall in my home. But I wouldn't be naked or only partly clothed would I?'

'Goodness, no. You'd be fully dressed, maybe in something that looks as if you are mythical!'

'That sounds fine to me!'

'I take it you agree then! We now need to work out exactly what you should wear, exactly what angle you should sit at, relative to looking ahead, what expression we want on your face. Do we want you to appear proud, modest, sad, smiling, regretful, weary and worn? Do you want to sit or stand... or even lie down? We need to decide what to highlight in your portrait, your hands and your face, perhaps... or just your face? I want this tablet in the scene,' he said, pointing to a square piece of wood. 'So there is a lot to talk about before we go near the canvas.'

At my next sitting, we decided exactly how I would appear. I relaxed in the hands of this master craftsman who knew everything about his art, not only about painting but also about getting the very best from his sitter, even to the nuances in facial expression. While he worked we talked about many things, my mission to France, his engagement by the king, only a few years before, what this mysterious mission could be that the king had in mind for him. 'He will send you to Portugal, to assassinate the prince!'

'Me! An assassin! No! A diplomat maybe!' He grimaced.

'We'll see... but you must swear to tell me when you know what it is!'

'I swear on that bible! There's one in that picture over there!'

Long periods of silence floated by as he, with taut and straining brow, struggled with the palette or the composition. I soon became adept at knowing that to tease him or to speak would be an unwelcomed intrusion. I spent these times contemplating where my future might lie. I had brought myself, through a magic combination of luck and hard work, to enjoying the riches of a wealthy woman. I had reached the age of forty. I had made love to thousands and thousands of men. Counting each time I'd been with a regular, maybe as many as forty thousand. My God, the very thought. Five times as many as a Spinóla army!

A recurring question challenged me: should I continue or should I retire and enjoy my wealth? The wealth I had only just gained. Retirement drew me towards its carefree indulgence. But I had to think deeply about its implications. I shared a beautiful house with Beatrix and the others. They'd be distraught to have to manage without me. Or would they?

Maybe they'd see my departure as an opportunity: a stronger future with fewer to live off the proceeds. Several days of reflection, helped by an interesting idea, led me to a decision.

***

'Esmeralda, you cannot leave us. You are our leader and we cannot do without you,' said Beatrix, on the verge of tears.

'She's right,' said Dulcina. 'If you've had enough of serving the customers, you could act as our madam and manage the finances of the business.'

'I already do that and that's something which I'd have to hand over to you girls. You may need to employ someone to help you.'

'I'm so sad,' said María. 'It won't be the same without you here. Are you sure your mind is made up?'

'Yes. I'm finishing. But I've thought of something which may make it attractive to you. First, I will give you my share of the business and all of my customers. Second, I will buy you a new house which will be yours and only yours. I would like to live in this house so, not only will I buy you another one, I'll completely furnish it and give you a thousand *ducats* into the bargain.'

'You haven't got that kind of money, Esmeralda. You know you haven't!' said Beatrix.

'That's where you're wrong. I took a great gamble when I went to France and it's paid off handsomely. I've sworn not to tell anyone about the details but the result is that I'm worth over ten thousand *ducats*. So I can do what I've promised you and have enough left to enjoy a reasonable level of comfort in retirement. I shall do some instruction in lovemaking to keep in practice and to earn the odd bit of cash.'

Dulcina laughed. 'So you're not going to retire your *vava* completely then?'

'I feel let down, Esmeralda. You are making us a promise and you can't tell us where your money came from. Did you steal it from that Frenchman?'

'Please, Beatrix. I may be lots of things. Including a killer. But I'm not a thief,' I said, angry at her reaction to my offer.

'I really don't know what to think and I wish you'd tell me more. Can't you tell only me? We've been friends the longest and if I were happy, Dulcina and María would be, too. Yes, girls?'

The others confirmed that they would. 'Right. I've an idea. I'll see if I can be released from my promise. Give me some time because it may take a week or two. But, in the meantime we should find another house. In this street if we can.'

***

'No I can't see him agreeing, Esma. You could try him. But he won't budge. You'd have to tell her you are a special agent and that just won't work. Unless he made her one. She could be the second woman agent! Or you could tell her yourself. And then you'd have to kill her!' said Diego at our very last sitting. He understood my problem well and was trying to be helpful, but characteristically sprinkling his response with humour.

'I can't go to see him, just to ask him to let me tell her.'

'No need to. I've told him I've all but finished your portrait. He wants to see it and you'll be here when he comes. Ask him then!'

Within a day or two, I was summoned to meet the king and Diego in the studio. Diego had placed my portrait just a little way inside the door; far enough in to give the three of us room to stand but not so far that we'd have to walk past other paintings to see it.

Diego and I were chatting with the door open when we heard animated voices outside.

'No, Private Secretary, I don't need you at the meeting. It's not for you to record for posterity.'

'I'll go then, Your Majesty!'

'Good. Off you go!'

The king entered the room. He was carrying a tiny box which he placed on a table. I curtsied and Diego bowed. 'These damned people think I need a nursemaid. But I've been king long enough now...' He looked at my portrait. 'It's beautiful, Esmeralda. Diego has produced a masterpiece. I love the way he's angled you away from the viewer, your slightly dishevelled hair and the idea that you are saying something or about to. And that youthful glow on your cheeks.'

'You are flattering me, Your Majesty. But Diego has done well; and I even like it myself!'

'What are you pointing at on that stone?'

'Aha, Your Majesty! She is making a prophecy. We cannot read it so who can say? The tablet may be blank,' he laughed.

'I shall arrange for it to be taken to your house and hung wherever you want it. Maybe you can see to that, Diego.'

'Of course, Your Majesty.'

'You won't have heard the latest news, Esmeralda,' said the king. 'General Spínola has captured Breda. It's the greatest triumph in the war and by far the biggest in my reign. I'm ecstatic! And do you know, Esmeralda? It's in no small measure because of you!'

'I'm not sure I follow, Your Majesty.'

'The general needed fifteen hundred more troops to attack Breda. So I sent them up the Spanish Road. You told us about the French near Metz. So we sent a small advanced party there three days before our men were to get there. They set alight to the French camp. Nearly all their troops were killed or so badly injured they couldn't stage a *comedia* let alone an attack.'

My heart almost stopped as I realised that my mission to France had led to these deaths and injuries. I became consumed in a dark blanket of self-disgust. Would I have accepted this mission, if I'd realised the outcome? It reminded me of my killing Dulcina's father, after the awful death of Susana. I felt sick.

'Don't look so sad, Esmeralda.'

'I can't help it, Your Majesty. I feel ashamed and guilty that my mission for you has led to all this death and injury.'

'I thought you might and I almost didn't tell you. But by getting the information you did, you most certainly saved a huge number of Spanish soldiers. Maybe all fifteen hundred. And they went on to join up with Spínola's forces in the triumphant capture of Breda. We've longed for that for years. The credit is yours, Esmeralda; or a good share of it, anyway. That is why I'd like you to accept this gift. It is an emerald ring. It was my mother's. Now it's yours. I'm going to call it "The Emerald of Burgos". It fits your name completely!'

The king lifted the little box from the table, carefully removed a ring and placed it on the middle finger of my left hand. I then lifted my hand and moved it to and fro to admire the emerald's cheerful, glowing beauty. Its many facets shone in the morning light which poured through the studio window. The bright diamonds in its setting amplified its glorious colour. 'There. It looks magnificent on you. Fit for a princess!' Suddenly, my grief at the death of those Frenchman vanished. The king had made me feel so much better, explaining the importance of the mission and giving me this special present. I truly seemed a princess and a prophetess at the same time.

'Your Majesty, I cannot thank you enough. It's beautiful. The emerald is perfect and the best I've ever seen. And those shining diamonds. The ring fits my finger well. It is such an honour for me to receive it. Especially as it belonged to your mother.'

'You deserve it, Esmeralda. Truly! What do you think, Diego?'

'I agree, Your Majesty. With both of your points. What an amazing result for you. Congratulations on the capture of Breda. Well done,

Esmeralda. You are a true heroine!' He didn't use my abbreviation, not in front of the king!

'Your Majesty, I now want to ask a very special favour of you,' I said. I explained Beatrix's doubts about my newly acquired wealth.

'Normally, I would refuse you outright... but I have a suggestion. I will agree that you tell her that you went to France, at my request, and that I paid you ten thousand *ducats*. But you must tell her no more, either about being a special agent, the mission, the information you obtained or what we did with it. Tell her that if she tells anyone else, I will personally see to her execution.'

'Your Majesty, I am so grateful.'

'Don't thank me, Esmeralda. Because there is a price I will take from you. I want Diego to paint another portrait of you. Your eternal beauty will again be the subject. I will privately tell Diego about the detail of this commission!' He chuckled. 'Are you happy with that, Diego?'

'Whatever you demand, Your Majesty,' said Diego, apparently wondering exactly what the king had in mind. I could easily guess.

'At least we know each other well, Diego. I won't be the least bit embarrassed at whatever the king wants. We'll be continuing our teasing together!'

'I might have known what you two were doing!' said the king, looking accusingly at Diego.

'I'm not sure how to respond to that,' said Diego.

'No need to!' said the king.

***

'I simply don't believe you, Esmeralda. I don't. You are lying!' said Beatrix.

'I'm not sure how to convince you,' I said, resisting my urge to become angry.

'Tell me how it came about.' So I explained my summons to the king. That he saw me as the best candidate to accompany the Monsieur to France. But said that I couldn't tell her what I did for ten thousand *ducats*. And that the king would see her executed if she told a soul about any of what I'd told her.

'Are you saying he would kill me? Personally?'

'Probably not. Not kill you himself. But he'd make sure someone did!'

'I'm now beginning to believe you, Esmeralda. I'm sorry! I should have known you would not lie to me... not really lie. So you didn't set up a brothel in Paris or anywhere else for that matter.'

'No. But I had to give you a reason for going that did not betray the truth. To protect the state.'

'All I can say now is thank you for your wonderful offer. Dulcina and María will agree that we move to another house, at your expense.' She accentuated the 'at your expense' in a way which I found awkward and uncomfortable, almost as if the three of them were deserting me. But I had to accept a certain distance if only because we would be living under different roofs.

***

It took a number of months to find a suitable house, only because the lovely properties in the Santa Clara rarely appeared on the market. So the four of us continued working together, serving our customers, in just the way we did before I went to France. In a way, I quite enjoyed serving them and always gave them my best. The sessions with our customers was, of course, punctuated by my need to visit Diego Velázquez in his studio.

'Tell me Diego, exactly what does the king want. What aspect of my beautiful body does he want to capture forever?' I asked on my first session with him.

'I have no choice but to tell you, Esma, otherwise you won't be able to pose for me! But it is a little difficult. Maybe it won't be so bad for you! After all, you and the king are intimate acquaintances and he wants something... well... very intimate.'

'Come on Diego, tell me! You cannot embarrass me, I assure you. Even if you tell me he wants a picture of my...'

'You've guessed, Esma! But maybe you haven't. He wants me to paint a similar, if not identical portrait to the one of the sibyl. But... but he wants you to be naked.'

'So I didn't guess at all!' I said. 'But if that's what he wants... I haven't got a problem...that is, if you haven't!'

'How do we do this, Esma? I'll need your help and advice.'

'As we did when you painted my portrait, you'll have to work out whether I should be completely naked or only naked from the waist up? Will you need different lighting to bring out my skin colours? Will you want to accentuate my face again or my hands or breasts?

'You are already making me feel at ease, Esma. I'm even looking forward to it now!'

'Which one of you wouldn't be!' I laughed.

'One thing. I'll lock the door while you are posing. We don't want anyone interrupting us!'

Diego behaved like the perfect gentleman while conducting this commission for the king. He treated me in exactly the same way as he did while painting me as the dressed sibyl. He made few remarks about my body, even though I posed naked, other than to utter quietly and occasionally the word 'beautiful'. He took great care over the angle he wanted me to sit and over the lighting and shade. I found the respect he showed me quite touching. We each took the task quite seriously and hardly teased each other at all. 'I cannot tease you from such a position of advantage,' he proclaimed. The completed picture impressed me greatly. Somehow Diego had made this portrait even more spontaneous than the previous one. It made it look as if my nakedness was uninhibited, natural and that clothing would be something foreign to my body. Both works were masterpieces, at least in my humble view.

CHAPTER 30

The Stranger

We eventually found a house for Beatrix, María and Dulcina, right at the far end of the Calle Santa Clara. It stood proudly, facing the sun, on the opposite side of the street. The previous owner was a Portuguese banker who wanted to return to Lisbon with his family to care for his ailing mother. His anxiety to leave Madrid meant that we could buy it for a very acceptable price.

'I love it, Esmeralda. And I can't believe your generosity in letting us have it. Are you sure you want only us to own it? Will you want a share in its value?' asked Dulcina.

'No. It's your house. The three of you will own it. You should each have an equal share. I will be staying here – in my own house – and will have no financial interest in it.'

'That's wonderful, Esmeralda. You are kind,' said Beatrix. 'We will all love you forever. But we must all stay in regular contact. We mustn't lose each other as friends, not after what we've done and been through together.'

So, with the ardent support of my colleagues, I went ahead and purchased the property for them. We vowed to be friends for as long as we lived.

***

It felt strange, reaching the point at which my career was to finish. I had to think about what I would do with this ocean of time, this uncharted territory of opportunity, which would appear before me. I firmly promised myself that I would go to Burgos to find my brother. I would certainly not resign my position as a special agent for the king. While still enjoying a teasingly intimate relationship with him, I felt sure that he would engage me on other challenging 'missions' in the furtherance of his security and that of his court. I hoped that none would require me to travel abroad. My poor frame had suffered enough at the beckoning of the ruts, potholes and fissures of the roads of Europe, including, of course, those in my travels to Lorraine.

So, too, were my encounters with our wonderful customers coming to an end. The day the business was to move to the other end of the Santa

Clara, on the other side of the street, would be my last of earning a living lying on my back – or in any other position of indulgence for that matter.

It happened the day before that final day. Dulcina told him that I would, of those three of us available, be the one to entertain him. None of us had set eyes on this handsome stranger before. I was sitting on my bed as I heard a quiet knock on the door. I shouted, 'Come in.' The door opened and he stood there facing me.

'The lady said your name is Esmeralda,' he said. He came towards me. 'That's a pretty name. Would you please stand up so I can see you better?'

I didn't know what to make of this man. He had a vaguely familiar look which I soon dismissed. I felt certain he'd never been one of my customers before. He looked straight at me and followed my every movement as I stood up to greet him with a handshake. It seemed as if he was studying me, perhaps anticipating how I would perform while serving him. He looked me up and down. His eyes paused on my breasts then looked again into my eye. I could not remember a customer whose gaze so exactly traced my steps, even as I walked over to close the door which he had left partially open, oddly so in the circumstance of his visit. Something strange exuded from this individual and I had to determine what it could be, before I could commit myself to serving him. Could he be violent, aggressive, want something painfully unusual; could he be concealing a weapon of some sort; was he looking for an opportunity to dispose of an experienced whore? These questions troubled me to the extent that, before I served him, I would explore him in conversation. My heart sank as I thought that it was my misfortune to have to face a difficult customer on this, my last day.

'Don't remember seeing you before, señor, even though you seem slightly familiar.'

'No. Never been here before.'

'What is your profession?'

'I'm a lawyer.'

'Do you regularly practice in this town?'

'Not exactly. No. But I have worked here before.'

'So you are here for a special purpose then, a special case maybe?'

'You could say that.'

'Dare I ask for elaboration?'

'I don't see why I can't say more,' he said after a perceptible pause. 'I'm here to defend one of my clients in the criminal court. He had been accused of evading tax.'

'A serious offence.'

'Indeed.'

'Who is he?'

'I'd rather not say.'

'He will be named in the court.'

'Yes, but not before.'

'Is he guilty or innocent?'

'I don't know. He says he has paid all his dues but I'm not so sure. If I do my job well, he will be found not guilty.'

I didn't know how much longer I could sustain my line of questioning but still felt I needed to know more about this man. I could not help feeling suspicious and uneasy, unprepared to be intimate, at least for those tortuous minutes.

'How is it that you've never been here before? Has someone recommended you?'

'Yes, a friend. He came here a few months ago. Enjoyed it,' he said with hardly a trace of emotion.

'So you live in Madrid?'

'Oh no. I'm only here for this case.'

'So where are you from?'

'Burgos.'

My mind began to race. Should I tell this stranger of my origins? A lawyer who could be familiar with the killing of the *hidalgo* and who would want me arrested and taken back to Burgos to face trial? But I committed that crime some twenty five years before so surely it would be forgotten by now. And why should he suspect me, even if, by some coincidence, he knew of the case. The only way he could know of my involvement would be through my confession and I was not about to deliver that to him. I could take a tiny risk of arrest, if he could tell me something of the fate of my brother, even if it was about his demise. I'd told Régulo de Aracena of my origins in Burgos and that had cost me nothing – other than finding that my killing of the *hidalgo* was premature and pointless – so I'd tell this man that I was from there and hope, however small the chances, that he might know something about my brother.

'You are joking. I'm from Burgos, too!'

'Tell me more,' he said. 'But can that be while we are making love. I'm beginning to feel that you don't want to serve me.'

'Nonsense, señor. How could I not want such a handsome fellow?' I could not see how I could delay the intimacy of this encounter any longer. I had, after all, spoken to him for a good few minutes and could find nothing tangible in this interview to deter me, at least not at that moment.

'Come and sit by me, on the bed,' I said. He joined me and awaited further instruction.

'So where did you live in Burgos?' he said.

I still felt hesitant about saying too much to the stranger, even though I was as confident as I could be that he wanted to do me no harm and that he could not be interested in my relationship with the *hidalgo*. He wanted no more than a casual chat, as many customers did, and this could be at any time during our encounter. 'I lived in and worked for an *hidalgo*,' I replied.

'Lots of youngsters found work for such people. The wages were poor but at least they had a roof over their heads,' he said, still sitting next to me on the bed and crossing his legs. As he did so, I could smell a cedar wood perfume on him, a sure sign of a man of quality.

'He was a horrible man and I ended up escaping from him and coming to Madrid.'

'Where did you live before that?'

'In an orphanage,' I said. 'I escaped from there too.'

'I did the same,' he said, making no motion to begin but seeming to be settled on my bed. 'I escaped with my twin sister, María, who I think is dead.' he continued.

'My God' I shouted, my mind in total tumult. 'You are my brother! I am María. And very much alive!'

He stared at me with a look of astonishment which turned to muted joy. 'I don't know what to say. I'm shocked and confused. I was about make love to my sister then?'

'Yes, Pedro,' I said, by then with tears of utter fulfilment and happiness running down my cheeks. 'We have found each other, in the strangest of ways. We have much to tell each other.'

'But your name is Esmeralda, not María. I am still unsure.'

Suddenly, there was a loud knocking on the door. 'Are you all right in there? Why were you shouting? Shall I come in, Esmeralda?' It was Beatrix.

'Yes, come in!' Beatrix entered.

'Let me introduce you to my brother, Pedro.'

'So you changed your name! We do look similar you know!'

'Esmeralda, you've said so much about your brother. I'm so pleased to meet you, señor. But I can't believe you have met again in this place. What is the chance of that?'

'Life is so full of coincidences,' I said, now partly recovered from this amazing encounter. 'I'm sorry to disturb you. It was the shock of realising I was about to commit incest, to make love to my brother!'

***

The next few hours were packed with excitement and emotion, mainly joy, and much hugging. At first neither Pedro nor I could believe that we had found each other without even searching. My explorations had not even begun and Pedro had taken me for dead. We exchanged explanations and experiences from our inexplicable past. Some facts, previously mysterious, became at least clearer, if not completely transparent.

'So who kidnapped you, took you off the streets?' I asked.

'That's a difficult one, Esmeralda. Hard for me to tell because I thought I was going to die. Do you remember that the day before I disappeared, I agreed to meet some beggars near the cathedral? They said they'd got some jobs for me and would pay me well.'

'Yes, I remember that. But you went and that was the last I saw of you,' I couldn't help myself from letting out a sob, even though he sat here, in my drawing room, talking to me.

'I met with the beggars who wanted me to steal some pots and pans from a tinkers' workshop, not far from the cathedral, in the Calle de Santa María. They'd pay me two *maravedís* for each one I stole. They told me exactly what to do. I was small and could easily hide. So I would sneak into the workshop and drop down behind a bench until I had a chance to take some pans. Then I'd sneak out. And return for some more, the same way.

'I found my way into the workshop by climbing through a hole in a wall at the back. I was about to go out of the hole when I dropped one of the pots I'd picked up. The tinkers heard me and three of them caught me as I tried to escape. They started to beat me and I begged and pleaded for mercy. They soon stopped but by then I was bruised and bleeding. They tied me up and took me to their camp on the Madrid side of the town. I was terrified. I had no idea what they would do to me. Day passed into night. And I was worried about you and Simón who would be missing me by then.

'Anyway, they left me tied up until daybreak when they gave me some food and water. Then one of them said they were going to sell me as a slave to some other tinkers, near Bahabón, on the road from Aranda.'

'Did you say, "Bahabón"?' I asked, remembering my and Susana's night in the gypsy encampment and our fortune being told by the fat soothsayer. How true her predictions had become!

'Yes, near there... There was a gypsy camp nearby and they tried to sell me to the gypsies. The gypsies tricked them and said they'd buy me... but they didn't mean it and intended to let me go. I spent a night with them while the tinkers waited to be paid. I remember a fat fortune-teller. I told her all about you and María and Simón. And that I wanted to get back to Burgos to be with you.

'The following morning, just as the gypsies put me on a wagon to take me back to Burgos, the tinkers came and took me. They were so angry with the gypsies, I thought there was going to be a big fight. But before the gypsies could do anything the tinkers put me on a horse and rode out of the camp towards Madrid. So I was back in their hands again.

'That explains so much, Pedro,' I said. I told him about the night Susana and I had spent in the same encampment, maybe a year or so later. I explained that we had seen the same fortune-teller who had apparently made a connection between me and Pedro and guessed I was his twin sister. I told him about her prediction that we would meet up again at some time in the future.

'That is a truly amazing story, María. First, I stumble into you. Then you tell me about this woman who predicted that we would meet. Not that she could be sure of anything. But even after that amount of time, she made the connection between the two of us coming from Burgos. Mind you, we may as twins have looked more similar then. And I didn't have a beard!'

'She said so many things, but that was the most incredible. But the thought that we would meet again has helped to keep me going. I cannot possibly say in words how thrilled I am to see you again. It's truly wonderful.'

'So you keep saying, María, but I do not tire of hearing!' It was hard to get used to being called María again.

'What happened to you after the tinkers came and took you from the gypsies?'

'That's the worst part of the story. They took me to Madrid. It took three days to get there. They then sold me to a Moor who took me to the Maghreb. It must have been the worst sea crossing ever. Everybody on the galley was sick, including the captain who was from Cadíz. I became a servant in a palace in Tunis. I thought they were going to castrate me and turn me into a eunuch. Just like they did with many boys. But I was too valuable as a stable hand, working for a Moorish prince.

'I spent six years at this palace. Life there wasn't too bad. They fed me well, mainly because of the importance of my job. But they paid me nothing so I had no independence. I had no chance of escaping because, apart from treating me like a slave, I could not pay for my passage back or anything else. Then the prince decided he would make a visit to Madrid. I was the only one at the palace who spoke good Spanish so he decided I should go with him. He made me swear on pain of death that I wouldn't escape from him and his entourage and go back to Burgos. Eventually, we ended up in a tavern, close to the Plaza Mayor. The prince believed he could trust me but I proved him wrong. During the second night there, at about three o'clock in the morning, I left the tavern via a door at the back. I soon found my way to the road which leads to Burgos. At daylight I got on a cart and the driver took me *millas*. Within about five days I was back in Burgos.'

'What a story, Pedro! You did well to survive. And in a foreign land, too!' I smiled and hugged him again. I still couldn't believe we had stumbled across each other. What satisfying luck. 'How did you become a lawyer?'

'That's another fantastic story. I must have been about sixteen or so when I got back to Burgos from the Maghreb. I wanted an education so I went along to the orphans' college and asked if they'd take me in. I explained that I'd spent time in Tunis and that I'd just returned to Burgos. They asked me what I wanted to study. I said law only because it was the first thing that came into my head! So they made me take some tests and, much to my surprise, I passed and they gave me a scholarship. Three years later I graduated. And here I am, a defence lawyer, working in the criminal court!

'What about you, María? I must get used to your new name! How was it that you left Burgos? How did you become a *puta*?'

I saw no point in trying to conceal anything from Pedro. After all he was my brother and he'd find out from someone else if I didn't tell him the truth about my past. I told him all about the *hidalgo* and why I had killed him. I cried when I related the story of Susana – Lucía to him – and he cuddled up to me in sympathy. I told him about our work as *putas*, before and after Flanders, and about my imminent retirement. The one important detail that I did not and could not relate was that I was a special agent for the king.

'Esmeralda, I want to ask you a special question. Will you come back to Burgos with me? We can then make up for all these years apart!'

'I cannot, Pedro. I'm sorry. All my friends are in Madrid. And I'd always live in fear of being arrested for the killing of the *hidalgo*. I feel safe here! But I shall regularly make the journey to see you. And you can come to see me! Anyway, a handsome man like you should be married and you will find a wife, I'm sure. I would be in your way!'

'If they arrested you, I would get you freed. Trust me!'

'We must accept that we live in different towns. We will always love each other. Now that I have found you, I have another reason for living. Tell me just one more thing, Pedro, just to satisfy my curiosity. About a year ago, I had occasion to travel through the Puerta de Santa Barbara. I was sitting in a carriage and as it sped through the Puerta I glimpsed a man in a heavy overcoat. He stood by the side of the road and I think our eyes met. My instant thought was that the man was you. Could it have been?'

'Yes, I was in Madrid about a year ago. It was cold and I wore my coat wherever I went. I don't remember seeing a carriage passing through the Puerta but do remember standing there looking vacantly at the passing traffic. It was a favourite pastime and I would stand there contemplating the speeches I was to deliver in a tricky case I was defending...'

'How I wished now that I had stopped that carriage!'

'But we eventually found each other, María. That is the important thing!'

Pedro and I exchanged our sad farewells, the day the trial finished. I cried as he turned back to wave while walking away from my house in the Santa Clara. I would surely see him again.

**

Not long after the girls started up their new business further up the Calle de Santa Clara, Beatrix rushed down to see me.

'I'm so excited, Esmeralda. I've had a letter from Antonio. From Flanders!'

'But you haven't heard from him for years. What does he want?'

'He's retiring from the army and wants to marry me! I can't believe it. He's on his way back to Madrid.'

So Beatrix and Antonio were married. What Antonio didn't tell Beatrix was that he had been shot and had to have a leg amputated. But that made no difference to Beatrix. She left the other girls and set up home with Antonio. They never had children but they were always in love. They frequently visited me and we talked of our old friends in Flanders and our exploits there. Antonio told us that Carlos Pinero de Albuquerque, our trusted wagon driver had mutinied, just before the capture of Breda. He was eventually arrested and sentenced to ten years in an Antwerp prison. Sadly, he hadn't been heard of since. The story of Felipe Sanz made us smile. Apparently, he convinced a rich woman in Brussels that he was a Spanish nobleman. They were married in the cathedral in which Ion and Susana were married. By the time the rich lady discovered the truth; she had produced three children by him. She loved him so much she forgave him.

The other two, María and Dulcina, soon found a new colleague. Against my advice, they engaged Melchora Cabello, the *puta* singer. She took to working at the upper end of the market like a hooked fish thrown back into its pond. She absolutely loved it. She never again went back to singing for a crust of bread.

Colonel Régulo de Aracena found it quite difficult to accept that I was no longer professionally available to serve him. But we remained close friends and he would visit occasionally and we would make languid love in my boudoir. He constantly flattered me with his extravagant praise. Nothing changes.

***

Antonio Hidalgo, my special agent colleague and itinerant musician, came to see me one day to ask me a favour. The following day he brought his clever son, Juan, to my front door. Juan played the harp and composed music. I showed him in and his father left. He showed obvious signs of nerves so I gave him a tour of my house. We returned to the drawing room and sat down again.

'Do you know why you are here?' I smiled while asking him.

'Not really,' he said with a quizzical look on his face. 'Is it anything to do with etiquette, perhaps?'

I stood up and walked towards the window, working out what I would tell him. Of course, I knew exactly why he was here. 'You have a wonderful father,' I said, giving myself more time to find the words.

'Yes, he has been a great help to me, especially with my music.'

'Well, your father has asked me to help you with an aspect of your education and etiquette is not far off the mark,' I said, turning back towards the lad.

'What exactly does my father want you to do?'

So I told him in emphatic terms. 'I am a whore. To be more exact, a retired whore!'

'Really?' he said, in utter astonishment.

'Yes. I'm going to teach you how to make love.'

Glossary of Spanish words

barrachel	army lawyer
burdel	brothel
caballero	middle ranking member of Spanish nobility
calle	road, street
carcel	prison
cazuela	part of theatre auditorium, solely for women
chacona	dance
comedia	a play containing tragedy and comedy
consolador	a dildo
crisantemo	chrysanthemum
ducat	unit of currency: 1 *ducat* = 11 *reales*; 1 *real* = 34 *maravedís*; 1 *ducat* = 375 *maravedís*
electo	elected leader
encantado	greeting: pleased to meet you
gitano	gypsy
hidalgo	lowest level of nobility
hombre	a man
libra	unit of weight, about 1 pound
legua	unit of distance, about 5km or 3.5 miles
maestro de campo	field marshal in a Spanish *Tercio*
mancebía	brothel
maravedí	unit of currency (see *ducat*)
milla	unit of distance, about a mile
paso	unit of length, a step or about a yard
pie	unit of length, about a foot
placer(es)	pleasure(es)
plaza	a square or market square
plazuela	a small square
puerta	Door, gate
pulgada	unit of length, about an inch
puta	prostitute
putaría	brothel
real	unit of currency (see *ducat*)
tasca	a small drinking house
tercio	Spanish infantryman
Tercio	Regiment of infantry men
titulo	member of the landed gentry

vara	unit of length, about a yard
vava	abbreviation the girls used for 'vagina'
villa	town
vulgo	the people, population